PRAISE FOR *IVORY SHOALS*

"What a grand adventure, beautifully told, marbled with wickedness and small miracles, glowing with heart."

—Jack Pendarvis, author of *Movie Stars* and *Your Body is Changing*

"John Brandon writes with a simple-looking declarative thrust that rarely permits subordination, or what Ian Frazier calls "riders," and riders make for fey yammering. Brandon tells you what his characters want, and you want it too. The effect of this strong forward telling is not entertainment, not story, but hypnosis. Brandon does not yammer. You won't put the book down, you won't want it to end."

—Padgett Powell, author of *Edisto* and *The Interrogative Mood*

"From shades of Homer and Twain, Cormac McCarthy and Charles Portis, John Brandon has conjured a poignant and heart-racing adventure story all his own. Twelve-year-old Gussie Dwyer's journey across the ruins of post-Civil War Florida feels at once as old as time and mysteriously modern, as we navigate our own wounded American wasteland."

—Brett Martin, *GQ* correspondent and author of
*Difficult Men: Behind the Scenes of a Creative Revolution, From
The Sopranos and The Wire to Mad Men and Breaking Bad*

"I opened John Brandon's new novel and fell hard. An adventure full of grit and wonder, far-flung and yet uniquely, specifically American. I hope I never recover."

—Daniel Handler, author of *All The Dirty Parts and Bottle Grove*

"John Brandon is a marvelous storyteller. With diamond-cut elegance and wit, Brandon's suspenseful tale depicts a young man's search for kinship in a beguiling and often terrifying world. Ivory Shoals is a book of grit, heart, and intricate beauty."

—Patrick Cottrell, author of *Sorry to Disrupt the Peace*

IVORY SHOALS

McSWEENEY'S

SAN FRANCISCO

Copyright © 2021 John Brandon

McSweeney's and colophon are registered trademarks of McSweeney's, an independent publisher based in San Francisco.

Cover illustration by Keith Shore

ISBN 978-1-952119-17-0

10   9   8   7   6   5   4   3   2   1

www.mcsweeneys.net

Printed in China

IVORY SHOALS

A NOVEL

JOHN BRANDON

McSWEENEY'S

SAN FRANCISCO

BOOK I

THE WATCH WAS AN eighteen-carat, rear-winding Waltham. The gold of the casing was smooth and by now warm in Gussie's fingers, the weight of the piece an unexpected comfort as he wheeled it this way and that in the scant light, the hands frozen at mid-afternoon, the black numerals quiet and proud as country deacons. Close to hand on the table was the deed box that for so long had housed the watch. The lid stood open, the velvet lining inside torn loose in places from the wood. The box had never been shut with a lock, only a length of twine, and that string now sat loosely coiled at the bottom like a starved serpent.

Gussie swore he heard the slow *theck, theck, theck,* but the watch hadn't been wound in many years, the key long lost. When he held the Waltham to his ear, the sound vanished. Above the tiny hole in the plate were engraved the letters M J S. Gussie brushed the pad of his thumb over the initials to and fro, wanting the slight scratch, to and fro again. He arose from his chair and crossed the room, closed the watch and enfolded it in one tattered dustcloth and then a second, crouched to his pack and buried the piece at the bottom of it.

When he stood again, he looked about himself lost and awed, as if the humble cottage parlor were a vast square in some foreign city. After a time, he turned and walked back to the tiny hind room that served as his quarters. His mattress there on the floor, stuffed with brittle beech leaves. His battered one-drawer bed table. He picked up his canteen where it rested in a corner and returned to the parlor, padding in bare feet over planks he'd scoured the day before with hot sand, leaned the canteen next to his pack. He'd polished the rented table with linseed oil, scrubbed the larder shelves pale. The whole of the premises was spotless, save his mother's room, which he'd scarcely set foot in these past days.

He sat back down at the table, nudged it flush against the broad front-facing window. He shut the deed box gently and drew closer his paper and pen and ink. The light outside was spectral, gray day giving out to gray night, the alley obscure and lifeless behind the window. Gussie took the pen in hand. He picked up the nearest sheet and read what was already there, word to word and line to line, then replaced the sheet atop the others and centered them on the tabletop. He slid the pen back in its quiver. Gifts of the past Christmas, these scribe's implements. His mother had scarcely convinced him to use them, so highly he prized the set. They would be sold now, not things he could take along. He picked up the pen again and struck a line. Struck the next. Struck an entire paragraph. He'd recomposed the letter a half-dozen times, the prose growing handsomer but the sentiments no more suitable.

He situated a fresh sheet and ventured a sentence or two, then his hand stilled and shoulders slacked. The wind picked up, the verbena outside the window whumping its heavy blossoms against the panes, momentarily breaking the quiet. Quiet in the cottage. Quiet out in the empty alley. Quiet, it seemed, up and down the coast and over the length and breadth of the great peninsula. Quiet, perhaps, through the whole of the vast, smoldering, bested Confederacy.

He was the only person who knew, and this made the knowledge feel suspect. His mother had carried the secret so many years, and now had passed it to him like some priceless seedling that must be kept alive. Gussie felt sly and desolate, the lone soul aware that this man named Madden Joseph Searle—the name itself supposititious, marbled and outsized on Gussie's tongue when he pronounced it aloud—was his own natural and rightful father. This man, Madden Joseph Searle, had no inkling he had offspring on the opposite coast of Florida, a stunned, scraggly boy of twelve who was at this moment endeavoring in vain to write him, to wave an arm in the crowd, to call in the night. Searle had not the remotest notion. An inventor by trade, Gussie's mother had told him. A personage of great learning, in command of a lavish garden of intellect. Whatever unfathomable math and philosophies the man's mind held, it did not contain the fact of his own child. The fact of Gussie.

He arose and fetched a candle and lit it, set it at arm's length on the table. He could see only himself now in the window. It was hot in the cottage and he stripped off his shirt and raised the window, then went and raised the back one. His mother had felt chill at all hours these past months, even after the brief winter had chased off, and Gussie had grown accustomed to sweating in their closed-up rooms. He looked at his mother's shut door. Behind it, part-burnt candles still slouched on the bed table and on the sill and about the floor. Gussie had been unable to straighten up, to take inventory, to strip the bed. His mother's friends, the other ladies who worked at Rye's, had come over the afternoon after her death, and he'd begged them not to touch the place, to allow him to tidy and sweep in his own time. He'd accepted their offerings of puddings and allowed them to sit with him that first night. None of them knew Gussie was leaving. They'd been dropping by in pairs and threes, gloves clutched in their fists, exhausting him with their sad ogling and drawn sighs.

Gussie took up his pipe. He plucked a match from a box on the mantle and wrapped his forefinger about the pipe's stem and puffed the bowl alight, set the matches on the floor next to his pack along with his half-full leaf pouch. He picked up the candle from the table and wandered into the kitchen.

He didn't wish to make an opera of departing this humble dwelling where he'd grown from a child. It was merely a place, he told himself. Walls and roof and chimney. Somewhere to spoon up meals and grab shut-eye. Scores of folks had occupied the cottage prior to Gussie and his mother, and scores would live here yet. Other books.

Other worn rugs. Even through the pipe smoke he could smell the cold, black stove. And the walnut water with brandy his mother had taken for appetite. He could see in the candlelight a dent in the floorboards from a kettle of lamb stew she'd dropped trying to cook for Gussie when she was much too weak.

His mother had been on the mend after the last frost had lifted. Or so it had seemed. She had begun taking strolls to the docks on Gussie's elbow in the strongest sunshine of the day, keeping down an egg for dinner, humming along in the kitchen as the neighbor children sang down the dusk in the weedy yard out back. And then suddenly she was ill as ever, abed long hours, shaking her head at offered plates, shuffling out to the porch but never stepping off it, as a hound tied short with rope. Then the week of ceaseless, drumming downpour from which her lungs never recovered. Those rains that turned her eyes docile as a sheep's. She'd held on until the end of April, until the close of the war, the formal surrender of the state, as if satisfied at last that her boy would see none of the front. As if the abeyance of hostilities were permission to let go.

Gussie sat motionless before a late supper of stewed prunes one of the ladies had left him. He'd unwrapped a soda cake with currants, and it sat neglected on the parlor table, as tempting to him as a round of soap. His mind was half-numb and seemed to keep a distance from him, more elusive the harder he chased, as wild turkeys in a wood. He had attempted over the passing hour to spur himself into gathering his mother's possessions for sale, but still her door stood closed. Her fine quilt, checked toast and cinnabar, tossed unfolded into the bureau. Candlesticks and snuffers of pewter. Purses and shoes and nine types of hats. Hanging in her wardrobe, tobacco leaves tucked into them to ward off moths, were her silk dresses, her corsets and bustles. Beneath the window, a wicker basket of tat-lined shawls. In the washroom, bottles of eau de Portugal she'd brushed into her hair, the wee casks of melon-seed face cream, legion rinses and blossom waters. All of it in a lot might draw a sum—something at least. There were still those of the shore islands with means. There was Jacksonville. St. Augustine.

Gussie spied a dark-glossed ant trekking across the table, describing a jagged course toward the cake. There was a colony otherside the window that enjoyed the shelter of the verbena. Gussie had routed the hill and found it rebuilt, routed it and found it rebuilt. The ant had no fellows Gussie could see, a lone scout on the range. He poised a thumb overtop the antic little creature and it paid him no mind. He did not press down, and after a moment withdrew his hand. He waited until the ant was very close to the cake and then broke away a morsel and left it there, watched the ant begin to drag the sustenance away.

He fetched his busted, stitch-bare boots and slipped them on and yanked the laces. Stood and buttoned his shirt and smoothed its front. He moistened his fingers and brought them to the wick of the candle and then felt in the dark for the door handle, drew it to and stepped out into the night and shut the door behind him, waited a minute on the step until the familiar forms lining the way emerged—all the low, plain, flat-faced homes; the leaning palms; the rocking chairs on the weather-warped porches. He strode his way into the alley and then up toward Palmina's chief thoroughfare, peace prevailing though the hour was not so late. The uneasy cries of gulls were absent. The scents on the air were of things sun-beaten and now cooling—tin roofs, weeds in bloom, the dusty alley itself.

Gussie walked past a darkened coppice of plum trees where on his workdays he'd often taken shade of a dinner hour. Past the masterly facade of Sirk Hall with its mosaic of a knight on horseback, his oblong shield concealing all but his armored boots and helmeted head. He saw the town bureaus, a large coquina structure that glittered madly in the day sun and remained faintly aglow even now. A block of failed clothes shops. And soon he began to hear the boisterous din of the Night District, an assemblage of taverns and plate joints that had collected about Rye's place and used that steady establishment as their anchor. Lamps were lit in the windows. Horses at the rails. The clinking of glass. Gussie heard jubilant hoots he knew in a moment could turn bitter. Drinkers on porches regaling their companions with tales from the contested wilds. Men made the butts of wisecracks, fleered in full, hoarse chorus. Rounds treated and the favor returned and returned.

Gussie lingered a beat on Rye's front steps, hitching his trousers and blowing out a hard breath, steeling himself before this interview with his mother's longtime employer. He held himself high and straight. Wiped his forehead dry. This would be his final visit to this particular house. There was strength to be drawn from the thought. The very last time in his life he would set eyes on this place.

He ducked through the cramped coatroom, unused this time of year, and entered the high-raftered and noisy barroom. A line of men posed along the thrown-open windows, their drinks resting on the sills. Others teetered in ladderback chairs or hunched forward over tables arranged haphazardly along the inner wall, whose fleur-de-lis paper was yellowed and peeling. The bar itself was deserted but for two gaunt-faced men leaning on the far end, their hats perched on their heads at impish tilts, their faces wan and shining with sweat.

Gussie approached the bar, and the tender—a man called Fozzy—set down a glass he was wiping and tucked the rag neatly into it. By degrees he deigned to lower his gaze to Gussie. It was a look Fozzy called upon often, that seemed to size the world as brimming with persistent, predictable annoyance. But in the next moment, remembering Gussie's circumstances of grief, his face softened a share.

"What're you doin here?" he said. "You're well aware mister don't abide youngins here business hours. You huntin somethin for your belly?"

"Huntin somethin for my billfold," Gussie said.

Fozzy's face wrinkled tight under his trimmed salt-and-pepper hair. He folded his powerful forearms against his chest. Gussie had seen him plenty of times before, but the two had never said more than hidy. Gussie knew Fozzy had come from inland, a runaway who'd shown up and claimed for himself all the least pleasant tasks at Rye's, who'd worked himself into Rye's graces and now found himself brigadier of the busiest barroom in half the county. Gussie's mother had taken this as another demonstration of Rye's unequaled cunning: taking on an escaped slave would ingratiate him with occupying Northern forces and moneyed Union sympathizers, but knowing Fozzy could hope for no better situation, Rye paid him no wage.

"I do wish you best of luck," Fozzy said. "This ain't no almshouse, far as I gathered. Money comes in. It don't go out."

"I ain't needin no alms," Gussie said. "Just needin to shut my mother's dealins."

Fozzy tugged the sleeves of his coat in place, a smoking jacket detailed in satin that he'd adopted as his uniform. The tinny gong of tobacco in the spittoon could be heard. A man sitting near the windows yawped for more whiskey, and Fozzy tilted his head in acknowledgment.

"Set'n yonder chair and be out of the way," he told Gussie. "Most usual he comes out to the bar to do his figures. You just keep put till he calls on you. Just like school."

Gussie nodded. If he had to wait, he would wait. He walked over and sat where he'd been instructed, feeling jittery and exhausted. He watched Fozzy limp whiskey here and there and collect money and make change from the till and rinse glasses and at regular intervals check himself in the mirror that backed the bar. Every so often a man would scrape his jaw with his arm and saunter down a narrow hall and out of sight toward what Gussie knew was an inner parlor where the ladies waited. Fozzy would pull a cord that rang a bell at the back of the house so Miss Ardelia could ready the room. The lovesome wares, Rye sometimes called the ladies—they weren't allowed in the barroom and the men didn't retire to the parlor until they were set on doing business. Gussie knew full well this was only because Rye didn't want any carousing he couldn't charge for, but his mother had often cited the practice when she felt the need to defend Rye. He never let anyone get rough with his girls, they ate and drank like heiresses, had a doctor within the hour for the asking. Gussie had heard it a few too many times.

On a tabletop nearby sat a shallow pan of poisoned sugar water, a means against flies. No victims afloat. Gussie dipped his fingertip into the pan, unsettling the malign little pond. He sat straight, slouched, sat straight again. Whenever the disordered party along the windows quieted, Gussie caught snatches of talk from the two men at the bar, their voices clear and hardy, mismatched with the haggard aspect of their faces and posture. They spoke of Nassauville, which was now being policed by Black Union troops. The mayor couldn't do a thing about it—he was trying to rule a foreign land. Soon they'd be the ones in chains, one of the men said, fondling a great gasper of a cigarette that he left unlit. White men like them with no pot to piss in. The man spoke reverently of islands in the Indies where one could live on the fruits of the jungle and fish in crystal lagoons. No fighting. No churches. No taxes. No mayors.

Gussie had a hankering for his pipe but refrained. He stared up at the rafters, stared down for a time at his boots. Scraped clean his thumbnails. The monotonous minutes dragged by like wheel-broke wagons, parties arriving and departing, the smell in the place growing closer and closer, and Gussie nearly started from his chair when, finally, true to Fozzy's telling, Rye strode forth from the narrow, shadowy hall, clicking over the planks in his shined half-boots and wiping his mouth with a handkerchief, and installed himself front and center, sitting at the near side of the bar like a customer. Gussie arose, but Fozzy, who'd been wiping down tables, took a lumbering step in front of him and said again to stay put till Rye called him.

"He knows you're here," he said. "He's well aware who's in the barroom."

Gussie returned to his seat and Fozzy went back to his work, running his rag in circles under his big, stiff fingers, limping to the next table and the next. Gussie didn't know what meanness or mishap had caused his lameness, but he couldn't imagine the man whole. The slow, herky progress he made across rooms was part and parcel of his being, the dignified insolence it allowed him, the illusion of his own sweet time.

Gussie tried not to stare at Rye's back. His pressed suit. His combed hair. The man seemed to have always come directly from a shave. He was a barrel-chested sort, though short in stature and with thin arms and bandy legs. Fozzy made his way around behind the bar and poured Rye a measure of clear liquor, which his employer took no notice of. He produced an ash dish and rested it near Rye's elbow.

Rye lit a cigarette and turned to some loose papers he'd arrayed aside his ledger. When he turned askance on his stool, his belt buckle glinted like a sport fish in the lamplight. He ticked his finger line to line, ignoring the dish Fozzy had set out and letting his ashes fall where they would. Times beyond number Gussie had mustered false smiles for this man, and he regretted them each and every. Gussie was no longer beholden. His mother had taught him to be sparing of those deemed vile and leery of angels, but Gussie did not hesitate to hope ruin upon Rye. He'd never witnessed him threatened or cowed, had never seen him brought to a moment's disadvantage.

Gussie watched as Rye dropped his cigarette on the floor and leaned to step on it, as Rye raised up straight and partook of a full breath, tipping his head to crack his neck. Gussie believed his time had come, finally, but a young man appeared from the hallway and stepped over and arranged three large picture boards on the bar. They were sketches, and the man who'd brought them out was apparently the artist, his hands sooty to the wrists with pencil dust. Rye dragged his stool out of the way and raised one of the boards to the light, and when Gussie discovered its subject, he looked away. A nude woman. Gussie kept his eyes averted—gazing vacantly toward the empty table next to him but still seeing in his mind's eye the breasts, the bare button of the woman's stomach—as the artist pointed out details and Rye nodded and chuckled. The first picture to the next, and the next, until all three works had been inspected and approved.

Rye stacked the boards on the bar and dismissed the artist with a clap on the shoulder, then took hold of his liquor and emptied the lot of it. He placed the glass on the bar and twisted at the waist and found Gussie with his pale, stony eyes and beckoned him with a pitch of his chin.

He watched Gussie until the space was closed between them, the two standing with boots near to touching, then he turned back to the sketches and hoisted one upright. Gussie knew he ought to shy his eyes again but that was not what he found himself doing. He found himself staring, mesmerized and ashamed, at the girl before him, who was perhaps only two or three years Gussie's senior. His chest went tight, his hands warm. The hullabaloo from the sodden troop at the windows was suddenly distant, like shouts from an opposite shore.

The girl's hair was arranged in a scalloped shelf. In one hand she held a shallow teacup, and with a finger of the other hand she stirred the contents. Close on the table before her was a bowl of sharp-cornered sugar cubes. A pair of pebble-grain slippers laid one flopped over its mate near her naked feet.

"Simple of mind, I'll grant you," Rye said. "But awful complicated to look at."

Now Gussie did look off toward the coatroom, angry with himself, and Rye brought the board to rest on top of the others and sighed.

"Trio of hard cases from the Home for Wayward Girls," he said. "But you'd never know they were hard cases. Guess that's the whole trick."

Rye's bowtie hung loose from his collar. It was of lustrous silk embroidered with coral flowers.

"Your momma—she wasn't never in need of advertisement. Just more hours in the night. Till her health turned, of course. Sad business all around. Sad, sad business."

Gussie didn't want to be angry. Didn't want Rye strumming more notes on him. He stood tall, only half a head shorter than Rye.

"I come to collect what she set apart."

"Have you now?" said Rye. He coughed in his fist and then granted himself a sweeping, listless audit of his barroom, washing his gaze over the rowdy and the solemn, over Fozzy, who stood sentry-like with hands clasped behind his back, out the windows where tied horses nickered and lone men pottered about the hard-packed street.

"How about we hold this pow-wow in my office?" he said.

He left the boards where they were and set the stool he'd moved aside back in place. He started toward the hallway, rocking side to side on his bowed legs, and Gussie followed him down the dark-paneled corridor, soon hearing sounds from both ends, the voices of the men he'd been hearing for nigh an hour and now the laughter of the ladies from the parlor—some throaty, some girlish. Rye trod a loose plank and it groaned; Gussie, in his turn, found the same plank and the same complaint resounded.

Rye opened the door to his office and stepped aside so Gussie could enter. A lamp was already lit inside, hung from its bail on an iron hook like in a stable. Rye pulled his bowtie free and tossed it on his desk. He sat heavily and motioned for Gussie to take the chair opposite. But for the broad desk of blond wood and the pair of chairs, the office was nearly bare. The window behind Rye was dressed in stiff drapes the bright, deep red of a new barn, and in a doorless and otherwise vacant closet sat a squat, burly safe with its stubby legs and thick crank handle.

"So," said Rye. He unfastened his collar buttons and worked his neck around. "I'm to understand you aim to do some bankin."

"You understand correct," said Gussie.

"And the account under consideration, I assume, is that of the late Lavinia Dwyer?"

"You assume right."

"And you before me are the lawful heir, Gussie Dwyer, beloved son of the deceased?" Rye laid his hands and wrists limply upon the desktop, like drowned rodents. "And your intention is to liquidate said account and transfer all proceeds to those there trouser pockets you most times use for hangin your thumbs?"

"I come for my momma's money," Gussie said. "You put it pretty as you like."

Rye reached into his vest and came out with another cigarette. He felt around for matches without success, then opened a drawer of his desk and shifted the contents about.

"You'd suspect a man what can operate a prosperous vice outfit, especially in these lean times, you'd expect that man could keep track of a match. Now wouldn't you?"

Rye's face was pink and fleshy. He set the cigarette down gently on the desk next to his bowtie, which he then stretched out and smoothed flat.

"How many ties you think I own?" he said. "Give us your best estimate."

"No great hand at guessin games," said Gussie.

"No, I reckon you ain't," Rye said. "Reckon you're still waitin to find out what you're a great hand at." He used a careful thumb to move the tie just so on the desk. "I'll tell you. Six dozen. That's the answer. Last count, anyhow. I'm liable to add to the total any time the mood strikes. Maybe before long, one for every day of the year."

Gussie's hands were clenched in fists, and he straightened his fingers and dried his palms on his trouser legs. Rye had left the door to the office wide open, but Gussie could hear nothing from without. He heard Rye's breathing and the creaking of the man's chair.

"I'd donate you one—can set a boy apart, presentin proper to society. But a dock rat such as you wearin a fine tie like this—why, people might take it for a stage costume. They might take it you were spoofin your betters."

Rye smiled a moment. When the smile gave way, he appeared bone tired.

"What you reckon you'll put it toward, these new-got riches? Hope you don't mind my askin. I know it's not rightly my concern."

"First things first," Gussie said. "I got to get it before I can spend it."

"Some ain't got a mind for lofty schemin. For thinkin ahead. It's the way of the world and can't be different. Somethin comes natural to this one is a mighty struggle for this other. I did always think you got dealt your share of horse sense. That's better than no sense at all."

"I ain't turn up for advice, nor no bowtie."

Rye drew himself forward coolly, his elbows on the desktop. "Be a relief to me to hear you hadn't worked up no ordained ambition for that money. That you don't have your heart set on some special shiny play-bauble. That way you won't get overly distraught."

Rye waited, his face expectant.

"Distraught owin to what?" Gussie said.

"Owin to the couple-three debits on the account in question. Debits you maybe ain't apprised of."

The office had been growing closer since Gussie entered it. His head felt feverish. He was sweating under his shirt, the lamp radiating heat like a bonfire.

"The furnishin of an oil heater and repairs to said heater, for instance." Rye put a finger to his lips. "Human nature to forget all these expenses, but the ledger remembers. That special tea we had to send out for, calmed her lungs down, she swore. French shields ain't free. Customer cigars—yes, she was months behind there. Launderin ticket, she liked that done every day—some do every two days, three. I don't believe I'm breakin a headline your momma wasn't one to turn a penny over and over."

Even the backs of Gussie's hands felt hot now. His attention was fixed upon the bowtie on the desk, the repeating florets brilliant against the dark fabric they adorned. There was the shut window. There was the safe, which surely contained within its hollow a quantity of notes from which his mother's due would constitute the thinnest cut.

"Took to orderin brandy brung up this past winter. Feeble a winter as you get in these parts, she was forever catchin a chill." Rye had no notation book out. He swung his eyes this side to that as he detailed the expenses, totting in his mind's eye. "And lest we neglect the safe-keepin fee, hiked considerably, I admit, with the ongoin heightenin of hostilities, and payable upon withdrawal."

Blood was rushing through Gussie's brain, pulsing in his fingers and ears. He should've known. He should've known this could go no other way. Rye—at once far off and right in Gussie's face—was assuring him these sorts of setbacks were typical in the realm of free enterprise. He was counseling Gussie against hard feelings and grudges. "It ain't your time to be settin terms, is all. You hadn't sold a thing but your own sweat, and sweat is cheap. Me, I sold a whole lot of the dearest commodity on God's earth and done it for a lot of years."

Rye stood up and dug in his trouser pocket, and Gussie was somehow on his feet as well. Rye was saying it wouldn't do to send Gussie off with an empty hand. He reached a fist of loose coin out toward Gussie and then Gussie was holding the paltry offering, weightless in his two clammy palms.

"I was you," Rye said, "I'd judge myself fortunate Miss Ardelia's willin to take me in. Claimants for helpless boys are hard to come by just lately."

"I maybe ain't as helpless as you think," Gussie said.

"I didn't have nobody take me in when I was your age. Nobody sweet as Miss Ardelia, that's sure. Bastards like you and me don't often have a carpet rolled out. Miss A, she'll counsel you same as I have. Cool heads will prevail."

Though Gussie needed whatever meager capital he could get, needed it as much as anyone had ever needed it, he parted his hands and allowed Rye's coins to fall onto the desktop, the first couple thunking down singly and then a plinking song of copper and silver that rang outsize in the low-ceilinged office. His mother had kept her savings with Rye because nowhere else was secure, banks unbacked against fraud and fluctuation and folding left and right, house robberies growing routine in the lesser sections of town. Gussie wished she would've entrusted it to him but knew why she hadn't—because if something happened to it on his watch, he never would've forgiven himself. Something had happened to it anyway. And whether or not he ought, Gussie felt responsible.

In the quiet after the ring of the coins, Gussie heard the men out front again. He let his hands to his sides. Rye did nothing. Just grinned. He said Gussie had a streak of rashness in him and that wasn't cause to deride a boy. Told him he might come to something yet.

"There them rascals are," he said. He brought his hand up, clutching a brass match safe.

"So, that's the tale you're tellin?" Gussie said.

"Long and short," said Rye. "Stout and skinny." He had a match lit and the cigarette pinched in his lips and then the steamy office was filling with colorless smoke.

"You and I are meant to be done here?" Gussie said.

"I won't take insult if you dispense with shakin hands. Won't be the first time. Folks think it's soft crabs runnin a notchhouse, but I'm here to tell you it ain't. Was, everybody'd be doin it, now wouldn't they? I can answer that—yes, they surely would."

Gussie managed to sidle around the chair, breathing shallowly the sour air. He made himself steady on his legs and again wiped his hands on his trousers, then strode with gathering determination to the doorway and, without looking back at Rye, wheeled swiftly out of the office and up the hall, hastening toward the yellow light of the barroom and past Fozzy and his drinkers, still hearing Rye's assured chuckle when he was out of the building and still hearing it when he was well clear of the Night District, when he was back on the otherwise quiet streets that led to the home where he would no longer live.

He managed to get the prunes into his belly, pushing them into his mouth mechanically with three fingers. The soda cake he stowed in his pack. He tapped the dottle from his pipe and packed that, too, along with matches and the remainder of his tobacco. He had made peace with his letter and put down his signature and sealed the envelope. It rested on the desk now, patiently awaiting its orders.

Gussie sat down in the middle of the floor in his stocking feet, his mind a muddle. He thought of the careful-stepping white cat that had graced his mother's service. He thought of Rye's bowties and the new ladies from the Home for Wayward Girls. He tried to form a vision of his father, with Gussie's own sharp features but bespectacled and wearing a groomed beard, poring over tremendous old volumes by lamplight, tepid tea at his elbow. Gussie looked at the candle flame across the room, still as if painted. His mother had told him never to steal so much as a button, but all the same to never brook so much as a button stolen from him. And Rye had looted them both. He'd looted the Dwyers good.

Later, in the tranquil predawn, Gussie did not feel skittish. His hands and legs were ready to serve, his mind exhausted beyond all prudence. Gussie would not mislead himself. Whatever compensation he managed would certainly be missed, and reparation sought. So be it. It was a trouble for tomorrow. Numbered amongst his advantages, though, would be his early setting out and the fact that not a soul was privy to his destination. He felt not a grain of quibble as he shouldered his pack and picked the envelope up from the table. He extinguished the candle and slipped outside and eased the door silently back into the jamb, then followed a side road to the post hutch and slid his letter through the slot and listened to it flap to the floor inside. The moon was still bright above, lit underwise to resemble the bowl of a ladle. The lesser byway Gussie took was lined with stout, dusty palms that appeared made of stone. Gussie traversed the playlot of the Catholic grammar school, a path worn white in the weeds where the boys ran races, another spot trampled where they smoked after morning refreshment. A pang shot through Gussie that he would be unable to bid Miss Emily goodbye. He would have to send word of himself as soon as he was situated. Send word contradicting whatever Rye was sure to say, painting him the knave, the no-count thieving runaway.

Gussie made water at the mouth of the back street, then strode down the center of it and stepped through the open gate at the hind of Rye's property. He minced around a broken-down tumbrel, lowered his head for the thorn-decked branches of a Jerusalem tree. He scaled the back porch and let his pack down until it met the wood, then he held still, quiet a true minute, his ear perked for waking life inside. He stepped over and raised the already cracked window inch by inch until there was room enough to guide one leg through and lever his shoulders inside. He pulled the trailing leg in behind, then again stood motionless, again hearing not a whisper nor creaking hinge, before marking his first light steps through the rear foyer and into the parlor. The divans and club chairs, scattered about the room without apparent order, were only dim shadows. Gussie knew the room was bathed in rich color—the walls curtained and tables clothed, plush rugs on the floor, elegant tapestries—but all was dark now, the ladies retired to the upper stories with the evening's last clients, Rye long departed for his rooms at the Fribley House. It was only the ladies with children who kept their own homes, and these numbered but Gussie's mother and Miss Ardelia, whose daughter was grown, and another lady named Miss Cloyce who had lost her son in the early days of the fighting.

Gussie picked his way across the parlor then stalked on the balls of his feet down the long hallway, running his fingertips lightly along the batten. The door to Rye's office was closed. The safe inside likely held the bulk of Rye's proceeds for the week, but Gussie knew Rye didn't trust anyone else with the key, never had, and this was Gussie's leg up: tonight's receipts would be locked in the till until tomorrow, awaiting Rye's late-morning arrival. Fozzy would be resting by now in cramped quarters behind the bar that had once been a kitchen of sorts.

Gussie lengthened his stride to avoid the noisy plank and crept into the barroom. The air held the strangely sweet stink of hard-used men, of woodsmoke and whiskey and sweat. He heard the buzzing of a fly. The neighing of a horse from a few streets over. He passed down the length of the bar and soon heard Fozzy's snoring, like paper lazily torn. Another sheet. Another. Rye's ash dish still sat out, the moon so strong through the front windows that the stipples in the ivory were easily seen. Gussie rounded the bar's front end and shuffled forward until Fozzy's narrow chamber was in full view. The tender slumbered flat on his back, one arm flung over his chest as if in allegiance. Gussie couldn't make out his expression, but he couldn't imagine it different than the one he always wore, of forbearance and spite-edged superiority. The man took his rest on a leaf-stuffed mattress upon the floorboards, same as Gussie. Clutched what pride he could, same as Gussie.

Gussie's searching eyes flicked left and right and found what they sought, hanging there on a wall rack tucked into the nearest corner. He widened his stance and leaned in from the doorway, not keen to step foot in Fozzy's domain. His fingers found the lapels of the smoking jacket and then the collar. He upraised it from the peg and drew it toward him, the fabric shishing against itself, backed into the barroom proper and crept behind the bar stooped low and pushed his hand in each pocket of the jacket one by one, each slick little purse cool to his searching fingers. And here it was, in the breast, long as a dessert spoon. Gussie held it before his eyes, its teeth showing in the angling moonlight. He folded Fozzy's jacket over his arm and laid it on the bar. Found the hole in the till drawer, his hand tense but patient, a single scratch of metal on metal. When he turned the key, a low click. The drawer slid to with a rasp. Gussie glanced toward the street. Listened again for Fozzy.

He left the coin unmolested, fearful of its rattling, lifting from the drawer instead a drift of limp notes. Small makes, but Yankee bills all the same. Something. Enough to declare he wouldn't bear serenely Rye's theft. Enough to sustain him a while on the road.

He rolled the notes tight as a rug and snugged them into his trouser pocket. Left the key where it was, did not click shut the drawer. He headed toward the open end of the bar and rounded it, willing himself not to over-hasten and outpace his own feet. He waded in the direction of the long hallway, retracing the stool-side length of the bar, the amber bottles posted glumly on the shelves, his mind whizzing ahead in exhilarated relief, already clear of this place though his body was not. And in the next confounding instant, pain exploded through Gussie's shin, biting hard and bringing a groan out of him. A hollow clangor in his ears, the meat of his hands thumping the swept wood of the floor as if he'd been smacked unknowing by a great ocean wave. The spittoon. It was wobbling upon itself now like a nimble-dancing drunk, calling up a jarring racket from the planks. Gussie lunged to still it, getting to his knees, but only managed to knock it into a new course, out into the middle of the room where it caromed off a chair and a table leg. He clambered after it, frantic, sprawling prone, finally embracing the bowl of the spittoon with his two arms, knees and elbows smarting, heart thumping in his chest like a trapped animal.

In the new fraught quiet, Fozzy's snores were no more. There was a long, empty moment, and then a panicked stirring was heard, the slap of bare feet, and here was a hulking form before the windows, head swiveling this way and that, strapping shoulders silhouetted. Gussie found his feet and saw Fozzy's eyes grow big at what they beheld. Saw the man's attention tick toward the toppled spittoon, toward the till, back to Gussie.

"Be dog," he said. "What demon got in that brain of yours?"

"Gettin what's mine rightful," Gussie said. "And not the whole tab, neither."

Fozzy whistled weakly.

"No demon," Gussie added. "Just gettin square."

"No demon and nothin else beside. Full load of post holes."

"This ain't your affair," Gussie said, herding his balance under him.

Fozzy's eyes went beady again. He cut them toward the entryway, the airless coatroom that let out on the street. "I let you slip off, it'll be my affair. Mister will judge it my affair. He'll shit a jackfruit, he finds his till light."

Fozzy was edging forward piecemeal, his able leg leading. "I know you're heart-heavy, but this ain't the way to gladder days. You give over whatever you swiped. Your wits ain't about you, so trust in old Fozzy."

At the man's next cautious gain, Gussie scurried in the other direction, toward the rear, dragging down barstools in his wake. He loped down the long hall, spending all available hurry but feeling hindered, stymied of step, as if slogging through the sugary sand of the open coast. He could hear the ruckus of Fozzy clearing his way, skittering stools across the floor. Gussie cut his gait through the parlor lest a rug fly from beneath him, his arms straight out in front of him for obstructive furniture. He needed only to flee the building. Fozzy wasn't fit for a street-winding chase. Gussie didn't look behind. He barreled into the foyer and kicked a leg out through the window, no wish to haggle with the door lock. He jerked the rest of himself through into the night air, his boot catching on the sill and sending him careening over the modest porch, shot his arm down and caught up a strap of his pack with his fingers and yanked the weight of it along with him, aiming to gather himself into a great leap down into the yard, and in the next mute, airborne moment he was alive limb from limb with both the dread of being collared and the glee of escape. The pack hauled him askance on his descent. Gussie's boots met the ground at odds and he tumbled over himself, his pack sailing above him and snatching him into a splay, the heels of his hands taking the worst. He felt no hint of pain. Was back on his feet again in a blink and wrestling himself under the pack and bowing to dodge the thorny Jerusalem and swinging himself around the gatepost. He flashed a look and saw the back door of Rye's place thrown open. He saw Fozzy leaning on the doorknob like on a cane, saw him halt at the porch's edge and peer out under the flat of his hand as if the noonday sun shone bright above.

Gussie raced as if spellbound, his pack for the moment no more burdensome than a sack of feathers. Vagrant cats were the only other life on the streets, and they hunkered mid-step as Gussie whipped past them, the *fump fump* of his load waning and then gone. He glided beneath a pair of beleaguered sassafras trees that leaned together at their heights. Whizzed over one crossroads and the next, measuring his steps to leap the wheel troughs. In a flash he was advancing up his own slender lane, and his pace did not slack as the cottage loomed up beside him. He couldn't keep his eyes from flicking over the verbena in raving bloom, the battered roof. He'd proven unequal to the task of disposing of his mother's possessions and they sat inside yet, abandoned. He was relieved, despite himself, at having an alibi to leave it all behind, but he understood too that he never would have dealt with any of it. He'd been making neat arrangements in his mind, but he wouldn't have taken his hands and amassed the remnants of his mother's life, the woman who'd cared for and fed and tutored him all his days, and toted the goods to shop row and hawked them like ditch-found camp trinkets. Given years, he could never have brought himself to do it.

Soon, Gussie's sprint lagged and his lungs began to cool. He could feel the weight of his pack again, the tug on his shoulders with each bootfall. He passed the inland terminus of Palmina's prime canal, the water below a still, dark double of the sky above, the yawls cozy at their docks. Beyond the canal, a covey of whitewashed cabins. Beyond those a tailor. A steep-roofed blacksmith shop, its yard treeless, its porch heaped willy-nilly with marlinspikes and grubbing hoes.

The boundary of town was a shrubby lot on which resided a couple dozen mules. The exhausted animals snorted in the darkness as Gussie paced by, and then all at once the dry, dependable earth of the coastal climes gave way to a plot of marshland grown over with panic grass and dotted with shallow, stinking pondlets. This was Morfit Slough. A built-up wagonway bisected the damp, mosquito-clouded district; Gussie knew if he kept at least a trot he might reach the other side without being bitten to a pulp. He kept his eyes trained on the ground before him, alert for snakes. His face was slick, the salt of his sweat in his mouth and eyes. He slipped his thumbs up under the straps of his pack, cushioning their pinch, until his thumbs themselves began to hurt. Humped on. Humped on. Lead trees with their yellow pincushion flowers. Snakebirds resting up for the next hunt.

By the time Gussie cleared the slough, his pace was much diminished, but he would not allow himself to walk. The first leaching of the night's darkness was afoot, the mosquitoes thinning in the sour fog. He told himself that though he was lost to the only world he'd ever known, he was also free of it—for the first time, an emissary of his own fortune. Enough rope to hang himself, and perhaps he had already done so, but any gains were also his to keep. His own lefts and rights, his own starts and stops. His stomach had begun to growl, but he paid it no mind and before long it gave up its gripe. He traversed a nondescript couple of miles on a footpath edged in carpetweed, the daytime collecting about him in the branches of lopsided live oaks, the arriving heat seeming to radiate from underfoot, lone brazen horseflies darting about in anger or play or because they knew no other pastime.

An hour later, Gussie approached a crotch in the trail that meant he was near Panama Mill. This was the farthest he'd ever ranged from Palmina, and that was some years past, when his mother had taken him to a traveling menagerie featuring a dwarf hippopotamus and a two-headed constrictor and a Jesus Lizard that earned its meals by scampering the surface of a long, tin water tub. He slowed and came to a stop, the first time he'd stood still since facing Fozzy across the barroom. He slung his pack around front and removed his canteen, warning himself against the greedy glugs he craved. He sipped. Breathed. Sipped. Clouted the stopper back in place and squeezed the canteen into his pack and cinched the cord. The way south would deliver Gussie to Jacksonville and beyond, along the path of the St. John's as it widened into its bays and coves. Gussie knew he didn't wish to be pressed against the coast, his potential courses halved and settlements abounding, so he dallied not and started up the other branch, heading north and west into the seemingly more open destiny of the inland peninsula. A holiday stroll was all his legs would yield now. He made plodding progress into a flat pineland with sparse underbrush, the trees lean-trunked and swaying in breezes his skin could not feel. The ground hard. The sky a deep sapphire now, close and cloudless.

And later still, he crossed on plank bridges a succession of thin creeks that barely purled at their weaving little bights, angry prick bushes lining their banks. He encountered nary a soul. The dry shlucks of his boots on the wooden walkovers reached Gussie's ears as if from afar. The buzzing of the circling flies became muted. He was mindful of a low and constant thrum. It came down from the crowns of the trees and up from the creeks, but it was also the dutiful lub-lubbing of his blood. In his fatigue he was growing inseparable from his surroundings, yet it was too soon to rest, and so he pushed and pushed into the day, the pineland rolling out endlessly before him.

Gussie removed himself farther from the east-west pike, leaving what was left of his footpath and traipsing through an expanse of thigh-high ferns, the brittle stalks snapping readily at the weight of Gussie's step. He trained his course upon a spread of thick shade several throws distant, and then suddenly he stopped, frozen, the sunlight resting atop his head like an empty glove. It had dawned on him, what he'd forgotten. In a rimmed mahogany tray, slid under his bed table—his Peter Parley, his *Putnam's Monthly*, his grammar primer, the reader of Bible stories Miss Emily had given him as a gift. He would not have been able to make room for the lot, and would not in truth miss the primer, but a fast heat was running around his head at his failing to stash at least a Parley or two in his freight, and the slim volume of church tales with its cities razed in a fingersnap and wives cursed into pillars of salt. The thrumming wail that had become a part of Gussie grew louder, common crickets now pitching in. Cattle drives and train sackings galore in the Parley. Fires lit under recalcitrant mules. Wolf trappers falling partial to their prey. Gussie closed his eyes, feeling a lonesomeness too great to understand. He caught the fullest breath he was able of the warming breeze. He looked down at his legs, then up at the sky—they were somehow opponents—and lurched himself back into motion, lacking even the energy to curse himself with the wanted gusto.

Step gave way to step until he reached the delicious shade of a holly tree whose limbs shot straight out from its trunk like the spokes of a parasol. Gussie shimmied out from under his pack and let it slump to the ground, then found the earth with his backside. He searched out the soda cake first, bit it gingerly so as not to crumble it. He could feel the first swallow scrape down the length of his throat, could feel his belly getting about its eager work. He tipped his canteen and finished most of what remained in one go. Rummaged in his pack until he came out with some strawberries the neighbor children had picked. The fruit grew wild in the untended lots of Palmina, and the youngsters had made a thrifty habit of foraging them and selling them door to door. Gussie's mother had always taken a sackful, and he now held a batch she'd bought a few days before her death. The fruit usually came pale and hard, and improved in flavor after a week's time. Gussie bit them away from their stems one after another, savoring the drip of juice each held. He had half a dozen barks of dried beef, and he chawed through one and the better part of another. One more toss from the canteen, then he rested his head against the holly, flattened his spine against the smooth bole of the trunk. Stared at an anthill an arm's reach away, seemingly dormant. That perfect uniform ridge collaring it. That perfect round tunnel in the center.

Gussie heard the faint yapping of dogs. When the breeze died he heard nothing, but when it returned he again heard the yapping, plaintive and throaty. He'd heard tell that all the highbred hounds of Georgia had been stewed with onions and eaten merrily on crackers by the Yankee soldiers. These Gussie heard now were perhaps escapees, they and their brethren deploying southward in nervous parties, their covenant with man dissolved. In flight, same as Gussie, no option but to presume themselves hunted.

Gussie felt childish for anguishing over his stories. A luxury such as that. An amenity against nothing darker than tedium. When he could see, as plainly as if the man stood before him now, his pursuer. Gussie Dwyer, a prey item. He could see the one who would gain on him each time he rested. The one called August. The one Gussie's mother had construed an artist for his harboring no ambition to rise in the world—no aspiration but to exercise his genius for tracking and for cold-eyed violence. The one who groomed his Spanish mustang mare with a whalebone brush and fed her ripe fruits by hand, who carried a pistol of monstrous caliber with a handle trimmed in onyx. One needed not sight him often to recall him. His burnsides unpaired, one thick and the other attaining patchily through a mottled scar. His beard stiff as wire. His kestrel eyes. His muscle-roped forearms the color of toast. Some claimed his ancestors hailed from an island of the South Pole where men worshipped mysterious creatures of the sea. Some swore he'd ranged southward from the barbarous hollows of Kentucky. Some cited a connection to a band of savages that haunted the mountains of Mexico and fashioned gay little whistles from the bones of infants.

The afternoon sun Gussie walked toward was a white wound in the lesser heights, the sky a faded green behind it. He'd picked up a faint backland trail that could've been beaten by deer, the pines growing taller and thinner yet, the country adorned with sun-addled myrtles whose bright flowers whirled gently to the forest floor. The trail widened and disappeared and then, just as Gussie began to despair, returned beneath his feet. He spotted the ruined remnants of a pit oven, the roasting rocks scattered and an upset chair sinking in the weeds. The scents borne on the air were kindred—the daily fresh flourishing of new growth along with the decay of the deadfall. Bird feathers. Clean old bones.

At length, near to pitching over for need of sleep, knees wobbly and hips stiff, he veered off through the path-side bracken and found a flat of barren earth carpeted thick with fallen needles. Got quit of his pack. Removed his shirt, sweat-soaked and sundried to stiffness now.

Instead of hanging it, he spread it on the ground and collapsed atop it, his boots still on. Against all reckoning, he did not immediately feel sleep drawing near—a city he'd forsaken that now forbid his return. After a time, he raised himself slowly to sitting. Hauled his pack upright against his body and retrieved his pipe. He filled the bowl and struck a match, watched the smoke waver up like a charmed serpent.

He dug in his trouser pocket and pulled out the notes he'd commandeered from Rye's till. He counted them, turning them rightwise as he went, then neatened the stack and pressed it flat with the edge of his hand. Rolled the bills tight again. Hiding as he was, he indeed felt somewhere in him the craven spirit of a common thief. He wanted to be rid of the money and to be done with Rye. He could scarcely wait to have it spent. To turn it over for boiled peanuts and ginger beer. For a berry tart and fresh milk. Stewed oysters and hot bread. If they even had oysters in the interior. Prune meringues. A roasted woodcock. Pepper pot and cornbread. He could've eaten it all at once, his appetite had returned so loudly, eaten it all and then slept for days.

Rye was roosted at the bar eating a custard in heavy orange syrup when, well past noon, Fozzy finally returned with August. Through the windows, Rye watched the bounty hunter bring his mustang to a halt at the rail and alight from her with the offhand aplomb of a lighter, younger man. Watched him scratch the steed beneath her muzzle and watched her toss her silvery mane. Rye heard Fozzy clomp through the coatroom with his mispaired steps, and then his employee crossed over and assumed a post at the far end of the bar and took up a deck of cards and laid a hand of rube-at-the-cherries.

Out front, August gave his horse a final affectionate pat and then stretched himself to height and panned his eyes uproad and then unhurriedly down. He wheeled around and stoically scaled the porch, disappeared from sight a moment in the coatroom, and here he crossed the barroom in his stiff duster with footfalls quiet as a child's. He showed Rye his straight white teeth, bright and clean as wedding china, and leaned equably against the bar.

Rye's spoon produced a delicate tink when he set it in the half-full custard dish. This day he wore a teal bowtie, and he'd sat for a shave to hasten the minutes along while Fozzy was out on his errand. The man across from him wore a long, matted beard the color of trail dust. He smelled of whiskey and horse and sea brine. Rye had heard the fellow had a taste for still-gasping fish straight from the canal but had never seen this rumor take life. Rye had been August's primary client since the war began and had grown to trust the hunter without making progress toward fathoming him. August had once earned coin chasing runaway slaves but had been in no small hurry to get shut of that traffic. He said there were too many slave-trackers already—you had to race to the quarry like a jockey, and once you had it, had to race it back where it belonged before another hunter ambushed you and snaked the bounty. He liked to work alone and thought it insulting to be pitted against others of his occupation.

"One-item docket today," Rye said.

"Just the kind I favor." August twisted a lock of his beard roughly with his index finger. His knuckles were as knotted as old tree roots.

"Dwyer boy. His momma finally passed. Came in face tight as a drum to withdraw the estate. Tally didn't rise to expectation, as it most times don't, so he came back later and raided me. One whole evenin's revenue. Right through the back window."

"Got better of your guard dog, huh?"

Rye and August turned their heads to look down the bar, but Fozzy gave no reaction, his eyes rapt on his game.

"Loyal," said Rye. "And prompt, seein as he beds on the premises. Not much for chasin, but that's where you come in."

August reeled his attention back from the card-playing barkeep. He rested it on the bottles against the wall. After a moment, Rye grabbed a tumbler and glugged in a few fingers and pushed it over to August, who took a dainty preliminary sip before tipping his head back and draining what remained in one easy draught.

"Dwyer boy, huh?"

"Never been no irk. Though I won't say I was overfond of him. Had a bit of the goody-two-shoes about him, but I never believed it. Knew it was always an act. He's got crazy in him, like you'd expect from a whore's son."

"If it was an act, seems he gave it up." August worked a finger around inside his whiskey glass, then plunged the finger inside his cheek.

"A botheration such as this," Rye said, "gives chance to ward off forthcomin trouble. All them scrounge artists out there. All those back from the front. Crisp reply in this matter will tame their notions." Rye breathed deep, then returned to his custard, finishing it off with quick spoonfuls and licking the back of the spoon clean. "He's beyond the age for a wrist slap. I want chastenin in full. Tall levy. Lot of folks with hardships of late, but precious few daft enough to revenge it on me."

August offered no rejoinder, nor even a nod. The after-dinner street outside the windows was reawakening with the chink of harness, the creak of wagon wheels. The spaced, considered flips of Fozzy's cards could be heard, and then he sighed and collected the deck and shuffled it in his slow hands.

"You prefer I return with a captive or a tragical story?"

"I want him brought," Rye said. "And if he ain't fribbled away his plunder, you can seize that and call it gratuity."

August sniffed. He stepped over to the windows to spit, then strode back to his spot.

"On foot?"

"Assume so," Rye said. "Unless he saw fit to add horse-thievin to his repertoire."

August scratched his burnside. "Won't get hemmed on the coast if he's got half a brain. He'll clear the river inland. Past there, it'll call for study."

"Got this from yonder where they stayed." Rye reached under the bar and dragged out a careworn coat sleeve, torn away at the seam—bigger than a child's, smaller than that of a man.

August accepted the article. Folded it in half once and then again. He gave the bar two quick raps with his tortured-looking knuckles, made a clicking sound in his cheek, and turned on his heel to take his unceremonious leave. After a moment, Rye and Fozzy could see him outside, tucking the coat sleeve into a pannier and then freeing the mustang from the rail and mounting with a nimble bound, as if hoisted with unseen wires. He reached forward and gentled the animal's poll, then swung her around and started her westward and away, leaving no evidence of himself, nary even a cloud of dust.

Fozzy left his game spread where it was and came over and removed his employer's custard dish and replaced it with an ash dish. Rye looked away from the window. He got a cigarette and lit it and blew a plume of smoke straight out in front of him.

"He cross at you rousin him?"

"No," said Fozzy. "Said he'll hide better next time. Gave a grin then up splashin water at his face. Came right behind."

"I don't reckon he gets cross," Rye said.

"Don't reckon, sir."

"Lion ain't cross chasin a deer." Rye took a long, covetous draw on his cigarette, then flicked the ash down near his boots. "Thing about him—ain't bloodthirsty, ain't blood-guilty. That's a rare circumstance. All the same to him. He don't think a whole lot of himself, see, but he thinks even less of everybody else."

"I've heard it told he's a twin," said Fozzy. "Other one March by name, owin to bein mild and quick-passin, while August is mean and takes his time."

Rye chuckled. "I heard that one myself," he said. "I heard that one and a whole lot of others."

———————

Next morning, under a sky blushed with a mustard hue, Gussie jibed his route northward, wanting more distance between himself and the rail tracks that led to Baldwin. He negotiated a parcel of meadowland suffused with eye-high fetterbush, the lithe sprigs hung with limp blossoms of ruby. Ferreted out another faint aisle slicing through the wilderness, and another. The boy felt fortified from his rest, his legs dully aching but resolute, his feet battered but resigned to their grueling office.

At another of the inert, scum-surfaced waterways snaking through the otherwise dry country, Gussie happened upon a mother and son, or so he took them, seated on a clean white log and looking upon a clogged brook as if upon a resplendent rolling sea. He passed a single-file line of girls in collared day-dresses, unbathed and slumping toward the coast, toward the land he'd fled. Here were the people. Boys with dogs. Old women walking with their faces in their hands. And cloistered beneath a soaring wart-trunked hardwood, a clutch of Black men reclining this way and that, heads rested on one another's shins, arms flung along the ground like neck-broke snakes, their exhaustion seeming contagious, an illness one might contract by passing downwind. These were freed slaves. Some had stripped their shirts, and Gussie could see plainly their dark, raised scars. He guessed these men had hoofed through the night, snoozing now while the sun showed, fleeing the plantation lands. Gussie heard a thin upscaling wail and realized first it was a song, and then that it was a song he recognized from the docks.

I'm castin my sins out middle of the sea,
with all the troubles of the world.
I'm castin my sins out middle of the sea,
they sank to the bottom like pearls.
Yes, they sank to the bottom like pearls.

In the letter Gussie had written Madden Searle, he had urged the man not to send anyone to meet him because he knew not where his course might ramble. Now he felt an idiot for having written this. As if Searle would leap to his feet after reading Gussie's words and dispatch an escort to ensure the safe arrival of some questionable alien dock rat. Gussie had drafted the missive twice, thrice, and again, and yet had not set it right, had not rid it of presumption. He had told Searle of the watch, explained that it had fallen down behind a bureau during his visit and only been found weeks later. His mother had chosen Searle, Gussie had written. She had chosen him for his kindness and had been pleased, despite the adverse circumstances the baby would be born into, to find herself with child. Yes, pleased. Yes, in her heart grateful. Gussie had relayed this sentiment but had kept to himself his mother's assurances that she'd met Searle well before the war's poverty had forced her to Rye's, her assurances that Gussie was the product of real affection and not a base transaction. Gussie, in his letter to Searle, had made his own assurances—that he did not reckon on money, that he aspired only to put eyes to his father and return the man's property. But any son would desire more. Who would believe otherwise? Who would look upon such as Gussie with anything but doubt and misgiving? His mother had built Searle up as a man of uncommon virtue, but how much could she have known? She'd sketched him as one whose familial woe had turned him regardful rather than bitter. A man of courtesy and a rational man. But who in Searle's strange position, no matter how noble, could be expected to acknowledge a penniless adolescent? What reason would he have, aside from a heart soft as a saint, not to lock the gates and return to his work?

The day was warm enough, though it was but early May, and Gussie heard again that droning din in his skull. He'd ceased sweating, his skin run dry. His spit was foam. His beaten trace of a trail wound him through dandelions and daisies, a world throbbing and hectic with bees. Sorry pond apples. Out-of-place pineapple palms hung with yellow-green fruit like rosaries. He danced his pack around and ate another bark of dried beef, chewing and over-chewing it into a splintery meal on his parched tongue. He drew forth a poke sack of raisins and shook out little palmfuls and tossed them back until the sack was empty. He kept on. The soft, monotonous cadence of his bootsoles. The shluff of his pack with each step. Above, birds so high in the sky they appeared fixed in place. Below, the rustling weeds.

"They sank to the bottom like pearls," Gussie said, his voice rough and strange. "All the troubles of the world."

Gussie's pack straps had by this time worn his shoulders raw, and by turns he hitched them up toward his neck, then spread them sideways onto his upper arms. It was one modest leather pack, the whole of his earthly grip. There was Gussie himself, the boy, his growling stomach and withering throat, his senses that seemed to grow both duller and keener by the minute, and then there was all Gussie owned jouncing in time against his back. His canteen. A flipper of matches. A folding knife that hadn't been sharpened in an age. A goodly helping of pork skins. Madden Searle's watch, of course. Tobacco and pipe. One fresh shirt in reserve, one pair of stockings. He kept in his pocket the money he'd appropriated from Rye, but at the bottom of his pack rested a smaller amount that he'd earned and saved for himself at the docks. Rye was right—his sweat was all he had, and how very cheap it was.

The pines began to relinquish the land, however miserly, to oak and persimmon. Soft beds of clover. And then the trail swelled and an unpainted post-and-rail fence drew up alongside Gussie. On the other side ran more untamed woods, but Gussie kept on until a house winked through and he was skirting a raked yard of dark soil. The fence was teased about with Calusa grape, tight green flowers on coiling tendrils. The vine thickened, doubled itself once and again, until in time the fence was engulfed and no trace of it could be seen.

Around a bend, Gussie came to the open gate, inside which a man was sorting the contents of an overloaded, slat-sided dray. The man turned his head toward Gussie, his brow gathering sharply as if the fact of Gussie was beyond his ken. He stood tall from his work, tapping the peen of a hammer into the soft of his palm. A dog with a corn-colored coat was casting its head about in the greenery nearby, searching out a scent worth tracking. The man wore denim overalls, the bib unclasped and hanging down about his waist. A livid wound marked his shoulder, only partly bandaged, couched in dark bruising.

Gussie introduced himself, and the man dropped the hammer into an empty scuttle near his feet.

"Awful thirsty," Gussie said.

"I reckon so," said the man. "Well out back. Only thing workin shape on the whole claim. Got a canteen, ain't you?"

Gussie said he did.

"Can't furnish much in the way of mess." The man's teeth had a gray, almost transparent cast. "Been gettin by with critters and onions. Run dry on onions yesterday."

"I'm fixed for grub," Gussie said.

"Step on in. Don't stand on ceremony."

The man picked a few loose tools from the ground and pitched them into the dray—augers and awls, darkened about the handles with use—then started up toward the house. He gave his knee a whap, and his dog jaunted out of the foliage and fell into position. Gussie skipped ahead and caught up with the man, and the two of them strode past a column of ash trees, their blanched flowers like burst stars. They rounded the house and Gussie noticed a pair of busted windows, remnant shards of the panes sticking in little jags from the frame.

The man said this was a good enough spread when somebody was around to beat it silly. His lemon grove was intact, but the fruits were hard and juiceless. All his seed had dried. Goats stole or run off.

"I got tobacco to trade for the water," Gussie said. "No jackpot, but more than a pinch."

The man scoffed. "Whatever you got, you best keep."

They proceeded into the rear yard, a space lorded by a tulip tree no less than a hundred feet tall. The well was in sight, at the far edge of the tulip's shade.

The man swept a look around, then succumbed to a sigh. "It was fun first couple months. Slip the yoke. Kick some factory stiffs around. Plop it down at the fire and listen to the fiddler. When that fun took leave, it sure ran and hid."

The man turned a short, squat log on its end and sat down, and the dog settled in at his feet. Gussie drank his fill, dousing away the worst thirst he'd ever felt, trying not to swamp himself, the sweet, metallic water sloshing in his belly like in a pot. He took his breaths, drank again, then filled his canteen to overflowing and had to take up a slurp before the stopper would plug back into place. He felt his hands and feet cooling, relief running down his limbs.

When he turned around again, the man had a canister open and was rubbing unguent into the dog's joints. He slathered the forelegs, then moved on to the hind, greasing the animal's fur clear down to the paws.

"Tell you how I came by this here companion," the man said.

Gussie looked down at the dog's contented face, its seemly hazel eyes. He already felt he should be off again, fear a weight in his bowels calling him atrail, but the respite was savory—the friendly company, the shade.

"Old planter up the county seat here, he owed me for pitchin in on his pe-can harvest. Owed it me three years ahead of the hostilities. Asked on it once, twice, then left it be awhile and the war set in. Suspect he thought I gave it up, or it's liable he plum forgot, all was goin on."

The man replaced the lid on the canister and stropped his fingers clean on his overalls. His own wound was oiled over with an ointment also, likely the same.

"Any case, I came home after the surrender, took a day or two ponderin. Took stock of the old farm. Came across a jar I hid from myself, got into that pretty thick. Next thing, high as a buzzard, find myself hoofin up toward that old boy's concern. Close on an hour hike. I tromped up the porch and told who I was and pretty soon found out the mister wasn't home. He was off somewhere for the day. So, I tell the gettin girl to get me a glass of lemonade, meanwhile install my hind parts in a rockin chair. No singled-out intent at this point, you see. Then I'm waitin for my drink and I spy this pooch here, not payin no mind and nobody payin him none. I snap my fingers and gave the porch a thump and over he trots. Happened by luck I had a lump of salt pork I brung for munchin along the road, and I gave him that and he let me love on him while he was champin it down. Next thing I said here we go boy just like that and he followed me off the porch and straight on down the walk. Mister wasn't home but the lady was. She stormed out on the porch and gave me a tongue-strafin for the books, hollerin every oath and slander. How sorry I's going to be. Callin the dog by name and him not so much as twitchin an ear. When she got quiet for half a blink I said to tell the old man he ain't in debt no more to Lester out on the creek run."

The man drew himself up from the endwise log, seeming rickety and weary now when only moments ago he'd been spry.

"About got his new name stuck," the man said. "Ain't that right, Doak?"

Gussie arose too, grateful he wouldn't have to make a rude exit, and the party left the shade of the tulip and began rounding back to the front yard, the brimming dray rising into view. The man leaned over toward Gussie, brandishing a flat hand to shy his voice from the dog, one eyebrow ticked.

"Seldon," he whispered. "'That's what they were callin him."

"No wonder he wasn't answerin to it," Gussie said.

August had passed the night in a third-fiddle bunkhouse a ways south of Jacksonville, had awakened before the sun and breakfasted on yesterday's Scotch hash, then had burned up the whole of the morning on the fruitless hunt, trotting south through humble bluffs tufted with sea oats and backdropped to the east by the blue sound. He had

made countless sallies away from the water, down one westerly spur
and the next, and backtracked each having found nary a bootprint,
nary a newly broken twig, nary a fruit stone. August had canvassed
a coterie of rum sots, stinking and beset with sand gnats, and had
yielded for his trouble only belched calls for his flask and offers to sell
him sour apples for his horse. Some Blacks had instituted a shanty-
town and August had interrupted their late breakfast of oysters and
heard from them no sir's. No skin-and-bone white boy with a bulged
pocket came by? No, none we witnessed. Plenty of boys passed, but
none lone and bareheaded and makin special haste.

Thereafter the dunes dissipated and gave out onto vast tidewater
flats pocked with crab holes. August encountered a very old man
hauling a skiff behind him toward drier land, a single drumfish lying
flat in the hull. The man told August all were lost babes to him, that
August himself was but a boy.

"About yay high," August said, holding a hand to his own shoulder and wondering if he spoke to a dullard or a sage. "Cheeks smooth
like creek stones."

But the man was already pressing on before him, drafting a line
in the muck that August would cross.

A couple or three villages arose, and he inquired briefly in each
and moved on, the trail growing colder. He crossed McGirt's Creek
and outpaced the flats and entered a bayside scape of sea grape and
flourishing wild cucumber, the setting growing pleasanter as his
mood soured. The afternoon sky was white and flat as a plate, the
early May heat doing its utmost to gain a hold. August slinked one
arm free of its duster sleeve, shifted and freed the other, rolled the coat
and wedged it secure behind him. He cuffed one sleeve of his shirt
up past the elbow, then cuffed the other and undid his collar buttons,
revealing on his chest an immense black brand of rising, hungry
flames that always itched when the day was hot but not humid.

The shadows were long when he clopped into an abandoned boon-docks that must've served the nearby sugar mill until the operation had closed. A corn snake crossed the way and August's horse halted of her own volition, betraying no nerves, until the terra-cotta creature had slithered from sight. After a moment she set herself again in motion, also with no bidding. Beyond these few hovels was the quiet water of Medicine Inlet, which jutted several miles inland and would need to be flanked if August wished to keep southward.

He bowed his head under a low-swept branch. Reached and found his whiskey and tilted out a long spill. The circling wind carried both the salt of the sound and the peat of the ancient, groaning forest. When the air stilled, he heard a dry hacking from within one of the rotted dwellings. The horse turned her head. Not abandoned in full, this lean-to burg. On a notch board nailed above the door frame was painted SEER of FORTUNES, then, beneath that, ONLY THE BRAVE SHALL ENTER. Nothing was visible through the windows. August put away his whiskey. He guided the horse over to a locust tree that stood passably straight amongst all the spreading, knurled live oaks, dismounted, hung the reins loosely around the trunk.

He approached the place and scaled its front steps lightly. This was the end of the Southern line for him. A checkpoint. A weigh station. He knocked at the door. When no answer came, he pushed it fro and stepped into a gloomy front room—stacks of frayed books arrayed sloppily about, a rocking chair heaped with cloaks and scarves.

A striped valance hung in the doorway to the rear room, and August took off his hat and brushed under it. At the creak of a floor-board the man inside started, his head jerking alert as if he'd been wrested from a reverie. He reclined laxly on a dais of sorts, in an attitude both slovenly and gauged for presentation, his garish rai-ment over-topped by a quilted jacket the slick color of a tree frog. His face was flushed, and in one hand he gripped a folding fan with bellows of translucent, veined parchment. Presently he collapsed the fan with a swish and tucked it out of view.

"You wish to inquire of the gift, good fellow? Do not approach lightly, for the gift deals only in bare truth."

"I suspect it's good and rested," August said. "That gift of yours. Ain't exactly a line out the door, couldn't help notice."

The man cackled mirthlessly. This was what August had heard from outside, not coughing. The man remained in his drifting posture and beckoned August closer with a fluid motion of his arm.

"What intelligence do you seek, my son? Mind, speak up clearly now."

August closed the distance between himself and the dais, hat held in both hands before him like a man arraigned. A jarred candle burned on the floor, and August could smell the tallow in the stuffy room. He could see, in the corners, weeds growing up through the floorboards.

"It's of an occupational bent," he began. "See, I'm engaged under decree of a man much grander than you or me, and this grandee in question had some money stole off him in the dark of night by—well, by a certain tender-aged reprobate who's took to parts unknown."

The man's eyes were shut, his palms upturned.

"I'm lookin to make them unknown parts known," August said. "So far makin as much headway as a hog swimmin upstream. Either he done vanished or I took a bum turn."

August took a small step back to signal he'd finished, and the man exhaled raspingly and let his attention resettle upon the carnal realm.

"Evil or afoul of luck?" he asked.

"Beg pardon."

"This boy. This reprobate. Be he a vile sort or a mark of misfortune?"

August scratched his beard. "Ain't for me to study," he said.

The man frowned affably. "Nor does it concern me, but we must provide the gift all it deems vital. Is this an innocent you seek to collar and bring to pain and ruin or a barb-toothed mongrel?"

"Don't know where you been spendin your evenins, but I don't happen upon over-many to be named innocent. Marks for bad fortune—now them's a penny a pound."

The man nodded in a reconciled way, as if to acknowledge an impasse. He drew his hand to his soft chin, squared his shoulders toward August. "Go with this, my friend, in grace and goodwill." He paused, eyelashes fluttering, fingertips pressed gently together. "In cornering this prey, his plight and your own will entwine as the vine which catches purchase upon itself. The both of you will duly taste the dust below of your own collusive weight."

August waited. He could hear the scratching of vermin under the floor and the tapping of his own finger on the crown of his hat. "That it?" he said.

"A bushel of counsel in a pin-tin of words," the man told him.

"Most get tangled with me, they wind up clipped. Always been that way. Don't know why it'd be different this time, after all these years."

"The future is not beholden to the past," the man said. "The past was itself once the future, don't forget."

"Past wasn't never the future. Past don't exist till we're done makin it."

"My dear child, the past is so hazy. Just try and look back. It's made of smoke. It's disappearing. The future—at least we can hear its drumming. At least it's coming toward us, not running away."

August put his hat back on his head and then looked at his own hands, these hard allies that knew always what to do. He widened his stance. "Should've shared it to start, I'm a fortune-teller myself. I got a way of foreseein if a fellow's soon to get whanged upside the ear. I don't require communin with unseen entities, see. If a fellow tells me somethin I want to hear, they most times don't get whanged. Tell me somethin other, well…"

The man's face lost a bit of color, a veil of worn tolerance now overspreading it.

"I won't rough you," August said. "Just doin your job, ain't you? Like we every one of us bound to."

The man was looking toward August but without catching his eyes. There was vast, unfathomable sadness in him.

"So, what's the damage?" August asked.

The man seemed not to understand.

"What I owe you for the sittin? Or the standin, as it was."

The man now made a reluctant inventory of August, to his boots and back up. The merciless eyes. The dark tattoo licking up above his open collar. "The gift hasn't need of man's currency, and I myself would hardly insult its exercise by assigning an earthly value. We accept such amount each addressee deems fitting."

August gave a laugh, but the man only took out his fan and snapped it open and fluttered it near the neckline of his vest. August went for his walking-about funds, then realized his duster was out with his horse. In the back pocket of his trousers he had some flat-folded, large-gauge Yankee bills and he slipped them out and peeled one and held it toward the man, whose fan stilled. The man looked at the bill warily—more money, likely, than he'd seen in some while—but August kept it there, and after a moment the man leaned himself forward on the dais and rose onto his knees and took the crisp tender and planted it, with forced coolness, somewhere in his bosom.

August split the seer a grin. "Ain't see that comin, did you?"

———

When evening fell, Abraham made his way out to the corner of the estate nearest the citrus, where a pack of freedwomen had taken up residence just outside the four-rail fence. Each morning they decamped and stashed their effects, and each sundown they returned, like clockwork, three or four pitiful females and their collective young. There was no work for them in town, Abraham knew, and so they pilfered fruit from the trees and melons from the patch, the children relieving themselves freely along the fence line, the women whispering in anguished committee deep into the night. They'd been so bold, in fact, as to help themselves to wood from the reserves for their cooking, Abraham was sure of it. The greater problem was that as word spread of safe squatting, only more penniless pioneers would amass. And if Abraham were to alert Mr. Searle of the intrusion, the master's response would likely be to raise a canvas awning for the trespassers against the coming summer rains. Softheartedness was all well for Mr. Searle, but Abraham was overseeing both house and grounds single-handedly now, and it was his duty to prevent the abstracted old fellow getting fleeced fore and aft.

He eased up behind the last row of grapefruit, training his ears on the clumsy rustlings, gladdened to have caught the offenders dead to rights. Through the leaves the women appeared as hustling shadows, retiring from sight then reappearing elsewhere, hissing at the children and flouncing about importantly. They had no lanterns but dusk hung about yet, and the moon had already made its luminous arrival at the tree line.

When he stepped into their midst, back straight and face hard, they froze, stricken, eyes aghast, releasing little gasps and then arresting their breaths altogether. The croupy wail of the lubber grasshoppers was loud in the grove behind. Abraham's watch ticked in his breast pocket. All at once the women fell to swooping about him, their purposes crossed and harried, plucking battered pots off the ground, ingathering what odd foodstuffs they'd managed to scrimp, swatting at the children.

Abraham raised a hand to still them; once they'd all obeyed, the camp half-packed already in a few short moments, he made a leisurely circuit around them, surveying, encircling them in his authority. The women wore coarse linen shifts and the children peeked out from behind them in soiled spoon bonnets. Their eyes, the whole lot, were yellow, their hair matted like wool. Abraham could easily pick out the head of the sorry party. Not the eldest nor fairest of the women, but the most intelligent looking. He took up a position front and center the huddling troop, then lowered an eye to this woman until she stepped forward. She was less afraid than the others, something shrewd in the set of her mouth.

"You'll carouse no longer upon this acreage," Abraham announced. "The master will not tolerate the befouling of his abode. At present he does not wish to bring legal recourse, but that generous position depends on your immediate and permanent flight."

The woman Abraham had singled out wanted to speak, and Abraham, with a gesture of his hand, granted her permission to do so. The woman kneaded her skirt in her leathern fingers, her shoulders gathered about her neck in agitation.

"If you see fit to grantin us one night more, we'll clear out in the mornin like we were never here. We'll be quiet as mice, then gone as a body can be before anybody wakes. The young ones are fallin out tired, but we'll make our hurry-up as soon as light breaks."

A breeze washed in from the Gulf, lisping through the grove. Abraham breathed the moist air. He brought a thumb to his lips, pretending to consider the woman's request. "I admire your boldness," he said. "Let it not be suggested you lack in that area. If I'm to understand, you wish this estate to bear your unlawful encroachment further than it thus far has. You propose a continuance of the offense.

You propose that the estate's reward for allowing your imposition to go unpunished be yet more skirts full of stolen fruit? Is that the bargain? Shall I fetch a paring knife and dining china?"

"We only take the ones fallen to the ground. That's truth I say to God himself. The ones ready to rot and then no good to nobody."

"What's yet to ripen on these grounds and what's gone to rot is no affair of yours," Abraham said.

The woman cast down her eyes, and perhaps there was something of anger about the tightness of her brow. A child behind her began to cry in sniffling pants, and another child endeavored to soothe him.

"We only take for the little ones," the woman said. "Never could suffer hungry little ones."

"I never could suffer them under any condition, starving nor fat as Christmas hogs." Abraham rested his hands on his lean hips and put a bit of starch into his posture. "And now," he said, "I've other matters to attend. This is not the United States Congress and we shall not debate further. You'll collect your holdings and quit this spot at once."

The youngest of the women, an overgrown adolescent, broke formation then. She wore blunt-toed boots that rode loose on her feet. Her hair was pulled back severely from her face, trussed tight at the rear of her olive-shaped head.

"And where are we off to?" she said. "We're to leave from here, but where are we to get to?"

"The devil, as much as I care," Abraham replied. "So long as there's no trace of you here anymore."

He was pleased enough with his course of action, with his execution of it, could see himself already back on his little portico enjoying a cigarette, but he made the error of looking too closely over the ragtag clan, abject and imperiled, thin to ribs, women without menfolk, faces hung like empty sacks. Pitiful, indeed. He indulged in a sigh. Brought out his handkerchief and drew it down his face and neck. "Haye Branch," he told them. "At Haye Branch they're to dole out provisions to the indigent. The announcement will be made in the morning, I happen to know. I could get in trouble for telling you that, but if your lot isn't indigent, I couldn't say who is."

"That's twenty miles if it's a step," the young woman said. She cut her eyes toward the little horde of children, who'd begun to fidget and speak low into one another's ears.

"And here you stand," said Abraham, "squandering the cool evening hours rather than making headway. Quit your dawdling and you'll start the line."

"If it ain't a lie and we're first to get nowhere. We've heard plenty of lies without yours."

"I've no motive to lie to you," Abraham said. "Indeed, no reason to speak further to you at all."

The young woman spit. She had more to say and went ahead and said it, and her elder companions piped back in likewise, but Abraham stood unflinching, still to his fingertips and eyes cold, until they gave up their entreaties and began testily assigning this one tote this and that one that, hanging knapsacks from shoulders and nesting lesser pots into their larger kin and prodding the children into a march and huffing off at a defeated, jangly shuffle. Abraham did feel for them. He understood they bore no blame for their position. He felt for all the newly freed. Cast off with nothing. Abraham felt he had never benefited from the ugly institution, had not owned a slave, had never had one in his charge, but now he would bear the brunt of its overthrow—desperate droves looking for work, looking for handouts. And when neither of those materialized, looking to steal. Abraham had spent the last years fretting over white looters—hiring young cane hands to defend the place at every fresh round of rumors, finally understanding that the boys themselves were the primary source of those reports—and now he would worry of dark-skinned thieves, men and women tossed ill-equipped into the cutthroat arena of American survival.

When Abraham could hear no more rattling, no more cursing, he started up the mild slope, his large hands clasped loosely behind him, through the citrus and past the tomatoes and squash. Beyond that was a bristling grove of butterfly palms, anomalous amongst the eatables, that had once been tenants of the house. Mr. Searle had ordered them brought in two to an iron tub and dispersed throughout to every room, a stunt inspired by his once-wife's combined wishes to be amid the splendor of tropical nature and to not venture out of doors. She'd claimed to suffer acute allergies to flowers and herbage of all stripes, could not endure direct sun, was grimly ill-disposed toward insects. She was the individual responsible for Abraham's being brought on, way back when. She had insisted upon a live-in staff, and for months Mr. Searle had minced about his home in utter embarrassment at the presence of servants. It had taken him longer still to grow accustomed to the monstrous house itself. After his wife had left, Mr. Searle had given Abraham instructions to clear the place of the spiny green plumages, to have them planted outside where they belonged.

As he climbed the steps to the porch, Abraham gained a view of Mr. Searle's workshop off on a flat that spanned the western flank of the estate. It was framed by a shoulder-high hedge, its windows blackened by dark fabric. Whatever the master was working on, he'd become more engrossed these past months and also more covert. He'd made his fortune in air-cooling, but his fascination with that subject had seemed to ebb even before the start of the war. Now Abraham could only conjecture his master's projects, could only guess wildly. Nothing that arrived in the post gave him a clue—it was only supplies related to candle-making, a diversion Mr. Searle had become smitten with during the Conflict and which took up more and more of his time. Oil of vitriol. Bitartrate of potassa. A mince hatchet for tallow. Mr. Searle had hired workers from the village and even charged a nominal fee for the candles he produced, just enough to cover expenses, Abraham assumed. Volumes on the properties of stearic acid. A biography of Joseph Morgan. It wasn't uncommon for Mr. Searle to take up recreational interests—he'd spent a summer constructing Egyptian reed kites, had fallen into earnest study of the Ancient Roman justice system—but usually these pursuits were indulged on Saturdays, a reason to escape the workshop. If the chandlery were meant to benefit his health, it was a failed venture. If anything, Mr. Searle was more ashen of late, less steady on his feet.

Abraham went indoors and made his way to the larder. When he drew the door, it whined—he made a mental note to soap the hinges. He also meant to scour the salt rime from the sills and mix up tobacco water for the ants if time permitted. Some time ago Mr. Searle had let go the maid, and not long after that he'd sent off the woman who'd cooked and kept the kitchen. After Ruth's departure and then Julius heading off to the Western Theater, there wasn't enough work to require a permanent maid, and once the maid was gone there were few to cook for, and Mr. Searle's waning appetite to boot—indeed, supper was the only meal he had regular appetite for anymore. It couldn't be overlooked, too, that the master had grown cagey about his affairs to a queer degree. Abraham had marked the change in him. He didn't want extra pairs of eyes about to witness the failing of his physical robustness, to fret over his ague or his occasional fainting—in short, didn't want anyone fussing over him. Didn't want, either, questions as to his daily activities, whether they were healthful. Didn't want anyone snooping around his workshop. Didn't want to do anything but keep private what was private and leave the rest to Abraham.

Abraham stepped inside the larder and set neat the jars of chutney and molasses and pickled carrots. He was as handy in the kitchen as that cook had been—it was only a fact. Perhaps he'd roast a chicken tomorrow to match with the mango preserves. He plucked a pair of sweet potatoes from a basket on the floor and an onion from another. Stepped around a case of spruce beer someone had sent Mr. Searle as a gift—too sweet for the master's stomach, if not his taste, it had sat there one bottle shy for ages. Hominy. Perhaps with sausage in the morning. No sense reckoning on Mr. Searle's breakfast. He'd get down what he could of a wedge of cantaloupe, washed back with four or five cups of coffee.

Abraham retired to his quarters at the back corner of the house, pausing on the way to straighten a hall runner with the toe of his boot. He lit a candle. On his chest of drawers, on a copper salver, he kept a bottle of sherry and a thin-stemmed cordial glass. He poured a measure and carried it out to his portico, which, though private enough, lacked for view, looking out upon the untended property abutting the estate—a weed-choked pasture marked with rotten troughs and disarrayed coops. Mr. Searle's broken-down old quarter horse was out there somewhere, too. The owner of the land, though refusing to sell the parcel, had given free rein to graze the animal.

Abraham tipped his glass to his lips and let the sherry pool in his mouth before swilling it. The evening sky was starless. On the pasture's far margin, silhouettes of bending palms and banana trees. He heard the rising shish of the pasture weeds. When the breeze reached him a moment later, it carried the scent of scorched sugar and bougainvillea. He saw something white moving toward him and soon could tell it was an egret, poking along the overgrown fence line with its halting strides, stabbing the tangled mean greenery with its sharp beak. He finished his sherry, then scanned the pasture for the quarter horse—stoic and standoffish ever since its bout of straggles—but saw no sign of the beast. He overturned his glass above his open mouth, tapping it with a finger, and a last drop fell onto his tongue. He'd been with Mr. Searle a dozen years now. He could remember meeting the man for the first time, after a stop-and-start train ride all the way from Kentucky. Remembered meeting the languid, petulant lady of the house, a singer of some renown. Remembered meeting Julius, only a boy but full of cunning, already both wryly pleased with himself and terminally bored. He'd seemed to take to Abraham, at the onset, because he paid the boy so little attention. Abraham had never had an affinity for children and couldn't be baited by their ruses nor charmed by their naive flummery. Julius would hang about as Abraham ticked down his list of duties, and Abraham would grudgingly allow the boy to accompany him on errands. Julius had no friends at all and was unbothered by this. When not following Abraham about, he passed his hours hunting vermin with a slingshot or leafing through his mother's magazines de mode. On many occasions, Mr. Searle had dragged him out to his shop and tried to ignite the boy's interest in the inventor's arts, but this was a misery for Julius, who would always take the first opportunity to slink away and back to his solitary devices. Nor did the child take any pleasure from time spent with his mother, those afternoons when she felt tolerably well and would summon Julius to her room and have him read aloud from a box of adoring letters she'd received over the years. She would lecture him on matters of taste, on the nuances and niceties of an evolved personal aesthetic. She had a handsome tome detailing her family's history, complete with gold-leaf frontispiece, and she would hold him captive and pore over generation upon generation of what she considered the grand musical eminence of her bloodline.

Soon enough Julius wasn't a boy anymore but a young man. In the course of time and affairs—Mr. Searle's increasingly crowded schedule and the flight northward of Mrs. Searle—Abraham and Julius had become what might be called friends. The young master was nothing if not a snob, and yet he seemed not to pay the slightest heed to standard distinctions of class. His snobbery was all his own, by turns capricious and systematic, and could be provoked by his contempt for his own kind—the lazy and softly reared and unproven—as easily as by those who quested after money, those who put on airs, precious artistes, from the hollowly pious to those dazedly sincere of faith. Somehow Abraham eluded his harsh appraisals. Always had. And perhaps that itself was the heart of friendship. Perhaps it boiled down to sparing a fellow your barbed verdicts. When Julius' mother had finally made scarce, the boy had been of sufficient age to choose whether to remain at Ivory Shoals or follow the Mrs. to Chicago. Mr. Searle and his son hadn't a stitch in common, so when Julius elected to stay put, Abraham had mulled over—hopefully, he admitted—whether he himself were the cause. But those conjectures could carry only so far. Julius, who'd never anguished at the parting of his parents the way a usual child would, had undoubtedly been held in orbit by the gravity of his father's fortune. A financial decision, in the end. Abraham knew the boy well enough. If debating current events over port with his father was the price of securing his future—feigning interest in matters of science, in the greater good of mankind, in medicine, in local lore—if this were the cost, Julius had settled on paying it.

And at some point during these war years, with desperation spreading like a slow fire all about the region and Mr. Searle's health flagging, Abraham had come to appreciate that any prospect of means in his own future, of social standing or even simple security, was fast joined with the prospects of his young comrade. The mercurial heir.

He thought of those last months before Julius' flight, all the drink-fueled card games in the stifling afternoon shade of the front porch. The hostilities were by then well underway and Julius' loitering about the estate was growing more indecent by the day. In the late hours of one particular gaming session, during which Julius had no mind for his play, the overgrown boy flashed a wily smile and revealed to Abraham that he meant, finally, to join the effort. He was going to serve the proud Confederacy. He knew this would irrevocably win his father's favor, who had of late been leveling long, disappointed looks upon his laggard offspring. Abraham could recall his own speechlessness and could recall the reproachful wink Julius had given him. "Come now," he'd said. "You think I mean to see any real fighting? Do you fancy me carrying a musket to the front, trudging over the still-warm carcasses of my illiterate brethren?" He'd then drained his glass and finished the game with an elegant face-card book.

His father's constitution had only just begun to falter then, and Abraham had kept Julius apprised of Mr. Searle's decline these past years. Julius, for his part, had kept Abraham informed of his true whereabouts, if not his true pastimes, with a breezy correspondence every few months. And he'd written his father also, devising from whole cloth secretarial appointments that took him to Missouri and Kansas, light-wristed posts he knew were more plausible for him than marching into battle. Mr. Searle would share the intelligence about town with a gaudy pride that nearly caused Abraham to pity him. Mr. Searle had never been ardent concerning any particular secessionist creed but did find odious the idea of able-bodied young men lounging greasy-chinned while their peers faced bloody hazard.

Abraham held no ill will toward Mr. Searle, indeed he admired the man for his expansive mind and pertinacity, but the fact was that Abraham's life of servitude could come to a close only when Mr. Searle passed on to the next world and Julius took the helm. To Julius, he would not be a servant but a right-hand man. An equal. A friend.

Abraham, though he knew the feeling was perverse, had begun to resent Mr. Searle's benevolences, to resent that they quaffed the same wine at the same dinner table, to resent the holiday gifts far out of proportion—silk hats and calfskin boots and most recently a fine hand-me-down portmanteau. Because, indeed, both parties knew that's what they were: benevolences. Because Abraham would seem the ingrate if he didn't perform a great fuss of thanks. Mr. Searle had gone so far as to institute an arrangement for the conservation of Abraham's wages, imposing thrift as one might upon a child. Abraham received an annual raise—generous in spirit but of no transformative effect on his fiscal footing—on the condition that he set aside one half of what he earned for savings. Since Abraham of course paid no room or board, it had never been a monetary hardship to reserve the income, but the system had come to feel like an affront to his manhood. As did the fact—Abraham had no proof of this, but no other explanation could be found—that Mr. Searle had conspired in some backroom, had flexed his favor as a man of means and notoriety, in order to stay the conscription agents from calling Abraham to duty. Abraham had waited and waited for that dark day, waited untold weeks and months before he understood that Mr. Searle had marked him for protection. What he had failed to do for his own son, likely because the young gentleman's honor was at stake, Mr. Searle had done for his servant. Lowly Abe who had no honor to lose, whose fate dawned and dusked with the whims of his employer. When Abraham first surmised what Mr. Searle had done, he'd felt relief, but now he could not look upon the action as anything but another undercutting benevolence, Abraham's very breath a charity, all of it decided without his consent, and Mr. Searle the wise, kind savior who sought no credit.

Abraham heard the unsettled call of a mockingbird, mocking he knew not what, and when he brought his eyes into focus he saw standing on the other side of the fence the grullo quarter horse, bowing its ewe neck to reach some knotgrass that had taken hold around the base of a post. When the animal became aware of Abraham watching it, it stood to height, peeking out from behind a wild forelock with a daft, coquettish look, then turned about and ambled down the property line toward the high-weeded darkness where none would know its movements, where none would look upon nor judge it.

———————

Gussie crossed the rail tracks at what might've been dinnertime. He emerged from the woods into the straight-cut corridor, stepping up onto the shallow clay embankment where the rails ran side by side as far north and south as could be seen. He wiped his face on his shirttail and took a seat on the clay, ate the last of his beef, wet his whistle. He wanted a train to pass so he would know the world was working, still viable, wanted to see the speck grow and grow and unblacken and finally roar past clanging and chuffing, hauling with it its own wind and spicy, scorched odor. But minute after minute and no train came.

He arose and shouldered his pack and plunged down into the full shade otherside the corridor and continued to wend his way westerly, farther away from any realm known to him, the squirrels working diligently above him in the oaks. The trail was neither sandy nor damp—a steadfast needle-bed that Gussie kept at with pert step, his pack lighter now because a great quantity of its holdings had been reassigned to his belly.

Farther on, the land began to open, the woods marbled with luminous wards of scarlet-budding milkweed. A queue of wind-darkened silos, no associate farm apparent. A great pyramid of bluish stones, easily triple Gussie's height, the monument's function a riddle. For a time in the shade and then a time squinting with head prayer-bowed and then the loving shade again—like this for what Gussie would've rated five miles, until, from nowhere, he heard a chattering din and found himself closing toward a throng of perhaps a hundred pilgrims disposed in a loose camp on the opposite shore of a shimmering, egg-shaped pond. To Gussie's squinched eyes, the camp across the water was a scatter of thrown jacks, but as the sight and sound of the settlement came near, Gussie rounding the muddy banks, he saw that a number of the congregation were engaged in spirited debate, their hot-blooded rhetoric and hearty guffaws carrying on the air, while others were dead asleep under trees or sulkily fishing the reeds with stiff cane poles. Gussie stayed out of sight beyond the forest line as he cleared the pond, making to bypass the straggled colony at a wide berth. He took the group for Georgians, close to the neighboring state as he was and with all he'd heard about citizens routed south by the town-load at the hands of Sherman and his rowdies. They were headed toward family or just waiting it out to return home or perhaps they meant to found their own little crop-swap right here. With their two-man saws. A huge woodstove they'd managed to lug into the wilderness. Their hive of chicken-wire playpens into which a dozen or so tots had been herded. Maybe a commune like this was where Gussie would wind up once his mission failed, once he ran short of supplies and spirit. At a camp like this, a willingness to work was all that was needed. All it took to be incorporated. A willingness to work and, in Gussie's case, a willingness to give up on true family.

Yonder the pond, Gussie had his pick of trails. He chose the central, but it was of no import because after a spell the others rejoined it again. Gussie halted and stripped his soused shirt and walked on bare-chested through the balance of the afternoon, swatting single, brave mosquitoes as they landed, the sun tightening his skin, and at dusk he came upon a busted wagon racked at an angle between the trunks of two gray-barked oaks, three of its wheels up off the ground as if to discourage someone dragging it off. The arrangement created a humble scarp and Gussie took the excuse to rest himself, scaling the wagon in two climbing steps and then settling himself in the bed, getting slightly up above, if for a short spell, the ceaseless, hot, table-flat hectares of the Florida outback. He drank the rest of his water save a single shake, pressed his palms against the splintery boards. Five minutes in the wagon. Ten. His neck and calves uncramping. The humble vista he'd achieved pulled his mind to a treehouse he'd many times climbed up into back in Palmina. Boys Gussie had never met had built it decades ago, in an indomitable oak that leaned out over the gaming grounds. He remembered seeing the structure as a wooden palace in the sky, wishing to be allowed entrance like the older boys, and he remembered, years later, being one of those older boys himself, seeing with more seasoned eyes what a ramshackle promontory it really was, with its rusty nails and rotting planks and roof of brittle fronds that blew off at each ocean gust. In recent seasons, the entertainment at the grounds had devolved from displays of horsemanship to contests of hunting dogs to, eventually, such baseborn spectacles as cockfighting. In time, the place was abandoned altogether, people's craving to see violence, even between birds, exhausted.

Gussie might've been beguiled into slumber right there in the wagon had the mosquitoes not begun arriving in waves. He had hung his shirt from a strap of his pack, and he unknotted it and redressed and with a resolved sigh got moving again, vaulting down from the wagon and then gently hoisting his pack over his head and onto his sore shoulders. The mosquitoes descended in earnest, causing Gussie to flap about his ears like a madman and raise his collar high and continually wring his hands. Flap. Wring. Flap. It was not until the moon was high, bedded in its misty corona, that the spleenful insects saw fit to lighten their attack.

Next morning, he was up and humping at first light. He knew that August—his mustang and his pistol and the sneer hidden by his shaggy beard—could be chasing his tail in some wrong county or just as easily could be a quarter-hour back, closing fast, smug and relentless. Gussie's only answer was to tax his feet, and he did so, fleeing a sunrise which attained behind him as a bruising of the eastern sky—an hour, another, until the above shown cobalt, the sun golden, the few clouds wispy as musket smoke.

He'd woken up ravenous and had steadily grazed the remainder of his foodstuffs and had only wound up hungrier still. At times he could swear he smelled breakfast on the air—lard smoke and grits and sausage—but he knew this was his nose's hard-up fancy. He slurped the last drops of water from the neck of his canteen, deflating his spirit while failing to dwindle his thirst. The wood about him, over the course of the morning, began to look overly vivid, lurid in its wildness and stored heat. His hands, he found, looked unfamiliar before him, large and slow. His scalp smarted unaccountably as if pinpricked all over, and when he swallowed he felt his tongue would be forced down into his stomach. Thirst—blurring his vision. Coming on hard and pressing his brain. How far could he have made it since the dog named Doak, the generous well beneath the tulip tree? He hadn't stopped yet. Walking and walking still. How far had he made it? Farther now than before. And now farther still. Thirst dogged him and dogged him and hunger was nowhere to be found. Thirst was the only thing. His heaving breaths like sawdust in his throat. Another forest furlong. Another.

And fate again rewarded him for keeping on. Not long after the sun reached its loftiest seat overhead, buzzing its power down on everything below and sapping Gussie's last stores of resolve, that scent that was like clean bird feathers rode the air and found the boy's consciousness and perked his pace without his even knowing it, and then he was shaded by oaks and by maples turning silver to red and he was, like a dream, standing on the packed bank-mud of a wide and flowing river. Yes, it was a river. Gunmetal blue. Washing past with a sound like happy gossip. He submerged his canteen and let it gurgle full and drank off half of it, spilling down his front. Made himself wait, watching the feisty green herons police the bank opposite. Breathing the sweet air. Feeling again, that easily, strong. Feeling that this water was only here because he needed it—somehow, some way, it had been put here.

He kept the river in view when, some ten minutes later, he resumed the march. He saw lone fishermen, rods clamped in the crooks of their arms and hats pushed low on their heads. He saw a shoeless boy walk right out into a neck in the waterway and swim for the other side, paddling one-handed because the other gripped a jar of moonshine. All was normal again. All was possible.

He passed behind a series of defiled manors, each spookier than the next, windows shattered and doors wagged open, gardens horse-cropped, porches adorned hundred-count with brown bottles. These wealthy families had fled farther inland, or some of them, Gussie had heard, straight north, right up clear to Virginia, the belly of the beast, where at least there might be an army to defend them. They'd lost what they'd lost. Gussie had lost what he'd lost. Others had had nothing to lose to begin with. None of it was fair or unfair. They just had to keep going. Everyone. They had to keep going toward whatever there was.

That afternoon, far now from the north-turning river, a series of sloppy homesteads broke the wilderness's monotony, their grounds dragged with all manner of degraded tool and plaything and castoff clothing. They came in regular succession, the dip-roofed tea box dwellings. Clotheslines festooned the tree trunks. The trail became a path and the path a wagonway, where Black and white and young and old rambled idle or steamed ahead with aim. When Gussie made the humble eight-plot grid of the town proper, a sheet board hung roadside. In black varnish: BAYA.

Gussie kept his eyes to himself, suddenly keenly aware of the cash rolled up in his pocket. He pressed his thigh with the heel of his hand as if to flatten the wad. In the alleyways, men unloaded crates with no urgency. Others, not so lucky, sat on porches and looked about and spat. Gussie rounded a gaggle of Black women in waisted linsey dresses of pale celery and radish hues, distracted unto themselves in their dour mutterings. A shop front advertising a law office and after it a dress shop, both dead inside, the dress shop populated with nude, blank-faced dummies. And then the dry goods shop—*Dry Goods of Finest Quality*, the legend on the window claimed.

Gussie pushed open the door and stepped up into an anteroom that contained only a bare hat rack fashioned of antlers and a bucket over-spilling with cut twine. He walked on through to the main shop floor, sidling past a near-empty display of brass-topped kerosene lanterns. The shop's shelves were patchily stocked with pickles and preserves, with loose-lain wire brushes. A jar with a single mint stick leaning inside. In a corner stood a pair of brooms that appeared secondhand. And then Gussie saw it—a low, deep shelf on the far wall laden with a line of garden baskets. Dried fruits, salted nuts, smoked meats. Bakery goods. Vegetables.

The clerk did not stir. He was perched on a high stool behind the counter, sifting through a disordered pail of bolts and washers. He wore wireframe spectacles and a forked beard. A stub of cold cigar was plugged into the corner of his mouth, a pencil tucked above his ear.

"Set your luggage down right there, you don't mind." He didn't remove his cigar to speak, his attention in his pail still.

Gussie unshouldered his pack and shoved it near the wall with his boot. He felt flustered at the sight of food, and he nodded to the clerk and then set about filling his arms with nuts and salt pork and dried apricots and a half-loaf of gingerbread and a sack of corndodgers and several peaches, straining his courtesy to keep from starting in until it was totted and paid for. He added a pair of plums and a pair of boiled eggs and a tin of vinegar beets, the clerk's eyes behind their lenses taking more and more interest in Gussie as he buried the countertop with his selections.

"Need a bigger ration sack," he said, once Gussie had quit fetching and stood before him at the counter.

"I plan to dispose of a good sight of this right here in Baya," Gussie told him.

The man seemed ready to smile. He drew a small writing pad from somewhere and pulled the pencil from his ear, tapped his spectacles farther down his nose. He began scratching up the total, lips tight, resting a hand on this item and that as he included it in his figure. He paused and narrowed an eye at Gussie, and Gussie said, "I can pay. Don't worry yourself."

Through the open window behind the man Gussie could see a trio of mules jessed to the trunk of a toothache tree, each staring dumbly in its own direction.

"Top that off with a newspaper, you stockin any."

"No, sir. Ain't nary a gazette in months. Keepin abreast on hearsay."

"Be happy with an old edition," Gussie said. "Any readin fodder. Theme ain't no consequence."

"Ain't got a thing at present," the clerk said. The man's cigar was pinched tight in the crease of his mouth. His pencil worked its strikes and loops.

"Well, you know what?" he said. Suddenly he was standing erect, a finger aloft. "Do got them tracts that fellow left. If you ain't choosy, like you say. Adventist, if memory serves. Would of thrown them out, except paper bein so scarce."

The man took a step back from his counter and scanned beneath it, crouched, shifted things this way and that until he stood again holding a stack of dog-eared pamphlets bound each down its spine with yarn. He handed one to Gussie and Gussie thanked him and glanced at the cover, on which a pair of hands were joined in prayer.

Just then the door moaned on its hinges, and next thing a man was dragging a voluminous wicker basket up into the shop and directly to the counter, limping with the awkward load and then letting it drop with a dusty flounce to the floor. It was crammed full of some root-yanked weed, prickly stemmed and with flowers of violet.

Gussie gave ground at the sight of the man. His free arm, not the one he'd been dragging his load with, quavered in manic jerks, and his eyes were estranged so that he seemed to regard with equal attention Gussie and the clerk. He doffed his hat with his good arm.

"Lordy," said the clerk. "What's it this time?"

"This here's a commodity certain," the man said. "Folks pay real money for this here."

The clerk stood tiptoe and leaned over the counter. "You ever brung this before?"

"I'd brung this, you'd remember it due to makin a rash of sales. This is God-honest ripe Florida burdock. Full bloom."

"Does what again?"

The man feigned astonishment, canting his head and slacking his shoulders. "What it does, exactly, is chase off every devil a man can invite unto himself. Alcohol sweatin you and bad stomach crampin you and even keep a fellow's hands up from his nethers. Done worked on me, true as my blood's red."

The man's rocking eye seemed to monitor Gussie, but he'd given no acknowledgment of Gussie's presence.

"Talkin truth," said the clerk, "most of my customers spend

considerable effort runnin down devils such as you list. Opposed to chasin them off."

"Soon to be many a man turnin over a fresh leaf. Mark my words. Many, many a man."

"Maybe right," said the clerk.

"Right as a rooster."

"Well, leave it out front there. I don't want to smell it all day. And don't be botherin back every hour to see if any sold, hear?"

"Suits me," said the man. "Couple days the whole lot'll be gone anywise."

"Fellow could dream," said the clerk.

The man made a chipper cluck against the roof of his mouth, then took hold of the basket handle and lugged his burdock back out to the anteroom. He pulled a chair in from the porch and set his wares up prominently and fluffed the top-laying switches. He called hidy-now and then the hinges were heard again, the tump of the door as it closed.

"Always tryin to peddle somethin, mornin noon and night," the clerk said. "If I had as many customers as them tryin to foist what-all on me."

He took up his pencil and accounted Gussie's last items. Put his fingers to his cigar for a moment, then took them away and left it where it was.

"Now let me ask this," he said. "You coast-bound or swamp-bound?"

Gussie's face grew hot at the question. He didn't wish to make news of his plans and also wanted to get himself alone with his new-bought feast. The mules out the window were getting testy, shuffling their hooves and tossing their heads.

"Them the only choices?" he said.

"Unless you headin Georgia way. Don't imagine that's the case."

"You don't mind," Gussie said, "I'll just keep my routes and schedules to myself."

The man got hold of one side of his beard, then the other, tugging each down smooth like milking a cow. "I ain't nosin," he said. "I'm askin because if you're swamp-bound, there may be another thing or two you'll be wantin."

Gussie looked into the man's bespectacled eyes, saw an eager pin-head gleam in each.

"I ain't aimin on no swampin," Gussie said. "Ain't aimin on that as it stands. But if I was to change mind, which I likely won't, what would these things be I might be wantin? Just for general knowledge sake."

"If you was to change your mind and head that way, which, like you say, you don't intend on, then firstly I'd question whether you got a match safe."

"And the answer I'd give is I got the thumber they come in and that's been doin me fine."

"That won't get it, young fellow. You want dry lucifers out in the swamp, you'll need a water-tight safe made special for them conditions."

"Things made special for conditions, in my experience, come dear," said Gussie.

"Not overly," said the clerk. "Not for what good it does you. Starts rainin out there, there ain't no nothin to get under. Set your pack down, next thing it's half-soaked."

"How much swamp out there?" Gussie asked. "Just out of curiosity."

"More than you'll want. Days and days on a straight march, but it ain't many manage a straight march. Once you get to corkscrewin, ain't no tellin."

"Glad I ain't goin there. Don't sound too appealin."

"And there's one thing a fellow wants even more than workin matches." The clerk stepped over past the window and pulled something off a nail in the wall. He held the item in two hands and examined it proudly, then held it up for Gussie to see. "Very last one."

"Heck is it?" Gussie said.

"This here's a horse-mane swatch. Old half-Indian gal weaves them. Soaks them in some philter she mixes. Now this'll keep the snakes off while you're camped. Snakes are awful in the swamp. Awful. Killed them all and piled them up, you could climb to the moon and take a bite off it." The man took off his spectacles and swabbed them clean on his sleeve. "Worst part, once you're bit, might not die right quick. Be sick as a dog day and night, day and night, till them gruntin hogs come along and find you."

Gussie pulled his pack near the counter. He went on and loaded in the beets and apricots and nuts, nestling them wherever they would fit.

"There's always luxuries, of course, but you don't strike as the luxury type. You got fire and that swatch, there's hope for you. You'll get lost, but everybody does. You'll get skeeter-chewed and most probably spider-bit, but ain't no help for that neither."

Gussie took all the peaches but one and pressed them gingerly down in with the rest of his grip, his mouth watering at the sweet smell. He slid the churchly literature in flat against the canvas, then arose again to the clerk's pleased face, the glare from his spectacles, the staked stub of cigar.

"Go ahead and add them," Gussie said. "A fellow never does know where he might wind up, does he?"

The clerk penciled in the new charges and announced the grand sum, and Gussie took out his roll and passed over what was needed. He stored away the specialty items and shumped his pack onto his back, then he gathered what remained on the counter into his arms—the peach, a plum, the salt pork and eggs, the corndodgers in their dark-stained paper bag.

"Luck to you," said the clerk.

"I'll take it," said Gussie.

He stepped out to the anteroom, now thick with the peppery whiff of the healing herb. He minced about until he was able to nudge the door open without spilling his load, guided it shut behind him with his foot, then he backtracked the main drag and cut south along a dirt alley and found a secluded alcove of shade where he sat down and filled his belly to bursting. The stone fruits dripping juice down his chin. Nearly choking in greed at the salt pork. The corndodgers golden-brown and lacquered with grease.

And only when he'd finished and caught his breath and felt heaviness overtake his limbs did his thoughts return to the swamp. The serpents lying in wait. The spiders heavy as kittens. Alligators, patient as the seasons and without scruple. A foulness of air Gussie knew he could not imagine. The very sump of the world, true enough. And yet, though the swamp spelled all this strife for Gussie, he knew also that his encroachment there would yield certain benefits. As he arose, sated, and began to walk down his meal—first toward the pump well he'd spotted near the center of the village, then off again away from civilization and comfort, the yolky afternoon sun sliding out front to lead him—he pondered that there existed vast quarters of the swampland where horses were of no use at all, nor money, nor good hats and good boots, quarters where all men, guilty or innocent, seasoned or green, rich or poor, were brought to equal terms on the legs and guts God had provided them. On their determination. On their luck.

Plenty of daylight remained when August decided he'd over-corrected northward and began cutting inland, with and without trail, his mustang fording with no hesitation brittle, thorny drifts of vine and mucked fields where wood storks panned. The sky above was the color of lime juice in a glass. Raccoons clambered up trees when August approached and peered down on him with their primed rascal eyes. Oil-scaled snakes shied off into the greenery. He rode the fringe of a compound of four or five raw-lumber cabins, snaggletoothed children spying him from the dormers. Pines thin as ramrods. Dense clots of palm from which the tocks of woodpeckers sounded.

For a time, he followed the towpath of a lethargic black creek he could've leapt over, and when he quit the creek the sun was a warped disc, low on the tree line. And in this long-shadowed hour, along a loamy length of trail that exhaled no dust at his horse's clops, August picked up a promising set of smallish boot prints, walked out in unvaried step one rod to the next, dying out in the sandy basins and reviving with the better earth. It had not rained these past days. Nor even had the wind risen. August stopped and dismounted, weighing whether to keep at this trail though he would see no prints in the dark. To make camp at such an early hour was a distasteful prospect, his blood spiced with success and the whole of the cooling night ahead.

He took a lumpy, pale-topped eggplant from one of his pannier bags and then slipped a foreshortened trench knife from its scabbard on his calf. He carved out a neat square of fruit for himself and then a larger one for his horse. Another for himself and another for the horse, both parties champing hurriedly and swallowing hard. And when he flung the woody stem trailside, he noticed, near where it fell, a fern with its fronds snapped on one side. He stopped chewing, his piqued eye following to the next injured plant. For a sign as plain as this, the twilight was adequate. August closed up his knife with the rough of his thumb and sheathed it. He went down hands and knees on the trail to confirm the tracks gave out here, and this was indeed the case. He stood and dandled his mustang under her cheek, took up the reins and told the animal easy now and led her slowly into the bracken.

He followed the harassed ferns without haste, one to the next, some half an hour, brushing each plant's foliage with his fingertips, until the brake disgorged him onto a weak westerly ribbon. It was full night. August sighed. He knew he should camp. He felt an almost corporeal desire for more tracks, but he would have to wait. He led the mustang to a clearing just off-trail where the countless frozen stars could be seen above. And from there, ready to tie her off and spread his duster on the grass, he detected in the thickening dark a low hut of rough make just otherside a loose copse of what looked like persimmon trees.

He led the horse behind him through a gap in the branches and stopped there and let his eyes attune. The dwelling before him, when it fully materialized, was no bigger than one room and appeared to lack windows, made of sloppily tacked flat-boards riddled with knots. The whole structure was craned forward, like a child peeking over a cliff's edge. August took a few more steps, then stopped when the breeze found its wings, bringing with it the tinkle of soft-jouncing bells, a little jangle in the rhythm of horse gait that went away a moment and returned and grew louder. Louder still. August remounted and centered his weight atop his mustang. He made his pistol handy. Listened to the regular, blithe music draw closer, his horse's ears pricked also, neck still and stance sturdy. No voices. Only the music.

When they came into the yard, the tin folding lantern they carried bathed August and his steed in bronze light. They were a party of two boys, one thin and wearing a flat-topped straw hat and the other soft of feature and pale, with hair as purple-black as a buzzard. The thin one held a half-grown cat against his front, lounging lazily on his forearm, and the fat one carried the lantern. Between the boys was a brindle mule. The mule stopped in its tracks at the sight of August and his mustang, quieting the bells abruptly. The lantern swung by its bail in the fat one's hand, swaying the shadows of all present one way and the other. One way and the other. The mule flared its nostrils. It stamped its hooves against the soil, raising less sound than it hoped to. The cat made to get on its feet on the thin boy's arm, and he soothed it back down by stroking it ear to rump.

"Bears?" said August.

The fat one, curious and uncertain, looked out through the curtain of his straight, dark hair. "They're shy so long as you don't sneak up," he said.

"Supposin I ain't got no bell," said August. "I just whistle a tune passin through here?"

"Some with young this time a year. Them's the meanest."

This one speaking had a trusting face. His sausage-like fingers gripped the lantern bail. His teeth were large and gapped. The other was quiet, fondling his cat with a thumb as it reclined against his shirt of beaten leather. A musket was strapped onto the mule's back, and the thin boy glanced at it and decided to leave it be.

"Happened by your castle here," August said. "Had designs on it myself, but now I see it's occupied."

"We been here since before it got cool," the fat boy agreed. "Watchin over till they get it runnin again. The lumber concern."

"Guardin for raiders is noble duty," August said. "I do admit I'm surprised all you got backin you is that one fire stick."

Now the fat one turned and looked at the musket. He didn't reach for it either. "We done all right so far. Ain't nothin took."

"And just that one pretty mule passin for y'all's conveyance?"

"How can we be of assistance?" the thin boy broke in. He had a nervy but faltering voice. He pushed his hat back on his head and August could see his canny, light-colored eyes.

August leaned and snorted clear one side of his nose, leaned the other way and snorted again. "I'm in a kindred line to y'all—makin sure assets stay where they belong or get back where they belong, dependin. I'm charged with detainin a scullion whore's son and returnin him to justice. Done searched hell to cake and coffee, finally gettin a bead here recent. I got reason to believe my fugitive passed through your territory here. And you boys keepin a vigilant eye like I know you been, I was hopin you caught sight—maybe tell me which way he headed out. Dark hair but not so dark as you got. Younger than y'all. On foot, most probably."

The thin one dug a knuckle up under his chin, a sly grin taking shape on his face. "What sometimes burns the fog off my memory is a swat a blind tiger." The boy leaned and spat, wiped his mouth.

"That so?" August asked. His voice was sincere, friendly.

"Yessir, it is."

"Your memory work that same way?" August asked the fat one.

"Yessir," the boy said.

August nodded. "It ain't an uncommon condition, I find," he said. "Let me see if I can't accommodate you boys."

He twisted at the waist and got into his panniers and came out with a dull, clamp-top tankard that sloshed when he waggled it. "This here's my auxiliary reserve. To my ear, that's a helpin for each. Step right over."

"Hang on," said the fat boy, his face glad and pasty. "Hang on a minute." He rested the lantern aground and crossed the yard spryly and went through the door of the shack. August moved his hand to his pistol but soon saw there was no need. In short order, the boy returned with three pony glasses.

His thin comrade led the mule over to an empty wood stand and tied him off one-handed, the other arm still engaged with his purring cinnamon pet.

The boys came over and August apportioned them all a scant two fingers and turned and put the empty tankard away. He began to raise his drink when the fat boy held up a palm.

"We got to toast," he said, a bit panicked. "We got to clink, or that's bad luck. Him failin to clink soon loses one friend—what they say."

"Reckon I'm immune to that," August said. "But I don't want nothin comin between y'all pair."

He and the boys brought their glasses together—he reaching downward from his position atop his mount, the boys reaching up—and then they tipped their heads back and swallowed. August gave back over his empty glass.

"Seem to do any good?" he asked hopefully. "Thin that fog any?"

The boys' faces were in shadow, the lantern behind them across the yard. The fat one looked to the other, who was smacking his lips.

"This ruffian you're trackin—he go about no lid right in the noontime?"

"Ain't wrong," said August.

"And maybe he want to pipe-smokin?"

"Ain't wrong neither."

The boy was plying the cat's ears with his fingernail, the pleased animal thrusting its tiny skull upward under the affection.

"I may got a right trusty idea which way that particular little'n left out." He wasn't looking up at August. "Course, now we're promotin from whiskey to that what can be given over for whiskey."

August beamed at the boy. "Y'all's luck just won't give out tonight," he said. "I so happen to be carryin a divvy marked special for this sort of expense. I'd say that's good news for one and all."

"Exceptin that outlaw," said the boy.

August winked. "Exceptin him." He raised up off the saddle a few inches to get at his money.

"If them's state notes, you may well fold them back up. We ain't needin no stove tinder."

"I carry crisp Yankee paper, son. Put one of these to your nose, you know what Philadelphier smells like."

The thin boy in the hat turned his shrewd, purse-lipped look on his compatriot, and the fat boy grinned. August counted out a number of bills and halved them. He handed them down to each in turn.

"Now before y'all turn over the intelligence, only fair I explain in full the agreement bein entered." August rested one fist atop the other on his thigh. He waited until both boys looked at him. "Acceptin a drink from a man's one thing, but once you go acceptin legal tender, that's a whole nother affair. See, right here where I could reach it easy, I got a piece of equipment I consider germane if I find out somebody lied to me. Like if they viewed a certain young criminal true enough, but don't have no notion where he's headin and decide to tell fiction in order to enrich themselves. Type of equipment with a shiny barrel and black handle, bring a fellow to give up the breathin habit. I know how nice that capital tucks in your palm, but it don't feel as good as gettin blast full of holes feels bad." August rubbed his mustang's neck, giving what he'd said some air. "Follow me?" he asked.

The fat boy spoke up, close to stuttering, saying they'd seen the kid August spoke of true as all the Bible just a couple noons since and had tracked him until he cleared their land. The other boy only counted his stack, one arm crooked around the cat, which appeared to have dozed off.

"Your pussy there puts me in mind of a story," August said. He took a gander around the yard, at the shack, at the proscenium of pine shooting up black behind the tiny dwelling.

"This was back when. I was a tiny fellow in short pants. Had a litter of kitty cats down under the back porch. Mama wanted rid of them. Had an elder brother, but he must've been off raisin the devil. Had a daddy somewhere—everybody does—but ain't never laid eyes on that cuss. So, it's left to me. Mama, she brung out a pail and filled it on up with that clay-shade water our well give up, sets it down in the dirt. Told me get my narrow hindside up under there and get them varmints, then went right on back inside to study four walls and talk at herself like she often done."

August paused a moment, and the absence of his voice seemed to wake the cat. It lifted its bony head and mewled once.

"I get on my belly and wretch up there and wrap a tail on my finger and give a yank. Toss that one down near to the pail. Get another tail and yank it. Seven of them. Wee pink noses, slit eyes. Tell you somethin, though—had all the claws they ought and knew how to use them. I went on with my duty and dunked each a fair turn and each gets a share of blood from that puny hand of mine. Once they're under the water, they dig in for all they're worth. I like to scream out. No thrashin—just dig in and cling and the water gettin red as a cock cardinal. Next one clamp and after a minute goes limp. Over and over. Pilin them there aground like three-cent walnut sacks. How many'd I say there was?"

"Seven," said the fat boy.

The other boy's face held traces of its assured mirth, but a crease was deepening between his eyebrows. The cat's pragmatic attention was riveted on August, its eyes charmed and icy.

"Very last one, maybe he knew to be scared owin to what befell his siblins. Put them needles so deep in my thumb-meat, had to pull them out one by one like pins in a cushion. I set there lookin at that mound of loose fur and tiny bones and I felt sadder than I could remember. Felt like somebody done kicked me and stole my favorite toy gun. Welp, after a minute it dawns on me why I feel so low. Wasn't from drownin them poor creatures. No, sir. What vexed me was there wasn't no more to put under."

———————

Gussie had resolved to veer south and enter the swamp before he reached the town of Barbers, making this day the last that he would tread a forthright and dry path. He still progressed westerly, the steeping jungle below him and the vast farmland above. He walked a strip of border between the two, and each seemed to press ever harder, tapering Gussie's passage, so that he smelled on the air by turns the bitter rotting quagmire and the tamed, plowed terra firma.

It was well past the supper hour when he passed an outfit of workers at rest from harvesting cabbage palms, the stout trunks piled up neat on buckwagons, the sheared fronds tossed in sloppy drifts. The men reposed in the shade, playing at cards, drinking from cups fashioned of woven reeds and wearing Dixie bonnets of palmetto. A hand ended and there was no celebration from the victor, whichever he was, nor lament from the losers. On past, not very well concealed in a path-side spread of dollarweed, a rattlesnake defrocked itself in a patch of late sunlight. Past that, a boy not much younger than Gussie kept watch over nine umber-coated goats, sitting with his back against a pine trunk, legs asplay, his thick tongue lolling loose from his mouth as he ate from a pink calabash.

The sun sliding earthward, Gussie livened his pace. He marched alongside a boundless field where indigo plants had been left to grow into a wild sea. He walked and walked, the blue leeching from the sky, walked until the trailside turned eerie in the moon glow, until the lesser creatures took rest and the shuffling he heard in the brush was hogs or something worse. He was by now no stranger to the trailman's nightly quandaries: when to cool his heels and where to make camp. The program was most often to await a nod from the countryside itself, some hindrance or harbor of note, and this night Gussie's signal came in the form of a stone edifice that he knew upon sight, though it was without steeple or decorative statuary, was a chapel of some brand, and which, he discovered upon peeking in its large, low-set windows, was at the moment deserted.

Upon finding the heavy front door closed but unlocked, he pressed the handle and ventured a few steps into the shadowy, spacious hall. He dug blindly in his pack and got a match lit. The chamber, he saw, was empty of pews and altar, void of all ornament or symbol. Dauber wasps bumbled about in the rafters. On the scarred wood floor sat a pair of candles, one new and the other burned squat as a johnnycake. Gussie struck a new match and got the tall candle burning, and now he could see all the way to the rear of the building, which was bare but for an upturned cistern someone may have used as a stool. There was a doorway, and Gussie carried the candle up toward it. He could see mangled bolt holes in the floor where the pews had been wrestled out, darkened ovals on the walls where sconces had hung. The air smelled not of Sunday clothes and dusty hymnals—only stone and wood and trapped air.

He reached the plain door at the head of the great nave and pushed it open to a barren sacristy. On the floor were a few empty sardine tins, old enough that he could smell no vestige of fish. A broken chair leg lashed lightly in place with cobwebs. And in the center of the floor, as if set there for admiration, an undamaged pocket edition of Genesis. Gussie reached down for the wee opus, dusted it off, carried it out to a corner of the main hall. He let down his pack and rested the candle and shucked off his boots and thereby claimed this nook of the sanctuary as his domain. He ate a piece of fruit and a hunk of gingerbread, walked to the front door and pitched the pit outside so it wouldn't draw ants to his bed-place. He reclined on his pack and lit his pipe and flipped open his humble share of the Good Book—the dawn of all that was, the familiar solemn sorcery of the original light, the first beasts to creep under that light and birds to soar up into it. The lovers. The fruit. The fat of the firstlings. The cursed ground.

Gussie knew these verses topside and under, but still they were preferable to the tract the clerk in Baya had given him, which had proven little more than a collection of pleas regarding the keeping of the Jewish Sabbath and adherence to a righteous diet. Gussie felt for a giddy drifting moment that he was back in Palmina, in the cottage, propped on an elbow on his mattress and reading on a mild winter night. A client had given his mother a costly French cologne—when she was still hale and reporting to Rye's—and she'd gone the very next day and traded it for a bedside lamp for Gussie. He'd spent uncountable hours under its light, scanning one line to the next until his eyes drowsed, uncountable weeks, months, seasons, living safe and beloved in his mother's house. The luckiest of boys. He saw it in a way he couldn't before. And he could admit now in his deepest heart that she was gone from him. He'd needed this long flight away from everything tied to her in his mind, had needed to find this place of quiet sanctuary amid the engulfing peril. She was dead and gone. Her heart had refused its work and she had been buried in the ground—her kind fingers gone limp and her sweet voice stolen off to some other realm. She would never speak to him again. He could recall the day—nine years old, he'd been—when she'd told him she would scold him no more, that he knew right from wrong and industry from idleness, what was decent from what was low, and she'd waste not another minute fussing at him. She hadn't known then how few years remained. He saw the reserved, sleepy look she used to give him, a corner of her lips revealing her pride. The way she would use her thumb to tuck an unruly lock of his hair behind his ear. The way she would kiss her fingers, when she thought him asleep, and press the kiss gently onto his forehead.

"Truth be known, I'm thankful for Sherman," the clerk said. "Finally put a halt to it."

August stood before the counter, his sack of radishes leaning there on the wood. He'd been informed of the price but had made no move for his money. It was a scene so familiar to him. Inquisition. Endless inquisition. He would shove as hard as the fellow bade him—his cold blue eyes or the cold steel of his pistol. Success would be his because men could always distinguish, in life if not at cards, an empty bluff from true resolve standing before them.

"Course, I wouldn't try and convince that lot up the lake." The clerk hitched up his trousers. Touched the pencil behind his ear.

August had ridden into town that morning under a stubborn bank of clouds that still hadn't betrayed a drop. Gentle thunder rolled in the distance.

"I'm all for Yankee-hatin," the clerk said. "Ought to be taught in grammar school along with ciphers and pomes. But Lordy, when you're beat, you're beat."

August felt the itch for something to drink at the hatch of his throat. He looked past the clerk and through the window. Three mules stood still and mute on earth parched to cracking.

"Story reads thus," he began. "Suppose to bring to justice a little scamp name Dwyer. Travelin light of his own two feet. Nothin but bones and bad ideas. Thievin's what he done. Likely done else he ain't prone to tell the pastor, but thievin's what he done concerns my employer." August shifted his weight. He pushed his duster open to rest his hands on his hips. "Good luck done sniffed me out here in Baya. Ran into this cordial fellow with a bum arm and stray eye, told me you may had the misfortune of servin this truant's needs. Him payin you with them stolen dollars he carries about cool as like he earned them."

The clerk drew in a breath that seemed to pain his chest. He unhooked his spectacles from his ears and set them on the counter near the sack of radishes, and they looked like two parts of some unlikely set.

"Wish I could help you, but I had a fair run this week. I don't make no habit of committin every shopper to memory. Just tot and make change and mind my own."

August nodded, as if in sympathy. He worked his eyes around the quiet shop, peered out into the little front room where he'd left his hat on a rack made of antlers. The clerk's cheeks had colored above his beard.

"A fair run," August said. "I find that hard to credit. I think you're in the same canoe as me. I think business been slow for a good, long while."

"Well, I'm one that's known for woolgatherin besides," the clerk continued. "Like that since a boy. Schoolteachers get on me about it daily. Tell me somethin, next day I can't remember a word."

August advanced a half-step so that he loomed over the counter. He didn't speak. He wriggled his fingers into the mouth of the radish sack and brought one out and placed it on his tongue. Ground it up in his back teeth and swallowed.

The clerk looked aggrieved. "Anyhow," he said, "I ain't under no bond to aid nobody else in his trade. Nobody never aid me. I ain't accountable to conspire with no lawman nor no man above or below the law. Ain't no duty of mine."

The clerk's voice was defiant, but he'd hedged back from the counter. August took another radish and chewed this one as slowly as a caramel. Pitched the leafy stem on the floor. He rolled the gritty, loud-flavored treat in his jaws, his nose smarting.

"Appreciate your position," he told the clerk. "Now if you'll allow, I'll explain mine. It ain't hard to follow. See, if I don't get no guidance as to where to fix my prow, then I got no choice except dockin up right here in town, and you may have noticed, there ain't a great much in the way of di-version in this sort of outpost." August crossed his arms on his chest. "Knowin myself way I do, reckon I'll get mighty dull and, if history holds, ill-tempered to boot. You can tell, my temper ain't in high repair as it is. Might not make that long night without needin somethin to occupy me. Somethin mean, it most time proves to be. Somethin along the line of findin a shopkeeper to maltreat in an inventive fashion."

The clerk was fidgeting now, unable to keep his boots planted. He picked up his spectacles with both hands and put them back on, and his eyes looked wide and strained.

"You makin a threat?" he stammered. "You walkin in here and makin open threats on an upstandin citizen?"

August frowned. "I'm just tellin what's to unfold. Just shootin a fellow straight. Just equippin a fellow to make an informed decision."

It was plain to see the clerk was angry. A lone bird alighted on the windowsill behind him and began to titch and hop about.

"You know that boy was here," he said, "but I ain't in possession of the first hunch which way he lit out. I seen him exit right out yonder door and not a step farther."

August ate another radish. This one he hardly tasted. "Aside from edibles, what he happen to purchase off you?"

"Not a thing. Just a whole scad of trail grub. I didn't know how he was going to tote it all."

"Think hard now. This ain't the time to be sufferin no lapses."

"I ain't sufferin lapses. Nothin to suffer. Done told you what I know."

August performed a resigned whistle. "Sure ain't overmuch to go on. There's all Georgia sittin up there. Could stay dry to the northwest and make for the Gulf. Double back on me. Stow himself right here. Nope, believe I'll need to bivouac in your fine town. I'll get out your way time bein and visit you again tonight, see if anythin come back to you."

"You'll be wastin your time," the clerk warned August, his voice cracking.

Out the window, nothing moved. The little bird had gone on its way, and the day seemed darker than only minutes before. August kneeled down and hiked his pant leg and slid free his trench knife. He rose back up, the knife's handle loose in his hand. The clerk was frozen, blanched. August dangled the blade by two fingers, letting it sway like a clock bob, his countenance baleful yet composed. He smiled, showing his strong white teeth.

"Thing holds a sharp like the dickens," he said. "Keen as mustard."

"If there was somethin I could tell you, would you take leave? I'll tell you if you'll get gone from here."

"Ain't a thing I'd fancy more."

"Mean men. All that's left in the world. Chasin down poor young-sters ain't got enough fat on them to make a biscuit." The clerk scratched his cheek hard with his thumbnail. His lips were dry. "Well, that there boy..." He brought a moist cough up from low in his throat and swallowed.

"The hour for girlish shyness done past," said August. He touched his thumb to the blade, seemed impressed.

"That boy you're seekin, he may have purchased one or two items a fellow would need for wrestlin the swamp. Left out on a path that picks up south end of that alleyway yonder."

"This here corner?" August said.

The clerk didn't respond.

August sighed. His look seemed to say there must be easier ways of meeting the goal, but at least they'd met it. He crouched and put the knife back where it belonged. Stood and dug out a palm's worth of coin. "I done forgot what I owe you for them tart-roots."

"Just take them," the clerk said.

"You sure? That's awful nice."

"Just get gone and do what you'll do. Don't matter nowise—we're all better off dead."

August wrung the radish sack closed and tucked it in the pocket of his duster. "Appreciate your contribution to restorin order," he said.

"Just go," said the clerk.

"I'll do that," August said, "but you got one farther thing to instruct me on."

"What?" said the clerk.

"Where a man can secure himself some half-good whiskey in this roarin metropolis."

The letter sat before him on the desktop next to its envelope, which had been turned inside out by the sender and sealed with honey that Abraham could faintly smell even in the musty study. The paper on which the letter was scripted was heavy and cream-colored, the penmanship so careful it was clumsy. Abraham folded the missive at its creases and smoothed it flat. He sat straight-backed in a great upholstered armchair, surrounded floor to ceiling by shelves of thick volumes bound in Russian leather. The hour was getting on to noon, and out the window the wind from the Gulf was tumbling cottony clouds across the sky. In the foreground was a stand of yellow trumpet trees, in the distance the familiar slow-swaying palms. A gust found its way through the open window and Abraham pinned the letter in place with his fingertip.

For some time now he'd been charged with sorting the estate's post. Aside from occasional reports from Julius, Abraham received no mail himself, but, as an inventor and a rich man, Mr. Searle was inundated with crackpot inquiries and cadging solicitations. Abraham was in the habit of sitting down every few weeks to the lot of it—he'd begun using the master's study for this duty, now that Mr. Searle could be depended on to stay out in his workshop or with his candles the whole of most days. He rested aside the legitimate business correspondence, which mostly came from the Applewhite Law Firm—documents, Abraham imagined, pertaining to royalty and patent minutia—and set apart also any letters or packages from Mr. Searle's friends. Abraham had license to review—and often took license to discard—anything of a frivolous nature, any advertisements or public invitations, and he had taken upon himself the inclusion in this latter class of calls for charitable donation. His employer had a reputation for generosity, which was, as Abraham saw it, one of the most injurious marks a man can have on his character. Now and again one of these panhandling entreaties would slip past Abraham, the latest from a league working on behalf of ex-slave children. Mr. Searle was now an honorary founder of this organization, and Abraham could only shiver at what sum would've warranted that title.

But this before him was an original bother—a youthful brigand announcing himself en route, sending afore him assurances of his lack of interest in Mr. Searle's assets. Dwyer. Gussie Dwyer. Duval County. His mother a serving girl named Lavinia. September 1852. This was no supplicant, but worse, a possible heir. Abraham was numb to think of it. A divider of inheritance. A mouth to feed and brain to school and overall deflator of wealth. He lifted the envelope, letter now back inside, and stared at it. The address of this property he oversaw. The mark of postage. He was at a loss. He could already see, as if gazing into a teller's globe, the son Mr. Searle had always coveted, or had not allowed himself to covet—industrious, wide-eyed, grateful, tagging close at his father's hip, full of earnest queries. Abraham could see too the boy's mother's kin emerging from near and far in twos and fives only after the boy had fully enchanted the lovestruck Mr. Searle. This timepiece the letter mentioned. Abraham didn't know what to think about that. Mr. Searle had never said anything about losing a watch, but then he owned four or five of them, all gold, and wouldn't have been distraught at having one fewer. Might not even have noticed.

The remainder of the mail sat in orderly stacks on the desktop, held in place with jade paperweights. A pamphlet outlining advancements to the dishwashing machine. An invitation to speak at an amateur chemists' club. Another to grand marshal a boar hunt. Abraham opened a drawer and pulled a sheet of paper from atop the new quire within. Pulled to hand the lustrous, veneered inkstand and a quiver of pens, the set a gift to the estate from Jackson Morton himself. He shifted in the spacious chair. Wrote *Most Dear Julius* at the head of the page, then paused. Abraham could no longer smell the honey from the boy's envelope. He could smell the open drawer, lacquer and faint coconut. The desk had been shipped all the way from the Orient, made of some blond shipwood, lashed at the joinings with flat, strong vine. Abraham crept his gaze about the room, this hushed apse that remained dim and grave even at the height of day. Crystal bookends. Specimens in amber. A chess set Mr. Searle had received just before the war, the pieces of camel bone—the prim bishops and dashing knights, the willing pawns. Webs had taken grasp in the high cornices. Abraham must remember to fetch the stepladder and clear them away.

He felt a headache taking hold, a strain behind his eyes. He'd used up the last dose of his Mexican remedy and had failed to replenish his supply. From the chair, he leaned around for a look out the window toward the workshop. He squinted beyond that, to the steep-roofed barn Mr. Searle had ordered raised for his candleworks. No way at present to tell which he occupied. Abraham hoped, with little confidence, that it was the workshop. He hadn't caught a glimpse of his employer since breakfast and wouldn't, he knew, until past dinnertime, when he'd turn up wanting only tea.

Abraham took up the pen and bit his cheek, feeling both the pride of his loyalty to Julius and the shame of his disloyalty to Mr. Searle. This was not intelligence he might rightly keep from the master. Not rightly, but he was going to keep it anyway. He set his jaw and put down the lines that needed putting, stopping often to dry his writing hand on his sleeve, surveying in his mind's eye long-distant seasons when Julius was but a tot, when he would slip the boy Turkish delights on evenings he'd not eaten enough supper to please his father. Abraham's repeated bids to entice Julius into the outdoor diversions he remembered from his own youth—knurr and spell, hide and seek—only to be begged back inside for endless hands of cards, on which Abraham would wager half-cents and make no endeavor to ensure Julius won more than his share. The afternoon Abraham had found him secreted away with a leaflet of lewd paintings and had discreetly disposed of the contraband, the day he'd harbored Julius in his quarters after he'd been barred from school for snooping at another's exam. In time, they were drunks on the prowl. Those evenings when Julius all but dragged Abraham inland, near to the county line, to a falling-over cathouse where Julius would pay Abraham's way and just about lead him by the hand toward one or another of the ladies.

Mr. Searle made his appearance as usual, stinking of wax and salt-peter, his shirt soaked through front and back. Abraham put on the kettle and offered the master a slice of squash bread, which the older man turned down. Mr. Searle's cheeks were gaunt yet slack, his eyes webbed with red veins, his face and hands pallid. When the tea was ready, he took it leaning against the kitchen counter, staring out the window with an attentive vacancy, dabbing mechanically at his forehead with a stained blue handkerchief.

Abraham said he'd go on and run the clothes to the washwoman before too long, while the weather was fair. The other man seemed not to hear him. After a few moments Mr. Searle placed his teacup silently on the counter and turned toward Abraham, his expression clouded, and said that as a young man he'd owned a single suit, of a quality much lesser than the suit on Abraham's back, and he would don it to tutor wealthy children in computation and drafting. It would go months between cleanings. His pupils had never taken to him, he told Abraham, anxious as he'd been, continually fearful that the boys wouldn't progress and he wouldn't be retained.

"Well, you've a train car full of suits now, sir. From London, no less."

Mr. Searle transferred his teacup, half-full, to the basin. Mopped his face with his handkerchief and folded it and tucked it into a pocket of his shirt, which hung loosely from his slender shoulders. Abraham's own wardrobe was fitting less snugly of late—when Mr. Searle's appetite was absent, as it normally was, Abraham most times did not bother to prepare a proper meal and found himself nibbling whatever leftovers came to hand.

"The post is sorted," he said. "You'll find it on your desk."

The other nodded. "Still no word from my son, I take it."

"No, not this time," Abraham said. "Soon, I would venture. Could be the mail's to blame. Not to be depended on here, but in the theater states, an utter shambles."

Mr. Searle blinked experimentally. "He'll turn up soon enough, don't you think? He can't stay gone forever." With an uneasy chuckle, he added, "If for no better cause than shortage of funds."

Abraham rejoined this notion with a grunt. The master had outwardly praised his son since the morning he'd departed for the effort,
had beamed witlessly over the reports the latter had sent home, but
Abraham wondered if the old man truly believed Julius' narrative,
which, to Abraham's senses, unclouded by fatherly sentiment, was
dubious at best, if not downright preposterous. In any case, the licen-
tious loafing the younger Searle was partaking of would cease soon
enough, the minute Abraham's letter arrived.

He announced he'd better get on his way, excused himself with
a bow, and left Mr. Searle alone in the kitchen. Fetched and shouldered
the jute bag stuffed stiff with laundry. He walked out to find the
quarter horse and spotted it beneath a flamboyant lavender jacaranda,
its head hung over the fence. At first the animal gave him a look like
gentry suffering low company, but Abraham patted its croup and
moved forward to coddle its muzzle. He led it toward the shed for
saddling, his hand instinctively checking the letter concealed in one
of his pockets and the money, secured in another, that he would use
to pay the express service.

The creek Gussie had been following gave out before him in a fan of
sandwash, disgorging itself down into a damp field of white-wanded
bugbane. For the first time on his campaign, dark clouds prevailed
above, a ridge of them directly overhead that resembled the under-
flank of a bull. An hour had passed with no rain but only the gathering
threat. Air so heavy Gussie could feel his arms move against it, the
mist sticky upon his skin.

He tromped on through the field, disturbing dozens of drunken
orange butterflies into the air, the briers clawing his trousers like
brazen street cats, Gussie stepping high, his boots sinking in the soft

earth—through this expanse and on into a yet lower, wetter holm where strap ferns thrived in drab bursts on the trunks of fallen trees, and then beyond this place too, to where it began: the morass proper. The great naked cypresses towering above, while their smooth-skinned knees jutted up from below like lost monks in their robes. Yellow-tongued cow lilies and floppy canna flowers. Above, a bodiless ceiling of ash. Gussie heard the chupping of frogs and the plop-splash now and again of a rotten branch falling from above. He hawed his course this way and that to keep his ankles half-dry, avoiding the clotted black pools. Used his hands to forge passage through green vines that shot crosswise and upward without need of a hold.

He had just finished persuading himself of the coming rain's benefits—that his burnt skin would be spared more sun, that the downpour would obscure his tracks, that he might set his canteen open for filling—when he halted still, struck by a shaft of strong sunlight, and gaped transfixed at the heavens while in a matter of minutes they faired completely, going white then blue, a soft color like the inside of a seashell, the dank soot that had hung there at arm's reach all day full gone in no time like a fatuous notion some shortsighted god had seen the fault in. Gussie wondered if what he felt could be true—that the air had cooled a degree, had thinned with the new sunshine. He kept on his way, surprised to find the sodden landscape more laborious to navigate under bright skies, mottled harsh white against deep shadow as it now was, the spiderwebs catching the light like jewels on an ingenue. The canopy thickened. Gussie could see his footprints behind him like impressions in an artist's mold, but there was nothing to do but make more of them, more of them, through the fat of the afternoon and on through its thinnest hour—his endless, squelching, veering steps.

At the waning of day, he was predictably lit upon by the mosquitoes. He buttoned his collar and cuffs and kept his mouth clamped shut. He could hear the insects bumbling against one another in his ear holes. One and then another got stuck in the wet of his eye and he struggled to swab them free with a fingertip. He spanked the backs of his hands against his thighs as he strode, snorted and shuddered his head like a mule. When he mopped the slurs of sweat from the back of his neck, the soft grit of bug bodies rolled beneath his palm. And his feet all the while did their work. Steps—the only things he could make, and he'd make them forever, his dry-rotted heels pushing dent after dent in the earth.

With evening upon him, Gussie broke his vow to wait till morning and took three long, noisy gulps from his canteen. He unbuttoned his shirt and flicked away what mosquitoes had drowned against his chest. Thumbed out his ears and rucked his hair. He had not seen a parcel of ground the day through apt for a campsite. When he could no longer see or when his legs gave out, whichever first, he would prop his back against the driest tree and hope for the best. There was ample light yet to sort patches of sky from the dark clots of high brush, to spot an occasional moon-colored orchid perched above the fray of the swamp grass, dumb and poignant as a toy boat.

Finally, near the dark profile of a strangler fig as tall as a lighthouse, Gussie laid a bed of sticks and twigs for his pack and himself, and after some minutes at rest he saw but did not hear, as if in a dream, on a branch so low he could have reached it at a leap, a woolly, white-jowled bobcat pad forth and survey its realm and flick its cow-licked ears, its shoulders rearing with each step like spade-blades, its straightened condition a matter of no great distress—a point, even, of pride.

Morning. On his feet again. Pack shouldered. The insects awake to him. Gussie checked westward best he could, tramping over sodden ground through blue-flowering weeds and past odd, persecuted hardwoods, the sun small and remote and seen only through a crowded latticework of leafy creeper. The tips of the fern fronds were coiled tight in the vaporous air. The striped ribbon snakes cleared way for the boy as he footslogged toward them, dragging their tails behind them like afterthoughts into the low growth. Above, from the mist-scarfed arms of cypresses, cottonmouths hung torpidly, dark-backed, staring with flinty eyes. No more the leggy white egrets, but only disheveled raptors that hid in their own shadows, faces purple and beaks hooked. Gussie had run out of tobacco but continued to draw unmindfully at his dead pipe. He'd shaken the final drops from his canteen hours before, and his belly roiled like a thing trapped inside him and wanting escape. He'd worked through the better part of his foodstuffs more quickly than planned and was beginning to consider in an outlying recess of his mind that he may need, before he could escape this ghastly ward, to hunt for his meals. He who had never hunted anything but a wage and a story to read. He thought of the knife buried in his pack. Thought of driving the dull blade into some creature's fleeing flesh. Folks roasted frogs, it was a fact. Roasted them and peeled their legs straight to bite their rubbery thighs.

He toured along mechanically, falling subject to that peculiar honing of the senses that befalls those running lean in a foreign terri-tory, and his hunger and thirst blurred into one and dwindled into the backdrop and he knew only direction and the black-green roof above and the hoarse bird cries and wet limb cracks that served as percussion to his march. He spotted a crude critter trap that held pinned beneath its sharpened stalks a clean-picked skeleton Gussie guessed a fox's. The animal's appendages had been gnawed off. Its skull rested a rod away from its ribcage, face tipped up so that it gazed into the backlit heights above. Gussie daydreamed vacantly of chilly, clear, dipper-drawn well water. He'd taken it for granted all his life and now it was his daily worry. His thoughts rolled bemusedly toward the past—back to before his run-in with Rye, his ill-devised flight, all the way back to before the war. He retook one of his walks with his mother, when she had spoken to him of self-pity, this after a week in which a coat of hers had been stolen and their stove wood found wet under a leaky tarpaulin and a wedge of cheese they'd saved for Sunday had gone moldy before its time. Resistance to self-pity, she'd said, was a true measure of worth. Gussie's mother had never pitied herself and she'd never pitied Gussie. She had granted that counting blessings could be an empty exercise, but counting misfortunes, to be sure, was a vice. There was never due cause, she told him, to quit doing what one knew was right, to quit serving the season and the hour with every grain of vigor one could gather, to quit bravely taking on the next task or trial.

The compass mark of the sun his guide, Gussie went on and went on, and in time encountered a great discouraging zagwork of spume-choked channels, too broad to leap and too numerous and wide-wending to flank. He could not steel himself sufficiently to plunge a bare foot into the rheumy muck and disturb whatever purblind, barb-toothed creatures might lurk below, and so he rolled his pant legs and stalked booted through one and the next and the next of the opaque creek fingers, his heart tripping each time he disappeared a calf into the dark water. He strode on, not looking upward, fording water when he came to it, fingering the insect bites on the backs of his hands carelessly like numb old burns. And when the soupy arteries gave way again to distinct black pools that could be skirted and hedged, Gussie's way was shown only by a gauzy glow in the tangled understory. He wiped the swamp dross off his legs, then scraped his palms clean on a cypress trunk. Unrolled his pants. Strained farther west in his wringing-wet boots.

Throat pinched and brain parboiled, in the last breath of light he entered a quarter where all vegetation was lifeless, where the vines dangled limp and untwined and fraying like weathered rope. Furry, stunted palms were suddenly all about, fronds hanging against the trunks like sun-stiffened brooms. And in this beaten, moonless parcel Gussie made his second swamp-bound camp. He took care with each step as he broke low branches off a pop ash, the tree long dead and the limbs falling away under the mere weight of his arm. He constructed his fire and delicately hung his wet boots aside the lick of the flames. Backed off a pace from the heat and scraped a plot of marl clear and set himself down, the horse-mane swatch he'd picked up in Baya nestled at his hip. He told himself good water was a dilemma for the morning. Reminded himself again what his mother said about self-pity. He thought of the last nights his mother had been alive, waiting up through the hours for the rare spells when she would awaken half-lucent and speak softly, a tender frown on her lips. She would speak of her cousins, her first playmates, all of whom had passed away young for one reason or another. Of playing whoop and hunt-the-slipper. Seeing a mummy displayed at a library in Georgia. Hearing a lecture on astronomy at Davidson College. She'd witnessed a bullfight, had seen kangaroos spar. Had passed many fall nights on a widow's walk that pressed up into the branches of a colossal bay tree decked with blooms bigger, she swore, than Gussie's head. She had spent the whole of a day and night helping to bake thousands of almond cookies for an arriving fleet of merchant ships that had been believed lost at sea. Had cheered the loggerhead mothers as they hauled themselves ashore at Cape Malabar to bury their eggs. She told Gussie that, despite all she had done, she had not truly been living her life until the evening of his birth. Told him she would trade all the time she'd spent on Earth for one more day with her son.

The night blackened as Gussie's fire lost gusto, the brittle ash stalks going up fast, and he could not rein his mind from the day of his mother's burial. In a half-sleep he saw the grove of grand nut trees composing the western border of the cemetery, and beneath them a line of uniform dogwoods, their dropped white blooms blanketing the ground. He heard the clop and snuffle of a distant horse. Felt a weak breeze not swift enough to flutter the garments of the mourners. Saw the steely sky, reigned over by an oyster-colored cloud front that had stalled at land's edge rather than advancing out to the Atlantic to be forgotten. He saw the fire burning in honor of the deceased, who had been lowered into the grave by ropes in a simple casket of poplar. Saw the wiry, quick-wristed diggers slumped respectfully at some distance, waiting to cover over Gussie's mother with soil as loose as rice.

The gathered men—Gussie recognized a few from Rye's and a few from their shops in town—had arranged themselves at like intervals around the gravesite, erect as pilings, eleven in number, and the women, ladies from Rye's each and every, stood a few paces distant in a loose party, black rosettes in their hair. A couple of the men had succeeded in formal dress, wearing shoes of soft leather and pigeon-colored waistcoats, and most had sat for a shave, the smell of the soap rich on the air. The attendants, men and women alike, had shed for the moment their commonplace greed and grouses, their hungers and thirsts. None were anxious in their fingers or throats for tobacco, whiskey. None suffered aches in their heels, cramps in their bowels, fever in their temples.

A begrimed white cat strode casually to the edge of the burial plot and looked down into it. The creature retreated a step and stood twitching its ears. The men paid it no mind as it wove its way through their ranks, steering its nimble hips left to right to left through the interstices of their panted legs. The cat made the close perimeter of the plot, then paused before Gussie and changed its course, seeming to avoid passing him as one avoids walking under a ladder. It trotted off across the flat scape of stone markers, its progress easily tracked until it stepped into the thick ground cover of fallen dogwood blooms, their soot-pearl coloration a perfect match to its coat.

The sexton strode down the sandstone walk, his black Bible clutched tight in the pit of his arm as if he feared it stolen. The path was lined with blooming monkey flower that obscured the sexton's legs and made him seem to float like an apparition along the mild curves that finally led him to the mourners. His footfalls could scarcely be heard, this plump minion who'd learned to tread lightly.

One of the men in fine dress hummed a dirge, his song growing louder and louder without his spending any effort, each note pulling itself up at the expense of the one before it. And louder still, building upward until it ceased abruptly, the last low strain making its escape from the man's quieting throat. Then the man looked exactly as before. As if he'd done nothing.

The men nodded at Gussie, knowing not what to say to him, then loped off in a jangling company toward the distant road. The ladies, each in turn, caressed Gussie's elbow or cheek and moved on, their satin dresses whispering as they departed. The smell of the dug earth. The tallest tree, dead and bare of leaves, its branches stitched coal black against the overcast.

He'd at least dozed. Not proper sleep, but enough rest to set himself off again into another scorching day that pressed him from all sides and caused him to labor for breath. He walked through the mud swales, crossing belts of better earth if they could be so called, where vetch struggled up under its eyelash flowers and pokeweed made its course, dangling its poisonous berry bunches like tiny chandeliers. He walked in damp boots still tight from their fire-drying, the stiff leather creaking like saloon doors, his toes pinched at each step. He could feel at his heels and on the flat tops of his feet the cool tingle of rash. Could feel his pulse in his temples.

He shed his pack and took a knee and began emptying the contents one item at a time, setting them in a close circle around him, until he discovered at the bottom a shake of peanuts that he gnawed and dry-swallowed, and a couple pinches of old gingerbread crumbs hard as gravel that he held in his mouth until at length they dissolved.

Gussie walked through the web of a silk spider and for an hour felt the sticky vestiges in his hair. His forehead and fingertips grew clammy and his stomach tightened to a cramp, his hunger settling lower and lower. The trees were not only dead but tortured, the bark flayed from their trunks. Some inner voice whispered that Gussie would find no issuance, that this place was his home now because this was where he would meet his end. His direction was fully lost now, the corkscrewing the clerk in Baya had warned of—he divined his course only by seeking the next thicket, the next.

And finally, body overmastering mind, all other cards played and the hand lost, Gussie knelt at one of the mirrored, sable pools and gently ushered the lacy green surface froth away left and right, trying not to disturb the dregs of the reservoir, staying his tired eyes from examining closely the water before him, this putrid buzzard bath. He cupped his hands and let them fill and drew them to his face. The water was a grade warmer than his tongue. His throat, disused and dumb, worked the slosh down. His hands, on some other authority than his own, cupped up another share. He could feel it slopping down inside him, like flood water in one of his Wild West stories rushing down into a dry gully. This would sicken him, he knew. This would exact its toll.

He rose with an effort to his feet and hauled his pack behind him to the shelter of shade. Slumped, an arm thrown protectively over his grip, his chafed shoulders and weary neck wedged at a crimp against the marble-hard trunk. Above him he saw the sparks of titi blooms and beyond that the green leaves and beyond that the impartial forever. And he saw the crumb of currant cake he'd left for the brave ant. The sketch of the nude girl holding her teacup. Fozzy standing bent at the waist out on the porch, peering after him into the night like a man who'd missed his train.

Gussie couldn't say whether his eyes were open. There was light and there was shadow. There was movement. There was a breeze carrying a scent he'd well known just weeks before but that now could not be real. The ambrosial spice of bottled cologne, of rinsed hair and hard-scrubbed clothing. Women. The scent of women. Gussie understood that this was the deluding labor of his own olfactory, parsing out the sweet strains of this flowery hell. But then he heard the shuffle of footfalls in the groundcover.

He heard, "Lazarus in a pine box," and an impressed snort. "What we got us here?" The voice was coarse and full and somehow shrill despite its bass tone.

And he heard another voice talking of scratching up belly timber before the fire went full out, this one of a lilting quality.

His eyes had indeed been closed, because when he opened them, he saw the two figures, hip-cocked and squinting above him. One was as tall as a mast, and when she came into focus Gussie met her eyes, which were dull but ready, like a put-upon dog with something to defend. She wore baggy cotton trousers and her fingers were long and battered, one set wrapped around a finished hardwood staff and the other gripping a canteen. She handed the canteen to the other woman, who handed it down to Gussie.

"Suppose we're a welcome sight," said the second woman. She was short of stature, her soft golden locks cropped up to her chin.

Gussie quaffed near half the canteen before handing it back. The tall one asked if he'd drunk swamp water and when Gussie nodded he had, she handed him back the canteen and told him he might as well finish because they wouldn't be drinking after him.

He felt buoyant despite the ache in his belly, looking at this pair of angels floating above him. The tall one wrapped her fingers around a strap of Gussie's pack and hoisted it onto her shoulder. The short blond one crouched and hoisted Gussie himself up by the elbow, and soon he was limping along between them.

"Leg spraint or what?" the tall one asked.

"No, ma'am. Just asleep."

"It ain't far," the other said. "Some thousand paces. You'd kept on, you'd walked right to us."

"Thousand paces for you and me," Gussie said. "About five hundred for her."

The tall one looked down at Gussie with no expression, then off again toward the westering sun. Swinging at her thigh, tap-tapping with each stride, was a sheathed machete, and in her hair hung three black feathers. The other wore a yellow chemise and boots fit in size for a small boy. Gussie kept up, his leg regaining agency. The tall one turned to the other and said Gussie could stay one night, out on the porch, and in the morning had to be sent off.

"I won't name him," the small one said. She smiled, but her companion did not return the look.

"I already been named," Gussie piped up. "I'm a stray for sure, but I do got a name."

"Don't want to know it," the tall one said.

"Gussie," he said anyway.

"I'm Joya," the smaller one told him.

She didn't introduce the tall woman, who was now sniffing the air with great concentration.

The swamp was growing less objectionable, seemingly with each step Gussie took. He could hear ordinary birds. The black soil beneath his boots was turning solid and there was a breach in the cypress where several red maples had taken hold, and under these was a homestead, built up off the ground and with a rope ladder that allowed to the raised entryway.

The tall one took her leave, stalking off into the wilderness with quiet, loping strides, an air about her of both hunter and prey. Joya sent Gussie up the rope and then followed. She stepped past him and led him inside, seating him at a table. Her boots she removed by stepping on one heel and then the other, and Gussie followed suit and rested his larger pair near hers.

"Now set back down," she said. "Ain't got no doctor out here if you lose bearin and break your head."

Gussie watched Joya assemble a little platter for him of fritters and bread. The preserves she smeared on the bread smelled of orange and ginger. She left the room to fetch more water, and he sat chewing fast and swallowing with urgency, gazing out a high window at the sheltering green boughs.

Joya returned with the water, and Gussie drank it. She asked if Gussie were misrouted or never had no route to begin, and he told her the former. He said he needed to get to the Bay of Tampa.

"Color's back in your face," she answered.

"What bit I started with."

"Guess it been a while since you chewed and swallowed."

"Real long time since I swallowed anythin good," Gussie said. "Hadn't had no sweet preserves recent. Sure no fritters."

"Couple hours you'll have turtle stew."

"Hate to think I died," Gussie said, "but glad to be in heaven."

He accompanied Joya outside while she gathered herbs from a little hanging garden the women had constructed. She picked what she needed and deposited the harvest in a pocket bag hung around her neck.

"People forever sayin inland folks don't know a boot heel from a Georgia peach, but I see that ain't true."

"Maybe some of us don't," Joya said. "Them with none to teach them."

"Think a country boy would take a week gettin trained for coast livin. It'd take a year for me to get trained up for the wilds."

Not much later the tall one returned, toting a water turtle she'd bound up by a leg. She dangled it from her outstretched arm for admiration, straining her shoulder, the doomed creature twisting slowly in the air, all appendages tucked save the tied one.

Joya said she'd go get the stew on, and the tall woman bade Gussie come with her. She said he was in grave peril of learning something. She said if he wasn't real careful, he'd leave a little smarter than how he arrived.

So Gussie watched her wait above the animal with her blade poised, watched the turtle finally believe itself safe and stick its yellow-striped head out to survey for egress. The next instant, that same head was rolling to a stop like a fallen nut, the eyes and little primordial maw still open. The woman held the meal aloft, wound-side down, to drain the dark blood. Gussie kneeled at her insistence and observed closely as she lay the turtle on its back and cut away the ground plate with a smaller knife, making several short, deft incisions, then sawing here and here and there. He watched her hack off the legs and tail. Watched her soberly strip out the organs and set them aside in a neat pile like deer sign. With determined, wiry fingers, she peeled the meat from the carapace.

She looked at Gussie through the fleeting light of dusk, handed him the warm, damp mass. He held it a little warily with both his hands.

"You put me in mind of this fellow I knew who's uglier than a shot buzzard," she said. "But you put me in mind this other fellow, too, who's handsome as the devil." She reached to collect the dismembered limbs and the small heap of organs and dropped them in the overturned shell. "Can't decide which you favor more."

"The handsome one, if I had to guess," said Gussie.

The woman laughed. She stretched out her long back and then put away her blades. "You could do this yourself now? On your own?"

"Got the know-how," said Gussie. "Don't know as I got the stomach."

"Yeah, that's the way with a lot of things," she said. "You don't know you could do it till you got to."

The stew was served with sparrow grass Joya charred up with parsley. It was heavy on Gussie's stomach and he felt himself growing drowsy right at the table. After supper it was dark out and the tall woman took Gussie's boots and excused herself to go waterproof them with mutton suet and linseed oil. She returned while Gussie was sipping tea and soon after that the three of them were smoking and soon after that Joya was running palmfuls of lemongrass oil over his arms and onto the back of his neck for mosquitoes. He was then led out to what they called the night porch, a cubby of a room that hung off the rear of the house, web-slung top and sides with broad fronds. Gussie felt like a beetle inside a curled leaf. Above, through the thin creases in the fronds, he could see seven stars, eight, a faint ninth, and he could feel Joya's kiss seared upon his forehead and could still hear the tall woman clacking her tongue and saying, "All right, then" as the women retired into the main house, holding hands like schoolgirls.

Next thing, he was blinking into a sharp morning light that poured through the green roof of the porch. A sheen of dew covered his skin, beading on the lemongrass oil. The day's heat had not yet taken hold. He stood and pulled aside a frond and saw a swath of white clouds stretching across the sky like fish scales. He was done with it, he hoped—done with the worst of the swamp.

When Gussie went in, the women were up and about and his breakfast was waiting. They filled his canteen and packed up corn-bread as he ate, Joya apologizing in jest for giving him more freight to buggy. They walked him outside and told him he needed to head southwesterly as best he could, to Alachua County. Told him of a pond he ought to see before noon—a proper pond, not subject in the empire of the muck. They asked about his stomach and he said the main thing was it was full now and the rest was fuss. He paced off their plot in his newly treated boots—both sad to leave the women and heartened with food and rest—and back into the wilderness. After a minute he turned and saw Joya there alone and still as a statue, unreal, posing amid the hardwood oasis in her flimsy yellow chemise.

Soon enough, he passed the riffling pond the women had prom-ised, the sight of which warmed his chest. The ground was reliable, enough so that Gussie again had to consider his tracks. His wits and strength about him, he thought to faint this way and then retrace through the weeds and proceed the other, and to repeat this ploy on the quarter-hour through acre upon acre of the moist yet solid turf. And no sooner did Gussie see with his mortal eyes clear proof that he had attained pleasanter climes—the cypress now mingling with tall, leaning palms and oaks of many stripe, squirrels, blue jays, a possum—than a lukewarm gale began to hiss in from the west. It was a headwind for Gussie, trawling with it a low scowl of clouds that looked like something huffed from the lungs of a great, diseased beast. Gussie heard the limbs of water hickory and live oak straining, the old trees giving way in small measure in order to keep upright. On his tongue, that metallic foretaste. He knew this was no idle show, that this time the skies were about business. He humped straight, pushing near a gallop, abandoning the ruse of his tracks and tossing his pack against him with each stride. Arms swinging, eyes on the storm.

The clouds still held when Gussie approached the first settled borough he'd set eyes upon in many days. The wind desisted in the tangled world about him, the calm heralding the storm's onset, and as he stepped onto the packed clay foundation of the colony, the cypress spires behind him appeared as a city of terrible old churches, haunted, eternal. A city Gussie had escaped.

He passed a woman pulling her young son toward a low, brick house, both attired in costumes of mourning. A man cajoling a pair of cows through the dark maw of a barn. Gussie quickly reached the center of town, and then came the thunder that he could feel beneath his boots, and finally the rain itself, slamming the tin roofs like dove shot. He scurried up onto the nearest porch, which fronted a general store and was cluttered with chairs and barrels and dried Indian corn hanging low from its beams. He set his pack on one chair and sat down in the next, grateful for shelter, and looked out into the sheets of downfall, the thunderclaps and lightning flashes too frequent now to match.

The porch held one other occupant, a man of perhaps fifty who wore an old court suit and crop-fingered gloves. He waited for Gussie to settle, then picked up his Gladstone bag and his hat and carried them over and took a seat at arm's reach, his mouth set in a benign sneer.

"I'd offer you some wax," he told Gussie, "but them boots look far past what a blackin brush could help. Probably do more harm."

Gussie could smell liquor on the man. His hat rested on his knee precariously, and the rain angling in under the porch roof splattered his feet.

"Ain't got none to sell you, anyway."

"Ain't got no money to buy it with," said Gussie.

"What's that on them?" the man said, squinting now.

"Some gals put it, keep the wet out," Gussie said. He was leaning away from the man slightly, a hand on his pack.

"Do the job?"

"Reckon to find out soon as this rain flags."

"Gals, huh? Looks to be many a Sunday since them things were suitable for mixed company."

Gussie looked at his companion's own boots, which were surely nothing special. The man leaned back and gazed out into the silver rainfall and, as if Gussie had asked, began telling him of days before the war, when he was the headmost drummer from Ocean Pond to Okeechobee, when shop owners would grin ear to ear at his approach, treat him to dinner and light his cheroot afterward. He'd bring all the new remedies before anyone else had hands on them. Everything from children's games to pepper sauce to liquor straight from Europe. Luck pieces—alligator tooth necklaces and the like.

"Sold out cart and all for a handful of coin," he said. "Sounds like from the Bible, don't it? All the world for a handful of coin."

The wind flagged, then picked up stronger, slurring the rain farther onto the planks of the porch. The lightning was blinding. Gussie shimmied his chair backward, but the drummer stayed where he was, his pant cuffs darkening in the downpour.

"And a boy such as you," he said. "At the world's scant mercy. A good boy, I could tell." The man looked down at his whipped old bag. "Ain't no place for a good boy no more. Lucky enough to grow into a good man, no place for that neither, not that I could find." The drummer exhaled, seeming to deflate into a smaller figure, shoulders slumping. "Ain't no place at all."

August dragged himself up and put himself outdoors as soon as the sunlight in the bare window awakened him. He got out on the mud ground with his heartbeat percussing in his skull, a few stoic, yellow-gilt clouds hanging in the sky above. He'd boarded his horse two days before, the mustang no longer able to keep the skirting, dodging swamp-paths that led here and there and nowhere August wanted to go. The makeshift livery he'd found was a converted corn crib, opened up on two sides for a breeze, the roof looking sound to August's eye, the stalls tolerably clean-scraped, the man running the place—a wiry old fellow with a straight back who went naked from waist up save a sweat-darkened neckerchief—was as sound as August was apt to find these days. He'd given the man orders to feed his mare nothing but oats and fresh produce, and assured him he'd pay whatever expenses were incurred maintaining that diet. He explained that the horse wasn't to be saddled or rode, but was to be led on a walk of an hour's length each morning. August said he'd be able to tell, upon his return, whether his directions had been kept. He'd be able to tell just by looking the horse in the face. "And don't let no goats around her," he'd added. "She don't do with goats."

And so he again strode through the morning on his own two feet, over better ground than he'd had yesterday and much better than the day before that, crossing the odorous leaf-mold basins with determination if not high spirit, tender of head and belching up last night's corn whiskey. If his brain was working, it was work he overheard muzzily from another room. He knew a town lay ahead, or something akin to a town, and the sun still hung low in the tree limbs when they changed from the blanched bayonets of cypresses to the great green bowers of live oaks.

On the narrow way, August passed a woman plying that art in which a sketch of punctures is inflicted on a square of metal. She held the stylus like a boy grips a spoon, one cheek bunched in concentration. Next, he came across a fellow thumping sharp-ended iron wands into the clay ground, each strike resounding in August's temples, the man marking off a modest domain with some aim known only to himself.

August crossed the square toward the store. A quartet of Black men sat at one end of its porch and watched him as he scaled the steps and went on inside. Instantly he smelled coffee abrew. He stepped around a bushel of green garlic and asked for a dose of what was hot, and the clerk poured it and handed it over in a tin cup. August sipped. He breathed in the steam. He could hear someone outside tossing logs into a barrow.

"Y'all got an ordinance in this burg requirin folks to bang on things breakfast to noon?"

The clerk stood still. He was a short man in a black-collared shirt, his dark hair slicked flat to his head. "That's Elwen," he said. "One of them big old hickories died. Nobody knows why. Up and died."

August blew on his coffee, then tipped the cup and took down half of it. "Whatever y'all payin him, I'll give him double to quit."

The clerk pushed his sleeves up over his forearms. He had a tin cup like August's but filled with water. He picked it up and emptied it out a window and put it away.

"I choked down some adulterated coffee in my day," August said, "but I believe this here gets the ribbon."

"I don't make no claim for the kick-juice, except you can't look through it and read a newspaper," the clerk said. "Blend the old woman down the way scares up. Acorns and chicory. I reckon there's a pinch of real bean in there, but I don't ask."

"I'm pickin up hints of gunpowder," August said. He finished the muddy beverage and stood with his lungs full and let it settle. He stepped over and grabbed a jar of pickles off the shelf and set it gently on the counter. There were pig eyes near the till and August asked for one of those too, and the clerk unscrewed the jar and extracted the offering with a pair of tongs. He handed it over on a square of wax paper, wasting no time replacing the lid.

August paid the man in coins, then chewed up the slick pig eye until he could swallow it down wetly and breathe again. He asked for a nip of something to chase it, and the clerk produced a bottle of rye and August took a throw. He opened the pickle jar and ate several, one after another.

"Stimulatin night?" the clerk asked.

"Them bottles don't empty themselves," said August.

He picked up his pack and went back out to the porch, where the Black men were just as he'd left them, gazing cheerlessly toward whatever moved into view.

August spat over the railing. He moved in the men's direction and put his hands on his hips and asked where he could get a hound dog, and after a moment the fellow nearest him pointed vaguely across the square and said, "Rodgers, unless he's all sold."

August nodded congenially and waited, and the man told him blue door, six, seven houses down. Hedge of twinburry. Ain't no missin it. August thanked him. He left the rest of the pickles on the porch floor and turned and quit the scene without waiting to see what the men thought of the gift.

He ambled down off the square and up the wagonway and found the homestead he sought. The owner was in the side yard disassembling a metal cage. His face was broad and pink under his straw hat and he stopped whistling when August approached. He set down one part of the cage and then another. Stood up straight, clapping his hands clean.

"Shoppin for a hound," August said.

"Yeah, you're in luck then," said the man. "Only got one left for sale. He's the one you want, though. Lulu of a redbone."

The man took his hat off and swatted it against his thigh and motioned for August to follow him around back. He led the way under low branches replete with veiny green ferns like headdresses, and then to a hollow in the vegetation where pairs of tense, bright eyes could be seen in the dim. A line of heavy, dull pens sat under a thick awning of vine.

The man hoisted a shelf of the maypop with a forearm and with the other hand worked at the latch of the nearest cage. Once he had the door loose, the dog stepped out calmly and looked at August, then back toward his owner. His tail was still. He was a svelte animal but not skinny, his coat the color of wet flour.

"His daddy's a right famed runaway-sniffer," the man said. "Acorn done fell pretty near the tree."

August went down on one knee and the hound edged toward him. He put his hand out and the dog sniffed it briefly, then retreated a step.

"That case, surprised he ain't gettin more excited sniffin me," August said. "Got plenty of that type of blood my own self."

He looked up at the man, whose pink face was turning florid now, his eyes worried.

"Told that by my sister," August said. "She ain't tell no lies, that one. Part Black blood and part Dutchman, she say. Scotch-Irish for a roux, where I get my cheery disposition. Still remember when she told me. Probably looked about like you do right now."

The man touched his hat brim and wiped his hands on his trousers. August let him step around in place like a nervous horse for a minute, then he stood up to height and asked after the price.

Once clear of the settlement, August stopped and pulled from his pack the coat sleeve Rye had given him back in Palmina. He got hold of the hound by the scruff and pushed his muzzle into the stiff cloth. When released, the animal snorted and wheeled, but after a minute his eyes seemed to quiet and he began snuffling about dutifully. There were only two trail mouths apparent and at the second the dog found what it was after, nose to the ground and legs churning.

At midday August followed his guide into a world of broad views, of spill plains inches deep and wide to forever, of stiff grasses that pitched near to the ground in the weak breeze, clacking against their brethren. Legions of tiny snails gripped in clusters to the stalks of every growing thing. Catbirds swayed on their shaky perches. Because he was closing in after all these many miles, August's energy did not flag. He drank empty his canteen and munched dried fruit one sweet morsel at a time. He'd brought a sack of biscuits soaked in lard for the dog, but he wasn't going to interrupt the little tracker, tripping along so able and eager that at times August trotted to keep up. The hound kept at his task for another hour and another, past nary a sign of human life save the modest artery they trod. August stopped the dog twice and forced him to drink when he noticed a clear enough slough. The clouds from earlier in the day had burned off altogether. The breeze was warm, and now and then rallied itself into a gust that carried the encouraging scents of tilled field and manure. August was in full sweat, his beard a sopped, thistly sponge. The dog veered onto spurs, then doubled back to the main way, fording drifts of razor grass that painted bright thin streaks of blood on his muzzle. The creature paused to sneeze, then continued on as before, until he brought them to a tormented ward of shallow bluffs where the grasses were yellowed and the fat deer flies whizzed about scornfully. The path went on to the northwest, but the dog had no interest in it.

August took a seat on a swath of grass that crackled beneath him. He waited as the dog picked his way in figures of eight through the mangle of half-dead reeds. August untied and retied his boots, rolled his head around on his shoulders. The sun was slanting in now, landing stronger than it had all day. The hound went out of sight for a time, but August could hear him ruffling in the low brush, rooting in the soil rot. August's lungs felt pinched from hurrying all day to keep up. He sat with his eyes shut, listening to the dog triple-checking and grunting and turning upon himself, until the noise ceased and here was the pretty sportsman before him, panting, head upright, dull brown eyes seeking further command.

August squeezed his beard, then shook dry his hand. He blew clear his nostrils and tilted his head to match the dog's. "Suppose I can manage from here," he said. He chucked the dog under the chin and turned and dug in his pack with both hands until he found a coil of leather lashing. He rose and walked down off the path a ways, striding long and sometimes leaping to keep his boots dry. The dog followed behind at an easy gait, perhaps relieved a new undertaking was afoot, until August stopped at the edge of a pathetic stand of cypress, a vestige of the real swamp that was now a day's walk behind. He knelt and the dog padded close and stood still as August scratched his floppy ears. He tied one end of the lashing snug around the dog's neck, then secured the other to the trunk of one of the weary cypresses. Gave it a tug to test. "Ain't in the market for no pet," he said. "Nothin personal."

August loped back to the wasted bosk where Gussie's trail had given out and sat again on his nest of grass. He took out the biscuits and gobbled them two bites apiece, listening absently for that forlorn wailing hounds were wont to perform and hearing nothing of the sort. Hearing only the wind. Belly full, he shouldered his pack and forced his way into the thicket and scouted what seemed the highest of the burnt swells and from that vantage could see the sweep of his surroundings in every direction. He saw the countless scars in the pale green expanse that were alligators biding their time. The far-off shimmers in the hot sky that were osprey taking up their rounds. And to the southwest, he guessed three miles on, he saw a parapet of good trees—full, broad-crowning—like the beginning of a rich continent at the edge of a sea. Perhaps closer to two miles. Nothing between but the steaming marsh. His blood was light with knowledge of his prey. Gussie's scent had disappeared here because he'd taken the water route. August knew he had to set out now, at once, and at a tenacious clip, if he wanted to make the crossing before dusk fell. And he wanted, swear to his name, to make the crossing before dusk fell.

When the runner arrived, the proprietor was on a stool at the end of the bar near the windows, crooking his head to regard a scorpion imprisoned under a glass tumbler. Rye looked up at the messenger for a moment but said nothing. The windows were shut against the angling sun, the establishment not set to open for another hour, so the air in the room was stuffy and still. Fozzy was at the other end of the bar, emptying a crate of liquor bottles onto a shelf.

"Fetch me somethin he can sting," Rye told his employee. "Check them mousetraps in the storeroom. See if we got any live ones."

Fozzy stopped what he was doing. He held three bottles by their necks in one hand. "Might not be keen to tangle with a mouse, sir. Mouse might put a fright to him."

"What then?" Rye said. "Roach bug. We can scare up a roach bug."

The scorpion was thorny and opalescent in the strange light under the tumbler. Its tail arched up over itself, its stinger resting above its back.

The messenger stepped over and slid his parcel onto the bar. "Just this today," he said. He crouched a little, getting a better look at Rye's specimen. The messenger had close-set eyes and wore a flattened cloth hat like men wore in bustling Northern cities. "Find one of them in my boot on occasion, but never half the size of that one."

"They fight them," Fozzy said. "Like roosters. You need another one just alike."

Rye picked up the envelope and opened it. The message inside was scrawled on the back of a bottle label. He had that very morning been thinking he ought to have let the Dwyer runt run free just for having brass enough to rob him, and now just for staying alive as long as he had. Rye hadn't known the chase would drag out, and he needed August back in town. There were common debts outstanding, and one of the girls had run off with a Union petty officer. Of course, once August was on the hunt, what power could pull him off early?

Rye unfolded the label and scanned the lines, his face impassive. He leaned and scratched with his fingernail at a blemish in the grain of the bar.

"You're the bearer of bright news," he told the messenger.

The man touched his hat. "That get me a drink?"

Rye laughed. "Know what, Fozzy? Go ahead and pour this fine workin man a hit on the house."

Fozzy came over and grabbed a bottle and popped the cork. He set up a short whiskey glass and poured out a long swallow.

"Tell you what else," Rye said. "I believe we'll pardon this little sucker. From injury and from entertainin us. This creature of God here. Dwyer's fixin to meet a bad day, but we can pardon this fellow."

"Mm-hmm," Fozzy said. He pushed the drink across to the messenger, who nodded his appreciation.

Rye lifted the tumbler the slightest inch and began shimming the liquor label underneath bit by bit, the scorpion, seeming aware somehow that its fortune had changed, lifting its legs politely to let it pass beneath.

August reeled in Gussie's markers greedily, losing him in the low-land sweeps where the earth turned to sludge, regaining him in the scrub plains where palmetto thrived. The air was still, August the only moving life in the landscape, as if he'd stepped into an artist's rendering rather than into the place itself. The trail was free of leaves and needles, so his footfalls made no more noise than his breathing. He stopped and sat and in no more than a minute downed a meal of dry white beans and tepid water, and when he rose again his legs felt strong. Another hour of tracking, the bootprints sharp-edged and unmistakable and matching in size to August's hand, then he partook of another brief recess to swab his gun and change out his stockings for dry ones. Sweating freely under his hat brim, he carried it in his hand for a spell and unfastened another shirt button. A new breed of palm, taller and scaly, infiltrated the belt-high palmettos. August brushed through and brushed through the fronds as if pushing open an endless succession of saloon doors, and when he emerged again into open passage found himself in view of a cluster of barns and cribs newly painted with clay and buttermilk. Pruned trees. A well in seeming good repair. The path skirted the property. August saw no house nor stock nor sunning cat from his vantage. No person in sight. He kept along in spotty shade, the trail straight as a fallen pine and hardening near to stone, and not a dozen paces past the spot where August lost Gussie's prints, he shot his eyes up-path and caught a figure in the hazy yonder ahead, slighter than grown and with a weary gait. Hatless. Pack freighting the hauler's step as if loaded with sand.

The boy did not look back and it did not seem he ever would—his whole future absorbed in his next step, now the next, the next—but August kept his distance until the path doglegged, at which chance he redoubled his pace. Another straight stretch forced him from the trail. He picked through the groundcover, biding, biding, then retook the pale, hard way, stalking low and fast. Back to the sparse woods, choosing his steps but nearly trotting, outstriding his quarry even through the morasses of dry vine. The boy kept his steady progress— past a withered fence that would've fallen with a shove, past a clearing of fetterbush with its urn-shaped blooms. Beyond the clearing the way began to wind like a snake, and August soon whiffed the rich pipe smoke on the air and soon after that was walking through the pale chuffs still floating knee-high in the stillness.

Loose corps of trees stood in every direction, and through their greenery to the northwest August glimpsed a wagonway flashing blanched and wide. The next bend in the path would deliver Gussie to the thoroughfare, and August did not wish him to make it that far. He snugged his hat on his head and secured his pack strap on his shoulder. Here was the final pursuit, the swelling horn music. But no sooner did August prod himself into full gallop, the boy left the path and high-stepped into a small pasture crisscrossed with fallen trees. August quickly veered course, falling away from the path on the side opposite, circling so as to flank in behind Gussie. He looped trailward, slowing himself, and came to a halt before the clay strip he'd been following the whole day as if it marked the border of a land forbidden.

Gussie had sat himself down under a clot of adolescent buckeye trees not much greater in height than August himself. He watched the boy pry open a tin and eat from it, and soon he could smell a briny tang on the air. The boy's head was small as a picked fruit and his gangly arms were like riding crops. His legs rested straight out in front of him, his feet in their boots splayed apart lazily, his deport- ment projecting the airy attitude of a tramp who'd boarded a barge.

August pulled his pistol from his pack. He lowered the pack by the strap and rested it aground, then wiped his fingers dry. The boy's head was rocking slightly with the effort of chewing. Less than a stone's throw off. The boy's gnashing would be loud in his ears, August knew. He took a few light steps across the path, then loped over one weed-swallowed tree trunk and the next, in and out of shade, until he was a horse-length from Gussie, directly behind him, and the boy stilled his jaw like a deer who knows it's been seen, his neck stiffening.

"Runnin won't help nothin," August said.

The boy turned his head and registered his hunter, and August could not have told for any fee what was in his eyes. He didn't seem to have given up the ship, nor was he scornful. Nor possessed by abandon nor even calculation. He started his jaw back rolling, not looking away from August, and August showed him the pistol without brandishing it at him.

"Ain't got one of these, have you?" August said.

Gussie shook his head. He swallowed and set the tin down beside him.

"Knife?"

"In the pack," said Gussie. "Not fit for more than cleanin your thumbnails."

"Take a scooch that way," August told him. "And no gettin sly with them hands."

Gussie slid away from his pack. He situated himself cross-legged, his head held upright.

August tucked his pistol at the back of his waist and got in front of Gussie. Close enough to kick him. This boy had been at the head of the line when they portioned out nerve but was so slight and so rawboned that August stood bewildered that it had taken him so many days and nights to corral the youngster. The hunter crouched low, a side-eye leveled, and took up the tin of fishes and stood and pinched them one by one by their shiny tails and dropped them down his gullet. The boy watched with no reaction. When August was finished, he tossed the tin spinning into the weeds. Swabbed his thumb and forefinger on his shirtfront.

"Three days' hump back to my animal. Long haul with your hands bound at your back. Don't guess there's no helpin it, though."

Gussie sat in August's shadow. He no longer looked up. In August's breast pocket was a length of leash cut expressly for the task awaiting. When he reached his hands up to retrieve it, fishing his fingers deep into the pocket, Gussie, quick and sudden as a rabbit, sprung to his feet and darted toward what meager tree cover surrounded the meadow. Three or four bounds, right past his pack, which he made no reach for, clods of dirt shooting up behind him. August had known he might run, but somehow it caught him off guard—he was still underestimating the boy. August made chase and Gussie led him leaping over logs and dodging around low branches and swerving about the thin buckeye trunks. Dashing along on instinct, the both of them. August was within arm's reach once, and a second time, but the boy skewed off in a sharp skitter on both occasions and the hunter had to start the chase anew. August could see he was being led toward a wall of forest where the boy might find cover to hide, and he resolved to make certain that hiding was not in the cards for Gussie Dwyer. This suspect had eluded his fate long enough. August closed in again and this time foresaw Gussie's gambit and dug left with the boy as if of the same mind and got his fingers under the back of the boy's collar and yanked him to a standstill like a mad pony, both of them stumbling for balance. The boy tried dropping to the ground to escape August's grip, nearly writhing out of his shirt. August hadn't chased anyone at a full run in some time—he felt at once relieved and a touch downcast that the sport was at an end. The boy squirmed, trying to clamber off, trying to roll along the ground, but August had him pinned with one strong paw. Hunched to a knee, he held the boy fast like a greased pig, and now the boy took a wild swing with his weightless fist and landed the blow on August's forehead. August saw his hat on the ground.

"I ain't goin back," Gussie squealed. His face was red and soil clung to his cheek. August could feel ribs under his fingers. He used both hands and got the boy's arms restrained, and next the prisoner fell to flailing his legs, trying to kick his way free.

"Some things ain't up to you and me," August told him. "Most things ain't. Now lay off this wildcattin or I'll make you wish you had."

The boy grunted and wriggled, but August had him. He said there wasn't nothin for it now but to simmer down, and after a minute Gussie seemed ready to accept this as fact. Both of them still breathed heavy. August hawked and spat over his shoulder. The boy went completely slack for a flicker of a second, but that was only in preparation to throw his head forward and sink his teeth into August's forearm. The elder combatant ripped away from his detainee, managing to keep him imprisoned with his other hand. The bite had barely broken skin, but August had had enough of the boy's stupid rebellion.

He reached back and got hold of his pistol by the muzzle, yanked Gussie over face down, and took a short swing, the onyx gun-butt resounding with a sick tunk against the little skull; the boy loosed a sharp cry that seemed to escape him before he could stop it. August wouldn't have minded one bit had the blow knocked Gussie out cold, but this did not happen. The boy squirmed all the more desperately, sobbing now. August was down an arm, hoisting the gun up and away so the boy didn't somehow get a hand on it, and Gussie managed to slip sideways and free an elbow and swipe it at August. The whole length of an arm followed, landing a hooking blow to August's shoulder that felt no more to the big man than a hearty greeting.

"Tell you what," August said. "I'll just keep hittin you in the noggin. Before long your brain will start workin or it'll give out once and for all."

He took another quick stroke, whipping the crown of Gussie's head, and again the boy emitted a cry like a stomped rodent and again he did not stop floundering or tossing his tiny fists. Snot was draining pale from his nose now and his eyes were closed tight, oily remnants of the sardines shining on his lips. August felt an unexpected fatigue wash over him. He raised the pistol again, annoyed at being forced to do so. He gauged this blow, wanting to strike Gussie's head at the base, just above the neck, a spot he'd had luck with over the years when aiming to turn an ornery body into slack payload. He meant to deliver the boy alive—a disgrace to his professional prowess to be sure, having to kill a ninety-something-pound punk in order to bring him in.

August pressed his knee across the backs of the boy's legs and pinned Gussie face down again. Pistol overhead, he held his breath the way a sharpshooter might and convened his concentration to a single point. Set his jaw and exhaled through his nose and drew upon a great share of his strength. And then, strangely, he did not see his arm fall before him as it should have. The weight of the weapon failed to flash downward and find its mark. His arm was still held high for some reason, the gun stuck up there like a weathercock. Something had gone awry with time itself, the minutes and seconds knotted in their own ropes. Time that made all debts due and overdue. Time that brought the dark forms of strange ships to the horizon. August was mindful all around him of an upbraiding clamor, a racket to fill all the wild pastures he'd ever crossed. The voice of his Lord, if ever he'd had one.

He was lying atop Gussie now, the boy struggling underneath him. August felt he was being drowned in a foot of water, held under in a warm, shallow cove. Fingers clawed at his hand, bending his thumb back, small and hard like a raccoon's paws, and August relinquished his grip and let the weapon be separated from him, knowing well what it meant to allow this. Gussie was beneath him still—it wasn't the boy who'd taken the gun. August could feel his hands but not the arms that led to them, could feel his heavy-booted feet down there somewhere, disconnected. The fingers that had claimed the gun tugged at his clothes, dragging at the meat of his shoulder, trying to roll him off the slithering boy. August could tell these little hands would not be able to move him, so he lurched his weight with a groan and the next moment felt Gussie slip away. The great hunter was on his back now. The fierce midday sunshine made it difficult to see the tree limbs not a rod above. Gunsmoke hung on the air, as natural a smell as the wildflowers. August felt the need of a whole breath. His front was soaked and hot and his head chilled. He looked aside and saw Gussie there, his shirt painted in August's blood, and standing next to the boy he saw an old woman in a collared dress and plain black shoes. He saw the long blue barrel of the old woman's shotgun. Saw her hands, the raccoon fingers that had clawed at him. The weapon was over her shoulder and August's pistol was in a big pocket on the front of her dress, the weight of the piece drawing her garment forward on her shoulders and exposing the tired, wrinkled flesh below her collarbones. August heard her tell the boy to sit down, but Gussie ignored the order. August could not stop looking at the woman. Hair ash blond. The skin of her cheeks as delicate as onion peels. He felt a need to touch her face.

"We sistren of the South been compromised," she said. "But there's still doins we won't stand for."

"Yes, ma'am," August said.

He could see the woman in every detail. She wore dangling around her neck on a short silver chain a dried spider set in a walnut shell. The pearly buttons of her dress glinted like coquinas in the surf. And now came the breeze. First of the day. Riffling her weightless hair.

"Startin to wonder I'd ever get a rest," he said.

"Think of somethin pleasin," the old woman told him.

August saw himself as just another of the fallen logs. The weeds would grow up around him and swallow him to nothing with a kind of merciless love. He heard bird twitter in the air around him and the old woman's fingers tapping on her gunstock. The world was dimming, a colorless peace descending. His last thoughts were of his mare, dozens of miles back the way he'd come, in the care of the kindly old man and his young woman. The oats and the fruit and the hour walks. He'd promised the animal—removing his hat and butting her affectionately with his forehead—that he'd return inside a week, a promise that would be broken. He saw his longtime companion waiting, waiting, day after day—this only friend, this only one who'd ever put herself in peril to aid him—growing fat but discovering betrayal, a thing as yet unknown to her. August should have given instruction for if he didn't turn back up, but he had always turned back up, and he knew not, anyhow, what instruction he would've given.

Gussie could faintly remember the old woman cupping his elbow lightly in her tiny, dry palm, leading him slur-headed out of the forest and onto a smooth limestone walk lined with kumquat trees. He could remember the thin buzzing of a single mosquito as he drifted in and out of sense on a fresh-sheeted daybed. Could remember, through his strange sleep, hearing the chaste little pats of biscuit-making, the thock of a cleaver on a chop-board, the old woman saying she hoped Gussie liked things spicy because the spicy was already in there and she couldn't very well get it out now. He'd been at table. He could see a vase of white flowers adorned on its bowl with an image of what appeared the selfsame white flowers. The old woman had told him she'd once had forty sheep. She'd asked him whether he was a Gustave or an Augustus or what, and he'd told her he was just plain Gussie.

He had finally awakened to true life, to supple light swelling in a window and the aroma of breakfast, and had thought of those morning hours when his mother was always near and belonged to him alone. His mother had managed to raise a breakfast for him without fail, except of course when she'd fallen too ill for kitchen work. Hotcakes. Grapefruits in the season, halved and dumped with golden sugar. Gussie couldn't help thinking of that last morning. How he'd slept late because the cottage was so quiet—no clinking of teacup and saucer, no coughing. Terrible stillness. He'd known before ever rising from his mattress. He could still feel the panic, pure as rapture, holding him in place.

Out on the porch, early evening, the old woman gazing about the property with her gray-blue eyes—the black nut trees, the ponds like ink spills, the limestone walk cutting off to nowhere. She had a pipe of her own she'd not used in ages. She asked Gussie if he could furnish her some tobacco, and he was glad at being able to give her something. Though the evening was warm, she pulled a muslin shawl from somewhere and wrapped it around her shoulders. Gussie got his pipe going and watched the old woman puff weakly at hers. She held the instrument aside and coughed, holding her tiny fist to her chin. Her eyes were watery, the skin on her face so thin that her cheekbones showed bluely underneath it. A pendant hung around her neck—a dead spider petrified in a nutshell.

"Wonder to ask about your charm there," Gussie said. "Not one I ever set eyes on before."

The old woman smiled faintly. She reached up and fingered the pendant but did not bother looking at it. "Daddy made me this," she said. "I was awful spooked of spiders when I was little. Hardly went outside. See one on the floorboards and freeze stone. Begged my elder sister go around with a broom daily for the high corners." The old woman let go the incarcerated creature and it came to rest at the base of her crepe-paper throat. Gussie saw the hairs on its legs, the false eye on its bulbous abdomen.

"Daddy caught this one in a drinkin glass and brung him to the ring-maker. Man thought he was potty. Had it set and strung and forced me to lookin close at it, next made me hold it in my hands, me shakin like a leaf. Soon as I was calmed down, looped it over my head... thought I'd die of fright then. He said I wouldn't be scared of nothin settin one inch from my beatin heart day and night."

"It worked," Gussie observed.

"Well, I still don't like them much."

"I don't neither," said Gussie.

The woman sighed. She took a moment to examine the backs of her hands, an air of resignation about her. "Came to understand there ain't nothin to fear but men. No stingin thing nor no sickness nor no devil's weather. Them things get you by accident. Men on the other hand—you know well as anybody, they out there huntin you."

BOOK II

THE DINNER HOUR HAD bloomed and wilted by such time Julius found his way back to the Barbary, that enclave of San Francisco known for obliging the indolent, the randy, the pestilential. The slate-colored cloud mass that roiled up from the Pacific each morning had disbanded into harmless factions, the mud of the roads drying hard. A wasted-looking mutt trotted past Julius, departing the rank ward as Julius entered it, the animal's head hung low to the ground scents, a pink and brown crust growing rapaciously over its belly. At the next corner, a busker worked his way into voice, hacking his throat clear of whatever had fouled it the night before, releasing trial strains of his piquant rhapsody up into the salty gusts. The man knew Julius, knew better than to hope Julius would spare any coin as he strode past in his wrinkled lounge coat and embroidered vest.

Julius pushed through a pair of battered saloon doors and into the Turncoat, his tavern of choice primarily because it was hidden on a side street and so usually peaceful in the sunlit hours. The proprietor, known only as Bitters, tidied the place less perfunctorily than was common to area establishments. Vomit and urine and stale spilled liquor were on the air, but faintly. The bar was empty of patrons save an ancient miner with shaggy mutton chops who sat at the far wall near a dormant fireplace, toiling with even temper at a Chinese box puzzle. Julius made noise with his stool as he drew it from the bar, and no sooner was he comfortably perched did Bitters appear from the back and set him up with a spilling stein of ale. Julius took copious gulps. Drink had a less and less conspicuous effect on him in the evening, no matter what amount he consumed—he had, from the beginning, been strangely unsusceptible to its wiles—but he now craved it mornings to start the gears turning, to stop him sweating through his shirtfront.

Bitters shook peanuts into a bowl and set them on the bar in arm's reach of both he and his guest. The tender had the black hair and dark, still eyes of an Indian, but the bushy brows and ruddy cheeks of a Scotchman.

"So, where'd the evenin wind you up?" Bitters was buttoning his shirt at the collar, a tuft of coarse hair springing forth nonetheless.

"Rincon Hill," Julius admitted. "In a townhouse built to resemble a wedding confection."

"Not been over there," Bitters said. "Have a view of us lowly folks?"

"I wasn't afforded the luxury of enjoying the view."

Bitters cracked the knuckle of each thumb. "I trust you was put through your paces."

"Limbered and run to a lather, my good man. If I'm not exercised, I become a danger to myself and to others."

"You can't get exercise in San Francisco," Bitters said, "you can't get exercise."

"Beefsteak with Sauce Robert for supper. Charlotte Russe for dessert."

"And only sweeter from that point." Bitters took a handful of peanuts from the bowl and tossed a couple in his mouth.

Julius needed to eat something, but the peanuts seemed an ordeal—his stomach just now calming with the beer, his teeth achy. "What madam lacked in pulchritude," he reported, "she repaired twofold with flexibility and a convivial nature."

"Flexibility?"

"Both physical and moral," Julius said.

Bitters stopped chewing.

"Had a pillory in the basement. Constructed originally, we can assume, for purposes of chastening. The irony was not lost on her."

"Can't say about irony," Bitters said. "Can say them rich ladies seem to got more ingenuity than I credited."

"Leave any soul idle, sweet perversion will find its avenue."

"All the ways to line a pocket." Bitters bit something off his thumb. "You found the green valley, didn't you?" He gave his head an admiring shake, then dismissed himself to fetch more nuts and wheeled through the rear door and out of sight.

Julius had a swallow of beer remaining and left it alone, not wanting an empty stein before him. He could still hear the pained mewling the woman from the night before had produced, her ringlets bouncing in time with his efforts. First, she'd commanded him to play the piano while she sat hands-in-lap on a nearby Sheraton chair, naked but for a tear-shaped pendant resting in her cleavage. She'd forced him to recite from an Italian language primer, punishing his uncouth pronunciations with swings of her wire fly swat. There were indeed more objectionable ways to keep the wolf from the door, and how many times, when he found himself flush, had Julius put himself at the other end of such a transaction? So long as one or the other was paying, bothersome attachments had no right to obtain. Histrionics. Promises.

Bitters returned, holding a sack of peanuts in one hand and an envelope in the other. He set the envelope on the bar.

"Came for you," he said. "Almost slipped my mind. Express post."

"Express?"

Bitters gave a nod. He turned and grabbed a bottle of whiskey and headed over toward the miner at the wall, affording Julius privacy.

Julius turned on his stool to survey the quiet barroom. Sunlight sloped in the windows and fell in rectangles on the dark, clean floor. Occasional rancorous shouts could be heard from outside. He took the envelope in his fingers, as white and sharp-cornered as if conveyed between the bindings of an atlas. It was no surprise it came from Abraham. He got the letter free and unfolded it before him. He could envision Abraham composing it with his long, red fingers, his brow creased in concentration, dressed up like a fool in Julius' father's castoff clothing.

He read the letter through unhurriedly, pausing halfway to swig the last of his beer, his mood souring, read it through from salutation to ambitiously flourished signature, and when finished he lifted his eyes slyly and stared ahead into the dully lit bottles on the shelf. After a moment, he refolded the single sheet without looking down at his hands, cozied it back into the envelope and slipped the missive into a pocket of his coat. His stomach had pleasantly deadened with the beer, but now blood drummed behind his eyes, his temples growing hot. He pressed his lips together and ground his molars, feeling a sweet pain in his jaw. Things happened in life—if one wished for that to stop, one needed to cease living. Things happened, and they were always either bothersome or brief.

Bitters made his way back behind the bar and Julius asked him for a genever. While he awaited his drink, he took out a stack of bills and counted a number of them into a smaller stack and those he folded in half and slipped beneath the heavy, empty stein. When Bitters turned and swapped out the stein for the genever, he froze.

"Get that out of my way," Julius said. "I detest a cluttered bar."

Bitters picked up the money and leafed through it with his thumb, still looking foxed. "Sir?" was all he could muster.

"For service surpassing the expected," Julius said.

"Well… but this…"

"Don't just stand there, put it in your pocket."

Bitters followed the instructions. He thanked Julius warmly, if warily, his movements a touch wooden. Julius was a notoriously poor tipper and the amount in question bordered on outrageous. Julius didn't, in truth, understand the gratuity himself. He felt anxious because of the news, fuddled, grateful to Bitters for delivering the letter, grateful for this haven away from the infernal caterwauling of the central drag.

"I'm going south," he explained. "This may be the last time you enjoy my company."

Bitters picked an unstruck match off the bar and tucked it in his breast pocket, where the money had gone. "Mexico," he guessed.

"Worse. Our own American South."

"Ain't that where you're from?"

"Everyone's from somewhere," Julius said. "Even you, I'd venture."

"What calls you?"

Julius slid his drink closer to him and slurped some of it up without lifting the glass from the bar. "Family strife," he said.

"You got a family, you got strife."

"Just in time for the heaven-forsaken heat to take hold," Julius said.

"Never been down there," Bitters said. "Not a once."

"You look down, you see a snake. You look up, you see an illiterate. You sit at table, you see cornbread."

Bitters took this in. "I'm partial to cornbread," he said optimistically.

"Yes," Julius agreed, "everyone's partial to cornbread." He filled his lungs and sighed. "And snakes can be run off with a rake and illiterates sent to school."

Julius lowered his eyes to his drink. He was sweating again. Like the lady he'd left this morning, he wasn't one for maudlin farewells. He'd turned his money over—it was time to depart. He lifted his drink and tipped the whole cocktail, finishing it with a shudder, then rested the glass on the bar. He stood, legs stiff, and rapped his knuckles on the wood, and Bitters performed a quick two-fingered salute and thanked him again for the liberal consideration and wished him swift travels and fair skies. Julius pulled his coat straight and turned on a heel and left the tavern, past the miner who was still engaged mind and soul with his puzzle and out into the sunlight of the afternoon, Bitters watching him, he could feel, until he'd cleared the front windows and disappeared from view.

Julius felt rushed, but also he knew the tasks before him were plain and sequential and beyond choice. Being absent from Ivory Shoals had in recent years been the best course, his proud father securely misled that Julius was pitching in with the effort. The weeks and months—he hoped not years—until he assumed his inheritance passed much more easily on the Pacific frontier than in Florida. More easily for everyone. But circumstances had changed. Opportunists were crawling out from beneath every rock, intriguers of every creed and age. Now one of these sought to slither over Julius' own unguarded doorstep. To poke its head in during the final act of Julius' father's life and see what it might coil itself around.

Julius scaled the dim staircase to his flat, a roost he avoided as many nights as possible, its single window staring close at the back of an apothecary, the air tainted with the gamey stink of the butcher shop below. He went straight to his bulky, steel-cornered trunk, emptied the thing, then wrestled it sideways down the staircase and through the cramped foyer and on across the street. He entered a low-ceilinged swap house, whose shutters were always closed though the place was always open for business, and traded the trunk, which he expected would hinder his travel, for the largest carpetbag in the dusty showroom— large enough, Julius couldn't help noting, that the peevish proprietor could've been folded double and stuffed inside it, showy curling mustaches and all. Julius had never cared for the man's manner, or rather, had never comprehended how a man who skinned the hard-up for a living and spoke like a dockworker should carry himself so haughtily. For principle's sake, Julius demanded that a cigarette case of stamped brass—which happened by mere chance to be sitting where Julius' eyes fell—be thrown in to sweeten his bargain, and after an over-rehearsed display of anguished whisker-tugging, the man grudgingly conceded.

Back upstairs, Julius gutted his narrow armoire, throwing the whole of what he owned into the carpetbag—cufflinks and hair-slick and razor and brush. He owned few clothes, but the majority, in keeping with the sartorial standard his line of work demanded, were of exceptional make. Two belts. Two pairs of gloves. He changed into his worn old boots and out of his goatskin pumps. Left the cigarette case he'd just negotiated for lonely on the dresser.

He would need send reply to Abraham before he set off, assuring the loyal old goose he'd be en route directly—assuring him he'd be on the way but also preparing him for the possibility that if Julius didn't arrive prior to this deuced interloper, it would fall to Abraham himself to intercede and sort the matter. To sort the matter by any means. To sort it in such a fashion it could not get unsorted. Abraham wouldn't like that tune, but he'd grow accustomed to it—if he had any talent at all, it was for growing accustomed.

No time for the tonsorial parlor, and to be sure no point, as Julius would be enveloped in trail dust soon enough. He took a last distracted glance about the room, scratching the back of his neck roughly, then rolled his shirtsleeves to the elbows and walked over to the window and hitched it all the way open. He unfastened the fly of his trousers and stood on the balls of his feet and made water down into the tight alley below, the splatter resounding satisfactorily back up to him, his efforts disturbing a woolly rat that skittered from beneath a crate and over the squalid stones in search of a more cloistered haunt.

Searle arose from bed gingerly, bracing himself on the night table to spare his seizing back. It would unpin to some degree, he hoped, once he began to walk about. He could see naught out the window save the slight inequality of darkness that marked the hedge line meeting the night sky. He picked up his watch and angled its face toward the feeble pall from outside—well past two and he hadn't so much as nodded off. He'd read awhile after supper—an account of the discovery of Neptune, one that dwelled more on its theoretical discovery than its subsequent sighting—but he'd never been one to grow somnolent in the pages of a book, the acquisition of knowledge only enlivening his blood. These bouts of wakefulness were nothing new to him, but the lumbago had begun only these past months, worsening with no warning then quieting for days at a clip, never departing completely.

He hobbled to his wardrobe and found a thin frock to pull over his bed shirt. Of late, even the tepid May breezes sufficed to run a chill through him. He opened a drawer and with his fingers located the key he needed and slipped it into his breast pocket. He retrieved his hickory walking stick from the corner where he'd left it, stepped into his slippers, then made his way up the hall, planting the stick lightly with each step so as not to disturb Abraham, the house somberly silent as only overlarge houses could be.

Sight came easier in the dining room, a whole broad wall spanned with soaring windows. Searle paused and leaned on the table. The effort of rising, and at such an hour, had stolen his breath. He knew he ought not pass outside without a nibble of something, but eating seemed a scabrous ordeal—everything always too salty, too cloying, too dry in his mouth. The village doctor had prescribed a pint of porter with supper to relax him in the evening and keep a bit of weight on his bones, but some evenings the porter was all the supper he got into him.

He went on through to the entryway. A looking glass hung on the wall near the hat rack, and Searle made certain not to glance toward it. He knew his face was gaunt, his skin dull. He knew his frock hung about him like a tarpaulin on a gatepost. He pulled the door ajar and stepped out onto the porch and descended the stone steps with care, the stars showing above him dimly along with the shy, burnished lobe of the moon. He found the path that led past the cocoplum hedge and followed it to the doorstep of his workshop, around which a fan of Venus-hair ferns had taken hold with their slumping silver-green leaflets. He drew forth the key and scratched it in place, stepped inside, struck a match and got a lamp burning. He picked his way through the clutter, shuffling in his slippers, to an escritoire in the farthest corner. Once seated, he hoisted the hinged desktop and removed a stout, heavy flask and next a bottle of Calvados. There was an amount of time he was forced to spend in his workshop, lest Abraham suspect the moribund state of his endeavors, and he had taken to smuggling bottles out in his coat pockets. It worked to his convenience that he'd always worked in privacy, and so obscuring the windows with dark dressings hadn't seemed out of the way. He despised the workshop now but tippling the sweet brandy could see him through a few hours, beside the fact that the liquor was more effective loosening the coils in his back than any other remedy he'd put to the task.

Once he'd filled the flask, he took a hearty pull from the bottle. Corked it and replaced it in the escritoire. How his eyes had grown weary of this place. What were upon a time the sanguine accoutrement of exploration now appeared only as a fagged jumble. Dusty beakers. Chemicals gone to vinegar like wines. The high drafting tables strewn with kettles and cogwheels and twine. Frowzy canisters of greases and oils. The disused scales. The postman's desk crammed with wire and filament of all gauge. Hand tools hanging dormant on the walls. Gloves balled unpaired and abandoned to molder like poisoned rodents. Stores of tungsten and lead, tribes of crucibles and test cylinders, rolls of foil, enough careworn volumes on metallurgy and botany and all else to cramp the shoulder-high shelf that ran the full wise of the shop.

In one corner sat Searle at the low, wooden desk. In another corner sprawled his halted efforts toward the development of an automatic typing machine. In yet another, the deserted evidence of his struggle toward an improved handheld metal detector. And in the final corner, heaped brooding on a hand press, were all Searle's legal notices. He'd left off reading them—had left off even opening them. Abraham dispatched his light post, weeding the frivolous correspondence and solicitations, but Searle had him set aside anything of an official or sensitive nature, and now that Searle had stalled as an inventor, this latter category was mostly composed of threats sent to his attorney from the opposing counsel in Rhode Island, forwarded on to the estate under the wax seals of Applewhite Law.

If Abraham happened to look out over the grounds now and see the swell of lamplight behind the darkened shop windows, he'd think Searle had been roused by midnight inspiration, out here hard at work. He needed Abraham, he knew, needed his firm hand managing the estate now more than ever. Abraham and his unfailing brusqueness with tradesmen and sellers. The clenching of his jaw at every instance of Searle's largesse. Abraham, ever the strict admiral, but if only he knew the secret water his vessel took on, the hidden rents in the hull.

Searle arose with his flask and snuffed the lamp and felt his way to the door and back outside. He turned and engaged the lock and returned the key to his pocket. Down the footpath he went, toward the chandlery studio he'd foolhardily had built from auction bluff oak. He could barely hear the soft murmur of the Gulf rolling in, the shore perhaps a quarter-mile from where he stood but blocked from sight by a thick swath of oak and loblolly. He made his way along the gently sloping earth, his soul lightening as the studio came into plain view, and soon his nose was full of the rich odors of saltpeter and beeswax, the rosemary and Balsam of Peru he used to scent the candles. Even the beef tallow on the air possessed sweet notes within its patent rankness.

He had founded the operation not long after the start of the war, when an almost instantaneous shortage had taken hold. He'd charged only enough to square expanses and spare an upright wage to the handful of workers who turned up from the surrounding settlements. Certain months, to be sure, he'd come short of the watermark, mostly by falling victim to his own experimental nature. He had been surprised at the degree to which he'd been taken in the craft's thrall, this age-old utilitarian métier. He'd felt from the outset, though he hadn't wished to admit it, that fashioning candles was a more honest trade than inventing—to produce a ware simple and time-tested and which folks inarguably needed, rather than aiming to persuade wives and farmers and bookkeepers that they were suffering a pressing shortage of some contraption they'd always gotten on fine without.

Searle, even now, did not consider himself a chandler, but the hours he spent engrossed in that art were his most contented. In his inventor's workshop, the best he could hope to feel was impotent, and at worst, trapped inside and gazing at the too-familiar equipment, the arrested schemes, that foreboding stack of envelopes, he would be overrun with a pitiable rancor, would feel utterly stultified. Past, present, and future would seem all a part of the same low, doomed scrimmage, until on occasion he would detect the keen, seductive edge of distemper—long hot afternoons after sleepless nights—and fleeing to the candle studio would be his sole recourse. His workers, two widowed mothers and a sweet-tempered old codger with bad feet, came thrice weekly and toiled with Searle dawn to dusk, and those hours flew by like spring geese.

But Searle went on past now, diverging from the path and stepping more spryly—his back, as expected, easing somewhat with the stroll and the dose of liquor—toward a bench he'd had placed in what, during daylight hours, was a shady spot. When Searle neared the bench, he saw the seat was sheened with dew, so he slipped out of his frock and folded it and rested it on the wood, lowered himself, shifted to discover an agreeable position. He leaned his cane against the armrest. He could hear the tame waves distinctly now, as one by one they unscrolled over the shells of the shoreline. He could smell from a mile up the coast the biting, saccharine odor of the rum distillery. Searle tipped his head back. The moon had drifted to an even remoter belt of sky, had paled up behind the big branches of Searle's shade tree. He closed his eyes. Sighed. Ah, Julius. These days he could not keep his mind from the boy for long. And was he to be blamed? The war over, Searle had naturally begun to anticipate his son's return, though he'd heard no news at all. He'd heard nothing, in truth, for a year now—the final communiqué had explained that Julius was to be sent far west for a secretarial post, that it would be difficult, where he'd be stationed, to put out letters. He said a missive had been prepared that would post in the event tragedy befell him, but in the absence of that dark notice, Searle shouldn't fret but should carry on with normal enterprise.

Fretting was Searle's daily bread, and the enterprise was axle-snapped, tipped nose first in a ditch. Searle was not the indulger of delusion he often, for appearances, let on he was. He knew it was unlikely his son had seen any real fighting, knew Julius was alive and most likely uninjured. Uninjured bodily, yes, but Searle's fear was that the boy, no boy but a young man now, was so stung of soul by his father's sending him off to war—a milieu that so grossly ill-suited him, a punishment for being the person God and Ruth Purifoy had made him—that he'd never show himself at the estate again. So bitter, and now a fellow who'd learned to live by his own steam—even if French leave had been Julius' course, he'd managed it on his own steam.

And sent him off Searle had. He'd leveed no ultimatum, but with his disapproving air and pointed remarks he'd no less than shoved

Julius down the front steps. Searle and his household had never, he had to admit, been in peril of being persecuted as sympathizers—he being a Virginian by birth and not one to speak his political opinions except over cigars amongst a trusted few. He'd known enough to keep hidden his lack of zeal for the Southern struggle, had known enough to keep to himself his scientific, logical views on the great clash: though he did not believe in karma, good or ill, he believed wholeheartedly in man's inability to wrest his nose from the lead of the dollar—whether his ways contradicted his Bible, his nation's constitution, his buried conscience—and that greed would always, in time, burn up its own furnace. But no, none had had reason to suspect the Searle family untrue to the Gray. It had been a matter more important than social perception. A matter of character. The matter of a wastrel son who lounged about the house, fine fare morning, noon, and night and servants at his call, a son whose milksop reputation was setting like clay in a kiln. The Culpepper boy had volunteered the first week. The Leggit boy, two years Julius' junior. The Trout boy. The Yarborough boy, and his family from Indiana. Searle had not been able to accept raising a coward, had not wanted an idle fop the carrier of his bloodline, and might now, as a result, have no son at all. It was meant for Julius' good, and maybe Julius would see the truth in that. It was possible in life for the same decision to be both right and wrong; it had been an unwinnable situation for Searle, and he had of course lost. If only the boy had possessed a scrap of initiative—if he'd been a fierce abolitionist, an adamant conscientious objector, if he'd had any bent toward staunchness or grit. Then he could've taken charge of himself and relieved Searle of the duty.

And some dozen months later, driven partly, he suspected, by guilt, Searle would find himself turning over a substantial regimental supplement in order to safeguard his servant. His servant, not his son. Searle desperate for agency, desperate to help someone. Abraham, according to the document Searle signed, was superintendent to the herds of cattle that Searle had owned but had never laid eyes on. Neither of them had ever seen the cattle in person. Cattle that had long since been slaughtered for the cause or stolen or had wandered off into the palmetto scrub to dangers inconceivable to them.

Searle took his stick back up and dug the tip into the friable soil. He leaned and spat. The story of his monetary hardship, simply stated, was his being sued for infringement by the family of his former associate, John Chloris. Dr. Chloris had been dead some twenty-five years, but still his name was attached to a number of groundwork patents pertaining to the air-cooling machines he and Searle had developed. Chloris was the elder to such a degree that there had been much of the mentor and protégé between them. When Chloris passed, Searle hadn't thought twice about continuing their work. The machines were intended to cool entire homes, offices, warehouses, and Searle had labored tirelessly at modeling new compressors, at making real the thermostat his colleague had envisioned, at liquefying ammonia more efficiently. Chloris was an old bachelor who'd never so much as mentioned any family from the North, and Searle had never thought any of his own actions clandestine or devious. In truth, he often imagined the pride the other man would've felt at the faithful rearing of his brainchildren. It had always been a fault of Searle's to think too little of practical concerns and live too exclusively in the atelier of his mind. All these years later, the family had been alerted—Searle still knew not how—that theirs for the lawful pursuing was a tidy fortune whose composition they hadn't had a moment's hand in.

After poring over the details of the case for weeks, Applewhite had grimly informed his client that he possessed no leverage and would inevitably lose in court. The war had commenced just after that, halting legal intercourse between North and South, but it wasn't long after Lee had rested his sword that the notices started up again.

Applewhite had assured Searle he could drag the proceedings out for years if Searle wished, with cashed favors and deferential agreements, but Searle wasn't of a stomach for all that. He'd agreed to fork over—to "settle the damages" as the opposing lawyer termed it—a sum large enough to require the eventual sale of the estate, the only condition being that the suing party agreed to keep the affair quiet. That was the sole satisfaction available, to keep the mess from public knowledge. But he would have to tell Abraham in due time, and of course he'd have to tell Julius as well, and he could only wonder with dread at either's reaction.

The most galling part of the whole muddle was that Searle had only ever yoked himself with this estate, into which so large a portion of his funds had been poured, to placate Ruth. It was no obscure truth, particularly in hindsight, that Searle had been a fool to marry her—this woman by profession a performer and by temperament a mischievous soubrette. From a distance of years, Searle could see that their association had been a tryst turned incautiously serious, she too alluring and he too promising for either to turn the other away. He'd bought her this house. These grounds. Had bought her a fine coach—its bench seats now full of mice, its wheels warped—for the purpose of conveying her the short mile into the village, which she grew dull on after a dozen visits. And then the virtuoso griping had commenced, targeting all from the absence of a passable wine shop to the abundance of ugly, pink-faced possums. Not a soul in the whole of the county could waltz, Searle amongst them. Not a soul in the county had read the Brontës.

He held the woman in disdain, to be sure, but he was apt nevertheless to find his heart aching when he dwelled upon her loneliness. Not only had she never remarried, but Julius, when she and Searle had parted, had chosen to stay in Florida rather than retreat with her to Chicago. His own mother, who had fed him at her breast.

And she'd seemed hardly to care, at the time. She'd departed the estate that bright October morning with much the air of an escapee from forced labor. Ah, the whole business was damnable. Rank to the essence. A foxtail stole of hers still hung in Searle's bedchamber closet, left behind when her possessions were packed, and he might've at any time removed it and had it shipped to her—though by this point the address would be well out of currency—or donated it to one of his female chandlery apprentices or even jammed it in the dustbin. But no, there in the closet it remained, where on occasion he would reach for it while dressing and clutch its feminine softness in his fingers.

His eyes had adapted to the darkness, and he could easily see the firework blooms of the nakedwood shrub at the end of the wall. He could see the blossomed vines that hung like roped iron from the oak limbs. He used his walking stick to scratch his ankle. Felt an itch also on his forearm. The mosquitoes had gained a bead. He leaned back against the bench, feeling a familiar despair. Loneliness was not Ruth's trouble alone, but his as well. Abraham was about always and he cherished the old governor, but Searle's parents were deceased and he had no siblings and his wife was gone. Most of all, he missed his son. Whatever disapproval he felt concerning the boy's libertine ways, a man's son was a man's son, and Searle longed to embrace Julius' stiff-set shoulders, wished to hear his voice, no matter how devilishly droll the words it rode, wished to sit down with the boy, now a man, and share with him a nip of brandy and a good smoke. Lord knew Searle had chided Julius on many an occasion for idleness, but now he himself was an idler of sorts, wasn't he, though unlike Julius he harbored no predilection for it, no aptitude. Perhaps the boy would cotton to Searle more readily once he knew his career was sunk, that the two had, if little else, an unknown future in common. Maybe they would get on better, Searle holding his cards of defeat.

———————

The old woman equipped Gussie with three peach tarts wrapped in pudding cloth and a big knot of salt pork, and when she asked if there was anything other that'd come in handy, he said he might trouble her for something to read if she had an old book laying spare. He said he wasn't choosy, but that he'd collected thus far an Adventist giveaway and a book of Genesis, so something of a non-pontifical bent would be welcome, for variety's sake.

The woman disappeared into the recesses of the house and returned soon after with a sheaf of bound pages that appeared torn from their cover. She explained that some years back the book had been divvied so that all the cousins could read it at once. The story wasn't the old woman's cup of cider, she told Gussie, but it might just work for a swashbuckler like him.

They stepped out to the front yard and the old woman outlined directions that would put Gussie in sniffing range of Gainesville, and when he leaned down and embraced her, she felt feebler than his mother ever had, even at the end—just a sack of hollow bones.

"Get now, boy," she told him, managing a soft smirk. "And don't waste no more time gettin beat on."

Gussie had much reason to feel light—being game no longer, his entanglement with the bow-tied pimp finally settled—and yet it was an act of grit to take the first step away from the old woman. His mind remained a beat slow and a shade muddy due to August's bludgeoning, and without the hunter's immediate threat to distract and prod him, the dubiousness of his future now cast a huge, dark shadow. Still so far to go, and for such uncertainty. He needed to thank the old woman and turn his back to her, needed to quit dawdling, and so he told himself that though his ultimate verdict was unguessable, that simply getting there, getting himself safely to Ivory Shoals—this was the business that by force of will he could conduct. That he had to conduct. He told himself his world was the scuff of the boot and the dust left behind and what else could it be—the scuff and the dust, his whole purpose. His grace. And with these thoughts herded hard to the front of his mind, Gussie started his feet moving down the limestone walk. He shuffled past the pairs and pairs of kumquat trees and trudged out into the cloud-scattered day before him, alone again.

Later, legs heavy and forehead reddening, Gussie's way tapered and gave out into a vast, defunct grapefruit grove. HANIFL CITRUS read an unpainted wooden sign. No end in either direction to the untended trees, so no choice but to begin down the straight central aisle that plunged into the stinking heart of the plantation, treading the soft, sweet rot that covered the ground. The fruits on the trees were too young, just sour stones, and those beneath his boots were of the season past. The smell as he delved on grew stout enough to start his nose running and eyes watering. Probably rodents beneath the rot, probably snakes to feast on the rodents. He pulled the sodden cloth of his shirt to his face, flies buzzing thick and delirious about his ankles, the miserly calls of crows filling the air.

Later still, weary in the heat, he took a knee trailside and drank from his canteen. He searched about in the depths of his pack for his pipe and tobacco, careful not to rip asunder the pages of the old woman's book. Gave his matches a shake in their tin. Revealed and hid the blade of his folding knife, keeping it limber. Here was the hair comb he'd brought along and had forgotten, a senseless and vain addition to his grip.

He arose, pipe in his teeth, meaty blue dragonflies zimming in and out of the sunlight. Pressed the trail south and west. Pressed the trail more. West. South. West again, he hoped. And it was on a monotonous, trounced stretch where birds hopped about the weeds for want of tree limbs that Gussie heard the strange wind and smelled the strange odor and began drifting, as if spellbound, away from his proper route. He left his trail behind, scaring the birds in his way off to other thickets. Yes, the high grind of the wheels. The clanging of the steel couplers. Gussie shuffled through the degraded woodland, quitting his pipe and breathing air laced with the twang of baked metal. He tacked and tacked until he was walking flush along the rail tracks—nothing now prohibiting him such conspicuous transport—and followed them for perhaps a mile, new vigor in his step as he trod the planed, raised apron, and soon he was led to a humble depot where three trains waited solemnly in the full daylight. One of the trains was being relieved of its cargoes by a team of men who whooped and called as they worked. Gussie kept clear of them, waiting in the trees opposite until the cars were unburdened and the engine put back to steam and the steel wheels began to creak and strain with their first revolution.

Gussie panned his eyes this way and that, assuring no one was about, then stepped over the gravel skirt and found a foothold on one of the scarcely moving cars and hauled himself up. He got settled at the rear of the box, where he enjoyed a plain enough view outside but was himself hidden in shadow. He nestled his pack to him with an arm, letting his legs idle and back rest, the train struggling to catch stride, bumping and wobbling, a couple roach bugs staggering out onto the filthy floor like roused drunks. The car smelled of coal and cut wood, but as it gathered speed, outrunning its own jostling, all scents were whisked away and the train rushed into a hammock overborne with fleshy cabbage palms and live oaks whose upper stories were clotted with mistletoe, rafters of turkeys milling about in the ground cover below.

The railway was meant to run the whole way to Cedar Key, but Gussie knew he wouldn't be taken that far. The Union troops had ripped up the tracks, commencing at the coast and working their way inland, Lord knew how far. He might get another mile without needing to reenlist his feet, he might get twenty.

Farther out in the hammock, too far distant from one another to comprise a settlement, homesteads appeared—log dwellings set up off the ground on piers of heart pine, hogs penned underneath. Roofs rusted assorted hues of orange. Alligator hides tacked to tree trunks to cure. In this stretch, no depot in sight, the train slowed enough to regain a bit of its totter and lurch. Gussie heard the fast shuffle of feet and was startled when a figure swung itself into his car, lissome and assured as a square dancer. The man landed upright dead center of the floor. When he noticed Gussie, he held him in a brief and neutral stare, then rubbed his eyes and sat himself down at the front end, facing Gussie but paying him little mind. The man's skin was as tight as hide and browned by the sun, but Gussie could tell he wasn't old. On his hip was a wound buckskin whip and for a belt he employed a length of broken harness. His chin was sharp and one eye wouldn't open as round as the other and in all ways he appeared tougher than a cob. He was a cow catcher. Gussie remembered them coming into town to trade, long rifles across their hips and liverish catch dogs in tow. They were rumored to subsist on charred rattlesnake and use turpentine as a mouth rinse.

The man removed his hat and secured it by its wide brim under the seat of his pants. He produced a purse of what appeared to be dewberries and flung them down his throat with three flips of his wrist, working his jaw in laborious rounds and swallowing hard. He had no pistol on his person that Gussie could spot but did bear on his waist a sheathed knife whose blade wasn't much shy of a foot.

"No call bein scared of me," he told Gussie, still not looking at him. His voice was sodden, as if his throat were stuffed with wet leaves. "There's them to fear the way you headin, but don't waste it on me. I'm no trouble till a fellow gets smart."

"Them to fear?" Gussie repeated.

"Aimin yourself at them overland pirates, what you're doin. Run some of them south counties so they may well be the law." The catcher grinned. "You don't look no choice fodder for pillagin, but maybe choice for sport."

He brandished a thumb and scraped the berry seeds from his failing teeth. He offered no further remark and Gussie asked him for none, and after a moment the catcher fell to gnawing his fingertips. He gave attention to all ten before he was satisfied, at which point he peered out into the hammock a long moment.

"Reckon this is about my stop," he said, neither pleased nor aggrieved by the circumstance.

He tugged on his hat and took his grip in hand and swung himself back out into the light, landing with soft knees on the trackside earth, and then the train left him immediately behind. Gussie was as startled at having him gone as he'd been at the man's appearance. He sat motionless for a time, pondering the catcher's warning. He wondered if it weren't the catcher himself who'd been sporting, with his talk of pirates. Amusing himself running a fright up a greenhorn. But Gussie wasn't as green as he'd once been and his fright not as ready. Of course, rascals and toughs lurked where they might—forever it had been so. Gussie should've told the man of August, August the Terrible now relieved the weight of his eternal soul—as imposing a villain as any down-county bandit. Gussie hadn't pulled the trigger, but he'd withstood the test all the same, his breath the proof.

The train kept on at its half-mind pace for another quarter-hour, and then the shrill whine of the brakes was heard. Fuddled birds blatted from the trackside treetops and the scents of old payloads returned. Gussie let the train slow before gathering up his pack and finding his feet. He edged to the lip of the car and crouched. Reaching low, he dropped his pack aground, then after a moment followed it down himself. Shouldering the weight, he stepped off again into the trees to skirt the trainyard wide.

From a distance he saw a passel of scrawny cattle in a makeshift pen, and nearby a dozen men sitting about a smoking scaffold-stove. Gussie smelled cornpone and bean soup, and his body wanted to linger in this savory air. Perhaps a lump of delicious, dissolving fat-back in the beans. He pushed himself on, striding uptrack in the shade all the way to the foremost train, which after a delay of a few short minutes began to strain against its heft.

Gussie crossed swiftly from the woods and mounted. Again he chose the rear of the car, so as to face the train's progress. This one smelled not of coal and wood but of turned vegetables, and Gussie was relieved when the train attained speed. He took the opportunity to dig down into his pack for the pages the old woman had given him, then shifted his position toward the slanting sun. He propped himself lounge-wise on an elbow, conscious not to lie down flat and drift to sleep. Gussie wasn't privy to the story's opening, but in only a couple pages he gathered that the young hero's family—he was apparently of the noble line of the Wandering Force, an order of Oriental men-at-arms who polished their swords to icy keens and raged against oppression—that this hero's family had been massacred by the Flaming Moon Cult, who coveted the family's book of secret combat techniques. The hero, Zhin, was now being informed by an elder, a longtime ally of the family, that the book the cult had absconded with was a fake. Gussie squirmed to a better position. He read on as the elder led the boy out into the wilderness and trained him from the authentic creed, instructing him to seek justice rather than vengeance, revealing the ways of the staff and star. He was teaching the boy to eat and walk with a still mind, and to read the wind as one reads haiku. The elder told Zhin there would come a time when he had told all he knew, and on that day he would return to town and leave Zhin to endure the winter in solitude, to survive many months in the bitter climes, and when the sun returned, as it must, Zhin would either have joined the chorus of the ghosts or the ranks of the true warrior.

Gussie sat back up cross-legged. He wondered what kind of cider the old woman liked if she didn't like this sort. His mind was already leaping to league himself with Zhin. Gussie wanted Zhin's courage, wanted to shake the dour pall from about his spirit. Zhin was being tested, wasn't he, same as Gussie? Zhin needed to survive the tough time, and better times awaited. Both Zhin and Gussie were trying to live by principles, Zhin's handed down from the elder, Gussie's by his mother. Both lived in a contested land that might burn forever if no one salved it. And Zhin would triumph, wouldn't he? Gussie had gleaned that much from Miss Emily's library—the hero always found a way to complete his mission. Justice was always served. Zhin would survive the winter and fulfill his great destiny, it was only a question of how. And Gussie would reach Ivory Shoals. That was his mission. The worst was behind him—it had to be. He was on a train, wasn't he? He had a story to read. He was an orphan, sure, but that was no rare condition and gave Gussie no right to despair. He had his health, which was more than many had. If he was going to starve, it wouldn't be today.

Not wishing to burn too many pages in a sitting, Gussie tucked the book back into his pack and returned his gaze to the passing country, where now slow runnels wound about great hardwoods. He sighted a fox shambling through a fern bed in an expert way, its jibs and jibes light and agile. The train encountered a stretch of ground not entirely flat. Its speed slackened on the mild upslopes and gained again on the falls, and at a moment when the cars were pacing no swifter than a brisk walk, a degraded husk of an old man limped up beside and latched his hands onto Gussie's car and began to grapple himself up, grunting and losing his footing. Finally, the man mustered his effort and heaved his weight aboard and dragged himself wheezing to the front wall, slumping to a rest and immediately succumbing to a fit of hacking coughs.

Gussie kept still. He felt a prick of guilt that he hadn't helped the man aboard. The train car didn't smell like a clove cake, but the added odor of the new passenger almost had Gussie coughing as well. The man's boots were ripped at the toes, his cap stained and flattened. His only grip was a tarnished flask that he presently wrested from his trouser pocket. He unstopped the container with his back teeth and swigged hard, his breath not yet caught—swigged again, then a third time. Satisfied, he twisted the cork back in gently, so as not to splinter it, then rested the flask on the dusty floor. The old man's face was revealed now, upturned under his lifeless hat, and Gussie was disturbed to note at once that his features composed a mirror likeness, only in ruins, of the cow catcher who'd shared his car just earlier. The one eyelid shy to open, the sharp chin, the beak-like nose. The eyes, yes—the younger man's clear but unattending and the old man's cloudy and focused to a fine point on nothing—they matched uncannily in their burnt-grass hue. The wrecked fingernails. The livid red ears.

The old man began to mutter under his breath, and after a time it became clear that he was singing, droning out a number that favored "Lorena" but was not "Lorena." Now and then he stopped and cawed in bemusement at Gussie knew not what, then fell back into his garbled verses. Gussie soon felt like an intruder and was gladdened to feel the train slowing further. He gathered his pack to him and shimmied quietly to the edge of the car, the man still chanting and squinting toward a dark high corner. Gussie saw he'd lost more teeth than he'd kept and observed now that he was also missing the ring finger of his left hand.

The train was moving slowly enough for Gussie to dismount with his pack shouldered. He stole a last glance at the old vagabond, who was still staring at empty space, and felt suddenly, deeply, that his tandem of rail mates were a grim foretelling of his own fortune—the cow catcher who stole for reasons he no doubt deemed just, same as Gussie had back in Palmina, and the elder, the walking dead, kept in spirit for breath only by the slosh of his flask, a half-man who was likely, same as Gussie, without family or connection. Both men, same as Gussie, riding what rails remained toward designs liable to blow away in the wind like dunes of sand. These men, Gussie understood, were the ones kindred to him, not the hero Zhin. Gussie had been deluding himself, thinking he and the young knight alike. Gussie had no community to defend, no one on which to spend his bit of bravery but himself. He had no stronger claim on any particular place than he'd had on the putrid train car he'd just departed. No sword nor staff, no great cause. Gussie and the catcher and the beaten old man were not in a tale—they were in Florida in 1865, where better times were a childish notion and justice a thing as remote as the cold mountains of Asia.

———————

Julius' stage journey had thus far been dominated by Midas' ceaseless babbling. Morning to night, morning to night. Julius had recognized the young fellow by sight when he'd first boarded, both of them frequenters of the same late-night haunts—he was said to be a poet, was known to grow brave enough on drink that he'd strip out of his clothes and swim nude in the frigid bay—but Julius had never spoken to him and soon realized that one didn't so much speak with Midas as provide an audience. Before the two-man party had even cleared San Francisco—that city now three days and countless miles behind them—the young man had detailed, whipping about for effect a hemstitched handkerchief, the principle foibles and grudgingly admitted attributes of several members of his family, what foods agreed or disagreed with him at certain hours of the day, at which shop exclusively he purchased his boots. Midas was being forced, on pain of financial marooning, he'd explained, back to Baltimore and the mind-numbing dullness of school, but as far as Julius could tell, the fellow had had too much schooling already.

As they'd sunk into the dusty warmth of the San Joaquin Valley, Julius had listened to Midas profess his admiration for the painter Millet, who struck without strain an unlikely accord betwixt subject and style. Ascending the Sierras, great quilts of snow visible here and there in the crags, Julius learned that real literature would perish with Dickens, that the old Englishman was the end of the Big Road, that the new novelists only cracked jokes or delivered homilies and often showed the bad taste to do both at once. At the tavern in Virginia City, Midas had accepted pipe tobacco from the tender and issued a warning that smoking was a whetstone to his wit, and moments later, as if addressing some urbane salon rather than a collection of worn, stunned miners, he'd begun discoursing on the virtues of the Barbizon school and plein air composition.

Julius, by this time, hated the sound of his companion's voice, but at least the self-important lecturing was a distraction from his own impatience. Omaha was worlds away and the stage driver—a wheezing coot with a knuckled forehead who kept a pair of shotguns on the board under his feet—performed every movement with maddening torpor and was pathetically averse to taxing his horses. Julius hoped to avoid turning over to Abraham such a delicate affair as the one he now traveled for. He knew too well what an honorable fellow his father fancied himself—if there wafted the slightest whiff of verisimilitude from the young scoundrel's tale, he'd be bestowed whole familial standing the very day of his arrival. And Julius would be expected to display not only gracious acceptance, but the joy of a united sibling. The little fleece held a more auspicious position than he likely knew, for he possessed the virtue of not being Ruth Purifoy's son. He was untainted, unconnected to the family fiascoes of Madden Searle's past.

Julius spat out the warp-framed window of the coach—too vigorously perhaps, because Midas paused in his monologue to look over at him. "Confounded dust," he explained.

The stage roved on, another day and another, slower than Julius could believe, through barren mineral flatlands where only sagebrush thrived, no water about save the odd sorry creek that meandered the desert floor like a kitchen spill. Colorless ranches ceded back to the wilderness. Lusty winds whistling in from competing corners, frosty or tepid by turns.

It was decided to wait on supper until they reached Salt Lake City, and by the time the stage wheels creaked through the outskirts, full night had fallen. Near what seemed the center of the orderly plotted town, a shaven-headed man with bare feet barked on about approaching boldly the throne of grace, about the surpassing exquisiteness of knowing the Lord, prompting Midas to lean toward Julius and with a drained expression say he found the old yarn of Christ mawkish in the utmost.

As soon as they drew to a stop, Julius excused himself from his fellow traveler with great relief, found a fast meal, then strode with purpose toward the humble vice section—east of town, he'd been told, toward the fort—and all out this way was eerily quiet as the hour approached midnight. He walked past a sect a few dozen strong who wore smocks of homespun wool fit for penitence, a pair of fat sheep tied up at a post like horses, rows upon rows of still, plain dwellings, some lit mutedly from inside with lamps. But here it was, the familiar, solacing sound of a parlor organ, easy enough to follow, the comic hew-hawing notes, the jangle and then the calamitous upsurge. And a block before he reached the music's source, a quiet, humble house of luxury. Julius could always pick out these establishments at a glance—a required skill in this instance, since no advertisement showed. Perhaps it was some secret endowment of succor in the aura of these places, or perhaps it was only the scent of women, which he swore he sniffed on the rushing air.

No porch, nor even a step. A trestle above the entryway was festooned with peppers hung to dry, and Julius bowed his head and passed under it and entered a sparsely furnished chamber with a low ceiling. No one was about. Little pots hung at shoulder height along the walls, bursting with coal-black flowers. Empty finger bowls rested on the sideboards and shelves, likely meant to hold Vinegar of the Four Thieves. Julius heard voices from deeper rooms, a feminine laugh, the tinkle of glass. Before he could decide how to make his presence known, a stiff-bustled woman he happily put no older than twenty emerged from the shadows and took him by the hand and led him down a long hall—no stop at a barroom, no stairs to scale—she striding pertly and formally, as if balancing some unseen burden atop her head, and he clomping, by comparison, behind.

Her room was even more plainly appointed than the front room, but the hostess herself compensated the lack of decorative allure. She had full, pink cheeks and eyes bright as dollars and buoyant, winsome breasts. A thin gold bracelet. Hair bound up tight with a clip-comb she claimed fashioned of jaybird bones, a gift from a Tennessean who'd visited some months back. She offered Julius whiskey and undressed as he drank it. She raised her fingers up to the comb, and Julius motioned to stop her, wanting to forestall the cascading of the dark tresses over the white arms. Julius was both soothed and unnerved now—he wanted this to take forever and he wanted it all this instant. Easier, in a way, to be the item bought than the buyer, easier to play harbor to perverse whims than to wrestle them over the wide seas.

"Move the bracelet from your wrist to your ankle," Julius told her.

"I'll try," she said, "but I ain't very sure it'll fit."

One of the three pieces of furniture in the room was a sofa of blue damask, and afterward Julius sat upon it, a tasseled pillow on his lap. He complimented the woman on the seeming genuineness of her excitement, and she replied that the fanfare was all to his own credit. On a high table sat an earthen gallipot painted with a ring of drunken pipers, and from inside it she drew a cigar, clipped and lit it, handed it to Julius. She stepped to the other end of the sofa and perched herself on the arm. The bracelet was tight on her ankle, biting the delicate bones.

"You shouldn't store these like that," Julius told her, holding the cigar before his eyes for examination.

"They don't stay stored long," she said.

There was a high window on the wall opposite, nothing outside it but deep night.

"You ain't from the territory," she said.

Julius spit a fleck of tobacco off his tongue. Watched the smoke rise like a line drawing itself.

"Most times I can place an accent. You're from a place with

learnin, but still unsettled. And near water, I think. Great big water."

There was a bronze ash dish on Julius' arm of the sofa, and he rolled the red end of his cigar in it.

"The Southern Keys?" she said.

"Not quite," said Julius. "Imagine the Keys with meaner breezes and cattle rustlers."

"Never been south of St. Louis, Missouri, myself." She slid down onto the cushion, settling atop her crossed legs and never losing her upright posture. Her hair obscured one breast.

"Were you in the fightin then?" she asked him.

"No," Julius said. "I decided to deny myself that proud claim."

Custom dictated he was welcome to stay until his cigar was finished, and all that awaited him once he left was a flophouse full of snoring men. He looked at the woman's naked waist, narrow as a greyhound's.

"I won't bore you with my own story," he said, "but I can tell you of a fellow I know who was picked up on his way to open lands by the Home Guard. A dashing, virile sort. Hung like a Shire horse."

The woman's eyes flashed at this, an amused grin taking purchase on her face.

"He was of course robbed of all monies, this handsome and intelligent chap. Derided for his fine manners. Spat upon. Fed next to nothing, and nothing that any but the starving would want. The thinnest corn samp, of a curious mud color. Stewed squirrel bones. He angered his captors by his preference of the lash to revealing his identity. This man I speak of, while not a prized ally in a barroom fracas, was possessed of rare tenacity and could swallow pain with any hill-born pioneer."

Julius reached over and touched the woman's ribs with his fingertips, and she straightened back to full erectness, correcting the relaxation she'd begun to fall into at his words.

"By the by," he continued, "he was transferred, this man, to a makeshift prison in the proud state of Alabama, a place where the air smelled of human waste and half-mad men wailed day and night as if repeatedly impaled with a rusty bayonet. The fellow, as he reported it to me, felt outside of time—felt, if you will, aside the map of sanctioned human fates. He hardly knew how many, but after some number of weeks, if I've got the story right, the officer in charge of the place took a shine to his strange inmate. An educated man, this officer. He fancied himself deft with the ladies and a raconteur. The officer would visit the man's cell, seeking a worthy conversant, and the pair would swap ribald yarns—the officer's stories often labored, overripe, as if he'd hatched them the night prior. Eventually, the prisoner would be removed on fair days from his cell so that he and the officer might walk while they talked, and the walks lengthened and slowed and before long the two men took supper together, the prisoner asked to apply his critical palate to the officer's weekly menu—this hardly past the first year of the conflict, mind you, before culinary paucity became the rule. The officer inevitably went so far as to take earnest evening leisure with the prisoner, who, I can attest, had a conspicuous flair in this arena, leisure which took them off the grounds and into town, if one might deem such a huddle of dump stalls a town. Habits formed, as they will. Habits many would consider profligate."

Julius paused to smoke, licked his lips for the bittersweet spice. This time he only ran his eyes up from the woman's hip and she pressed higher her already rigid bearing.

"I won't delve into particulars regarding the recreations these two favored, but the officer found himself sated, edified, reduced, and when the time was nigh, it was without difficulty that the prisoner ensnared him in, well, great potential embarrassment. The officer was obliged to accept the terms of an agreement by which knowl-edge pertaining to certain depravities would remain confidential in swap for the bestowment on the prisoner of railway credentials. As I understand, one of your professional colleagues was an invaluable cog in the scheme. As well as a crippled man preferring unnatural love who had once earned his bread climbing trees like an ape. The prime ingredient, of course, was the corrupt pith of the officer's soul. Always within us, the seeds of our degradation."

Julius ashed his cigar with a thump, then leaned and gathered a thick lock of the woman's hair and fitted it behind her ear, exposing the breast that had been hidden. A little purse of rice, the nipple wine-colored.

"You remind me of somebody on a stage," the woman said. "The way you talk."

Julius looked into her eyes. "Do you take me a hero or a villain?"

"I wouldn't dare say." She drew her hand up and wiped the corners of her mouth. Julius could smell the balm she used on her elbows and knees.

"You can divine from where men hail. Can you divine whether they're good?"

"Bein good is no profit, for then the devil regards you a prize."

"A client said this?"

"Men tell me all manner of things."

He offered her a turn at his cigar, now half-spent, and she leaned her head close and took the smoke into her lungs and released it in piecemeal puffs through her dainty button nose.

"Will it be a joyous reunion?" she asked. "In Florida. With your kin?"

"Feelings will be mixed, I predict."

"My mother and father are gone, dead, and my brothers won't have a thing to do with me."

"Joy isn't my greatest care, as pertains my return."

"It ain't?"

"A fox snoops about the henhouse—the henhouse, in this case, a sixteen-room estate nestled to advantage near the docile Gulf, a handful of valuable patents, groves, furniture, no small mound of capital."

"What sort of fox?"

"The sort to make dubious claims. The sort too young to know what's good for him. The sort to get strung up by his tail."

"Claims on what grounds?" the woman asked, concern on her brow.

"On the unlikely claim my father sired him. If it's true, I'm happily surprised at the old man. Didn't expect he had it in him."

The woman shook her head, and her hair fell again down the front of her. "You mean he might be tellin the truth?"

"One can't rule it out," Julius said.

"But if he ain't lyin, then he's your brother."

Julius removed the pillow from his lap, exposing his half-kindled manhood, and replaced the ash dish on the flat of his thigh.

"Just a boy?" the woman said. "String him up?"

"Let's not get operatic. We've lost a half-million boys."

The woman's cheeks had paled, her coquettishness waning. "But your father's estate sounds plenty to share. And the gain of a brother."

"I've no need of a brother, no use for a child underfoot. The estate is indeed bountiful, but that matters not a whit." Julius took a long, indulgent pull from the cigar. There was more there for the burning, but he upended it and tamped it coolly until no more smoke arose, then rested the butt in the dish and rested the dish with care on the wood floor. "One has what one is able to keep," he explained, the woman watching him with hot eyes, an arm crossed over her front and the pad of one foot on the floor. "This is the way of men and always has been. No fault lies in the urchin seeking his pudding, no fault in my repelling him. The victor has his spoils, the loser his wounds."

The woman's shoulders slumped. "A villain," she said, a bit inso-
lently. "I reckon you a villain, not a hero."

Julius narrowed his eyes at her, held her in his gaze, and she
betrayed no fear. After a moment, he nodded toward his trousers
and the rest, and she arose and gathered his clothing in her arms and
carried it all over and dumped it on the sofa. She went for her own
underclothes, but Julius told her not to, and so she sat on the bed
and sighed and appraised her fingernails.

Once he'd dressed, Julius told her she was free to remove the
bracelet from her ankle. He watched closely as she pinched the clasp
with care and peeled the thin chain of gold from her flesh, where it
left an impression like bright, red thread.

———

It was late morning when Gussie arrived at a town called Sattsboro,
which after so much lonely rambling seemed positively teeming.
Groups of Black men nodded meditatively at one another and leaned
away from their brethren to spit tobacco juice at the dust. A band
of boys several years Gussie's junior played batball on a worn, weedy
pitch. A lean man of undetermined age stood stiff and steely a few
paces off the wagonway, his face tart, peddling a stringer of shot
squirrels. There was a clear creek lined with sweetleaf shrubs, and
the short bridge that spanned the creek marked the entrance to the
town proper, which included a smith's and a saloon and a plate joint
already astir with dinner proceedings. On the square were tied off
fitter, grander horses than Gussie had seen since Palmina. Women in
good dresses and toddlers in dapper nankeen suits.

At the far side of the square stood a general store with a fresh-look-
ing roof of cypress shingles. Gussie ambled over and stepped onto the
porch, held the shop door as two women made their exit, then walked

inside and was braced at once by the rich waft of ground coffee. Gussie needed only a glance to be startled by the whopping breadth of the wares. Every strain of gewgaw and foodstuff reckonable crowded the shelves—picnic baskets, sets of dominoes, even speaking trumpets. A sideboard was decked to the inch with bachelor spittoons, many of them prettied up with etchings of songbirds or blushing belles with lips painted like rosebuds. There were cans of marrowfat peas. Pickled onions. High, proud loaves of brown bread. Plug tobacco. Tins of lard. Spanish fritters. Everything from oilcloth sacks to bundles of beanpoles to metal shoes equipped with wheels on their soles. A dozen dried meats. A giant pyramid of potatoes and another of corn.

Gussie didn't notice the clerk until he spoke—a young man whose cotton blouse was buttoned all the way to the neck and who had a fresh, powdered air about him. He beckoned Gussie over and handed him a tin contraption with a push-button on its side, told him where to put his eye. Gussie brought the novelty to his face and pressed, and the first card flapped down into view. After a moment, he pushed for the next card. Then the next. What Gussie saw was the image of a warship running headlong into a torpedo of rifle powder, and then the great craft sinking, piecemeal, into a stormy sea.

"The amount of cleverness dedicated to playthings," the clerk said when Gussie handed back the piece.

Gussie, stomach growling, only nodded. He stepped over to the foodstuffs and made his selections, totting the total in his mind so as not to overdraw and also gauging what would travel—dried venison and prunes and salted nuts. He arranged the pile on the counter, then wriggled free of his pack.

"Hell of a shop you got here, sir," Gussie said.

"It's a hell of a shop, but it's not mine." The clerk was already tallying Gussie's purchases on a clean little pad. It seemed to require only a fraction of his attention. He had long, orderly sideburns and pink lips. He looked at Gussie significantly and told him the establishment was property of Mr. Eli Acker, but that Mr. Acker was out of town on business. "Very pressing business," he added, his tone one of cagey awe.

Gussie asked for tobacco and the clerk retrieved it and dropped it on the counter.

"I had a position as math instructor awaiting me at the seminary in Tallahassee," he confessed, "but when the opportunity arose to apprentice under Mr. Acker—well, of course that was too attractive to pass on. A man of that stature. Didn't have to think twice."

"Sure," Gussie said.

"What do you mean, sure?"

"I mean I'm just agreein with you."

"Sounded more like a question, the way you said it."

"Tryin to agree, anyhow."

The clerk's shoulders went slack. "The name Eli Acker doesn't ring a bell? The cattle baron, Eli Acker?"

"Not as such," Gussie said.

"Not as such?"

"But I ain't from around here, so don't weigh it too heavy."

"I know you're not from around here. I can tell that much. You don't need to be from around here to know who Eli Acker is. He's got more influence in Florida than any governor they could seat." The clerk snorted. "He's a personal friend of David Yulee, who I've met and shook hands with right in this shop. Right where we're standing."

"Yu-lee," said Gussie. "Now that one I might've heard."

"You might have heard of David Yulee," the clerk said, as if to make sure his ears were working. "The man owns half of Jacksonville. The Federals detained him and that's exactly the business Mr. Acker is seeing to."

"I don't get Jacksonville way with no regularity," Gussie said.

The man paused. His expression was mostly curious now.

"David Yulee," he said. "That's his iron they're rebuilding the railroad with? I'll feel better if you don't walk out of here not knowing who David Yulee is. That'll be a comfort to me."

"My mama told me it's many curses to bein grown, and studyin politics is front and center."

"Your mother told you that?" the clerk said.

"Yessir."

"My mother told me not to walk around ignorant as the day I was born," the clerk said. "It's good fortune I didn't wind up in a teaching trade. I don't think I've got the patience for it."

Gussie's eyes had been wandering over the wall behind the clerk, hung so busy with merchandise, and presently they caught upon a small board chalked with pricing specials and the month and day.

"That today's date?" Gussie asked, and immediately he knew it was a mistake. The clerk, without missing a beat, embarked upon a routine centered on the notion that displaying wrong information on blackboards was his most beloved diversion, that he relished nothing in the world so much as causing pointless confusion for his customers, but Gussie scarcely heard the performance. His birthday had passed. He was thirteen years old and had been for two days. Thirteen. The first birthday he'd passed alone. The first that had gone unmarked. He bowed his head to look down at himself, wiggled his same skinny fingers and shifted his tormented feet. The same inner voice rang in his head, saying that surely he wasn't the same fellow now as before he'd left Palmina, that surely he wasn't the same fellow as before his mother had passed. The alteration, he reckoned, had little to do with age. He'd fallen asleep so many nights now without a soul to care what happened to him. Had awakened to that same circumstance, none to bother whether he perished snake-bit or for lack of drink. None to care whether he grew to a man, or, if he did, what type of man.

The clerk was still talking. He held a pair of suspenders and tossed them lightly atop Gussie's haul.

"I'll be all right without those there," Gussie said. "Got my doubts I could afford them anyway. This I got already gone scrape me."

"Those are on the house," the man said. "You're not hard of hearing on top of it all, are you?"

"I ain't hard for hearin and I ain't no charity case," Gussie said, though he was aware how much he'd thinned since his journey had begun, aware that his trousers sagged as though he'd stuffed the pockets with stones.

"Charity hasn't a thing to do with it," the clerk said. "I don't wish to see your drawers and I don't want any other poor soul to have to see them, either."

Gussie saw no advantage in pressing the conflict, and so went ahead and thanked the clerk, who gave him his total and accepted his money and, as Gussie packed up, continued to spoof him by inquiring whether he'd heard of George Washington or maybe of a fellow of some accomplishment known as Julius Caesar.

Gussie exited the shop and departed the square, heading due south and pausing at a public pump to fill his canteen, and soon Sattsboro was behind him, only himself and the trail again, and he thought of how his mother, even during the bad years, had made sure to furnish him lavish confections on his birthdays. Each May he'd been old enough to remember, right up through the last, one year and two days ago, when it had been a toffee roll adorned with marshmallows that he'd finished in one sitting. He pined now for his sweet and of course more deeply for his mother's lips upon his waiting cheek, and he doubted very much that he was grown, despite his losses and the calendar's decree.

He'd asked his mother once why men were mean—this after a drunken boatswain who'd been insulted in a tavern had slit the throats of the offender's prize goats—and she'd stared at him so earnestly he at first mistook her for cross. She'd set down her needlepoint and picked something off the shoulder of her dress, then leaned toward him, eyes firm, and told him that bravery and decency made men content. That they grew mean out of despising their own cowardice, their own villainy. Bravery, she'd avouched, could be raised with a bottle or with bruised pride, but decency could only be planted in a soul by God, and Gussie, she said, was flush with it.

And little remained of that same steamy day when he cleared a high-grassed crook in the trail and raised his weary eyes to survey the next hundred-count of yards before him, and he registered like a drunkard's vision the unreal form of the horse, the sight of which struck him still as stone. The traveler frozen mid-step. The horse frozen in the traveler's gaze. Gussie had strode free of the lofty hardwoods that afternoon and into a likelier landscape of palmetto and pine and the various scrappy oaks with their contorted limbs and dust-green foliage, the sun all day in a high bisque luster that had worn on him and worn on him relentlessly, and he had been testing his burnt lower lip with his fingertips when the palomino steed appeared in the waning light. Its white mane proud as flame, it recomposed itself and began again to crop the trailside carpetweed. A Morgan, Gussie guessed. He understood at once what he would do and possessed not the vim to counsel himself against it. He was close on bankrupt. Footsore and far from harbor. This fine a horse would be sought by its owner or whatever bandit had slain its owner or whoever had outfoxed that bandit, but if Gussie rode for just an hour, two hours, only to boon his day's progress before he quit for camp—he could stop at the next town and present the horse at the livery or some handy estate, turn the animal up as lost in the role of good-deeder. Just getting it off the perilous plain. Perhaps some wee reward would even be in the offing, above the reward of covering more than a day's distance between now and when the stars showed.

Gussie knew the tried course was to gain a horse's respect at once, to walk straight up with clear intent and exhibit a presumptuous mastery, but he couldn't risk spooking the Morgan. The animal would never believe Gussie's put-on confidence. Gussie surely wouldn't believe it himself. The best plan, he decided, was to appear without scheme, merely another incurious element of the woodscape. He needed to drift into the horse's proximity as if led by the innocent concerns of any forest critter, needed the joining as one to seem as much the horse's notion as his own. He had precious little riding experience. His history with horses consisted mostly of leading them gently down the alleyways of Palmina—extra money to be made at the livery when the docks were slow—and many of those horses knew where they were going and wanted to get there.

The Morgan stood at a slant and blocked the trail, facing more away from Gussie than toward him, and Gussie didn't want to approach the animal from behind. He stepped off into the grass and flanked ahead, raising his knees high for the weeds—ten yards, twenty. He reassumed the way again a good bit uptrail and then began, shuffle-step by meek shuffle-step, to put himself nearer. A pause, a look about, then nearer. A stolen glance at the great golden stray, then nearer. The light draining swiftly now, the thickets all shadow and the path soft-looking as wax.

The saddle had slipped skew. Gussie could see it clearly now—deep-seated and with a tall, shapely cantle, an empty scabbard dangling from it. He edged his boots a measure closer in the dust and lowered his pack to the ground, opened it and fished inside with slow fingers until he felt the last wedges of dried apple. He returned to height. Nosed and nosed, trying by act of will to tranquilize his breathing and heart. When Gussie stood no more than three strides from the animal, it quit rolling its jaw and looked at him frankly with its big, ready eyes. It issued a quizzical snort, then raised its hooves only to replant them, the muscles of its chest twitching and tail swatting its rump. It was into a stand of dwarf cherries, Gussie could see, and not eager to abandon the spot.

Gussie returned the horse's open expression. He outreached his arm, offering up his hand, the empty one, then stepped the hand close enough for the horse to crane its neck and sniff. Gussie had another hand in store, fat-fisted with apples, and though the horse snuffled these up and champed them without apprehension, it just as soon drew high again its head when it saw no more delicacies forthcoming—towering over Gussie then, breaking fully the brief moment of caucus. Nothing for Gussie but to tax whatever goodwill the apples had bought, and so he scuffed close and stroked the horse's neck. The horse shied from Gussie, still sidelong in the trail, its head strained high and vainglorious, the brass appointments of the elegant, slump-jerked saddle chinking. The reins were in reach, but Gussie resisted temptation. He couldn't have the Morgan rear. The horse took another retreating, labored chop-step, unwilling to turn itself rightwise in the path. It sharmed about as if in a stall, and Gussie kept along with it, kept stroking it neck to shoulder best he could reach. And with the movement, Gussie scented something in the cooling air—the musty, mineral odor of spilt blood. Gussie spoke to the horse, in that blasé whisper he'd heard the Black livery men employ so often, telling a horse as they had told all the horses before that it didn't need to do naught but unlax and hold its vinegar and it'd be as spoiled as a Hindu heifer, telling the horse it had a friend now and that was a good thing to have. Gussie was able to wangle around and view the injury—a musket's work, most likely, the wound half-scabbed and infected. The listing saddle was pressing close to the damage, and when Gussie hoisted its weight up away from the horse's hide, the animal wheezed, its ribcage flexing. The saddle was like a sack of bricks to Gussie's tired arms, but he searched his fingers to the catches and loosed the great cumbrance and tugged it as gently as he could from the hurt and finally heaved the thing upright. He snugged the stirrups, his pack slipping about on his shoulder. The horse tolerated all this, and once the service was performed, seemed to Gussie—seemed to this desperate, saddle-green boy trying to read the beast by its breaths and eyes—to have lost a measure of its distrust.

Gussie now reached for and caught the reins, and the horse did not dissent. Gussie stepped back around to the unharmed side, his optimism growing, and began to walk the horse uptrail, the animal testing against its lead and Gussie grasping the leather taut without ever wrenching it, as he'd been shown back in his old life. He walked the Morgan farther, a little farther, lulling the massive warrior into rapport, one spooky oak and the next drifting past. The trail was straight, and Gussie felt possessed of one final ration of pluck. He snatched up the reins anew and flexed his fingers about the straps. Put a testing bound into his step and drew a great breath that stretched his lungs. The horse's gait was even, but it wouldn't look at Gussie, its eyes fixed ahead.

Gussie minced his steps, reaching up for the saddle horn with his off hand as if for something on a top kitchen shelf, and as he skipped into a leap and sought the stirrup with his boot the horse chose its moment to pitch ahead, leaving Gussie without purchase, leaving him suspended in air a moment, most of his weight hauling on the reins. When his feet met trail he could do nothing but hit a few quicker, choppier strides and leap again, a sort of match-step glissade, the horse nearly at a trot. And again the Morgan lurched forward, again that moment of stopped time, Gussie hanging there, his weight on the reins, stabbing at and missing his target with the toe of his boot. But Gussie felt he had the measure now, and on the third crack he vaulted forward in anticipation, matching the horse, and this time his foot did strike the mark, boot-leather on iron—struck the stirrup, yes, kicked at it, yes, but alas only rattled around and around without managing to make the fit. And this time it was worse. This time Gussie was hung up aside the horse at near a canter. Perhaps it was the Morgan who'd taken Gussie's measure rather than the other way around, because it tossed its big head and jerked Gussie near endwise. Gussie felt his legs swing up under the horse instead of back to the earth, felt his pack-straps slide and catch and heard the canvas scrape ground. For a blink he still believed he could swing himself right-side with the aid of the horse's own movement, like a clock bob, but then the reins jolted again and he was head under feet and could feel his grasp slipping. A scrabbling flail for anchor against the horse's great, smooth underside. The moment, both slow-dawning and sudden, of appreciating his foolishness, almost as if some stranger had tossed it to him, the heavy object of his own folly, and now he could sit in a chair and turn it over in his hands. He was hard down on the trail in a cloud of dust, a searing smart in his shoulder, pain enough to keep him from moving. An awareness that his pack had come loose from him. Grit in his mouth. The Morgan's hoof reports, like wood on wood tlot-tlotting away. A different, fresher smell of blood, and then all was peace but the small birds whickering to and fro above him, roused by the aberrant tumult in their forest, slaloming with frightened abandon from high branches to low.

———————

Abraham struck the match. He held it beneath the folded letter until the flame caught and flared, then lowered the paper into a marble ash dish he'd set on the drink table out on his portico, watched the communiqué darken and diminish and disappear into smoke yellow as a goat's eyes. It was midmorning, the breeze halfhearted. The same view out toward the weedy pasture. The distant line of bristly palms. A tree in the middle distance denuded by some pestilence or another, standing white as ivory in the sun, groping from the ground like a ghoulish hand. Abraham raised the dish and leaned from his chair and dumped the contents, watched the ashes flutter to the dry, loose earth.

Julius had described the boy as an invidious cur, and those words now rolled about the pan of Abraham's mind like restless dice. Julius had lamented men of quality such as themselves drawn into such tawdry plots. He told Abraham he regarded the problem of the interloper as his own to dispatch, he being the blood heir, and pronounced in fervent language that all conceivable haste would be made. But he also stated, with no want of clarity, that should he not arrive in time, Abraham must be prepared to fill the breach. Resolve would be called for—cold, manly nerve. Julius affirmed their fortunes linked as with iron chain, affirmed his loyalty toward Abraham. When he mentioned his father's health, the intent was to remind Abraham of the urgency of the situation, rather than to beg an update on the poor fellow's decline, which he neglected to do. He signed off with the hope that in no long time the episode of the imposter would be behind them, left in the past along with dusty stage travel and meals of warmed-over beans, along with anxious coin-counting, along with Julius' entire exile, along with the whole dratted war—and the pair of them would again lounge together of an evening on the front stonelay of the estate, jacks and aces in one hand and dry sherry in the other.

Abraham should've been out front now, supervising the boy he'd hired to scrub that same granite slab Julius so prettily referenced, but he felt listless, leaden, felt tied to his fiddleback chair, a hand-me-down from the drawing room. He should've now been risen, sliding the chair against the wall, up under the overhang in case weather arrived. He should have been rinsing clean the ash dish, but he could not impel his body to stir, could not prevent his mind from slipping two days past, to an initially pleasant afternoon venture he'd made to a low-roofed sip room just the other side of Creek de Aza. He'd opted for the three-quarters-of-an-hour walk rather than bothering with the cranky quarter horse—indeed, he'd been in no hurry. The intent of that sort of outing, which he undertook monthly or nearabout, was new air and a change of scenery, to stretch the legs and clear the mind. And so he'd strode over—road unto trail unto rougher trail unto faint footpath—under a static, harvested-looking sky, and had finally spotted through the dwindling brush the Florida state flag, flaccid but hung high, and then a single hexed horse at a rail, one eye crossed and one ear scalloped. A doorsill of loose-stacked bricks. Inside, a few ignored tables, a couple hard-used divans. On one side a company of unwashed young men—blind at two in the day on what looked to be cane beer—pitched quoits and partook of big swollen fistfuls of peanuts from a darkened iron tub. On the side opposite, two men sat at the bar, one a straight-backed fellow with white hair but a face younger than Abraham's, the other a lanky sort whose hat boasted a pink curlew feather and who Abraham recognized as Thurgis, a sheriff who worked the nearby towns—how diligently, at this point, was anyone's guess. Abraham had seen him a handful of times, Thurgis in each instance slur-voiced with drink. He didn't expect the sheriff to recognize him, and this bore out when Abraham settled himself on a stool a short way from the sheriff and both he and the white-haired man tipped Abraham a nod, hardly breaking talk: a Vermont lumber concern scouting the area, all the abandoned salt works on the north Gulf, how small and bland the grapefruit were now compared to the old days. Whenever the sheriff spoke, no matter the theme, no matter if in accord or dissent, his eyes became possessed of a simmering outrage like coals peeking out from a newly banked fire, posing a continual dare to his listener to gainsay. His red beard was waxed slick, his vest snug on his thin frame.

Abraham had somewhere along his foot journey lost the taste for liquor—the heat, most probably—but he ordered one at any rate and let it sit unmolested before him as he listened to the white-haired man, partly blocked from Abraham's view by the sheriff between them, explain that his right arm had been ruined in battle and so he'd schooled himself to do everything lefty-wise. Cook grits. Write even.

"Shootin from the other shoulder?" the sheriff asked.

"No, sir. Not me. Ain't playin volley with no more lead."

"Wish everybody thought that way," the sheriff said. "My job would be a sight pleasanter."

"I count myself smiled upon." The white-haired man's enfeebled arm, Abraham leaned to see, hung close against his front like something pinned there and forgotten. "Got shut with only the arm here and a little scurvy. Still takin air, the main thing. Had me a limey sawbones, you like to think he never had so much fun as unbustin an arm."

"You're a good left at hoistin whiskeys," the sheriff said.

Abraham was not without admiration for the blind bravery of soldiers, but in his hidden heart he considered them fools. Those great waves of poor Confederate infantry that stood nothing to gain by victory. One was forever obliged to hear talk of honor from the rich and ranked. Always honor. Lee, who turned countless scores of hungry boys into musket fodder, celebrated for the poise and fortitude of deciding, once the struggle was lost, to spare the last few. And valor. It was all well to be valorous when one's name was assured to ring through history, but what of the piled pale corpses of dirt farmers' sons, fading already in the wash of time?

The sheriff raised himself off his stool and drew out a knife with a blade as long as a man's foot and cut himself a twist of tobacco. He pressed the wad into his cheek, then told the white-haired man—though he spoke louder now, inviting Abraham to listen—that he hadn't had a deputy since his brother lit out, no help in three years. Could have one, he said, if he wanted fourteen-year-old blood on his hands or wanted to drag around some graybeard militia fogy. "Nobody payin taxes," he said, "nobody payin for a license. This place here ain't got one, I know. Government tryin to collect tax so they can hire somebody to bust whoever ain't got a license. Askin money from people so they can bust them same people."

The white-haired man whistled, amused. The sheriff called out and the tender came and filled the sheriff a shot and filled the white-haired man one as well, and when he looked down the bar Abraham went ahead and drained his waiting drink and signaled for another.

"Heard tell of a youngster, no more whiskers than a cat could lick off," the sheriff said, "brought an abrupt end to this old bounty man upstate aways. Talkin about rough times for agents of justice. Meanest sumbitch ever born, they say, this bounty man. Folks afraid to even think cross of him. Flames branded all across his chest, how they knew it's him. Tracked this boy from Jacksonville way or such, week upon week and soon enough sloggin horseless through the swamps, catch up just to get a scattergun blast from the youngster and this hunched-to old lady took up for him. Worse sumbitch north of Sumter done in by a granny and a durn candy-suckin kid. What you deal with now. Ain't just got to worry of hard criminals—every last soul's hard now. Get stabbed in the belly by a nursery maid, wouldn't surprise me none." The sheriff had his hat with the pink feather on the bar and his long knife, and now he rested his empty glass there. "Told me the boy's name but I done forgot it already. Actin like I'm supposed to remember every truant in the state. Won't even get me a deputy. Gunther, I think. No, wasn't Gunther."

Abraham went on and lifted his fresh round and drained it. The glass was gleaming clean, nary a smudge. "Was it Gussie?" he asked. His voice was hoarse, so he cleared his throat. "The boy's name—was it Gussie, by chance?"

Thurgis the sheriff turned toward him, and the white-haired man was looking over too. Abraham set his glass down softly.

"Gussie," the sheriff repeated. "Yeah, I think that's it. Gussie. Now how'd you know what it was?"

Abraham pushed his little glass away from him, not sure whether he was done drinking or asking for more. "What did he... where was he making for, I wonder? Where'd he have mind to get to?"

The sheriff took a moment, in the way of sheriffs, to look Abraham over. His eyes. Clothes. Boots. Back to his eyes. "I reckon he's headed anywhere he wants to be headed," he said. "Anywhere he gets a mind to."

Abraham nodded, coolly he hoped.

"I reckon he's a free element in the new South," the sheriff went on. "Same rights as you and me."

The sheriff stared harder at Abraham now, as if trying to place him, and Abraham went ahead and stared right back until a caterwaul went up from the men pitching quoits across the way, cheers filling the place.

"Yes," Abraham said, raising his voice over the noise. "I reckon that's precisely what he is. I reckon he can go wherever he pleases, just like you and me, and hope for whatever reception the Lord sees fit to bestow."

Hot darts of pain ran down Gussie's back, and even the moonlight hurt his eyes. For a time, he saw only the woman, who wore a frilly blouse but trousers like a man. He saw, as if her face were spotlighted on a stage, her carven chin and mobile eyes. She wore a sun hat though it was night and hanging at her back like a quiver was a long, stiff braid. She had been talking without pause from the moment she'd roused Gussie from the trailside weeds, but he'd not corralled a great much of it. She took herself a constitutional every night after supper, clear to the trail where her property butts. Always took along a little sack of pecans—had some left if he wanted, a couple down in there at the bottom. The Morgan abruptly returned to Gussie's mind, the memory of his foolishness. His cheeks turned hot to think of it, his achy gut felt full of steam. Gussie wanted to speak. His lips were caked with dried blood—he could feel the rough edge and taste zinc as he swabbed about with his tongue. She didn't sleep much anymore, the woman told Gussie. She took to the bed out of charity for her feet, but her eyes didn't hardly close. It wasn't much farther. This part here was muddy.

As Gussie allowed himself to be led wherever this woman was taking him, the winds of his mind blew from afar the fact that he had been saved from dire outlooks by members of the fair sex not once on his journey, by Joya and her statuesque companion in the rank swamp, and not twice, by the old lady and her blessed scattergun, but now thrice: this lean-armed hero with her busy, dry eyes, who now supplied her name as Miss Elam—if his bell, she said, wasn't too rung to remember it. So long ago the swamp seemed, the turtle supper and Joya anointing him against mosquitoes. It felt more distant than Palmina somehow. The women of Florida had rescued him—from exposure, from enemies, now from his own stupidity.

Miss Elam tugged him to a stop and looked up, her grip firming. And he saw it, a snake coiled sloppily across the trail. After a moment he heard the quiet rattle, distinguished it in the din of crickets and toads like a student of music might a single note in a symphony. Canebrake, Miss Elam told him.

"Leave that one to next year, my papa would've said. Had to be long as he was tall or wasn't worth a stew."

She guided Gussie into the sedge, flanking the shimmering serpent, then was soon again at her soothing disquisition, her voice lithe, running over disparate particulars as a cat over river stones. Green peppers didn't agree with her, but red cleared her skin. A yellow moon meant a secret would out. Treat an enemy sweet, bees will never sting you.

Miss Elam's house was a dogtrot. She led Gussie up the breezeway and into the sundered kitchen. She didn't imagine, she said, that Gussie wanted to wait till morning to fill his belly. Boys his age, time you got the dishes washed they were sniffing around for the next meal. She knew. She remembered her brothers that age, remembered her mama saying it was one long mess service, raising boys.

From a food safe with doors of punched tin she retrieved a mince pie—made with beef tongue, she told Gussie—and sided it with calves' feet jelly and set close a glass of sun tea to wash it down. And when, only minutes after, he was through, plate clean and mouth wiped, she led him back outside, down two steps and up two, and into an entry where the pair removed their boots underneath a grand hat rack that held a large shelf-crowned thigh-beater fitting in size for a man. Under the bench were a pair of men's leather town shoes, worn ruddy. When Miss Elam saw Gussie glance at the shoes, she reached down and rested her fingertips on the shiny toes a moment. He saw now that she wore a simple ring of gold on her fourth finger, and when they moved on into the parlor, arranged there on a burnished table beneath a painting of a farmer hauling a roped bull from a lake, he saw a fine-looking pipe and its polished nickel implements.

"My husband," was all she said, and she went quiet for some moments before recovering herself with a brave breath and a quick clap of her hands. She told Gussie he was in for a bath, additional to his other trials. She waved off his protestations about the late hour, led him to a washroom, brought in full buckets at two a trip and dumped them in the tub. Gussie followed her order to disrobe and sank himself into the tepid water, which rippled about him in the candlelight. Miss Elam told him to rest his head back. She laved the water over him with an enameled cup, slow and careful, cleansed his scrapes and tested his bruises. Doused the blood from his jawline and ear.

"Whoever dusted you off, hope they took flight from these parts," she said. "I had my fill troublin with low types."

"No dustin off," Gussie said. "I was thrown by a horse." Gussie remembered in clear flashes slipping under the Morgan, scrabbling for grip, the moment of free fall, the hoofbeats fading. He'd fallen prey to the haste, so often spoken of, that preceded waste.

"So, you're down one animal?" Miss Elam said. "We can inquire tomorrow. Might could turn him up—stranger things have happened. Turn him up and take a switch to his tail parts."

"No, ma'am. I ain't down no animal." Gussie drew his knees up to his chest. He was grateful it was night, so the filth that must've collected at the bottom of the tub couldn't be seen. He admitted to his hostess that the horse had not belonged to him, assuring her of his genuine intention to ride the steed only to the nearest well-to-do homestead and turn it over. He'd only wanted to make more ground before night.

"I ain't no rustler nor hustler," he said. "No matter what Nealon Rye might tell."

"Who's Nealon Rye?"

"Nobody. Nobody of no import, far as I figure."

"I can divine myself you ain't a heister," Miss Elam said. "I could read that when I first led you from the trail. Always been a crack jury for character, though I do appreciate a fellow comin out honest. Ain't got to tell me no more, you ain't want to."

"I thank you for that," Gussie said. "And for the bath and the pie and for everything."

"Yes, well, it ain't no trouble. I had trouble before—fixin you up ain't it."

After a moment, Miss Elam leaned back in her chair and set high her line of vision, steepling her fingers. "Band of filthy layouts squattin right in these very rooms," she told Gussie. "I don't need to tell you they didn't find a lot of time for housekeepin." She turned her head aside as if to spit but only sniffed hard. "Took my damn mule. Warlock. Good old Warlock. Spite the name, only magic he did was disappearin a week's oats in three days. That's what I used to tell people. That was my joke. Keep an animal six, seven years, you get attached. Had no place to hide him. No help to fetch. All I could do was make myself scarce and watch they didn't burn the place to the ground."

The candle on the shelf began to gutter, so Miss Elam stood and lit another from the flame. With both candles burning, the room was momentarily brighter. Gussie held himself close, arms around his legs and palms on his ribs.

Miss Elam reseated herself and told Gussie of being forced to abscond to the woods out back of the house, where a disused smokehouse served as her residence for fully eight weeks. She'd gathered what she might, she said, clothes and foodstuffs and what meager keepsakes she could stuff in a canvas sack—her husband's smoking kit sprang to Gussie's mind, the shoes—and hid her money in a wall crack of the smokehouse. She'd slept on a rotted pallet, a dirk knife in arm's reach. In the end they hadn't looted overmuch, too lazy to lug anything heavy or maybe just not too interested in the curios and oddments of a plain old country woman.

"You're not all very plain," Gussie said.

"Oh, no?" she said. "You got one or two answers, don't you? You just might do all right, push comes to shove." A little laugh escaped her but didn't register on her face. "You ready to get out from there, your majesty?"

"Reckon I'm puckerin."

She went over and lifted a cotton towel off a hook and reached it out to him. Turned away while he rose and high-stepped out and began shucking the towel up one leg and then the other.

"Finally lit out, I was cleanin for weeks, scrubbin each square inch of this place. Them gentlemen never saw fit to wash a dish. Just leave them sittin where they may, or if they was real industrious that day, chuck them off the porch."

She handed Gussie a pair of drawers, far too big, and took the towel. "See if you can keep these up till tomorrow."

Gussie stepped into the crisp, white underpants and then folded the waist upon and upon itself until it stayed put.

"I'm sure sorry all that happened to you," Gussie said. "My mama used to say the South of this nation has better and worser men than anywhere the world over."

Miss Elam moved the chair back to its spot in the corner. "These were of that second stamp. The worser. Couldn't even bother with the outhouse. Just let water right out an open window." She went and grabbed the candle that was still aflame. "Consider myself lucky the weather was fair. Could have been January or Ju-ly."

She led him back into the parlor, quickly and expertly dressed the sofa, and bade him goodnight.

"I'll just be in there starin at the wall," she said. "Makin certain it don't go no place."

But when she retired to her bedroom Gussie heard her stirring for only a few minutes and then could hear nothing in the house save her even, feathery snores. She was worn out enough for a dozen ranch hands with grief and hard use and ordinary women's work—so worn out she couldn't tell when she slept. Gussie looked at the painting of the man and the bull, their eternal tug of war. He too felt sapped. He hoisted his pack up beside him on the sofa and tiredly audited its nonedible contents. His sorry knife. The horse-mane swatch, which could not be said to have failed him. He thought of lighting a candle and reading further of his Far Eastern gallant, and it was not only his aching eyes that stopped him doing so. He felt a strange lack of interest just then in the fictional fates of fictional young men. What had happened on the trains had somehow withered the part of him that wished to be buoyed by the overcoming of made-up perils, by the vanquishing of imaginary scoundrels. He didn't even want the Bible and its quaint miracles. Didn't want any version of life that had been crafted to fit inside a book's bindings.

He fished to the bottom of the pack and instead found the gold watch, held it sheathed a moment and then slipped it from its dust cloth and gripped it fast, ran his thumb about its clean edge and then over its three-letter engraving. Opened its hood. Snapped it again. It was the same warm as his palm, the same warm as the bathwater had been, the same also as the deep, endless night outside. His father had opened and closed this watch, had drawn it from his pocket after being lost in his work, had checked it waiting on a train platform before an important meeting. He had ridden west toward Ivory Shoals those so many years before, fresh off his encounter with Gussie's mother, disoriented probably, delighted and perhaps heartsore, and under the canvas of his carriage had made to pull the watch from his pocket for the simple, dependable intelligence it would bare and had discovered nothing there but weightless lint.

Gussie brought himself upright on the sofa. He still wore only the overlarge drawers and had to shimmy them back up his hips where they belonged. The parlor looked larger in the day, emptier. He wound his arm testingly in its socket—he could hold it only as high as his head, and this with a hard pinch in his shoulder. His pack. His boots. The painting. The meerschaum, the sight of which now lit a hanker in Gussie for his own pipe. He heard birds outside, and then behind the chirping was another family of sounds—the small, sanguine tapping of wood tools, the squeak of an awl.

When he stepped out back, barefoot and bare-chested, he saw it was well-nigh noontime. Miss Elam sat at a little table at the rear egress of the breezeway, turning a birdhouse before her eyes like a jeweler with a brooch. She brushed the steep little roof with her free hand and picked up a rasp. She didn't look toward Gussie when she jabbed her chin at an extra chair and said, "Take a load off, bronc-buster."

The birdhouse was a birthday gift, she explained, for the daughter of a couple who lived a few claims over. Georgians, but not chased south by Sherman. They'd moved down the summer before the war, and the father, due to a lame leg, had been exempt from service. They had three young boys and a teenage daughter, and mother and daughter alike were the fetchingest eyefuls ever to eat soup with a spoon. Necks like swans. Cheeks to make any Richmond debutante look like a miner at quitting time.

Miss Elam stuck her thumb in the door-hole of the birdhouse, pressed the digit in to the hilt and then fit a pencil in besides. She had upward of a dozen birdhouses of her own hanging about the yard high and low, and every so often an inhabitant would flash through the dappled light.

She set down her work and rested her hands in her lap, blinking her eyes gently after straining them so long in concentration.

"Never bore no children myself." She spoke with mild surprise, as if reporting weather that wasn't altogether usual. "Just worked out that way. I ain't heartrent about it, if I'm honest. My own mother had nine, and it didn't appear no great merriment. Most of the day sweatin puddles on the kitchen floor. For diversion, there was darnin shirtsleeves and puttin up preserves. She'd fall to snorin in her rockin chair with a baby on her and still be pushin to and fro with that one foot, dead to the world."

Miss Elam pulled her braid over her shoulder and rested it down the front of her, pressed a finger down the length of it, her knuckle tricking over each tight knot. She wore a fresh blouse but the same trousers as the day before.

"Course, it does get lonesome," she said.

She leaned away from Gussie and spat discreetly into a cup, then replaced the receptacle on the ground beneath the table. She sighed and looked out to the distant sky, past the Carolina wrens that busied about the yard, past the healthy trees that held the creatures' little homes.

"I think on him mornins," she said. "I stay abed hours, so I can remember without no distractions. Just lying in there watchin the light creep down the wall. This mornin I was thinkin of when he took me to Montgomery. Took me no special reason—chore leave, he said. He had people out that way. It was wintertime—least it was in Alabama—and there was frostwork on all the windows, like elves snuck out in the night and etched it. Everyone in their woolen scarves. I borrowed one from a friend of Sam's. It was white as clouds, with little blue stars done into it. Went on a wagon ride and Sam wrapped up our two heads like one, his cheek warmin mine and mine his. Once the horses got limber, their breath shot out in front of them arm's length. I can see it right now. You need to remember all these things, young man. You need to keep these things, or they're gone. Nobody'll remember for you."

Gussie held his pipe by the bowl with tense fingers. He could also see all that Miss Elam had described, clear as if in a picture book. But this was her book and he had to worry about his own. As did all. Their own sights. Sounds. Precious smells. The Atlantic at night, hushed crashes like applause. The crisp, salty smell of the sea breeze, gone by now from his clothes and hair. Miss Elam was right, things slipped away. All the delicious tales Miss Emily told of bygone Europe—what particulars had he already lost? The names of the boys he'd worked alongside at the docks—Clem and Sonny and Clyde—he still had those, or at least most of them. What about Gussie's mother? Might even the details of her, in time, fade? The gradations of her smile, from polite to exuberant to the anxious grimace she wore when, on occasion, a friendly customer would speak drunkenly to Gussie and pet his head like a dog. The soft bedtime verses she sang, like music was an orchard and her voice a quiet wind luffing through it. He didn't want the smallest part of her to drift off. Not even the look of her when she'd been sick. The sound of her coughing. He had to cling to those parts too. How about the times she'd been angry with him? She'd raised her voice so rarely. What did that sound like, her ire? Like when, as a tiny lad, he'd hidden the first mullet he'd ever netted in his dresser drawer. Like when he'd skipped out on Miss Emily's afternoon lesson to play cards with the older boys behind the customshouse.

"My mother passed," he said, startling himself. "She was a workin lady. She was a workin lady but there wasn't no better woman the town over. Wise as an owl and sang like an angel and made sure I never worried over gettin a meal. Not once. Taught me writin. Taught me more shoulds and shouldn'ts than I can count."

Gussie drew a greedy breath of the midday air, feeling dizzy and eager. He understood that this was the first time in the length of his life he'd volunteered his mother's occupation. He'd volunteered it to someone who otherwise would never have known and had not even asked.

"She said the foolin of oneself was a widespread pastime," he continued, "but her trade wouldn't allow it. Said if heaven and hell were real, there must be a third place, neither paradise nor pit, for her like—there'd be no bankers there nor assassins nor priests nor drunkards, none but them which sold what they couldn't help possess for reasons they couldn't control."

Gussie again gulped a breath. He felt unsteady but a measure relieved. He found himself going on, not able to stop, telling that his mother cooked dumplings like perfect little settee cushions that melted away on your tongue, telling how the street children gathered in her skirts just to hear her mildly scold them away, telling of the many dozens of poems she could recite from memory, that she could name every flower that bloomed.

When he paused again, he saw that Miss Elam was regarding him as one might an exotic, imperiled animal. He sat back in his chair and tried to regain his decorum.

"Maybe I ought not to have told all that," he said.

"Well," Miss Elam said, "seems like maybe you needed to."

"Yes, ma'am. I reckon I did."

Miss Elam put her hands back on the birdhouse and set it to a pretty angle in the sunlight on the table. She neatened in a row her tools, then drew up her cup and spat again noiselessly.

"Can I say something now?" she said. "Can I tell you just what I think?"

"Yes, ma'am."

She tapped her shapely little chin with her finger and then looked Gussie in the eyes. "What I think," she told Gussie, "is that whatever hardship your mama was under, one thing it didn't do was hinder her raisin up a fine son."

———————

Searle had sent his three-soul labor force home an hour prior, ample time for them to walk home before nightfall, and he sat now tending a fire in the small pit he'd built center of the estate grounds, his eyes trained upon the short logs of pine that were already seething orange against the dusk, their sap bubbling and hissing. Another long, wakeful night awaited him. Evening last, Searle had forgone even his bedchamber armchair, and instead had padded out of doors and spent the dark hours in the haven of his chandlery studio in a light-brained trance, dusting and sweeping and setting equipment to rights, tightening lids, polishing metal-ware, scouring the cherrywood troughs and greasing the wick threaders.

He could hear music now from upcoast, from the docks of the inlet out there past the estate wall and past a swathe of tangled oakwood and a field of muck grass. Harmonica and washboard. The basso of an elder rafting beneath the trill-flights of a young girl. Searle rose and prodded the fire with his walking stick. Added a log. Stood motionless some moments, listening to the pinesap pule and hiss. Ridiculous, a fire in this season. He never grew warm anymore. Would've worn his chesterfield day and night if it wouldn't look queer. He breathed in heavily the harsh, dense smoke. Held his wind and waited for the breeze to shift. After a minute he backed away a measure from the modest blaze and turned and began to cross in his stagger-stride the tract of sodded land that separated his camp from his laboratory, resting the tamp of his walking stick only gently against the soft earth with each right-sided step.

He calmly removed the key from his vest. Got himself inside. Quietly, without lamplight, stepped to the high, narrow table and for a moment braced himself against it. He then opened his arms and gathered to his person every shred of correspondence the table held, corralling the whole mess against him like oiled apples, the sharp-cornered envelopes pricking his palms. All those vile edicts in steady hand, foul injunctions mailed under neat stamps of wax. The sensible advisements from his own counsel, tinged of late with concern. Cold figures compounding outrageously in their neat columns. Requests turning demands turning threats. Motions and pleas, many predating the start of the war, curling from the humidity of four summers verging to five, prepared in the time before planters were colonels, before farmers were sergeants, before field hands were infantrymen.

Searle tucked documents in his vest and in the neckline of his shirt and in his trouser pockets and then his waistband, clamped them under his arms. His walking stick he carried clasped in his teeth, and in this fashion he strode unsteadily down out of the laboratory, the door left ajar, and made the return trip to his fire. When he came near the pit, he tilted forward and unburdened himself of his disagreeable cargo, a shin-high drift collecting on the thick, clipped grass. He cleared his collar. His pockets. He pulled the chair to and sat himself down. Rested his stick aground. And then, a single vulgar piece at a time, as if to grant each its miserly due, he deposited the articles of mail with a flourish and a recoiling of his hand directly into the growing blaze, a one-stunt mage at exercise, raising one flare and the next as if freeing golden birds up into the dark night air.

Another hour on, he sat inert, cinders before him, the exhaust from the pit so thin he could again smell the sulfuric acid in the sleeves of his shirt. His stomach was in upheaval. The night previous, he had finished the last generous slosh in a bottle of Calvados washing down a pair of limp yeast rolls, but this evening his appetite had wholly fled.

The meat of his palm had been clenching and falling slack of its own accord—this was new—and he watched the phenomenon with dull curiosity in the glow of the fire dregs. He knew it was time to rise and get himself inside, but he also knew that when he stood to height his heart would flutter for minutes on end like a trapped moth. His legs felt feeble as a fawn's, and his spirit was in no better condition.

Searle looked toward his laboratory, the dark reefs of moss depending from its roof edges, its black and depthless windows, its door yet swung open. He took up his walking stick and jabbed its end into the gray-red cinders, enlivening them, bothering up slow tongues of flame. He had lost all his money, or would soon lose it, but this was merely the insult. The people he'd lost—here the injury lay. His wife—a union doomed from the start, ended finally and hatefully. His son who might return any moment or stay gone years, this boy now a man whom Searle felt he hardly knew anymore, if ever he had. His mentor, whose memory was entwined irreversibly now with callous greed and ruin.

And there was yet another—one he rarely indulged his mind's eye to peek upon, and never in the daylight hours. He peeked upon her now. The only other woman he'd ever lain with. She who'd inspired such wounding tenderness in his heart that he could still feel the sting if he allowed himself. The plum of her mouth. The flushed, elastic cheeks. The tough yet tender set of her eyes. Silly to think of this, a single evening's fervor so long past. The instant understanding in the touch of hands. The succor from the cold feminine drafts of his own cavernous household—the warmth in being petted, being chosen, the thrill of flesh that answered his touch. Silly to think of it still, but sillier yet the guilt he'd forded, the inner disgrace over the flouting of his vows, tossing in night sweats for weeks on end. A destructive knowledge—to think one had known love, withered as that love may have been, and then to find out in a couple too-short Atlantic witching hours that one's whole marriage bond had been, from the beginning, myth and charade. Emotional frivolity.

Julius had been set to turn nine years of age, and because Ruth was unable or uninterested and Searle himself so utterly out of sorts, it had fallen to Abraham to arrange what sorry last-moment celebration he could. No entertainment. Three or four distracted neighbor boys. A maternal gift scavenged in town by a servant, a paternal scrounged from the workshop. This was the thing to regret: the neglect of the child. How credulous, how superstitious even, were marriage's promises. All promises, perhaps. Promises to country. Most of all, promises made to oneself—he'd guaranteed himself to rededication in the workshop, had pledged to himself to apprise Abraham of his fiscal crisis. They blew away in the wind, all these oaths. Blew up and away like pine smoke.

They had come down out of the high desert flats and passed through hills washed over with tides of dull white flowers and finally bottomed into the matted landscape of Nebraska, most of it cured to burnt hues and punched here and about with reservoirs the color of beef fat. The sky remained stripped. Wind rasped under the stage. In a bullied camp called Cayote, Julius had purchased, from a grocery owner whose tongue was too plump for its housing and hung free like an actor's playing at fatigue, a bone-handled bowie knife with the legend TEXAS stamped into the brass guard. Julius had clutched the knife through the night past and the one before, testing its edge compulsively against the skin of his knuckles, and now, seated next to Midas and across from a bumpkin fiddle band that had boarded that morning, he fingered the dark cut lines he'd inflicted.

The party had crossed and recrossed the Platte, and sometime that afternoon would see the last of it and reach Omaha, where Julius could quit the stage, thank panting deaf heaven, and also shake loose at long last from Midas, who planned to drag his grandiloquence and pair of overstuffed sea chests to Chicago. Julius would be expected to perform his half of a heartfelt handshake, resigned sighs, significant manly claps on the shoulder. Midas, this particular morning, cravat loosened and hat atilt, had delivered unto his benighted mates a suite of strictures denigrating the concerti of Joseph Woelfl and declaring devotion for Ignaz Moscheles. He'd heard one of the latter's compositions strafed by an inept piano instructor in Boston, he reported, and had managed only with great strength of will to restrain himself— and lucky for the piano instructor that he had—from challenging the offender to a fistfight.

Julius' mother lived in Chicago, as best he knew. He would not, he'd decided, send a letter along with Midas. He wasn't going to do anything of that sort. He could envision the woman perched in her cramped parlor behind rose curtains, scribbling her tart, futile memoirs on sheet after sheet of creamy mourning paper. Could hear the splishes and murmurs, from behind a closed door in the tiny flat, of her laborious toilette. And he remembered her at the estate, of course, showing interest for a time in commonplace concerns, expressing disfavor usually but now and again mild approval, and the old man would leap upon whatever had drawn the tepid praise and order heaps of the article brought—preserves of tangerine and coconut, single sabatias in flute vases, skin tonics contrived of shark oil. What he recalled more immediately were the drawn-out years when she was far gone to dreariness and outbursts, eating nothing but pastes. Caraway seed paste, meant to prevent hysterics. Fig paste for digestion. The soft, boiled onions that salved her throat. He remembered the sour, earthy scent of the pastes when he embraced her, and the way she shied her face up and away as if he were a dog that might lunge to lick her. And yet she never inspired pity, even in her own child, because her eyes never lost their lofty contempt. She never let Julius, nor his father, feel they'd done anything but injure her by their mere existence. It had been no vexing verdict for him when the marriage dissolved, both because he was better suited to the role of prodigal than of caretaker, and also because he'd known, even then, that Ruth didn't want him. What she did want even she didn't know, but she didn't want her son. That much had been plain.

The band that had crowded into the stage was of three members, the core of a mud opera that had come undone, and the moment Midas rested his case, the leader cleared his throat, apologized for his outfit's inferiority to such as Ignaz Moscheles, and, mostly to preclude further sermonizing, Julius guessed, kicked his comrades into a number that described an equatorial isle where the gods, when pleased, dropped covered platters of veal fricandeau from the heavens, but when offended, showered down angry white scorpions.

Gussie walked the hours of the day with no great fatigue, his shoulder only periodically remembering to ache, forging south but edging coastwise all the while and sharing the way with rising numbers of wayfarers. Detachments of small ranchers waiting trail-side with their soft-eyed stock. Woebegone back-grove pontiffs in robes fashioned of bedclothes. Lone fortuneless ex-soldiers, their faces beneath their hats truculent as gamecocks. Gussie kept his pipe and fodder buried in his pack, his eyes to himself. Men wore greatcoats in the feverish midmorning and men went with chests bare. Dogs were about the settlements now, growling at or consoling one another, licking the axles of wagons—sad bellow-ribbed greyhounds, tail-hacked retrievers. He passed through Gillston. Brine barrels of beef on the porches. A jousting ground, its overgrown track and quiet ring poles. At the butt end of town, the customary soothsayers and rendering shacks and peddlers of unlabeled elixirs. Buskin Crossing. Mascotte. Tainter.

At a crotch in the trail, Gussie veered into a wasted heathland of palmetto that was sewn under with still-green gouts of sandspur not sharp enough to grasp his boot leather. The way was pocked with anthills big as campaign hats. Down this way, fellows on the hike grew again scarce, and as dusk fell, Gussie's only company were the white-cowled eagles soaring above and the salt-and-pepper bobwhites fluttering up indignantly from the brush.

Upon the gloaming, enveloped in the familiar music of crickets and frogs, Gussie stopped on the trail and cocked an ear at another sound—the gurgling and purling of stream water. He stepped off and picked his way through gaunt, arrow-straight pines whose limbs grew only on one side of their trunks and came in short order upon a mellow slope that eased to a dark bottleneck in whatever obscure watercourse he'd found. He strode upbank, seeking an access free of sedge and whatever venomous boarders lurked therein. When he found the spot he sought, he let his pack onto his boot tops and drew out his canteen, uncorked, crouched to the welcome task.

"You ain't want to do that," a voice said.

Gussie felt instantly weary, but also unwilling to give way—the foolhardy courage of those with little to lose. He didn't turn around. He knew it was a Black man who'd spoken, perhaps two rods distant.

"Listen, cousin," Gussie said. "If you're so ornery you got to clobber me for makin bubbles in this here stream that ain't fixin to run dry no time soon, you may as well get to clobberin." Despite his declaration, Gussie kept his canteen poised instead of sinking it.

"Ain't nobody clobberin nobody," the voice said. "Least of all a stick-leg yearlin like you."

Gussie, from his crouch, drew his head around. His eyes flicked about the foliage but couldn't locate the speaker in the shadows—until he saw eyes, still as stopped clocks, yellow with strain.

"I got water for drinkin," the man said. He stepped out into view and Gussie took in his figure, over six feet and with thick-muscled arms. Waist belted lean. Boots as thrashed as Gussie's, laced high and tight to creaking.

Gussie reached out to shake and the man met the gesture.

"Acey," the man said.

"Gussie."

The clear-voiced stranger scratched one eyebrow and then the other with his thumbnail. "Weapons?"

Gussie shook his head.

"Truth?"

"Never owned no gun and ain't gone in for thievin one."

"Ain't been reduced, huh?"

"Not as yet."

"Well, that is somethin to boast."

Gussie nodded.

"Findin it a fuddle here recent, tell between thievin and foragin." Acey raised a foot and leaned to flick an insect off his boot. "Let's sidle back from the boat track, Gussie. You don't mind."

The man turned and began into the brush, but Gussie ventured only a step before hesitating. This man was his kin by misfortune, but Gussie was as defenseless as a traveler could hope to be.

"What taints it?" he said.

Acey stopped and turned, and again groomed his eyebrows. He explained an outliers' camp sat a half-mile upwater. Not outliers no longer, rightly. He didn't know what they were now. Forty in number, he gauged. Holding a couple prisoners, mean-ranking former Home Guard. They'd elected a Dean of Operations and a Chief of the

Hunt and what all. "Ain't got no program for belly soil except that south-runnin outhouse. I only use it for fishin. Clean them fellows to no skin at all and cook them black."

"Prisoners?" Gussie said.

"Coop lumbered up. Throw scraps in, bones to pick and corncobs. I spied them wakin one up from day-slumberin with a hot coal-poke."

Gussie took a step forward and Acey turned again to lead.

"In my best interest," he added, "keepin abreast of what nearby whites gettin up to."

"I ought advise you," Gussie said, "there's an old fold-knife bottom of my pack. Almost sharp enough to spread lard."

"That's all right then. Just see it stays there in your pack where it belongs."

Gussie followed Acey into the trees where it was darker, grateful at the prospect of clean water, glad for company in this shuddersome precinct of failing pine and razor-sharp palmetto spokes and aimless, hapless desperados.

He didn't realize until Acey sank to his haunches that they'd arrived at camp. After a moment, he sighted the ring of pale ash, cold at present, the little three-wall hut, no more spacious than a pantry, its roof a contrivance of pine brooms and marsh reeds. Gussie sat against the base of a tree and watched Acey root around in the deep shadow of the hut. His possessions above a cornhusk tick were spare, but included a complement of a half-dozen drink vessels, a few of them standard issue but also one as big as a field basket with the name CLAYNE embossed on it, another a small leathern sack seemingly meant for wine. "Give us that water tin," Acey said, then he filled it and handed it back and told Gussie to put it away. He came and sat near Gussie and they drank deeply and without hurry from one of Acey's canteens. Gussie insisted on Acey's acceptance of one of his ham biscuits, and Acey from his stores brought out black trumpets, the first of the season, and fragrant strips of dried hare, and for dessert several handfuls of squashberries that the pair picked out one by one from a pail as carefully as if picking spiders off the feet of an infant.

After the meal, Acey lazily tidied the camp. The stars above were finding their truces, holding one another fast in the arch of the heavens.

"I ain't waved you in to kick you back out," Acey told Gussie. "You dock here till mornin. I most nights stretch aground. Don't bother about the old villa unless the weather turns."

"Don't want to impose," Gussie said.

Acey sat down and straightened his legs and raked his eyebrows one to the next yet again. "I been so imposed," he said, "nothin you could do gone even make the report."

Gussie dug into his pack and brought forth his pipe, filled it and got it chuffing, then turned it over to Acey, who pucked his lips at it heartily and sighed his approval.

A few articles of clothing hung on a branch at camp's edge and Gussie could discern a tunic, the Union blue showing black in the night, suspending stiffer and prouder than the blouses and trousers near it. When Gussie asked Acey if he'd seen the fighting, the other's eyes rolled toward the uniform. Smoke seeped drowsily from his nostrils. He passed the pipe back to Gussie.

"We got ours most days," he said. "Yessir, we did." He cut his jaundiced eyes hard. Rolled his tongue in his mouth, as if chewing on it.

"Had me two brothers," he said. "The one perished in glory in a hail of musket shot, seen it with these eyes and heard it with these ears, chargin the gray line full throat, showin them boys what a yell ought sound like." He drew a line in the dirt with his finger, paused, then brushed away his work. "Other one, I ain't sure. Most probably he's murdered like a dog after they done repelled us at Ocean Pond.

Wasn't fit for no warrin. Used to drink himself limp at the farm—master give him the bottle all he wanted, then cut him short and he'd be three days with the horrors. Wasn't worth a damn no more. I snuck back after, back to the pond, but never seen hide nor hair. Rollin over bodies, lookin at the faces. Rebs wasn't puttin stock in Negro prisoners. That's Trowel, one I seen killed, and Nixon, the one I ain't. Suppose he may be out there somewhere. Can't be sure. We were never apart an hour in our lives, three of us. Makin up for it now."

Listening to this, Gussie felt shame. He felt it heavy, right in the middle of his chest. He had never in his heart considered himself a Confederate but also had never spoken out against the South. If called, which he would've been some year on or even sooner, he would've been hard-pressed to lay out. Perhaps this was what his mother had feared more than even his bodily injury: the choice between cowardice and fighting for a wrong cause. To have fought against men like this one before him—the thought deadened Gussie's innards. Thinned his blood to broth.

"I'm glad you were able to make it alive," he told Acey.

"I waltzed around with that same thinkin, but now I ain't so sure. These here days we're puttin up with are a sight closer to Hades than the other place."

Gussie restocked the pipe, pressing the dregs of his tobacco deep into the bowl. "You fought for your folks," he said. "You knew you were doin right."

"Tooth and nail," Acey assented. "Napoleon wouldn't lower himself to serfs for troops, but our captain said if Russian wheat hands held up like Alabama cotton hands, he might have swapped his view."

Gussie loosed his bootlaces. Rolled down his sleeves against the mosquitoes. Acey kept snug-belted, buttoned to the neck.

"We were feverin to get at them. Hearts swoll up like muskmelons. Beside all, we were promised land. Deeds inked in Washington and set in gilt frames—that's how it was sold. A homestead for your service. Own place, do whatever you see fit. Don't look as that prophecy comin to pass, unless Santa Clause take up the slack. Tell us we're supposed to go back same place we run from and ask about workin a wage—just enough for the meanest whiskey ever stilled by mortals and tuck off somewhere to drink it so it ain't confiscated. Had my fill of the lot of them. Politicians, pastors, sergeants—whole stinkin, leechin lot."

Acey still held the pipe but had forgotten it, and it was soon to go dormant there in his fingers. The smell of tired mud and the creatures that lived in it rode the air, along with parched pine, along with sweat—Gussie's and Acey's both, salty as rime on an old bucket. Some slow-rooting varmint skirted the camp, rustling patiently past and then out of earshot.

"About you?" Acey said. He patted for matches in his pockets and rekindled the pipe. "What got you to mistreatin your boots?"

Gussie's sinuses felt mucked. He leaned aside and cleared his nostrils with a sharp snort, wiped his face on his sleeve.

"Bein honest," Gussie said, "I'm lookin to unbastard myself."

Acey's expression was unchanged. "That so?"

"Lookin to be called son by my father one time. One time will do it."

"He expectin you?"

"Can't offer no certain answer. I'd bet no before I'd bet yes."

Acey gave a single, sluggish nod.

"I ever do stand before him," Gussie said, "my hand will be out, but only to get shook, same as I shook your hand. I'll have some tobacco, one way or the other, and I'll offer the man some, just same as I done you."

Acey loosed something from his teeth, spat it behind him. He reclined flat on his back and rested his hands on his chest, then produced a hollow sound in his cheek, as one yielding a point.

"Reckon I'd sooner a buried daddy to a breathin one I'll never lay eyes on."

"Yes," Gussie answered. "I share that same reckonin."

In the morning, the air was still. Gussie got himself upright and blinked his eyes to service and hoisted his pack and tread quiet as a fox away from Acey's camp, not wishing to wake his host, who remained flat on his back, hands still clasped with an air of placid ceremony atop his chest, boots laced and shirttail tucked. Gussie had not tendered a prayer since the final time he'd walked into the Catholic church—Miss Emily always bade him list the wondrous, the reliably kind in his life, to roll those of his acquaintance in need, to humble his soul—but once he'd retraced the thin river and mounted again the footway, he halted. He dropped chin to chest and shut his eyes and beseeched the Supreme to shine whatever favor could be spared on the sorrowful Union veteran who'd warded him from the thirst and lonesomeness of a bruised Florida night, and who'd endured already more than any child of God ought.

Gussie said amen and nodded his head to no one and then fell to his usual pace, picking up and setting down his calloused heels through greens of cinnamon ferns filled with hundreds upon hundreds of white-streaming spider lilies. The pines, always picketing the world. Again the gothic oaks. He would cross into Hernando County before noon, best he could plot, would march himself to toppling today and sleep on whatever supper his coins could raise and fret over tomorrow at such time as it stood before him.

But he had not been afoot a half hour when he looked up from his boots, at which he had been dazedly staring, hypnotized by their endless simple rhythm, and beheld, preparing to quit the trail through a tight cleft in the brush, a lean and shirtless man, slick-skinned in the humid blue morn, no hat atop his fluid silver locks, his upper arms cinched with gaudy tourniquets of garnet and yellow. The man went still as a spooked possum, crouched a bit. He raised a finger aloft, as if to quiet a room for music, then he retook the trail theatrically, with slinking, outsize strides. Gussie could see there was another man with him. This other made no notice of the first's funning—he stepped from the scrub with eyes trained dissolutely, almost serenely, on Gussie. He stopped and waited, this second man, his eyes glinting like glass and couched in a face as bloodless as a skinned potato. He was laden with a bulky, twine-baled pack, and he disburdened himself of it and stood it against his own firmly planted leg. Gussie knew these were not men one wished to run across. He might've woken a mere minute later that morning or strode a fraction less spryly, or he could have made sure to walk with his head up, vision at use, rather than ogling his endless boot landings like a dullard.

The pale-faced man had a revolver lashed to his chest and fingered it incuriously, and Gussie knew he was meant to see the revolver and to forego thoughts of running. Gussie was a mouse in the middle of the kitchen floor and here were the housecats. He thought of the watch, of course—once he thought of it, could think of little else.

The first man, the shirtless one with the flowing locks, spoke now. "Often one is obliged to clamber for the fruit," he said, "and other times one barely evades being hit atop the head." He took a tentative breath, regarding Gussie wryly, as if embarrassed at what he saw. "Tributes from the citizenry were bountiful last evening, considering the circumstances, and now here you, a sugared talmouse to punctuate the feast. What have I done that the morning sun smiles upon me with such grace?"

This last question was directed at the pale-faced man, but he gave no answer. The shirtless man bore no visible weapons, while his attendant sported, as companion to the pistol he caressed like a miniature harp, a painted wooden truncheon that dangled loose along one leg and a double-edged rapier that sat against his hip, its blade as clean and flat as December daylight.

"We'll dispense with traditional threats, oaths, and prostrations," the shirtless one said. His expression was tart now, scholarly. He wore spectacles with tiny lenses.

"You shall step forward and present all impedimenta front and center, attended by any consequential armament, then you shall step back and retake your position and indulge my perusal of said luggage. I don't expect more than penny-candy wrappers, but professionalism compels me. I judge not a hound by its baying nor a play by its billing. For all I'm to know, you're in desperate flight following a string of safe-crackings."

Gussie's thirst came hard, pointlessly, suddenly. He didn't know if he wished another traveler to happen along or wished to be left alone, unobserved, to his humiliation and abuse.

"What, pray tell, do you await?" the shirtless man said. "I'm not hostile to idiots, if that's what you be. I find their company pleasanter than that of many learned men."

"Ain't no idiot," Gussie answered, "and ain't got no arms." He slunk his pack to the front of him and walked it forward, dumped it in the loose dirt, stepped back.

"Come over here first," the shirtless man said.

Gussie went and stood close to him, face to face, and the man leaned forward and flatted his hand over Gussie's trouser fronts and then bent all the way down to his ankles, flicked his fingertips up to the pits of Gussie's arms one side then the other. He told Gussie to step back and told him ambition, a trait that often served young men well, would serve him very poorly in this particular instance. The man then surprised Gussie by lowering himself down softly, without touching his hands to the dirt of the trail, until he was sitting cross-legged like a schoolboy.

"Which day of the week is it?" he asked Gussie.

"Ain't sure," Gussie told him.

The shirtless man eagerly flourished his fingers over Gussie's dusty, seam-spent pack. "I don't suppose it matters. They're all my lucky days, aren't they, big fellow?"

The pale-faced man stood behind, unflinching.

"You'll kindly excuse my associate," the shirtless man said. "We've been appallingly short on sleep these weeks. The nature of our trade reduces us to nomadic modes of living, moving camp hither and yon, catching what daytime winks are to be had. After a while, it makes a man cross as a weasel."

He looked up at the broken morning sky, then sighed genially. Loosed the cinch of Gussie's pack with calm fingers. Began exposing one item and the next to the light, placing them about himself like parts of an antiquated game he couldn't yet understand. He pulled out Gussie's canteen and tossed it behind him to the pale-faced man, who caught it with one hand and glugged it hollow in a long, careless draft, dripping liberally down his dingy shirt front.

The shirtless man had Gussie's paltry coinage, jangling it as one shaking luck into his dice. The partial book the old woman had given him—young Zhin. The man thumbed it open and whisked his eyes over one page and then another, his brow pinching as if to name an odor. He looked at Gussie quizzically, then back toward the pages.

"'The outlaws had infringed upon heritage, which lived in the soul,'" he read, "'and upon family honor which coursed in the blood, and the prefect had summoned aid from provinces afield.'" He licked his chops like a hungry child over a lemon cake. Reached the volume around to the narrow of his back and snugged it in his trouser waist. Plunged his hand again and this time found Gussie's fold-blade. He examined the handle this side and that, as if for inscription. Opened and pressed the blade to the muscle of his shoulder, where it yielded meager results, then shut it and flung it to his comrade. The horse-mane swatch, at which he chuckled derisively. The suspenders Eli Acker's man had given Gussie, removed and shoved deep in the pack long ago for the added wear they put on his shoulders—the shirtless man untangled and stretched them wide before him as if testing the tensile strength, then let them drop limp onto the trail.

He gave the pack a shake to confirm it harbored yet more plunder, then sank his arm past the elbow and threshed his hand about like one hand-fishing crabs. Gussie well understood what remained to be dredged. It disoriented him, that this maleficent villain who so firmly commanded the proceedings at hand was stooped in the dust before him, that this burnished, hawk-nosed bandit had chosen of his will to sit aground childlike. Gussie saw himself, in a flash of mind, bounding ahead and punting the man in his smart, puckered mouth, snatching the straps of his pack while the watch still hid inside and dashing into the scrappy underwood, taking his chances with the panicked lead of the pale-faced man's revolver. But Gussie's legs did not stir to heroism, and the next thing he knew the shirtless man was undressing the Waltham of its cloth and dangling it before his eyes from its delicate fob, the casing glittering in the fresh light. He weighted the watch in his hand and then looked at Gussie and performed a long, impressed whistle.

"Bonnie timepiece," he said. "For the likes of you, bonnie time-piece indeed."

Gussie's ears were aflame. He wanted to batter this blackguard in his fussy marmish spectacles, bash his head flat like was done to vipers found on town streets. Gussie had put far more than half his campaign behind him, more steps than stars in the sky, swarms upon swarms of flies, lashing storms, the angry glaring sun, thirst and hunger, sleeping aground in fear of snakes, a malnourished wanderer out with the lorn hounds and red-skulled buzzards, besting bounty hunters and wrestling his grief, and now, of a fine morning in a quiet wood, this good-for-naught would rob him of the single article he couldn't make good without—rob him and look upon Gussie as if he'd stolen the article himself, as if Gussie were only a scale version of the larger scalawag before him. His hands shook and his vision blurred. His stomach struggled to clench, a broken-fingered fist.

The shirtless man flipped open the cover of the watch and inspected the face for a long moment, then snapped it closed. He turned it about and brought it to his eye, sighting it edgewise.

"This darling won't see general inventory," he said. "We'll dedicate her a personal objet d'art. Makes one consider wearing a vest, so as to pocket her up in due style."

He tipped his head back so he could see the pale-faced man. "No exception taken, I trust? If I confiscate this little dandy?"

The pale-faced man shifted his weight. He turned his head and looked down the straight length of trail behind him, then guided his eyes back around to Gussie.

"He's anxious we be on our way," the shirtless man said. "I can read his whims and tempers like a husband his wife's. He's a right enough chum, but if you've hopes of rousing conversation… well, better off playing croquet in the high grass."

He stood himself up and arched his back, stretching like a man awakening from a nap, then Gussie watched him slip the watch into his trouser pocket. Watched him nudge the ravaged pack with his foot.

"I shall leave you your pipe. I'm not without mercy. It isn't noble, taking a fellow's puff stick—particularly a fellow down on his luck, as most fellows are who've run into me. And not only, in my grace, do I spare your pipe. I bestow upon you a gift of one stuffed pouch of Carolina cherry, donated no more than two hours past."

The man dug into another pants-pocket and produced the pouch and tossed it on the ground near Gussie's feet.

"I let you free now to wander and make your fortune, doing so with the same shrewd clemency as the fisherman who releases the adolescent grouper. You strike me an industrious lad. Somewhere down the winding trail, we'll meet again."

The man took the time to advise Gussie, despite whatever hurry his second was in, to relish his journey, wherever it took him—to relish the grand delicious hardship of it. He said a young man's trial was sweeter than an old man's triumph. He ordered Gussie to gather his grip back onto his shoulders and to press on gamely into the lovely, peacock-blue yonder where his future awaited, and he watched Gussie do his best to follow this directive like some prideful sergeant observing a private he'd trained.

Gussie scuffed downtrail until enough ground was between himself and the site of his raid, then he stopped and faced about and surveyed the abandoned straightaway—no different, from this distance, than a thousand other stretches of trail. He stared, sniffling, blinking hard. Breathed the air that smelled both sodden and dry as a kiln. He stepped off into the grass. And then farther. Set down his pack and opened it and withdrew the stolen tobacco and cast it into the brush with a grunt.

He wiped his face roughly on his sleeve and began picking his way back from where he'd come, walking some thirty yards off the trail, warding away thorny branches with his forearms and mincing past toothed palmettos and stomping straight through the nodding staffs of lizard tail. He could feel the tears drying on his cheeks—insult and loss, and also the blaring sun, whose rays now shanked harshly through the branches. He bore on under the reproachful tisking of bananaquit birds, spitting automatically at the sand, waiting until well past the spot he'd encountered the thieves to return to the trail

and quicken his pace—easy to do under his scraped hull of a pack—
and he soon found himself at full run, back to the quiet river, up the
bank, into the shady wood where Acey kept home. When the man
glanced an intruder near his fire pit he leapt to half-standing—once
he saw who it was, he sighed, relieved, and relaxed back onto the
matted dirt where he'd been darning a stocking. He set the article
aside now, next to a hat of blade-stiff, tight-plaited palmetto fronds.
He bade Gussie sit under his slouching green roof and proffered
a canteen.

"Looks like you done seen a ghost," Acey said. "Or somethin
worse."

Gussie allowed his breath to settle, then enlightened Acey as to his
vile morning. He told of the pair he'd encountered, one speechifying
to beat the stumpers and the other beaming fixed and cold as the
Prince of Fiends himself. The blame fell in part to himself, he said,
for letting slack his guard. He told of the revolver and the truncheon
and the rapier and of the tobacco he'd jettisoned and indexed all that
had been looted, leaving the Waltham for last. He related to Acey,
less importantly, the fineness of the piece, and more importantly,
its unique value to him—irreplaceable. He told of Palmina. Of his
mother's collapsed health. The old deed box that had been the watch's
depository the whole of his life. The counties across which he'd carted
it. The engraved initials. And when he peeked at length up into
Acey's face, the man's eyes were narrowed and his jaw along one side
twitched like the nervous wing of a harmed bird. Gussie watched
him pick up the stocking he'd been mending and look at it a long
moment, then roll it neatly and place it away. When he spoke, it was
in faintly more than a whisper.

"I know them boys," he said. "Pons and his outfit. Thomas Pons."

"Thomas Pons?"

"Silver hair long as a horse tail?"

Gussie nodded.

"Ain't no other," Acey said.

Gussie wiped his nose and fetched a sharp breath. He watched as Acey slowly arose and moved about the camp woodenly, formally, with the stilted poise of one touched with dreadful wisdom. Acey unfastened his belt and jerked it a notch tighter, then stood very straight and peered out into the dappled foliage. He crouched and retrieved from a dig-out at the rear of his dwelling a sack of dried stone fruits, the remainder of the mushrooms, the last chaws of rabbit. He told Gussie with eerie calm to eat his fill.

"Don't feel much like breakfastin," Gussie said.

"I ain't ask your feelins. I told you put somethin in your mouth and chew."

Gussie picked out a brown hunk of fruit. It was tough as boot tongue and hid its flavor expertly. He worked it over best he could, eyeing Acey, who only peered from beneath his brow into the woodland day, making no move to eat or drink himself.

"And swallow," Acey added. "Thought you knew that much."

"You sore at me?" Gussie asked.

After a beat, Acey looked down at him. "I ain't sore at nobody. We just ain't got all day."

"We ain't?" Gussie said. He slipped some mushrooms into his mouth so Acey wouldn't scold him again, grabbed a canteen and washed them down.

"That de-luxe horse timer don't belong to you. Ain't yours to lose, far as I gather."

Gussie watched Acey sink to one knee and disentangle something from under the hut wall. It was a brass-hilted poniard, the blade straight and tapered at its end to a sneering point.

"Got to catch them belchin up dinner. Steal up siesta time."

"Hell no," Gussie said. He got quickly to his feet. "You ain't gettin tangled in this. I ain't asked it. Got nothin to do with you. You're livin peaceable and you're meant to go right on."

Acey didn't answer this.

"Hear me? You hear what I'm tellin you?"

Any trace of wrath had departed the man's face, as one listening with forbearance to a worn joke.

"God only guess what arsenal they got. Anvil worth a lead, I reckon. We ain't got a single firearm to answer."

Acey tested the tip of his poniard with his fingertip. "Somehow I ain't feelin no spirit for fussin," he said. He sheathed his weapon and lithely banded the scabbard about his shoulder on a length of strap.

"I ain't fussin, I'm tellin," Gussie rebutted. "I done incurred enough losses today. I'm cuttin them."

"I mean to get your heaven-forsaken watch back." Acey stepped out into a patch of full sun that was singing down between the oaks. "You do what you please. Lincoln said everybody's free to do as he please."

"See what you're at?" Gussie said. "You're puttin me in guilt for what'll happen to you."

Acey stamped one foot then the other, as if to prepare them for duty. "You ain't want no cavalry, you ain't should've blown the horn. Once it's blown, it can't get unblown."

"I ain't come back here to—I don't know why I..." But Gussie stopped, arrested by the sight of Acey's mercenary grin.

"Pons runs a skeleton crew," he said. "Never more than three or four. He ain't keen for splittin the winnins, way it's told."

"I'll be ate up," Gussie pleaded. "Top it all, blood on my hands."

"We all get ate up from somethin."

Acey stepped over and grabbed Gussie's limp pack and handed it to him. He tossed some rabbit in his cheek and worked his molars.

"Them boys a good sight meaner than us," Gussie said, his voice halfhearted. "Much regard as a rattlesnake. If you're a friend of mine, you won't do this."

"I'm fond enough for you," Acey said, "but there's a load more timber on my fire than your bitter fortunes. I done had enough of havin nothin, then havin somethin and gettin it took. I done had enough of all that." He squeezed his right forearm hard with his left hand, then after a moment reversed the operation.

"Besides," he added, "you ain't got the first inkling how mean I could get."

Acey positioned the poniard along his ribcage, made subtle alterations until it laid as he liked, then champed down the rest of the rabbit. Gussie, seeing the cards on the table and feeling twice defeated, reluctantly slipped his pack up onto a shoulder. He was fixed in the center of Acey's scratched-up camp that was fixed in the center of the most parlous county of this whole steaming, untamable peninsula, running fool's errand inside fool's errand around the endless miles of cunning dark and rash sun.

Acey stepped over to his tunic where it hung by its collar on a broken limb, elbows threadbare and lining tattered, and he took the rough fabric of its arm between his thumb and forefinger and tugged it so, to view its flat front. He rolled his eyes down the garment, shoulder to hem, his face inscrutable. After a minute he turned the arm loose and backed away. He pointed resolutely into his shelter, at the paling razor-frond hat that sat on its floor, and Gussie brought it to him. Acey set it atop his head and tapped it snug.

"Mr. Thomas Pons," he said, "fixin to be short one expensive minute-keeper or surplus two worthless carcasses."

Gussie slowed when they reached the infamous piece of trail, crawling his eyes along the wayside for the portal in the brush. No footprints—likely Pons and the pale-faced man had swept those away—but when Gussie stood in the place he'd been before, he could make no mistake. The drift of weeds where Pons had contemptuously slung the specie. A line of pumpkin-colored flowers along the trail's edge—Gussie remembered them peeking out from behind the pale-faced man's legs like children from their mother's skirt. Gussie nodded and he and Acey stepped through into the scattered shade, Acey holding down his hat. He touched Gussie's sleeve and told him they should drink their fill now and that Gussie should lighten up his shoulders, and so they emptied a canteen into their bellies and hung Gussie's shuck of a pack on a branch and began picking their way deeper into the dust-green growth, slip-striding around thickets and clearing with arm-length sticks the spiderwebs and thorny vines. They trained their progress intersectional to the trail, due east, skirting areas where pine quills and oak leaves had collected for fear of traps, flicking their eyes from the ground at their feet to the crowns of the trees and back down again. Neither Gussie nor Acey spoke. For a spell Gussie would lead and Acey follow and after a time they would switch, these swaps in position fluid and without preamble, both older and younger guided by an animal wit that laced their bloods like a tea. When they passed through the pools of shadow beneath vine-tasseled oaks they were near invisible, and when the sunlight again found them, they were plain as sails in a harbor. The heat and the absorption of staying quiet and keen had them sweating without cease, swiping and swiping the salty gushes from their foreheads.

After some twenty minutes they came upon a hog run. Judicious in their pace, they followed it as it sliced its way through the brambly vegetation until, after another twenty minutes, it petered in an abrupt loosening of the undergrowth. Gussie and Acey came to rest in an airy breadth of pawpaw and scrub pine—they knew they must hunt up the lair in short order or lose the cause. They tossed aside their sticks and stalked onward pine to pine, neither leading nor backing now, ignorant what sign or signal they might discover, stepping softly, eyes shifting this way and that, Gussie feeling naked without his pack despite his awareness of what precious little it contained.

They advanced over two more acres of pinewood that grew poorer and poorer by the ten-step, and at length came against a stand of redbuds huddled tight enough for a hedge. New scents were on the air—cut wood and dung. Here at the redbuds they crouched, peering through bright cavities in the foliage, and for a long moment both were still as posts, nothing moving but their eyeballs, the sun plumb overhead and teetering in its roost. The two trespassers cautiously crabbed back from their vantages to a distance safe to whisper, and Acey pulled off his reed-weft hat and shook sweat from the crown. They had spied a trio of colts, their legs unseen because they grazed at the fringe of what seemed a great swale, one horse coffee-colored and two golden, all dropping their heads down out of sight to crop the groundcover, all switching flies resignedly with their tails. Contented animals. In health, it appeared. Downwind the horses, the crest of a tent. Beyond the tent, they could only guess.

A nervous neighing rang out from below, and Gussie and Acey backed off from the redbuds, moving away from the colts. They gave ground and then described a generous bend about the deep end of the sunken camp, gaining no intelligence but running no risk, watching for brush thick enough to shield an approach. Around the rim. Around the rim. Farther. And here it was. They both knew at once and came to a halt. Acey retightened his boots and arranged his collar. They assumed knees and hands and Acey crawled in first, removing delicately from his path any brittle twigs. Gussie was on the other's heels, lifting and resetting his knees rather than dragging them. Acey waved Gussie up alongside and the two eased flat onto their bellies and from this outlook could survey the encampment in its every fact and feature.

Near the opposite reach of the sinkpit, above the colts, stood a weald of turkey oaks that grew spitefully into one another rather than to open sky. Brittle grasses sprung from the almost vertical nearer walls, along with the brown-singed appendages of prickly pear. On the floor of the depression stood unreflective pools of muck water, the largest of which could've kept a small fishing craft afloat. And then the three tents, arrayed offhandedly, their fly-flaps hung open like the tongues of desperate cattle.

The rector himself, Pons, reclined center of the scene, lounging in full sun on a berth of oat sacks, feet propped on a stump, reading something held lightly in his lap that Gussie soon pegged as the book that had been stolen from him. The pale-faced man was also present, lying aflank against a wall of the pit in the only strip of shade afforded at this high hour. And there was a third man, leaguing with the count of the tents and steeds, an Indian who had been tending to some chore near the horses but who now walked up toward the middle of camp, a heavy wooden rood tapping with each stride against his flat, bronze chest.

Cold pitch-torches leaned against the tents, and weapons of all stripe laid about haphazardly but near enough to hand—club-sticks to knives to a regiment of glinting, long-handled gaffs to what appeared a stout claymore driven down into the starchy earth near the entry to one of the tents. And some few rods behind Pons, alone on a square of rough, black fabric, rested a repeater rifle, a Spencer perhaps, reposed there in the inexorable sunlight like a head-struck serpent.

The Indian conferred with Pons in low tones. Gussie and Acey, from the high lip of the pit, could hear the deep, chapped timbre of the Indian's voice, though they could not make out his words. And

then the briefing concluded, Pons nodding his approval, and the
Indian went to his tent and disappeared inside. Pons folded a page
in the book and stood and replaced it in the hind of his pants, went
over and fetched the repeater and returned with it to his field chaise.
Gussie and Acey watched as he oiled the barrel and swabbed over the
stock, seeming to delight in the weight of the weapon in his hands.
He shouldered it, sighted near to far at whatever was handy, grasshoppers or eagles' nests or who knew what. He fetched ammunition
and loaded the gun and tapped the butt against the ground. Clothed
it in the black blanket and leaned it in a stiff, wide-leaf shrub where
it vanished from sight. Pons then removed his spectacles. He took
his own skull firmly in his hands and corked it on his neck, as if
meaning to detach it, and let go a chirpy snort. Twisted otherwise
with equal might. When satisfied, he let his head rock backward,
exposing his leathery throat, hair dangling past his buttocks and
face to the pearly sky. It seemed he asked nothing from the above,
no concern nor concession, but only faced it as a man might an ocean
he was soon to cross.

Acey moved his elbow to touch Gussie's, then craned his head near.
He began to whisper into the dirt, began to lay clear for Gussie that
he needed a commotion over yonder margin of the pit, an agitation
to draw eyes, and then he could slide down the wall otherside and
make fast for the loaded repeater.

Gussie nodded, but Acey's eyes were groundward. Acey said Gussie
should give off a ways like they had done before, then fetch up on the
ridge and don't say a thing till they take note of him.

"Then say what? Once they seen me?"

"Tell them you want to join up," said Acey. "Tell Pons you're
wantin a start. Say it's Saul they run into on the road this mornin."

"I done seen the dark," Gussie said.

"Won't need to be no drawn-out spiel."

Acey hoisted his head for a final survey of the pit, and Gussie did likewise. What they were doing was crazy, but they were sure as hell doing it. The pale-faced man, buried in sleep, hadn't twitched a muscle. Pons was back in his spot, chest pressed up into the sunlight, engrossed again in Gussie's book. At the far end, past the colts, the pit wall had been washed in and made for a mild grade. In the middle ground, the claymore stood so stalwart it seemed to have been planted there all along and the camp composed about it. The identical tents. The gaffs, as from a plundered whaling ship.

Acey and Gussie began to belly backward from under the brush. They could see scant little for a time, only the loose soil beneath them and the crowding umbrage above, and then the air opened and breath came easier. As they wheeled about, getting to their feet and brushing their hands on their trousers, they saw standing before them like an effigy another Indian, not the one from the pit, this one with his high-muscled chest unadorned and the bank of one cheek pocked deep with shot. Neither Gussie nor Acey did a thing except rise to height and face it. They were staring at the rude end of a blunt-barreled twin-blast, no place to run. Gussie let his eyes drift toward Acey, but his cohort did not return the glance nor even seem to register their misfortune, his eyes still and stark and hard under the broad brim of his cracker Stetson.

Pons regarded them bemusedly. He released an effete sigh and remarked on the inopportune ports toward which men convinced themselves to sail. Gussie and Acey sat with backs to the pit wall, twined at wrist and ankle, hands in their laps and heads bowed, in the same shade—though it now reached some many yards across the bare floor of the pit—in which the pale-faced man had taken his rest. He was awake now and sat near them on a split-back chair the party must've rendered from some citizen's porch. He rolled cigarettes one to the next and huffed them down fast and impassively, occasionally slumping his head over and leering at Acey with some twisted class of infatuation. He didn't wear his revolver, but hanging from his leg in a scabbard finished in calfskin was his trim, ready rapier.

The Indians had started a stew boiling, setting the cauldron on its hooks and building a neat fire below, and now they took leisure some ways off, playing what appeared from a distance to be an outland version of fox and geese.

Gussie and Acey had been captives an hour or more, and Gussie felt strangely clear of mind. He understood there was naught else that should've occupied him, nowhere else in the world he should rightly have been. He felt borne along like a wrecked seaman on the tides, drawn inevitably toward his fate. It was worse for Acey—he was being punished for virtue. He was bone-good and had done what good might. Gussie looked at the Black man sidelong, moving only his eyeballs. Acey had tipped his hat off his head and onto his lap and was picking at the plaited fronds with listless fingers, his face betraying nothing, peeling loose a strip and then in time another and harrying it to shreds.

Pons strolled over to the stew pot, swatting Gussie's book against his thigh as he strode, then dropped the pages without ceremony onto the coals beneath. Gussie saw the flames stoke up at the ready tinder, then watched the first dark curls of smoke rise slowly upward into the enduring vacancy above. The copy of Genesis had likely found the same fate. And also the tract.

Pons called his men to mess, which Gussie and Acey had been smelling on the settled air long enough, and the band gathered about the cauldron and Pons fished about and removed from the broth a bundle of sodden herbs, sniffed it, tossed it away without care. He served up bowls for his subordinates and dealt out spoons before he partook of the meal himself. Pons contented himself with his single serving, the Indians with seconds, but the pale-faced man took up the ladle some six or seven times over, until at length he stood gingerly and loosed a great belch that resounded like a horn blast in the earthen jar of the sinkpit.

Pons arose and released the grapeshot scout back up to the woods, and the Indian walked over and scaled the wall as easily as a squirrel up a tree trunk, hoisting himself without strain by exposed roots and exploiting footholds not detectable from where Gussie sat. The other Indian, he of the grand pine crucifix, thumbed up the waist of his scratchy trousers and set about clearing the supper ware.

Pons sauntered over to where Gussie and Acey sat and stood smirking at them from behind his spectacles, Acey's poniard strapped to his bare chest. Gussie's hindside was numb as a plank but he'd been combatting this by leaning one way and the other and tightening his knees to his chest, which way Acey now sat, chin resting on his folded legs. Acey was still busy about his hat, and by now had bothered it patchy at the crown and instituted a thick dandruff of fibrous, sharp-edged tatters all sides of himself. The pale-faced man had followed Pons and now crossed behind his captain and again took up the split-back chair. Again the cigarettes. Again the wicked leering.

Pons cleared his throat. He scratched at the pale of his inner leg with a short stick he'd picked from the ground. "Custom dictates a last meal," he announced, "but my hollow-legged colleague has disallowed you that luxury." He turned his mock-spiteful attention to the lead-boned alabaster figure in the porch chair, but the pale-faced man did not look away from Acey.

"I don't reckon it a pressing matter," Pons reasoned. "Hunger and thirst and such mundane concerns won't be dogging you two for any protracted term."

The floor of the pit was beginning to darken with the hour. The horses, some sixty yards distant at the shallow end, had been keeping to the shade of a winged elm that leaned out over the hollow, but now they stretched their leads out into the open and jostled and necked.

"You, my lad," Pons said, addressing Gussie, "will be eased into the hereafter as tenderly as a pet goat in lean times, the blade keen and hand steady, but the news for you..." He stepped toward Acey and delivered an almost mischievous kick to the captive's bulky, battered boot. "The news for you, freedman, isn't so sunny. I wish it weren't so, but as a leader of men I must make certain concessions to those in my charge." He stopped and waited for Acey to cock his eyes upward. "Disparate agendas must be made harmonious. Tasks divvied justly. Talents utilized and vices assuaged. I confide there are days I envy those taxed only with carrying commands forth, with merely marching the course rather than plotting it. In the turn of days, you see, I'm obliged to do what I might to buoy morale, obliged to honor such requests from my officers as might be granted without adverse consequence to operations at large. In our line of work, ordinary comforts are few, and so comforts out of the ordinary—well, at any rate, the petition germane to you, my poor dark dear, is that you be surrendered to the able custody and irregular enthusiasms of my Sergeant at Arms."

Acey glanced over at the pale-faced man, then reset his gaze upon his own midsection. The man in the chair seemed not to hear any of these proceedings. He brushed the red end of his cigarette against his palm, raised the ashes to his face, and blew them into the dead air. A feeling of torment at his own helplessness washed over Gussie, which he knew was exactly what Pons wished him to feel. His wrists had itched under the frayed twine since the moment of his binding, and now he scraped them freely against each other hard as he might, rasping the skin near to bleeding. The giddy confidence from up on the rim of the pit, the sly hatching of Acey's design, now seemed a cruel jest. Gussie hated Pons and feared the pale-faced man, but these feelings were like spurious small faiths that would prove of little aid in the gloom of night. There must be some action to take, any, no matter how assured of failure, some program other than being tractably ushered to the slaughterhouse. Gussie's eyes fell upon his own useless hands, then next upon Acey's, now limp on his lap but covered in small cuts from the busy destruction he'd worked on his hat, and then to the restless forms of the colts across the camp, and then to the pale-faced man's ripped shirt and dumb, enthralled mouth and to the Indian scouring a spoon with sand and to the trees atop the far edge that still caught in their upper reaches the rich evening light.

Pons tilted his head low to catch Acey's eyes. "My assistant here asked me, as we repasted, whether I believed a Negro possessed an eternal soul, and I replied that of course this was so, and he next took me aback by saying he wished to see this for himself. The soul of a free buck Negro. I could only applaud his curiosity toward such a matter as the invisible, theoretical essence of man, for his usual means of scholarly exercise, you see, is to trap woodland creatures in a narrow space and observe the quarrel."

Pons awaited a response from Acey but was not dejected to receive none. He scratched his leg again with the short stick, then reared back and threw it end over end almost straight in the air. Gussie tracked its trajectory until it was cut off from sight, and it made no sound when it landed up on the grass of the rim.

"There exists in some very few," Pons said, glancing over at the pale-faced man, "obscenity so pure that innocence is its close cousin. My confederate here is a true profligate. He's hardly useful to me at times, if truth be told, but other times his reputation and chilly glower save me untold trouble. And we all have our easements, do we not? Drink. Open-minded women. Philosophy. You'd soon have found yours," Pons said, settling a soft scrutiny on Gussie, "or it found you, had you only lived longer." Pons dabbed his forehead with the soft of his wrist, ran a thumb under the taut-hung string of Acey's poniard. He told Gussie to despair not, for the road to his Lord was near its end, told Acey that by morning the whip would be in his hand and the blisters in the planter's.

Above Pons' voice and above the strident calls of forest hawks, Gussie heard a roaring gale that did not play about Pons' streaming hair in the least nor brush against one another the crowns of the beaten oaks nor disperse the ribboned palmetto scree strewn under and about Acey's legs. Gussie wanted Acey to live and had no nameable wish besides. He wished to free his friend and suffer the atrocity of the pale-faced man himself. Another sunrise for the worthy. Another brimming palm of squashberries. Another chestful of free air.

The Indian lit a lantern in acknowledgment of dusk, hung it back among the tents somewhere. The pale-faced man had unsheathed his rapier. He paid no attention to it, like a man holding a newspaper he'd already read. Pons was now on to putting his own larcenous feats to scale—the Spaniards had stolen the peninsula from the savages, the United States had forced their terms at fifteen cents an acre. He himself was but a solitary bugler, while gathered under the mantle of empire in every corner of the world were great booming symphonies of avarice.

Pons made a cool bow and stepped off and showed the camp his bare back and groaned in relief, the sound of water meeting water plain to ear. A parson spider wandered onto Gussie's knuckles—its body slick, its amber-colored legs thistly. It ticked its weight low, then haunched up again. Gussie held stiff, and after a moment the spider went along on its way, across the boy's wrist and down onto the floor of the pit and over a range of tiny, dry fissures that would disappear with the next light rain. Gussie shuddered. He found himself thinking of the docks in the afternoon, of slapping down the gangplanks to empty the live wells of mackerel and bream, the whoops of his comrades mixing with the frenzied cries of the gulls. He saw Miss Emily's firm, sweet countenance, heard the French prose she sometimes recited, meaningless and beautiful to Gussie, sounding as though a rain-drenched sparrow had lodged in her cheek. He smelled baker's bread wafting above the cottages at daybreak. He heard the Black men beneath the hackberry lifting their haggard voices, sinking their sins to the bottom like pearls. Heard the expressive little squeaks of Miss Elam's wood tools. Heard the line, recited in Pons' mock-genteel lilt, "The outlaws had infringed upon heritage."

Next was a low grunt and a fast whusk through the thick, hot air. Gussie tensed to attention in shock, drawn back from his reverie, and saw from the corner of his eye a dark ghost surge through the shadows. The sound of boots on dry, caked sand. Dust in Gussie's mouth and his heart in his throat. His vision floundered to catch up, and yet he knew what was happening. Acey had found that something, that anything, that Gussie had not, that action to take on the walk to slaughter. The sickening, damp slitch of flesh giving way to blade. A flail of white limbs and a thud in the dirt. Gussie strained against his fetters, fell sidelong to the sand and lurched to right himself. The pale-faced man was aground on his back, and Gussie heard him insuck a wheezing breath, as if drawing the air through cheesecloth. He saw Acey, found him now in the tricky light, bounding toward the center of camp, covering the ground before him swift as a deer. And he saw Pons at a hitchy chase, trousers still unfastened and one hand holding them by the waist. The shrub was a smudge in the half-lit scape, a stain both distant and somehow near that marked, this night, the spin rod of all creation. Gussie's eyes caromed between Acey and Pons and then he saw the Indian, now closing on a vector of his own, weaving between the tents and out of the lantern light, his strides smooth and footfalls soft. Before Gussie could tell where the advantage lay, Acey lunged like a man diving into the sea and the branches gave way under his weight with an ascension of snaps and cracks. Then the echoless whack of the stock against Pons' skull. Acey whipped free the ticking and swung the barrel toward the Indian, who came to a halt in a single minced step and held still, waiting there at the ripe like a good hound called to stay. Pons was in the sand, one hand testing the damage to his busted ear. The pale-faced man remained on his back, a bent leg levering side to side, reaping what toilsome, thin breath he could, the handle of his rapier jutting out beneath his collarbone like a coat peg, rills of shining blood coursing down behind his limp, meaty arm.

Acey brought the Indian near him and ordered Pons to his feet. The Indian had a drop-point hunting knife on him and Acey had him toss it in the dirt, then picked it up himself. He escorted the small party over to Gussie, nearer the pale-faced man, and righted the split-back chair to get it out from underfoot. Then he leaned over, eyes and repeater fixed on Pons, and handed the hunting knife to Gussie.

"I was just about to whip them myself," Gussie said. "But I guess you were in some kind of a big hurry."

Acey had Pons slip the poniard off and easy-pitch it, never sundering his attention from his new captives as he donned the spry lancet.

The Indian tucked his chin and began speaking to Pons in his dry, blocky inflection, and Acey told him if he had anything to say he could put it forth in workday cornpone English and in a hearty voice. "My mama ain't abide no mutterin, and I ain't goin to neither."

Gussie cut himself loose, then blew air on his red, abraded wrists. He stood and shook wherewithal into his legs, his boots heavy as flagstones, then treated himself to a good, long look at the sharp-edged remains of Acey's sun hat, so much spiny confetti, nothing less than their salvation and nothing more now than a bear-chewed mangle of yellow-green.

"I may start wearin one of them," Gussie said.

"You can wear one," Acey answered. "Ain't goin to look as good as I do in it."

Gussie next looked over at Pons' face. If he'd been unroostered, there was no evidence. His eyes were clearing from the stock blow, the set of his face already reverent and suspicious—the air of an expert when confronted with a divergent rationale. He had the heel of his hand pressed hard to his injury, his mouth, for the moment, closed tight.

Acey told Gussie to empty the biggest pack he could lay hands on and load it again with whatever goods seemed suiting to a champion of innocents such as he, and to do it at a trot because they had no notion where that scarred Seminole was got off to.

Once Gussie stepped out of the way, Acey installed his prisoners in the same spot he and Gussie had claimed these hours and drew close the split-back chair and rested himself there with weapon poised and first finger snug in the guard.

"Keep your eye out for the twine ball," he called. "I seen them throw it in that tent yonder."

Gussie unhooked the bail of the lantern from its spindly cross-beam and it swung beside him as he ducked through the nearest button-flap. In a fumbling haste he fell upon a pack nigh as tall as he, upended it and jounced it empty of rumpled white clothes and stolen knickknacks, and began to grab at the tent's disorder for choice plunder. For his own part, he sought only what had been taken off him and not a sewing pin more, but on Acey's behalf he plucked up whatever ammunition came to eye, whether a match for the repeater or no, and whatever dried meats and canisters of nuts and bundles of salt and sugar and gladsome, heady-smelling herb reticules. He bustled tent to tent, and in the intervals out in the open he could hear Pons again at his orations, his silent period ended, no worsened for verve by the contrary turn in his fortunes, this time relating King Alfred's adage that men forget themselves in easy times and remember themselves only when hardship alights.

Gussie soon discovered his fold-knife and his canteen. The former he tucked into his boot, and the latter he filled to the neck from another vessel and set aside. He reached several jars of preserves down into the pack, stacking them tip-side like bricks—root vegetables, green tomatoes, eggplants—and soon was hauling the pack rather than toting it. Patches and mending thread. A wealth of matches. A spyglass. A knot of plug tobacco heavy as a purple onion. The dishes Pons and his crew had dined upon, the spoons and forks. And here was the pale-faced man's revolver, fearsome in its bridle. Gussie paused, but when he put his fingers to the weapon, he felt no lingering evil—only iron put to purpose, only another tool that could be used for terror or survival, depending upon who wielded it.

Gussie backtracked, breathlessly revisiting the tents he'd already pillaged, darting his eyes in the lantern light, and here in a corner, yes, tossed carelessly as an apple core, was the twine. Back to the second tent, the first... finally, beneath a raised wooden cot that must've been Pons', in a hinged gaming box tucked beneath a Mexican shawl, Gussie found a sheaf of browned maps, and quiet atop the maps, like a cherished egg in a nest, was the Waltham. Winking in the yellow glow. M J S. He slipped it roughly into his trouser pocket. Put a steadying hand against the tent wall, a shiver of dizzy happiness running through him. Patted his pocket to make sure, then breathed deeply what air he could in the hot enclosure. He unfolded one of the brittle maps and saw charted there all the farms and homesteads and shops and markets and worship houses of the surrounding shire, all overlain with a scatter of inked symbols that to Gussie's eye looked strangely childish—grain-sickles and nooses and moonshine bottles and sincere-looking Conestoga wagons with outsize wheels. Gussie stepped outside with the maps, out of view of Acey and Pons and the Indian, and tore the weak-folded parchments in two and four and eight and scattered the pieces to the breeze.

He could hear Pons presenting the litany of cities he'd worked, the roll of states he'd departed richer of both purse and discernment than he'd arrived. Gussie dragged the pack over to Acey, and his compatriot chuckled. Pons allowed himself to be interrupted. He appeared amused as well at the figure Gussie and his overlarge equipage cut.

"Judge by that grip, you're scheming for a colt," Acey said.

"Not me," Gussie said. "Got a hard line concernin that. You'd do well gettin me just to feed a horse a carrot."

"I reckon old Acey's the mule tonight. Won't be nothin new. But them chattels don't weigh so strainin when they belong to you." Acey spoke without unriveting his eyes from the pair aground, without shying his finger from the trigger.

"If you might leave us a single blade," Pons said. "I know you wouldn't bereft a chef the tool of his art."

"Oh, you're a chef too?" said Acey. "I'd get tuckered, bein clevered up so many directions."

"Perhaps it's not for me to say. Perhaps it's always to the diners to size the kitchen's talent."

Acey sighed. "Hear you chebberin on between my snores," he said.

"Couldn't find no yellow-boys or like that," Gussie said. "Got to be hid someplace. Probably buried, if I guess."

"We ain't foolin with searchin," Acey said. "I ain't givin this barb-mind sumbitch no more chance to wile me."

Gussie lowered the lantern until it rested in the dirt. At the edge of its shrunken halo, the pale-faced man still fought for breath, face up, whimpering, the earth beneath him spread dark with blood. Acey asked about the twine and Gussie answered and then the big man ordered his prisoners onto their bellies and told them to mate their hands at their backs. He said he'd hold the fire-stick while Gussie took care of the lashing, for if anybody was called to shoot a fellow dead, he favored it be him.

"Now that's how you bound a body up proper," Acey said, once Gussie had done his work and stepped back. Next Acey baled the pack up to his satisfaction, then secured the repeater crosswise through the straps. He swabbed his hand over his face, stroked down his eyebrows, then stepped off toward the pale-faced man and knelt at the demon's head. He removed a packet of cigarette papers from the breast pocket opposite the injury, inspected them and deemed them dry enough and slipped them into his own shirt. And when he put his hands to the haft of the rapier, the pale-faced man slowly raised his own hands and wrapped them weakly around Acey's and held his eyes open so as to look square in the face the ministering figure above him. And rather than struggle, the hurt man put what feeble effort he stored in alliance with Acey's and the blade slid readily free, accompanied by a pulsing dark sluice, and what weak light was left in the pale-faced man's eyes dimmed then, as a pair of lamps running the same moment dry of oil.

When Gussie and Acey judged themselves halfway to the trail, they held up and Acey mined the tobacco from the great pack. He was beginning to limp under his bounty but would not hear of casting off so much as a matchstick. Gussie refused the ill-gotten smoke yet, and this seemed to please Acey even as he partook himself. Acey's ultimate act as despot of the sinkpit had been to pluck Pons' spectacles off his face and hang them by an earpiece from his own collar, which, in union with his overstuffed pack and fastidiously tucked shirt, caused him to appear now a litterateur on some enlightening foreign expedition.

The moon was small and misshapen above them, and though Gussie and Acey strode with eyes dancing this way and that for the grapeshot Indian, fanning yon to dusky copses, sweeping upward to fat-jointed boughs, they failed to notice Pons' scout lodged motionless and snug in the crotch of a longleaf pine some handful of rods aside their course. The Indian, though he was aware of the wayfarers passing below, one at light and even step and one at a sweating hump, did not turn his face to them because he knew that to put eyes to a creature allowed the creature to see you, too. He kept his breath and spirit quiet until he was again alone. He knew that when he returned to camp and cut the rest of his faction from their tethers, in which he knew full well they waited because he'd heard no shots—he knew, once all were standing and had dusted their trousers, that he would be questioned of the stick-armed white boy and the brawny Black, and he knew that he would tell nothing of them and that it would be reckoned the escapees had elected to bushwhack rather than seek the pike by fastest line. He knew that the fanatic blue eyes of his chief, straining in the dark, would turn in short enough order away from beggarly boys and piteous ex-slaves and toward where they always turned, toward those with estate, toward the moneyed, the landed, the full of larder, the kindly starred—those with wealth, they were his cherished and enduring darlings.

BOOK III

JULIUS HAD BEEN BROODING in an abbreviated banquette, his shoulder slumped to the window of the quiet lounge car, gazing out at nothing more notable than the occasional overgrown racecourse in the pastureland, when a too-loud voice from behind him at the bar forced him back to the present moment. Too loud and also, Julius noted, half-drunken. A masculine voice, neither young nor old, faltering at its high notes. Julius listened as for the next quarter-hour the voice detailed the exploits of Bloody Bill Anderson and William Quantrill, and the tender, his apparent audience, responded only in grunts—the towns the villains had torched and the settlements torched in turn for abetting them, their beginnings in horse-trading and coach-sacking, advancement to slave-tracking, to armed rebellion, to the utter terrorization of the frontier's pro-Union citizenry. Julius could hear the fast tapping of the speaker's boot toe on the floor, the anxious drumming of his fingers on the maple bar.

A gulp of gin and tansy, now zestless, remained before Julius on his little table. He'd been nursing it most of the afternoon. With the city some two thousand miles behind him, he'd finally reached the true dregs of his San Francisco revenue.

He pushed his gin from him so as not to smell its clammy sweetness. Turned his head slightly from the window in order to sight the talkative drinker. Expensive coat, listing sloppily from a shoulder. Expensive boots, loosely tied. Red hair in dire need of trimming. Face redder than the hair. The man went on now about the scalping of Jayhawkers and the horsewhipping of defenseless women, his accent neither Southern nor Northern and much closer to college than to the farmyard.

Julius adjusted himself on his seat in order to inventory his remaining capital, plunged his fingers into his trouser pocket and wriggled them one coin to the next. Even less than he thought. An amount that, if not invested, might as well be slung out the train window. And now a scheme worthy of investment had tottered right into the room and docked itself at the bar. Providence. Not to be ignored.

"We mustn't lose sight," the man warned. "Savagery, in the end, is only garnish. The resort of the long shot. A measure to engender terrible dreams and weaken resolve." Julius watched side-eyed as the man gnawed manically at his red-blond mustaches and scratched about his wrists as though his coat sleeves were stuffed with hay. He watched as the man introduced himself to the tender as Troth, and the tender, failing to return his own name, stepped away from a bowl of punch he was mixing just long enough to shake hands.

Troth took a quick sip of his whiskey, not seeming to taste it, drew breath, and forged swiftly and without segue into the theme of his recent travels, leaving easily behind the wartime bad actors of the plains. One simply could not envisage the winters of the far north who'd not greeted them eye to eye, Troth told. He counted it a smashing success that he'd emerged with fingers in a full set. One could spit in the air and hear it tinkle like penny nails on the frozen ground. Bruise-gray noondays for weeks on end. His quarters had been a glorified wigwam, and so he hadn't thought twice about treating himself to a deluxe sleeper for this leg of his return. Heedless of the tender's tepid interest, he disclosed that he was employed by an eminent prospecting concern. Most eminent. He didn't wish to say which, if the tender would pardon, but the men whose interests he'd been advancing were of familiar name and considerable reach and wouldn't forget him when his reconnaissance bore fruit. Very familiar name. And considerable reach indeed.

Upon the thunk of Troth's empty glass meeting the bar top, Julius arose and stepped over and presented himself as Mr. Malcolm

Turner. William was Troth's Christian name, Julius learned—another William: Anderson and Quantrill and now Troth. Julius shook the man's hand, told him he'd overheard him telling of his fascinating travels.

"I find myself very curious to hear more," Julius announced, "and find myself also very curious about yonder broth in the king's porridge bowl."

Troth turned to get a look.

"La Patria," informed the tender. "Not without my own flourishes."

"An itch I intend to scratch," Julius said.

"Yes, my good man," said Troth, game if not steady on his feet. "Chart the course and stay it. No contravening of orders."

"I mean to get utterly wallpapered on that red nectar," Julius said, "if you don't mind my speaking frankly, and it's my heart's wish that you'll join me, sir. That you'll perform the courtesy of saving a fellow drinking alone."

Troth clapped Julius on the back. "We must let curiosity run. Coop it away from fresh air—that's when it grows mean."

He was perhaps half a foot shorter than Julius. His hide crusher sat on the bar at his elbow, and Julius could see from his superior height that, though young enough, his counterpart's salmon-colored hair was thinning through.

The tender ladled each man a quantity of the rose libation, and Julius and Troth withdrew across the narrow walkway with their squat glass mugs and took rest against a balustrade, loomed over at their business by a mural of two woodsmen limbing some grand, felled hardwood, hatchets in hand and visages content.

Julius insisted on hosting—Troth raising only the briefest of polite objection—and each man disappeared three or four mugs in short order, Troth submitting in this time his hindsight expatiations on the Great Conflict, venturing that if the South were to have any real prospect of victory they ought to have surrendered their precious Virginia at the outset and focalized in defense of deep Dixie.

"But all that brass from Virginia," he said, scoffing. "Enough to forge a belt buckle for every Chinese." A strain of Southern accent spiced his voice. Julius could hear it now—the high drawl born along on the drunken enthusiasm. "Richmond to a boy from the Louisiana bottoms may well be Prague. Georgia boys defending Georgia, I say. Carolina boys fighting in Carolina."

Julius glanced at the tender and believed he caught him smirking, a wiry man of perhaps thirty with freckles and a long, pointed nose. He'd already dipped the next pair of punches and had them waiting at the bar's edge, crouching there merry as carolers.

"The way I'm told," Julius rejoined, "the good senators removed to Richmond on finding they couldn't abide Alabama's uncivil climate."

Troth cackled wearily. "Moreover, the rebels should've offered freedom to the halest Negroes in exchange for their service—could've got the leg up on that score. Had they emerged the victors, they needn't fulfill any promises." Troth raised his glass and emptied it, sloshing a measure of the punch down onto the plank floor. "Pretext," he said aggressively. "It survives only the mild seasons."

Over the next two hours, Julius maintained a steady supply line of punch and Troth of wheeling, back-doubling colloquy, Julius beginning to register some buoyancy of head and weight of limb but still able coolly to steward his companion on to oblivion, to notice the excitable little man's arm quavering, to notice the thickening patina of sweat on his guest's face, the way his shoulders ticked and hitched inside his elegant Emerson frock coat. Only the lowest strip of the sky was visible from where Julius leaned—the windows fixed at such a height to accommodate sitters at the banquettes—and that low strip had darkened to sapphire and was hushing further by the minute. Passengers making their way to the dining car gave Troth as liberal a berth as they might, channeled as they were along the polished bar, some of the men leveling rebuking scowls, the women cheating glances as they quick-stepped past.

Troth, eyes wet, spoke at length of a revered auntie of his, May-belle by name, who when he was a lad had been an ally against his stepmother, the latter a cheerless tyrant who had carped Troth's father to unqualified submission. To his stepmother, Troth slurred, all was decay—from a hand of poker to a noonday quadrille. Decay! Execrable decay! A boy couldn't so much as swap the salt for the sugar or filch a tuile cookie without her screeching it up as the devil's own rascality. Their tiny Indiana town, a den of sin. Gomorrah. Banish Maybelle from the house is what the old shrew did, and so the nephew would steal out into the night barefoot and call at her boardinghouse and the two would sit down to tea at any wee hour they pleased. She'd passed away two summers ago, the blessed angel, and that's why Troth had taken appointment amongst the glaciers. "My stepmother to this day deems me a rake. A servant to vice, to proclivity!" For Maybelle, he pleaded—one arm raised for emphasis and the other gripping his drink—the church was a means to grace both earthly and...

"Otherworldly?" Julius helped.

"A means to magnamim, to mangan..."

"Magnanimity?"

"What elevates beats above men is not only a belief in the..." Troth motioned upward urgently with that same free left hand. "And aspiration to be sympathetic..."

"You're making perfect sense to me," Julius rejoined. "Preaching to the choir."

Troth's blinking was growing sluggish. When his eyes shut, it sometimes seemed they wouldn't reopen. "If won't make animals of atheists, will you? Creatures of wood who care nothing of legend... impulses of aid." Troth braced himself against the wall, his empty mug rattling against the balustrade. "I've considered that vice itself differentiates. Yes, vice itself!"

"A convenient notion," Julius replied, "but the proof of man's awful superiority is not vice. We only have greater facility toward it. The hound wants his belly stroked, the cat will lap itself sick on overmuch cream."

Troth nodded laboriously. He was listing with the gentle rocking of the train, chuckling senselessly to himself, and when Julius brought yet another helping of punch over from the bar he had to wrap Troth's fingers around his mug, waiting to let go until he felt his companion's hand recalling its habit. Troth sloshed a quantity of the stuff down his throat, belched, pawed at his vest. Julius judged with a quick jangle of his pocket that he had coin enough for one last round, but more drink and Troth wouldn't be equal even to the task of pointing the way to his berth. Now he was asking Julius what type of woman he preferred. That was, at least, Julius' best guess at what he was asking.

The man's mustaches were stained pink, and Julius, for a fleeting moment, was sorry for him. Vice wasn't his problem—but loneliness. Always loneliness. Julius told Troth he favored his women either young and soft as lambs or old and want-hardened. He almost whispered, bringing the drunkard before him into closer confidence, that he admired fine-boned fingers. Mouths small and plump. A reserved manner. A sallow look about the eyes.

He threw back the last of his own punch and took Troth's empty vessel from him and nested the first inside the second. Leaned across and snatched Troth's hat off the bar as he deposited the glasses.

"I favor them," he said, his voice chill, "nude and hungry and in unceasing but bearable pain."

And next Julius was hauling Troth car to car, the latter's weight near to dead, stopping once and then a second time to rest in unpeopled alcoves, fumbling in Troth's vest pocket, legging the door fro, dragging the limp load that was his drinking companion into the privacy of the sleeper.

Julius ignored the lamp. He slumped Troth into a cream fauteuil chair that dwarfed his form. Troth's features enlivened a moment with a witched look, then went dormant, peaceful. Julius stepped over and drew open the shade to the incurious evening, which seemed to slip past the travelers as much as they rushed past it. He surveyed the room, paying mind to Troth's breaths as they issued more slowly, then began to roughen in slumber. A party of half-empty soporific bottles rested in a wooden bowl on the narrow vanity, but save that, the chamber was tidy as a West Point dormitory. Handsome luggage, in a proper set. Hard to league with the frigid provinces earlier described. Julius removed a dark wool overcoat, heavy as a sheepdog—this fit the story better—from an ottoman and sloughed it in a corner. He crossed over to the tight little closet and found it empty. Found nothing under the mattress. Nothing in the unsecured footlocker. At length, with a not-unhappy sigh, he approached and knelt before Troth's slumbering person and reached inside the man's Emerson coat and ran his hand up and down, first the left side—nothing in the pocket but a loose match—and then the right... and here, yes, it was. Pay dirt. The worn but fine leather flapping so easily open. The stiff bills tucked neat. United States greenbacks. Hello, Mr. Chittenden. Mr. Spinner. Hidden away in the safest spot there could be.

Julius removed the bills and replaced the wallet in Troth's coat. He gave the unlucky fellow a kiss on his rosy cheek, then stood and stepped over and settled himself on the baroque, tasseled ottoman and gazed through the window at the monotonous fields, light lingering just amply for him to catch sight, standing fixed as a post in the acreage of grain, an old farmer facing down the iron horse as it clacked past him, motionless but for a hoe he balanced crosswise before him whose long handle rocked slowly in counterpoise, back, forth, as if he'd been charged with some dreary and everlasting keeping of the slow flatland minutes.

Many hours stood to be burned before day would break and the steamer would board, and Julius was obliged to invest the first of these in locating the Planter's Hotel, where a letter from Abraham awaited him. In perusing the letter before the foxfire coals of the great lobby fireplace, in finding that the letter bore no news of a prompt resolution to the threat. He penned an immediate reply assuring his old servant that with smooth travel he would arrive in time to complete all chores himself, that, in fact, if travel went agreeably, he might turn up prior to the letter he was at this moment composing. But he again reminded Abraham, again concealing his doubts as to his accomplice's ability regarding said office, that if nominated, he must run. Amongst other rhetoric, he reminded Abraham that it was in every man's God-given nature to shield his holdings against marauders, that even if in some mad flight from character the patriarch had indeed engaged a paramour, any resultant progeny was in all respects illegitimate. The boy was a stranger. A stranger preying upon an unwell man's tenderheartedness, as so many saw fit to do. Julius impressed upon his colleague the real possibility that the old man might disinherit him altogether. Who knew what spells the young sorcerer might cast once the elder Searle was under his sway? And if not that, who could say what fortune might be spent on the sharper's education and diversion? Study at fine institutions. Edifying travel. If Julius had his bet, the boy planned to fall in lockstep with all his victim's enthusiasms, pretending himself kindred with every fiber of Madden Searle's mind and makeup.

Julius held the two letters up before him, his own devil-may-care hand against Abraham's stiff script. Folded and tucked the one letter in his vest pocket and carried the other to the Planter's long marble counter. He bestowed a healthy consideration upon the clerk—compliments of William Troth—and this business done, took up his carpetbag and strode out onto the night streets, tacking lazily off from the river and into darker, less seemly quarters of the city, the heavens high and char-dull above him and the cobbled ways slick below his boots.

He passed a Masonic lodge with its forbidding air and lofty turret, a smith's shop and a tanner's, a series of fleabag inns, and at length found an unassuming tavern called Cousin of the Evening whose door stood meekly at the bottom of a half-flight of stone steps. He descended and went inside and commandeered the far-most stool, disposed of a hookerful of whiskey without ceremony and then settled in behind a glass of port wine.

The tender was a hulking sort with sleeves too short for his arms who, once he'd served Julius, sat low behind the bar on a folding campstool and restored himself to a periodical concerning, it appeared, hypnosis. The establishment's fireplace was cold, the andirons bare and black, and above on the battered mantelpiece stood a stuffed cock of radiant green and copper plumage. The only patrons aside Julius were a trio of greasy-collared men with stained hands who conversed in subdued tones around a table dead center of the room.

Julius partook of the slightest sips of the port, merely coating his palate, drinking now only to drive off a headache. He had perched his bag on the stool beside him, and now he slid his hand down inside it and extracted the knife he'd bought in Cayote and clutched it atop his thighs where it was hidden below the overhang of the bar. Pressed his knuckles against the flat of the blade.

He harbored nothing in the sphere of moral qualm, but wondered at the revulsion of forcing sharp steel into living flesh. The visceral perversity. The staring down of one's nerves. This was the means by which he would annul the boy's life—quietly, quickly, as pausing astride to light a pipe. If sighted, Julius would hail the youngster in greeting and amiably step near, perhaps pose a question as to his whereabouts, a lost but optimistic fellow traveler. But where? Where upon the body to strike? In the belly, if they faced each other, and then sidle about and draw the blade across the throat. Between the shoulders, if he were able to steal up. But what if the transaction were not quick as lighting a pipe? What if the little devil managed to scamper off, bent over his injury but fleet in his panic, hands clamped over a wellspring of blood, off the trail and into the brush? Julius would wind up clambering after him as after a stuck pig, tripping through the woods. He must remember to withdraw the knife quickly and be at the ready for the next thrust. Be ready to grapple. Ready to choke the boy by the neck if the knife should clatter to the dust and out of reach.

A shudder ran through Julius, and he drained the remainder of the port. Without inquiry, the tender stood and refilled his glass and said it would be the last before closing. He called the same warning to the threesome at the table, who glanced up but made no reply. Julius squeezed the weapon's handle, doubling his grip upon the instrument until his arm began to quake, released a long breath, and shoved the piece roughly back into his bag. It was one thing he'd never killed a man, but he'd nary even thrown hand into a proper fisticuff—nary a duel, nary a melee. The knives his hands were acquainted with had always rested, before his taking them up, on dining tables.

He straightened his back and drew a deliberate breath, the air in the barroom light for the open windows but fortified with the under-stench of spilt drink. He was enfeebled of spirit for lack of sleep—that was much of the trouble. A man could disquiet himself until nothing was left of him. Not only deprived of rest but soul-damp from overmuch gin and punch and now port. He was glorifying this straightforward act of self-interest that lay before him. Falling prey to romance, as a waltz-dizzied debutante at a soiree. He would do what he must when the moment arose. Nothing more and nothing less. Turn living body to corpse and drag the corpse from sight and continue on his way. Continue rightly to the claim he'd given up so much for. So very much. His only mother, to give example—the woman now a stranger to him. Worse than a stranger, in truth. Civility to a stranger cost little. Julius had forsaken her in order to cling fast to the estate, yet still had been brought to the sale of his carnal talents, the peddling of his very self, a play-pretty for past-ripe countesses. Softer words existed than whore, but what good were they? Illness—yes, he'd suffered it. Straightened quarters. When trade was slender, bad beer and bread crusts days at a time. Prison, no less—rancid, reeking, Confederate jail. He had dragged his person about this America by rough means and against his wishes. Had suffered fools, had stolen from them. His father might have prevented all of it, could've kept Julius away from the war, away from what had befallen him these years, but the old man had chosen not to. He'd chosen to make Julius earn his potential reward, and Julius, by God, meant to. He was a man now indeed, if not of the cut his father had envisioned. A man who would have, in full, what was his.

———

Abraham had commenced his journey directly after clearing the breakfast table—a chore accomplished mostly by the removal of the tea caddy—explaining his coming absence to Mr. Searle as a jaunt to Anclote to catch a variety program passing through their part of the world. He told his employer, taxing his powers of invention, that the show featured a contortionist from Scotland and a string ensemble from Hungary, and when asked the name of the troupe said he couldn't recall. Carver and something. Carter, perhaps. Mr. Searle, an odd expression tightening his jaw, said Abraham's absence would be no trouble as he would spend the better part of the coming days in his workshop, said he was making good progress with a couple of his newer projects. There was that half-ham at the ready. The olives and strawberries. Mr. Searle cleared his throat and shuffled his boots on the floor, the old altar boy struggling mightily with his dishonesty. Abraham knew that his master, despite the fellow's attempts to conceal it, had been spending far more hours disporting with his candle whimsy than he had at gainful exertions in his inventor's shop. Indeed, those ragamuffins he oversaw in the studio were near on full-time employment. "Best of luck then," Abraham said, not minding making Mr. Searle squirm a bit. "I look forward to seeing what you've been working on, when the time is right."

Upon meeting the prime wagonway, he'd turned south instead of northward, clopping slow on the quarter horse because he mistrusted both the horse's disposition and its brittle old legs. It would take the better part of the day to reach Tampa, and in the morning he'd go into Mize Station. He'd packed light—his straight razor, his toothbrush and orris-root powder, a change of clothes, and most important, a tidy sum of cash, bound up in an oilcloth poke bag and secured inside his trouser leg, tight-pressed against his thigh as some tumor that had grown there. Mr. Searle's bothered old bloodweed, who was costing Abraham in expediency, was an advantage in the sense that no brute or indigent, upon viewing the scraggy steed—its split hooves, its tan-gray coat as dingy as a hound's night-rug—would conclude the rider to be in possession of anything but the hair on his head.

Abraham rode a mile away from the estate, another, down into the white-blown salt marshes where critter tracks were woven into garbled runes on the parched path. Where branchless, crooked stalks rose from the dense mud like fascinated serpents. Where outsize water birds now and again rose up from nowhere and startled the horse, buffeting the air with their stiff wings, their ill-joined legs dangling beneath them.

In time, Abraham would assume Julius' old quarters—these were the things to think on—the attached sitting parlor and high-windowed den with its view out into the bottle-green boughs. His own room, come available, would be filled by a new servant. Abraham would call out to the man in a clipped, distracted tone and demand his afternoon refreshment, a nip of amontillado perhaps. But what had unexpectedly entered the warren of Abraham's mind and would not find its way out was something much less helpful—an evening some months before the start of the war, when Mr. Searle had hosted a relation of his passed-away stepmother who was traveling through to Monroe county, speculating on real estate in the Southern Keys. The old man, unaware that Abraham stood around the corner, had spun out a chuckle and remarked that Searle's "frowning, lank domestic" would make an able spy in the upcoming contest. Suspicious and discreet, the man explained, and a pinch bitter, too. Mr. Searle had not let the ungenerous appraisal stand. He'd said if practitioners of espionage were loyal and usefully circumspect and wielded the household expertise of three or four lesser subordinates combined, then Abe forecasted as a peach of a spy indeed. Abraham had wondered that moment whether, by skulking in the steamy little ambry between dining room and kitchen, he'd proven the old prospector's accusation correct. He'd wondered also if Mr. Searle had suspected him lurking near, and whether his employer's response would have differed if he'd been assured of privacy. But Abraham knew the answer. He knew that it would not have differed one word. He understood in an inconvenient, honest part of himself that Mr. Searle believed him wholly and perennially constant, and that this confidence could only obtain because master, too, felt devoted to servant. A purer devotion than Abraham's, apparently. A foolish devotion, it was being proven. But wasn't this warding off of the young adventurer also an act of loyalty? Not only to the legitimate son but the father himself, the one who had, after all, hired Abraham? It could be soberly argued, couldn't it, that to allow the resourceful lad to stroll free up the front walk of the estate would constitute a gross failing in Abraham's commission? He'd run off many with empty pockets and shadowy hearts, and here was merely the next. Abraham had on his hands a cunning survivor—did he not? A murderer no less, as hard-shelled a fortune-seeker as ever made trail.

Abraham pulled low his hat-brim and lit a cigarette, passing now on the raised trail a former citrus grove chopped low by axe, likely a Union detachment's handiwork, the uneven expanse of stumps reminding him immediately of the stove-piped rooftops of Cincinnati, where as a lad he'd many a time taken refuge on high with the pigeons. His childhood had been a blight. A pure blight. His father a broom maker who'd died of drunken exposure in the lowly hills of southern Ohio. His mother a dullard seamstress whose heart had given out before she'd reached thirty years of age. The appointment at Mr. Searle's had flown him away from that sorry history. Had given him a new world.

Think of the future, he scolded himself, the time when Julius would be king of the castle. Think of what life could be, not what it had been. Instead of catchpenny reviews, Abraham would spend the symphony season in New Orleans. Someone would chart his meals, clear his dishes, hang his suits of clothes. First order of business would be a decent horse—a gloss-coated charger that would inspire obeisance in the village lessers, a mount to stay all snickering. Good wines opened on his whim. Boots from Europe. Perhaps even women.

Why not? They were about for the taking now if they believed one could usher them toward safety and comfort. A full set of luggage. Tomato tarts sprinkled with rock sugar. Hampers of plug tobacco. Leisure. Real leisure.

In the morning, Abraham settled with the sallow old proprietor and retook the way, which was now lined on both sides by hard berms topped like feathers on a helmet with Caesar weed. He passed a troop of llamas brooding behind a split-rail fence, with their steep necks and lazy, harlot's eyes. The day's warmth setting its barbs, he crossed a deadfall-choked rill then ascended to a shady banyan grove, and just beyond the grove was the lone consequential structure of Mize Station.

He tied the horse to a splintered rail and crossed the yard, and after taking the four steps up onto the bare porch, he could see down into a clean, open wagon that stood near, could see the braces bolted into the scrubbed wood, only one still clasping its length of iron links. Abraham went on into the cramped lobby and searched out a placard that told him Sir William was on the upper floor. The building was quiet and Abraham's steps echoed on the stairs. The other doors were shut, but Sir William's was quarter-way open. Although of considerable fame, he had no secretary, no anteroom. Abraham rapped firmly on the door and heard a rasping but not unfriendly voice bid him enter. Sir William sat heavily behind his desk, which was really just a dining table, pen poised and head canted as if Abraham had only stepped in to drop off some bit of news. A tan duck coat, stiff with disuse, hung on a wall hook behind him, and a half-finished breakfast of pickled okra and prunes had been pushed aside on the vast table-top. Abraham smelled coffee but saw none and was offered none. He himself was freshly shaven, but the man before him had many days' shadow on his jaw.

When Abraham announced he bore a case for consideration, Sir William rested his pen on his blotter, showing no eagerness but neither any impatience. He half-rose to reach a finger of okra, which he deposited in his mouth and more or less swallowed whole. He pointed to a white-painted chair and Abraham dragged it over. The rest of the building had been vacant of personal effects, but Sir William's office was littered front to back with all manner of curiosity and keepsake. On a sideboard sat a fat, worn text for practicing the Spanish language. On the windowsill, a potted cactus. Against one leg of the table, a deep drum of what appeared to be cottonmouth skulls, devilish, stark-white. A tarnished knight's casque rested on its side. A blunt-beaked halberd leaned in a corner.

"Floor's yours," Sir William said, pursing his lips to listen. The slouch of his back caused Abraham to sit straighter.

"Well, to dispense with preamble," he said, "there's a fugitive, a criminal at large, wanted clear over the other coast and now fled toward this one. A teenager, a young man—aged enough to stir up all manner of trouble, anyhow. I've a notion where he's headed and a notion when he might arrive." Abraham rested a hand on the table, and Sir William looked at it like some peregrine article he might want for his collection, his eyes beading. "All you'd need do is have one of your men sniff him out and apprehend him and hand him over to me. Just apprehend, that's all. I'd assume custody."

Sir William moved his head, not quite nodding. "No more men," he said. "Not a one. Just yours truest."

Abraham could feel the pouch of currency against his inner leg. He'd not been able to decide whether to have it at the ready entering Mize Station or wait until it was wanted to extract it. He'd considered that he wasn't truly safe from bandits until bodily in Sir William's company. Or perhaps, deep down, he didn't wish to part with it. But that made not a lick of sense—such a small expenditure compared with the half-fortune it might preserve.

"Perhaps," suggested Abraham, "you could hire a good man, a discreet man, on a temporary basis, expressly for this piece of business. Or perhaps handle this account personally."

Sir William's expression of tranquil engrossment didn't change. He swabbed out an ear with his smallest finger.

"You say your name was?" he asked.

"Ben Shrader," said Abraham.

The other man smirked. "You a landowner, Shrader?"

Abraham's foot began to tap and he stilled it. "Nothing to speak of," he said. "Enough for me and mine, most years."

"Where about this nothin-to-speak-of plot, you don't mind my nosin?"

"Some way north of here."

"How far a way, would you estimate?"

"Well, that depends on the route one takes."

Sir William laughed contentedly. "Yeah," he said. "Everybody got his own route."

Abraham felt he was at a card table. Outside the window, the boughs of the trees were full of pearly light fine as nursery powder. The sash was lifted, but no birdsong could be heard.

"I've brought with me a down payment and have been assured deeper billfolds at the ready. Awaiting only a report of your willingness. I was told you were top in your field."

Sir William picked his pen up with two fingers, held it before him as if checking the balance of its weight. "I ain't chased nobody in years, Shrader. When a party's property goes missin and another party knows where it went, I arrange a meet. I help the parties settle a price for illumination of the truth. I might've been somethin hot out in the wilds in my day—if folks say that, I ain't callin them liars—but now I ain't much more than a broker. A wheel-greaser."

"You'd be serving the right," Abraham said, hearing the strain in his own voice. "Delivering a dodger to justice."

Sir William nodded. "I reckon justice a slippery word, Shrader. Slippery as an eel."

"Not in this instance. In some, I grant you, but not in this."

"What's the crime?"

"Crimes, Sir William. Numerous. General ruckus-raising, thieving from establishments, accosting the township's good daughters. Top it all, a violent streak. An all-over vicious specimen and unhealthful influence."

"Some of them good daughters want nothin better than gettin accosted. Pray for it nights between scripture and hair brushin."

"And he's been named responsible," Abraham said, flattening his tone into one of utmost gravity, "for the death of a colleague of yours. Oh, yes. And so, murder. You can add murder to the list."

"That is quite a list," Sir William said, not seeming impressed. He reached and popped another okra into his mouth. With a gesture of his wrist he offered Abraham some, but Abraham declined, trying not to show his frustration.

"I assume this is a white boy," Sir William rejoined, "since you ain't indicated one way or the other. No more slaves to turn up, so now I'm chasin down sorry white boys what snuck a bottle of lightnin or got cornered in the stables by a debutante or got some unlikely homicide fixed to their legend. I might've been that poor boy of a time, Shrader. Suspect you might've too. Catch up every boy shows a streak for mischief, won't be none left."

"You're getting it cockeyed," Abraham said. "This is a very bad sort we're dealing with. Daggers in his stockings. No, nothing like I ever was. He's at much heavier than mischief."

"I ain't got nothin cockeyed. Never do. Got it dead right, like usual. What's in your pink little heart, Shrader? Can you tell the congregation? I know what's in mine. I can feel them scaly things wrigglin around in their own sweet poison. I figured how to tame mine for use within the law, but serpents they be."

Abraham didn't know what to say to that. The air in the office didn't feel clean in his lungs. Impatience was mostly what he felt in his own breast, if he had to say. "Are you in business or aren't you?" he asked. "I've come a long way on tidings that Sir William Beth is a serious man who shies not at the day's labor, whether it be savory or duty's dry cress."

"You've come a long way," Sir William said. "From your home-stead a good way north, just enough for you and yours."

He drew a breath that filled him like a bellows, then rose from his chair and strolled to the window. He gazed outside, his back to Abraham, bending at the waist so as to peer up past the treetops. He remained a long minute this way, as if reading something in the clouds as they drifted by like untethered boats.

"Been out West?" he asked.

"Arkansas," Abraham said. "I've crossed the river. What of it?"

Sir William touched the pot that held the cactus on the sill, turn-ing it in the slanting light—a bulb cactus, its spines thin as dandelion dust. Next to the cactus sat a framed picture. Sir William picked it up and carried it over to Abraham, held it before him for viewing, angling it from the glare. The figures in the panorama were dark, the air too bright. Sir William leaned his bulk to Abraham, and Abraham could smell the pickled okra on him. He held the picture poised there behind its glass and used his other hand to point.

"That's a haciender," he said. "That there they call paddle cactus, that along the wall, and you can't see them, but we stand in the shadows of willow trees you might chop down for a bridge to old

Spain. Fellow standin front of the haciender, belly full with chicken in sweet chili gravy, that's my own self, Sir William. Off in the afterground is a mountain. Bunch of them, rightly." Sir William used his smallest finger, the one he'd used to clean his ear, to underline a shadowy ridge at the top of the composition. "You may hold the belief you seen a mountain, but you ain't. You get up top one of them there, horses look like tick-bugs and rivers like racer snakes. Can't work up a sweat no matter what you do, wind steals it right off." He leaned in closer, wanting a better look himself, touching Abraham's shoulder. "And that there, with the ever-pleasin curves and eyes round as chestnuts is a Miss Roderiga Garza. Wouldn't believe it, but she's always happy to have old Willy around. Cheeks plumpin like apples whenever I ride up."

Abraham nodded, feeling crowded, hoping the man would remove the picture and stop looming over him. "The real West," he said. "Charming, but I don't see why this—"

"Real villains too. That's important. See, way I figure, I got just enough pepper to do somethin Christian in this world. There's true-to-God outlaws in them open reaches. Not fellows locked up 'cause they lost the taste for hot lead. Not youngsters hunted up 'cause they got no Daddy and had to plunder up a dinner. A past is a past and everybody got one, but I'm about prepared to tiptoe away from mine." He looked about himself wearily now at the plentiful relics and queer trifles that overcrowded the office. "Plain room and a pretty girl and put a few in shackles what in truth got it comin."

"I thought you were too old," Abraham said. "The frail old broker."

Sir William bared his yellow teeth. He stepped over and restored the picture to the sill. Abraham had refused the okra and now could feel hunger in his gut. He felt suddenly distant from Sir William, as if the office were a vast arena, felt himself receding from the present moment. He felt removed from the whole morning, his whole journey.

"Is Miss Roderiga whatever-her-name part of the Christian program you so optimistically envision?"

Sir William was at the window, but Abraham could tell he smiled at the question. "No, sir," he said. "She visit the church house, suspect the place might catch ablaze."

Abraham could feel the plug of notes jabbing his flesh when he shifted in the hard chair, daggering his skin like a child's toy pikeman. A voice from a recess of his mind was beseeching him to reach into his trousers while his counterpart faced away. When the man turned back, Abraham might flourish the money climactically, a gesture of trump, to sell the aged slave-tracker on one last blessing for his stake before he shot westward. He'd learned, over the years, that men were often blood-seized at the plain sight of cash, often agreed to terms they hadn't wished to. But Abraham made no further flick of the foil, knowing that with this man before him it would be no use. His arms felt weighted. Too weighted even to reach for a morsel of okra.

"You can water that poor animal out back of the buildin," Sir William said.

———————

It was late morning, at a crossroads near Camp Ligee, when Gussie approached and could not help himself entering a vine-enveloped hash house called Po's. The tables near the big, west-facing windows were already crowded, so Gussie crossed to the far wall and set his pack in one chair and his own tired carcass in another. In a corner hunched an iron stove with a belly like a bull's head, in such long disuse that green creepers wound down its stack. A company of ladles and forks hung handily on a rafter, swaying ever slightly. The proprietress appeared—Po, perhaps. When she neared the party at the windows, they let up a buoyant cheer. Lemon brandy. Gussie saw it advertised on a crooked sign above the tight corridor to the kitchen. The woman refilled their glasses and scolded them sisterly for their impatience. A scar the breadth of a woodworker's pencil, which Gussie saw when she looked over and tossed him a wink, spanned her whole cheek and trailed off below her ear.

She brought him a glass of water clear as a jeweler's eyes, assured him the vittles would be out directly. Before she could whisk herself away, Gussie inquired how far on Tampa was, and when he heard her reply—for Tampa was south of Ivory Shoals, farther even than he needed travel—he felt suddenly rushed, harried, crowded.

"That's all?" he said.

"Unless they finally decided to move Tampa," she told him.

A handful of days, if the trail was sound. A handful of days and all would be decided. Just a few more nights at camp, spending the evening hidden away and alone, before he awakened to his whole future, whatever it be, before he walked himself right into his uncertain destiny. He ought to be happy, he told himself, but somehow he hadn't been ready for the good news. Somehow he wasn't ready for his work to conclude and his verdict to be read.

Po brought Gussie a bowl of cabbage palm stew and two fists of course-crusted bread, and Gussie calmed himself by digging in. The proprietress had served Gussie first and now sauntered over to the bulk of her clientele, who received her with a program of companionable taunts. She put their bowls to steaming and centered on each of their tables a platter of bread. Again blessed them with the brandy. They were young men all and seemed imbued with the wholesome mischief of boys on a church junket. One of them, upon sampling the fare, called out that a ball of yarn might flavor up the stockpot. The proprietress—indeed Po, as Gussie had heard her addressed—pulled back her shoulders blithely and decreed there'd be no guff regarding dinner. She said she'd grown up so poor that on many a night she'd quieted her stomach with beeswax. "Captain John Dickison himself occupied table here and he ain't lodge no complaint," she told them. "Suit your soft-soled lot just dandy." Po gave a sharp nod then returned to her duties in the kitchen, leaving the young men happily outdone and rendering Gussie happy that Po was the one to which he'd turn over the bit of coin he'd scratched from the wayside scrub where Pons had tossed it.

He soaked his crusts and listened absently to the rhythmic badinage across the room, which now took on a more serious humor. The men were ink-slingers, swapping flopped leads and travel advisements and accounts of reptilian run-ins. They filled out the whole catalog as to speaking accents but favored such congruent wardrobe they seemed in uniform—the oil-grain half-boots, the patterned cravats, even the long, thin cigars they'd stabbed cold when the food arrived. They conferred soberly on Lincoln's murder and the plotting that brought it off, discussed in awed derision Jefferson Davis' $100,000 personal debt, spoke of the new commander-in-chief, Andrew Johnson, who one of the paperboys charged had been illiterate until age twenty-one and another defended by his assertion that, in Tennessee, twenty-one was considered dangerously young to acquire such a frivolous skill as reading.

Gussie could only wonder at the cities these men hailed from, cities yet intact, straightened to some degree but enlivened with the gusto of victory. He knew, and wished not to begrudge it this lot, that to them the hardships of the world were only fodder for vivid copy. Adventures were bestowed upon them—a great one, in this instance—with no risk to themselves. They'd been temporarily called from home but each knew his family awaited, cozy rooms stuffed with books, blazing candles, soft rugs. Each one would feast upon his return. Each would rejoin loved ones to be clapped on the back and questioned thirstily on his emprises afield.

When Po returned to fill Gussie's water glass, he found himself asking where a fellow might find work if he sought it, feeling foolish even as he posed the question, for industry was crippled all over and he was nowhere near any metropolis or even a town. Po told him she knew of no paying work but did know where a young man might gain room and board if willing to keep the place up. No more than three hours on foot, she rated. Square meals and nights up off the floor, if you weren't stingy with your sweat. Based on some Northern religion or other.

"Northern religion?" Gussie said.

Po swept Gussie's coins off the table and dropped them in a pocket of her apron. She shrugged at him. "I reckon they're most all Northern to us, ain't they?"

Gussie pressed through the afternoon rain, and once the sun had returned he walked another hour, so that his clothes were near dry again when he approached the hostel. Gussie met the steward, or headmaster, or pastor—the man failed to offer a title, wishing only to be called Mr. Haines—but briefly, paid witness to said superintendent's changeless expression, one eloquent of humility but also of broad disapproval, was extended a dry hand to shake and asked only few questions about himself—whether he was suffering illness, how long he planned to room. A single night, Gussie said, trying to look the man in his eyes rather than inspect the pewter whistle hanging from his neck, its tiny cork ball housed inside. The man apprised Gussie of the two rules: instructions were followed at first issuance, and no sass-back was tolerated. He handed Gussie off to a soft-faced boy called Bith who was to act as his cicerone. Bith escorted him about the grounds, showed him the springhouse, the smokehouse— which was in no small disrepair—the twin outhouses, one for children and one for grown folks, both situated in a swale at the property's edge where welters of white-throated blossoms thrived. There's just the one grown folk, Bith said. He reported that Mr. Haines mostly left them in their own charge, hoping they'd reward his trust. Bith had only seen the man lose temper once, when a boy had mistreated one of the mules—Haines had skull-drug the luckless fellow down to the creek yonder and close to drowned him. Bith said they expected a rush once word got around they were back on their feet, but at present it was only Bith himself and one other boy who kept his own counsel and did solitary duties, mostly in the kitchen, peeling vegetables and scrubbing the supper-ware. Gussie had glimpsed this boy back in the house during his interview with Mr. Haines, a boy some inches shorter than Gussie and a match to him for jangliness of limb. Bith warned Gussie not to put a cross word toward the quiet third lodger, who'd been used most of his years as a child brawler in the barrier islands. Bith often caught him staring off where there wasn't a thing to stare at, like he forgot he was alive. "One thing sure," Bith said. "He could whip us two at a single service and not get to breathin heavy."

In the short hours before supper, the two boys stood the bedframes endwise and polished the pine floor of the vast, plain bedroom. They stripped the mattresses to their ticking and sprinkled them with lavender oil to ward off fleas. Then, the sun at long last relenting, they fed the mules and hogs and clambered up and swept clear the roof of the springhouse, which was matted thick with hand-shaped oak leaves fallen during the term of winter and dampened in place with daily summer showers. A faction of rotted sweet gums had been felled on the dry western dogleg of the grounds, the trunks sawed into sections that now wanted ricking for stove wood. Gussie and Bith had only just set to this labor when they heard the shrill but glad sound of Mr. Haines' whistle splitting the air, calling them to table.

At supper the boys were not to speak. They shoveled down their portions of heavy pinto-bean pie and gulped greedily from their water cups and listened as Mr. Haines recited Bible verses. The runty battler ate as quickly as anyone but did not finish his helping, instead sliding the remainder over to Bith, who dispatched the added nutrition without pause after finishing his own. Each diner cleared his setting, and then Bith and his wordless companion retired to an austere parlor at the back of the house, where they were to self-administer one-half-hour's learning and one-half-hour's diversion.

Gussie begged off from the indoor enterprises. He excused himself and slipped out the backside door and returned, under light of the moon, to stacking the sweet gum logs fore and aft against every firm-standing trunk in carrying distance, hauling them three and four at a go, halting his relay only to rank neat the stacks, his fingers falling numb and forearms rasped red as berries. He sweated through his shirt and shed it and continued to uncover ground, using the thickest lengths to base the piles and building them as high as his chin and higher, the crickets raising their nightly chant all about him. The lanterns within the house went dark one by one until only a pair remained, in the boys' room and in what Gussie surmised was Mr. Haines' study. The mosquitoes could hardly purchase on Gussie's body for the slurries of sweat, but they so banqueted about his ears and neck that when his task was at a close and he draped his sodden shirt over his shoulder and strode back toward the rear door, his jaw throbbed as though he'd been clouted each cheek with a yardstick.

Breakfast next morning was weak coffee and grits thick as plaster and one boiled egg per man, a repast Gussie attempted to refuse on grounds that he was departing that morning and so would not earn any further board. Mr. Haines had no patience for this notion and set Gussie's plate before him with the air of a man who hoped not to suffer more foolishness. He rested no kind hand on Gussie nor even kind eye, but once all were finished and had patted their bellies and wiped their lips and conveyed plates and milk cups to the basin, Mr. Haines summoned Gussie with a terse nod to his private quarters. He bade Gussie rest himself in a chair and revealed that he knew, because Bith had so informed him, Gussie was journeying to unite with relations and was loathe to turn up penniless and ragged. Without pausing for Gussie to confirm this, he retrieved from a desk in a windowless corner of the room an envelope fashioned of sugar sacking, and contained within the envelope, which was sealed with dark pitch tacky against Gussie's fingertips—contained within the envelope, Mr. Haines explained, was a tribute to Gussie's staunch back and busy hands. If delivered to a certain Landis Coker of Brom's Point, the missive would result in an offer of employment.

Gussie felt his face redden. He arose and shook Mr. Haines by the hand and thanked him profusely, all of which seemed to embarrass if not offend the severe old instructor. And once he'd weathered Gussie's gratitude, the man pulled his whistle off a nail in the wall of the study and donned it and stepped past Gussie lightly and summoned his remaining charges to him, the thickset and flushed Bith and the wire-armed and pale other, and began to deliver his orderly précis of the day upcoming, what activity would be expected and according to what timetable. And again, as he must have done each day for as long as anyone recalled, stated his pair of straightforward and invariable rules.

The new land Gussie forged into was one of brackish rivers overlooked from high perches by princely osprey. Always the pine. Always the sun. Gussie regulated his stride so as not to jostle his letter, which he'd cottered down into his pack in such a way it wouldn't be rumpled or bent or work itself open. Gulls flew here

and there, vexed, their cries weak with doubt. Patches of marsh.
The rivers splitting into canals lined with red-rooted mangroves.
And here on the air—yes, unmistakable—was the scent of the sea,
the scent that had so long now been only a memory, a kelpy, sweet
brine carried to and past Gussie on a breeze delicate as silk ribbon.
The smell of home and of heartache and of everything. The smell of
every Palmina child he'd grown up with, of every porch he'd ever
stood on, of his mother's hair after they walked the canals. And here
were the familiar pelicans roosting on the pilings of two-skiff docks,
the familiar oyster shells climbing the pilings. All became salty,
bracing. Gussie could feel the closeness of the Gulf on the backs
of his hands, could taste it coating his tongue, and soon he sidled
through an unassuming stile in the low growth and felt himself no
longer advancing, his progress stopped. He felt the stillness after
long transit that fills one like a secret. The busy, empty-headed hum,
as if the wind with its wordless verse could pass right through his
ears. A push of vertigo as his bootsoles settled in the silt bed. As with
the Atlantic, of course, no far bank could be seen, no resumption of
the realm of man, only the blue-black edge of the deeps against the
palest green of the sky. The tide was receding, Gussie saw, doubling
and perhaps yet to tripling the humble beach, leaving drifts of coarse
seagrass that glistened in the sun. The Gulf was calm, its surf giving
out in docile fans rather than crashing, no whitecaps offshore, the
shells on the tidal flat undashed, as if gently offered up in tribute.
Gussie's knees felt unreliable, loose in their halters. He slipped off his
pack and rested it on a crisp raft of salt grass, bared his feet, cuffed
his trouser legs. He waded to his calves in the lukewarm wash and
let his eyes dazzle at the countless, glimmering wave rows. Turned
and left the sea long enough to strip off the balance of his clothing,
then stepped out again and cuffed the water about his elbows and
shoulders and face. He submerged his head and licked the salt from

his lips. Waist-high in the slow swells, hair stiff and dripping, he turned his back to the fathoms and regarded the breadth of the parti-colored peninsula he'd conquered. There it sat. Humanity as wicked as one could conceive, or as worthy. Country both perilous and splendid. Showers and storms and the punishing surveillance of the sun. He was the selfsame Gussie Dwyer—the same two eyes he'd always kept open, the same two hands to forage and fight, the same two feet to carry him—but in his chest his fear was faint and his pride seasoned and quiet and sure. There was no novelty now in his being responsible for his person and for his own doings. Outwardly, he remained a boy, but he knew the journey he'd undertaken was not a boy's. The journey he'd undertaken, and now all but completed, was one that few grown men would wish for.

He picked his way south, his skin tight, the beach at intervals a narrow brown strip or a shapeless run of low dunes. At times there was no border whatever between the woody marshland and the sloshing expanse, so that Gussie was obliged to again go bootless in the shallows, the mud slick beneath his feet, the sheepish crests slapping themselves dead in the underwork of the mangrove stands. The clouds had ranked themselves high and were drifting landward when Gussie caught a whiff of fish smoke. Mullet, his best hunch. He knew he was hungry, and knew, more to the moment, that he was close upon Brom's Point.

No more than two hundred yards on was an inlet, pinched at its neck and tapering to a river and creek as Gussie tracked it away from the sea. Docks in fair standing and serving their purpose, cleating safe many battered half-cabin vessels with sails of hemp. The modest center of commerce, the four or five tradesmen indispensable to every hamlet. A general store, a rotten-roofed livery—not much of a town, but plenty for Gussie if work were to be had. He stopped an old man hobbling the opposite way and asked after Landis Coker's outfit, got his answer and tacked farther inland, across the rudely cobbled square and down a cindered lane along which the trees stood higher and heartier. The sky had been darkening as Gussie walked, and it pulled the curtain on its matinee just as he reached the shut-up gate, the cool drops pecking his cheeks. A bell on a post stood one end of the gate, and Gussie pulled the rope to sound his greeting. Immediately, a pair of spaniel mutts bounded up from the other side, barking and spinning about, uncertain whether to bite or lick the visitor, and it seemed it was the dogs' racket rather than the bell that caused a man to appear, loping over with a newspaper overspreading his straw hat. He snapped his fingers and gave each dog an amiable swat on the rump and they trotted together toward a tall, painted barn whose doorway gaped open. The man had one hand on his paper shelter—Gussie had seen the scribes back at Po's, and now he saw their long-missing product—and with the other hand he reached over to shake and then unfastened and pulled open the gate and bade Gussie follow. He said he bet Gussie was hunting work, seeming neither sanguine nor skeptical at the prospect, and Gussie verified this and told him he carried a letter of testimony penned and signed by Mr. Haines at the hostel in Weeki Wachee.

"I don't know from Mr. Haines and I certain don't know from Weeki Wachee," the man called from under his collapsing cover, "but let's get you up and let the boss look you over."

Gussie followed the man across the yard, his escort walking splay-footed and with a step too heavy for his frame. He left Gussie on a cramped but dry porch and entered the office, stopping at the threshold to fold up the now-soaked newspaper and remove his hat. He caught the door before it shut behind him and said he may as well deliver Gussie's note—he may as well add mail-donkey to his list of duties. He stood there and waited as Gussie uncinched his pack and delicately pulled free the envelope. Gussie felt a pang, handing the memorandum over to anyone but Coker, but there was nothing for it, and so he did as he was told and then found himself again alone, rocking heel to toe and picking at his knuckles, the clatter of the rain on the roof above drowning out any talk he might've overheard from inside. There was a window, but with nothing behind it but the still furniture of a vacant room. An empty glass tumbler. A cold fireplace. On the porch sat a solitary wooden chair, but Gussie elected not to rest himself in it, not wishing to seem weary before he'd logged a first hour of labor. He could hear the dogs barking from the big barn and occasionally the cackles of several boys—hard to tell how many. Did it mean Coker would need no more help, that he already had some number of grunts in his employ, or did he need what boys he had and Gussie too and even more if he could get them?

Finally, footfalls from inside. A cough. He stood back to leave way for the door to open, and open it did. This had to be Coker, this older man coming out now, folding the letter and tucking it away, stepping down onto the porch and appraising Gussie top to bottom.

"Elbows always that sharp," he said, his voice deep as a stage put-on, "or you been runnin lean?"

"A fellow gets short of wind," Gussie said, "carryin around all that muscle. I ain't got no such hindrance."

Coker smiled. He gazed out over the drenched front grounds of his operation, then sat down in the chair Gussie had eschewed and settled his arms on the rests.

"What can you do, especially?"

"Just work till I give out, then take a deep breath and work some more. Work without over-many waterin breaks. Know a tool from one showin."

"What can't you do?"

Gussie mopped his nose with his sleeve. "Bein honest, I got precious little mind for high math. I could read like a shed-fire, though. Never had no bit a trouble there."

Coker wore shirtsleeves, displaying fleshy, almost womanish arms that shook when he chuckled. He told Gussie they were clearing and plumbing for a depot. All the cuttings got jacked small enough for the mules to handle, mules dragged it up here, where it got sawed up pretty. Coker admitted the work was mean on the back and meaner still on the fingers.

"I happen to be in practice for rickin," Gussie said.

"So I hear," answered Coker, patting his chest where he'd slipped the letter. "If Haines is sponsorin, I'll believe you're right-handed. He don't hold with a lot of nonsense, that one. Don't hardly hold with pleasant dreams."

"No, sir," said Gussie.

Coker craned his neck to examine the clouds, which were shot through with yellow light but yielded their rain steadily nonetheless. "We can use you. I don't reckon you're wantin no more suspense. Lord knows we can use you." He arose spryly from his chair. "We do breakfast, the rest you root up in town. Y'all start up soon as the weather quits. I'll pay you today for today's hours so you got somethin in your pocket for supper. For now, them boys'll give you a couple gnaws of whatever they got cached in the barn."

Gussie watched Coker, watched his new boss, step back inside the office house, the door not quite latching behind him. He stood still a moment, trying to understand that just like that he was employed, that the letter had been a success. It had to be the letter—it wasn't the looks of Gussie. That was it. He had work. He would earn money, like back in Palmina at the docks. He turned and collected his pack and jogged through the rain to the barn and stepped inside the open doors, turned his name over to the assembly of boys stretched this way and that on the straw. They numbered five, Gussie the sixth, and they dealt their own names back at him brisk as a roll call. Alden. Finch. Robert. Harley—this boy sitting erect, eyes expectant in his great, round head, a wisp of blond whiskers on his lip. And a big boy, shoulders round, hair parted and smoothed as if for Sunday service, whose name slipped through Gussie's grasp. The barn was enormous inside, cavernous. It smelled of wet dog but there was no sign of the dogs anywhere.

Gussie had no intention of asking for food, but as soon as his backside found the straw, the one with the striving pale mustaches yanked a bark of jerky from a grocer's bag and reached it over to Gussie, and Gussie told him much obliged and that he'd make it square the minute he stood winner's end of a day's pay.

Gussie's benefactor held him in a look of wry astonishment. "You come in sidewise, we'd never have seen you."

Gussie was already chewing the jerky and didn't deign to respond. He'd had his fill of commentary on the languished state of his physique.

"Could use your arms for knittin needles. Get us some yarn and di-vert ourselves durin the showers."

Gussie got his canteen out to wash away the smoky pinch of the jerky.

"Launder our dirty shirts on your ribs," the boy went on. "Plenty of uses for you around here. Take Sunday work as a scarecrow."

A few of the other boys snickered, shaking their heads.

"I could work just like you," Gussie said. "Fact, I'd be surprised if I can't work better, fond of your own wind as you seem to be."

The boy was encouraged at Gussie's riposte, at life in his adversary. He nudged the bag of jerky nearer Gussie, and Gussie pushed it back.

"Ain't wise givin me no more belly timber if you got hopes of keepin up."

"Only thing needs worry for keepin up is your britches," the boy said.

Gussie could feel his color rising and knew this development was visible to his new associates when the big one broke the quiet with a chuckle and advised Gussie pay no mind to Harley, at least not any mind he could use for something better.

"He's a famous one for spoofin a fresh ensign. Go ahead, eat. He gets too far out of line, I'll ball him up and pitch him on the roof."

Gussie looked again at the boy who'd given him the jerky, Harley, saw the well-disposed orneriness in his eyes.

"Anyway," the big boy continued, "Harley gets plenty of work just haulin that pumpkin of a noggin about. He's workin anytime he's upright."

Harley scoffed. "Good turn for me it ain't a pumpkin—you'd have ate it raw already, stem to button."

One of the others piped up then with a grinning insult, then another joined the scrum, and so it went, round and round, until the rain abated and promptly the sun shone strong in the windows of the barn and the boys arose and stalked out to their labors. The hauling. The limbing. The chopping. The stacking. All of this toil a relief to Gussie—to put himself to purpose, to be of use. The cypresses, look-ing dead already, falling with great reverberate thumps against the damp earth. The sweepy whoosh of the longleaf pines. The tipping crunch of the live oaks, towed out in tumbling, unwieldy tangles by the mules. Laden carts to, empty fro, and picking their ways between them the vagrant cats, out of hiding in the drying early evening, ambling low across the busy paths and then high-stepping the thicketed outskirts of the property.

Later, when Coker handed Gussie his due for four hours' sweat, he couldn't see forking it over to the restaurateur. When most of the crew peeled left at the square, he continued on to the general store and procured himself a small put-up of the jerky he'd sampled, a spotted yellow apple, a pair of seedcakes, and a handful of rock candy flavored weakly of lemon. He filled his canteen at the well outside and spent the hour or more until bunk leisurely wandering the nearby environs, plucking his supper by the fingers-full from his bag and eating on the hoof, navigating only by his sense, often vague, of what direction the Gulf was. He swapped route whenever a fortification of mangroves repelled him, when a bridgeless canal appeared. This jaunt became Gussie's custom—the second evening, the third—this inquest of the eccentric passageways in the coastland brush. It was queer and disorienting to walk without direction, to walk as a fellow at loose ends with no greater goal than to unwind the clock until curfew. The colonies of fiddle crabs on the estuary banks, fleeing down their holes as he approached. The children at hide-and-seek, pressing pleading fingers to their lips. The alleys of sea grape that hitched and wheeled drunkenly before disgorging him onto unpeopled beaches. And when he returned to the barn in the gathering dark, day's work and day's razzing and day's wandering ended, when the boys lay flat in the hay, lost in the moony chasms of their dreams—at this lightless hour, two ancient Black men could be heard at the front apron of the grounds, feeding twigs and pine brooms and green acorn clusters and all other woody detritus unfit for profit into a quiet, hungry balefire that at dawn would still smolder.

After his fourth day of work, the others off to dine, Gussie sought out Coker and begged the boss to convey to the rest of the company his best regards. He had known he would depart once the workweek ended, his stake sufficient, but had not planned to steal away without bidding his mates goodbye. Today, though, the moment for farewells before him, he'd been unequal to it, to looking each boy in his eyes and shaking each hand, this corps of whom he had grown so swiftly fond. It was cowardice, he knew—the same true reason he'd made himself scarce of the dinner hours. He'd kept his distance because he was afraid of how he would feel, how sad to depart. And so he would abscond from this temporary home, would steal off like a timorous ghost. Friends. He'd again had, however briefly, friends. And he would again lose them.

———————

Baton Rouge, upon Julius' arrival, was as welcoming as a block-house. The few operable shops were shut up for the night, and the sorry men picking about the dusty pans of the downtown lots had taken leave of their senses or were making such vacation their prime ambition. The magnolia blooms had yellowed. Fog had set in, near as thick as in San Francisco. The only headway Julius could claim—after wandering the debris-strewn streets and questioning anyone capable of standing erect—was the irksome knowledge that he would need wait out the evening and acquire a horse in the morning. Jed Juel, a twitch-eyed old itinerant told him. Jed Juel get you sorted for hooves, but won't get back till daybreak. "Went to New Orleans," the man said. He pointed, finger shaking like a leaf, in the direction of Hunt Street, told Julius to mark the blue-painted silo in the foreyard of the fourth house at the right.

No choice but to satisfy himself for the night with the tippler's instructions, Julius gained entrance at the nearest boardinghouse and convinced the honorable directress, though the supper hour had come and gone, to grace him with a perfect farce of a meal headlined by the crumbliest pone he had ever labored to chew and many slices of melon so pale and flavorless that one could not, in the poor light of the slant-ceilinged dining nook, discriminate flesh from rind. A flea-ridden mattress. A view out the tiny window of a peeling plank wall. The scratch of desperate mice and the scent of their droppings.

Well prior to daybreak, the early risers of the district about their business to the light of whale-oil lamps and suet candles and the glow of their cheap cigars, Julius found himself rapping on the front door at the address with the blue silo. A man peered at him from behind a pulled curtain, unlocked the door, stepped outside. This Jed Juel, hidden beneath a cottony beard and well-worn gaucho hat, led Julius around back to a weather-darkened pavilion and pointed at a strawberry appaloosa, the only horse on premises not spoken for, an animal with a heavy rump and one ear hacked off and clear, iron-hued eyes. Julius was in need of a saddle, and Jed Juel said that was fortunate—Anton held a mighty partiality to the particular rig hanging on yonder hook. He had his whims like any of us, but if you took time to learn them, he'd love you fast and forever. Julius had thought to enlighten Jed Juel, but of course did not, that he didn't wish to grow beloved, rapidly or by grade, eternally or in brief, but only wished to get himself on from this underarm of a waypoint and nearer his fair tomorrows. He did not haggle over the price, did not bother to examine hooves nor mouth, and in response to Jed Juel's friendly query as to where he was headed, replied, "Here and there mostly, unless plans change." Moreover, Julius' complete lack of deliberation put Jed Juel off his ease, so that when the moment arose for the exchange of reins for tender, it was the seller whose hand was slow.

"Take it easy on him till he gets warm," Jed Juel warned, following Julius and Anton back around the side yard. "Don't let him drink too much when he's in a lather. And give him leave to di-gest after his meal—quarter-hour, at the least."

"Very good," Julius answered.

"He ain't over-fond with other horses," Jed Juel called. "You're best not to force him through a neck in the trail if a rider's comin immediate."

"Yes, yes," Julius said, and then in a whisper, "And I shall sing him to sleep in a restrained baritone and polish his remaining ear with a cashmere handkerchief."

Julius walked his new conveyance briskly to the humble yet crowded wharf, where he claimed and secured behind the saddle his seam-worn carpetbag. He mounted and found his bearing, cleared in some minutes the clots of foot travelers, then urged his steed faster and faster and put behind him the musty river and the lowly sections of town, good old Anton growing more assured as Julius prodded him. The morning awakened to meet them as they found top speed, merry Red Stick left behind, and over the next hours Julius felt he was getting the better of time, which slowed as he raced. When Anton took a notion to slacken, Julius clapped heels to his flank, and soon the horse seemed to share the rider's lust to be farther on, over the next pathetic ridge, across the next beaten flat, out of the next tangled wood.

And it was not yet noon when the untended farm country began, dusty green cottonfields by the hundred-count going wild, plows and shovels abandoned to rust. These were the bloated holdings of an era fresh ended. Tin plates and gather-sacks scattered. A forgotten boot. Julius was breathing Southern air for the first time in years, but this knowledge brought him no bracing feeling of home. His heart bled not a drop for the Confederate planters nor the feebleminded poor who'd been convinced to back them. Louisiana was a pit and Florida would be worse. Ivory Shoals—nothing more than the filthy outlands of Tampa, that pirate's stockyard. Lean alligators and fat buzzards. Cruel insects and reeking swamps. Droves of the unwashed, white and now Black also. But Julius had no constraint to the American

Gulf Coast, now did he? No, he didn't. None at all. He could secure
what was his, the whole of it, and when the patriarch passed to
green valleys could sell all and settle Abraham with an appropriate
sum and take passage to the continent—why couldn't he?—on the
most sumptuous liner New York harbor could boast, crowded with
prim-footed women reared in opera boxes who spoke five languages,
with men who spat their madeira on the deck should it disappoint.
London and on to Paris, as far away as possible from this wretched
countryside Anton now burned through. Ah, to be finished, once
and all, with Puritanical fiddle-faddle. Julius could hear now the
rollicking din of the Montmartre cafés. Slow holidays to a seaside
lined with fine hotels rather than heat-warped hovels. Vast public
greens kept neat as a pin, rather than the mongrel-trod mud plot
Ivory Shoals dared call a park. He could see mademoiselles dancing
a polonaise over waxed floors, their hair in soft, dark bales atop their
heads, their kittenish eyes flashing this way and that. The strolls
down Haussmann's fresh, broad boulevards. Awakened of a morn by
the honey-colored sun in an east window, no more by mosquitoes
mired in the sweat of one's brow. Silver-appointed landaus instead of
mule-drawn rattletraps. It was said the new wives of France were as
knowing as brothel girls, and the brothel girls on a par of innocence
with the archfiend himself. Circles awaited that would appreciate
Julius' charms—a rich American, a veteran of battle, a Southern
gentleman who could just as readily speak of the rough-and-tumble
West. Who could tell of Indians strapped with quivers of arrows and
bedecked with eagle feathers. Stage sackings and quick-draw artists
and saloon-room poker games. He'd be formally invited to balls at
great houses and his arrival announced in the front hall, rather than
being slipped in and out by a servant entrance and hustled down
a dark alleyway. Julius could envision a tasteful bachelor's quarters,
living out what remained of his youth with little need of molesting

his capital, his belly kept full by fashionable hostesses who might slap him playfully on the shoulder with their peccary gloves, who might wonder in grateful awe at the propitious tides that had washed him up in their part of the world.

Horse and rider were thundering an approach to Mobile when the game Anton, whom Julius had driven hard after heavy eating, had pressed to an all-out gallop every minute save strict passages through towns—it was nigh to Mobile that the horse slacked, ignoring Julius' kicks and oaths, slowed and hobbled and then recovered himself to a canter, slowed and hobbled again, walked for a time, then resigned trail for weeds and stood swaying this way and that like a sapling in a gale. When Julius finally dismounted to berate him face to face, Anton collapsed in a quivering heap. Muzzle frothed. Breath a rattle. The muscles of his hips seizing. The animal would not look at Julius, his eyes lolling wide of his most recent master, wider when Julius stepped to. He batted his foreleg in helpless defeat, stamping little depressions in the soft roadside growth. Julius wasted no time, the spade shown clear before him. Seeing no other travelers about, he detached his luggage—leaving the saddle, which was too heavy to tote—and humped over the next hillock with purpose in his stride and made his way diligently over the countless bridged streams that purged into Mobile Bay. He willed himself, hour upon hour slipping through his fingers, into the eastern cleft of Alabama and into and out of a series of encampments in which he found chances to fill his canteen, to nick odd fruits from street stands, and finally to surrender the lion's share of his liquid riches for a molly mule, Linessa by name, a sooty buckskin in color, flat-backed and long-eared and with such meager mane it seemed to have been trimmed after some arcane foreign fashion. The owner admitted Linessa was no majestic

courser but promised that for fording treacherous country her equals
were rare. Might whimper at a creek, he said, but that was how she
gathered her grit. The man titch-titched in his cheek and the mule
walked obediently near, her gait as hip-swayed as an aging whore's.

Once atrail, Julius saw that spurring Linessa the mule to her
untimely demise did not number amongst his concerns. He could not
entice her, by any passion of stinging boot heels, to maintain any clip
more urgent than a trot. And he did not possess the heart, half-starved
and short-slept and now fiscally reduced as he was, to turn about and
track backward and demand refund, to waste time searching out more
fitting transport. So he pressed on into the panhandle, which was
one immense thicket of brittle vine, denouncing his new trail mate
without any real vigor as a mangy poltroon and a yellow varlet and
a loathsome powder-hoof dawdler.

More plantation land. More crouched hamlets populated by bent-
backed women and men who spat down their shirtfronts and children
too dazed to play in the squares. The River Escambia, dull, still as
a slate roof. The town of Milton, hard eyes following Julius from
listing porches. Knox Hill. Holmes Valley. The disagreeing waysigns
for Shade Spring. To the east, Linessa. To the east, foul brute. Evening
overcoming afternoon, Julius passed through a wood enlivened with
an understory of blush-pink twinflower and came upon a supper
shack whose line of rising stove-smoke was near invisible in the
dusk, its dining room lamps glowing softly. He tied off the mule.
Sauntered stiff-legged up the porch steps. When he saw himself
in the looking glass just inside the door, he saw a man gaunt as an
apostle. A man with a holy air about his form—he who had denied
himself precious little all his years. He had not, ever before, been
owned whole by a mission. Had never bellied so in the winds of
purpose. Had never been driven by anything that at once touched
brain and bone, hand and eye, past and future. He'd give all to see

the boy's blood. Would give his own blood seven vials to one. The need filled him like love. The desire to grip the rudder of events. To rate worthy. This task that loomed close before him now, a task of rare repugnance that required rare spine. Who was this fellow before him? It was Julius Searle. He would always recognize himself. Perhaps would know no other soul in the world, really, but would know himself, no matter what happened to him.

Julius became aware he was being spoken to, welcomed. He was ushered toward a spread consisting in whole of a soup tureen—what variety of soup he was not apprised and did not inquire—and a crock of soft-looking peanuts that gave off an odor of wet earth. The dough-gummed matron of the establishment advised him that many went in for the congressing of the two offerings, and Julius followed this advice. He sat down and spooned and spooned until his dish was dry, paying no attention to the flavor on his tongue and little attention to the dull ache he felt pulsing through the whole of his lower jaw. He pushed the dish slowly away from him. A trio of kittens pawed about beneath the table next to Julius'. He leaned and watched them fumble about and trip on their paws. Bat clumsily at one another. He brought up onto his lap the feeblest of the litter and fingered about its ears, the light bones of its tiny skull. Held it up midair in order to feel the bite of its keen, slight claws in the back of his hand. The teeth improbably small and perfect, yet there they were, white as royal linen.

"And where is their dear mother?" Julius asked.

"Now she's a queer one," the old lady replied from her chair against the wall. "Goes out huntin in broad day rather than sunrise or sunset. Won't show herself without she got somethin for the little ones."

"They've no taste for the goulash?"

"Hope they don't never. Hope mama always comes back. Mine didn't, but I hope theirs always do."

A raft ferry at the Apalachicola. A girl child and boy, posted port and starboard, shoving off with poles before trading them out for long-handled oars that could be wielded from standing. Over to Axton Bluff, Julius motionless at the top of the locked companionway, Linessa's reins firm in his fist. Then back to the trail, the mud hardening to chalk, and into a familiar land of live oaks whose sagging limbs lent them the look of weary nurses putting infants to bed. Wakulla Springs. Carn Springs. Sugar Springs. Redleg Springs. Julius beginning now to picture in his mind's eye the sole approach to the Shoals from the north—a limb of land set hard along the sea and traced at its waterside edge by one clear path. A path too narrow at certain lengths for two men to walk shoulder to shoulder. A path choked tight even at its broadest.

———————————

The water purled evenly, never turbulent enough to lose its clarity, the white sand beneath—the ivory, as it were—glowing dully in the tinted afternoon light, the river's murmur near to inaudible as it mingled with the measured shushing of the Gulf surf some forty yards downstream. Any birdsong to be heard was papery, weak-hearted. Abraham could see through a tunnel in the foliage to where the waterway spilled out, could see the bobbing pelicans, boats moored at a sandbar in the green shallows. For the third day he had disdained his household duties. He'd postponed an appointment with a floor polisher, had left Mr. Searle to fend his own suppers, had not gathered bundles for the laundress. A tea service sat in the master's study, yet to be cleared, the cup likely stained. The front walk was blown with sand. The decanters smudged. Abraham's scheme was not lost upon himself. He wished Mr. Searle to chastise him—this man whose tartest brand of admonition, in years upon years, had been to doubtfully overlook his spectacles in Abraham's direction—wanted this man to grumble at his performance. Thus far, the cheese moldered in the trap. The distracted master had betrayed no notice of any delinquency, while the servant grew ever more agitated. Abraham's hands, limp in his lap, were damp with sweat, pale, as if languishing this quickly with disuse. He sat cross-legged on a fallen cypress, his pants seat assuredly sullied—he could not care, presently, about the condition of his apparel, nor, for that matter, his bodily hygiene.

Abraham dried his palms on his trousers. The dying day had wrought about him a small, dim chamber, a cell, a hold of shadows. The dusk's warnings were hollow, rote. Its symbols delusory. He had taken to providing himself with double and, today, with a triple dose of Mexican remedy, and this renowned cure had served only to cast all without the web of his thoughts as unreal, suspect, and to make all within the web bold and insistent. His joints were numb, his scalp hot. He leaned to the stream bank and plucked cautiously with first finger and thumb a solitary grass of Parnassus, broke it at the stem and drew it to his chest like a ceremonial flame, traced the veins of its wan, green flower.

He had bought a pistol. Less dear than hiring a man—this was the thin consolation. He had slid in a single round, thought better and loaded two instead. Then had gone ahead and filled the spinner to capacity, the half-dozen humble demons, heads bowed and hands at their sides. He'd told the old sutler it was for snakes, as if that crusty fence cared a bit what purposes his wares came to. At night, hidden at the rear of his closet, the pistol had felt as a serpent itself, curled behind Abraham's winter slippers and the long skirts of his housecoat and a dusty crate of secondhand crockery—a snake itself, coiled tight and head low, devising to attack him in his own quarters. His sleep was now only a vehicle for harrowing visions. He'd seen himself, the night previous, traversing a boundless swamp whose water was not water but, instead, none other than the dilute brown broth he had subsisted on at the orphan hall as a boy—those hundreds of shallow bowls, a single ladleful, no more or less. In life that broth had been free of any noteworthy chewables, yet in the swamp of Abraham's dreamscape, as he picked his way in high boots, terrified but compelled to seek—seek what, he now could not remember—his eye was drawn, now starting left and now right, to so many scraped hocks of bone that burbled drearily to the surface, clean and haunting. Delicate bobbing flukes, each fine little evidence gently drifting off out of sight in the mist, perhaps again to be sunk and again borne to the surface on a belch of the sour water.

The grass of Parnassus had wilted under his attentions. He dropped it gently into the current and watched it ferried toward the open water until it was swallowed by the darkness. Julius. Oh, Julius. He saw the young master as he'd seen him years before, his silken, dark hair threatening to curtain an eye, a single gleaming ring, its amber stone fat as a bumblebee, his wrists trim and grin sharp. His friend. His accomplice. This scarlet-mouthed youth whom Abraham had known from a boy. The youth whom, if absent from a day's school lessons, had been truant of his choosing, taking his leisure at Twyla Pass with a knot of tobacco and a mouthful of waggish observances for stray ladies—this, rather than Abraham's own fate, which was to be turned away with contempt from the schoolhouse, cheeks livid in shame, a boy of six with holes in his boots and squirrel blood beneath his fingernails. This boy, Julius, whom, if he hawked a coat had lost but one of a great company of coats, the proceeds wanted to replace bottles raided from the estate's stock, rather than, as it had been in Abraham's case, a lone coat sold for daily bread. This boy whose morning stomach upsets were the just returns of overmuch rum or Chartreuse, rather than the cramping brought by scavenging in back alleys for plate scrapings. This boy whose recurrent grievances toward his father pertained to the patriarch's predictable steadfastness, his resolve to work, his disapproval—mild as it usually was—of traits in Julius that no right father the world over would endorse, whereas Abraham's father, well, one was lucky to pry him out from under a dripping still. And the singular instance this budding heir might account the nobility implied by his style of living, might put to view some proof of mettle, he instead absconds to the foremost den of vice this nation can boast. His grand seminar in roguery.

Abraham shook his head and snorted, fighting his mind. The cards were shuffled. The cards were dealt. He could not fold. He had to stay in the hand, belly to the table and feet on the floor. Meanness was, at times, required—he well knew this. He wouldn't talk himself out of a disagreeable task. He'd done plenty of them, and for much scanter profit. And he'd rather be mean than weak. Would rather make his own fortune than continue tending another's. He arose from the cypress log too quickly, making his head light. Stood unsteadily at the bank of the Shoals, the handle of the pistol digging sharp into the knob of his hip. He strode out into the middle and set his feet. Faced the Gulf, which he could no longer see. Felt the wet in his boots and stockings, the sluggish current around his ankles, the calves of his trousers soaking through. He bent double and dipped his hands and rinsed his face and neck and ears. Stood again, a perfect, terrible quiet unto himself. He recognized, yet, that Julius could've spent his adolescent hours however he liked and had spent so many of them with him. Recognized that he was aware of Julius' wartime where-abouts only because Julius had chosen to make him so. Recognized, and none could outweigh this last, that Julius was offering to share his abundance, offering a fellow such as Abraham, a street scamp in boyhood, chance to rise in his middle age to near-gentility, to attain a class otherwise vetoed him, to make unlikely golden his late years. Julius was offering, in fact, what the whole rest of his schooled, groomed lot, his father included in the number, saw fit to horde away.

———————

Impassible screens of dusty sea grape. Curious powder-white ibises. Palms grown tall and thin, creaking in the breeze, thrusting their bristly coronets to the heavens. A settlement at the weedy debouchment of the Tramposo Verde. A lunchroom clinging to the rear of a fresh-painted church. The red steeple. Fig trees in the patchy yard. The waitress, heavy-boned, a tined blossom of canary-yellow tucked behind an ear. A helping of Nesselrode pie thick and hot as a new brick.

No afternoon rains, nor even a rumbling threat. Only a static blue sky hanging low over the throbbing inland and over the purple depths of the Gulf and over a strip of shops that tirelessly beckoned passersby with whitewashed porches and crowded display windows. Gussie's soul felt shadowless, composed of nothing but the colorless light that flooded the main street. A bellyful of nut pie, the proximity of others, the salt air, the looming form of the Lord's house. He was soft-headed and dreamy in the warmth of day, his steps quiet on the planks. Children below, out of sight, whispered to dogs unknown to them until that very hour, naming the animals, chiding them lovingly. Sand dollars broader than Gussie's open-stretched hand were propped up like portraits. Taxidermy swellfish, blown round, their spikes clean, suspended from wires and turned slowly about like planets. In an oil painting, a gaunt man struggled to prize a lock off a chest, a rail spike clutched in his sore fingers. Gussie stared, dazed, until some part of him was able to league this artwork with the one on Miss Elam's wall, the farmer at the pond, tugging uselessly at his colossal bull. And at the end of the long, common porch, a man in a field-stitched blue shirt buttoned tight against his throat crouched comfortably in the shade and folded banana leaves into toy cranes and tiny, dugout boats.

Gussie patronized a bath that was only a flagstone court stalled off with mats of vine. He declined to throw in extra for warmed water, feeling dandy enough paying anything at all to bathe himself, the Gulf waiting a five-minute walk behind. He wanted the rough rag and the peel of sweet soap, wanted the woman to pare his nails with her special little tool. When again clothed, he walked down the road and sat stiffly in a green upholstered chair while a harelip barber snipped here and there and back and forth, revealing Gussie's ears. Before he knew, the brush was about his cheeks, his chin, the barber's wrist flicking expertly like a bird policing its nest. A white beard in the looking glass. Out came the razor to its light labor, the barber betraying not a hint of irony concerning the procedure.

In a corner of the general store turned over to footwear, a man clad in a magenta vest and butter-colored trousers knelt before Gussie and unwound his inch-tape, leaned a keen eye, paid the tape back around until it was tight again. He disappeared, returned carrying a pair of secondhand boots that flashed oxblood in the radiance of the window—used, yes, but sound and glossy as all the world next to the disintegrating dregs of leather Gussie had walked in with. The man used his thumb on Gussie's sore toes. When he declared a fit, it was without any salesman-like flutter or braggadocio—a statement of plain fact.

"You got an estimate how far to Ivory Shoals?" Gussie asked him.

The man handed over Gussie's change in a neat stack between his thumb and forefinger. "You'll be one night atrail. Watch gettin onto the Indian Rocks bend."

"Watch for it to get on, or watch to keep off?"

"To get on, otherwise it's down and around and add an en-tire day."

"Appreciate it," Gussie said.

"Appreciate the business," the man answered. "Stow them new slippers for now if you plan on keepin them pretty. Wear the oldens till the land spreads back out—good track from there."

On a bench in front of a glistening coquina courtyard, Gussie heeded the clerk's advice and swapped out his boots—an unwelcome gambit because the new pair felt as clouds beneath his tired feet and the old like sprung traps. He nestled the fresh ones into his pack. Cinched it up again. Wiped the sweat from his chin. He was breathing deeply the warm, rich air—the smokers full of fish, the damp-rotted rope, the spice of men's cigars, and the cologne of the women in the square. His mother's birthday? Is that where these scents had alighted his mind? That old seaman—Gussie could see his grin—on holiday from the north, his standing burr of sterling hair. His gentle voice as he bartered an afternoon cruise, a "prowl" he named it, for Gussie's rasping of his boat's weathered hull. The old man was headed next to the Southern Keys, taking the trip while he still might, before the Stream was peppered with federal corvettes. Gussie saw himself leading his mother, who he'd kept ignorant of their destination, past the shuttered cheesemaker's and the shuttered hat shop and the smudge-windowed grocery, sneaking upon the riprapped harbor from the rear and halting before the old fellow's high-sailed sloop, Gussie hopping aboard and then offering his hand and steadying his mother as she strode the little chasm of tidewater. "All to deck who's comin to deck," the old man had called. He'd donned a cap of the type Gussie had seen rich boys wear on their way to the preparatory campus, with an abbreviated bill that spared one's eyes but wouldn't catch up in a gust. The fellow squeezed Gussie's mother's hand, then busied himself with the administration of the craft, guiding them out the river to open sea and then out beyond the sand bars, the water darkening and sky clearing completely. Gussie's mother perched herself in the prow, her color high with the sea spray. When the boat slid broadside to the swells for a moment and saltwater sloshed her stellas, she only laughed and loosed the laces and lightly kicked the shoes aside. She pleaded they go out a bit farther, a bit farther, so they might lose sight of land altogether, and the old sailor conceded. In the quarter-hour they spent in the detached limbo of the deeps, a repose stole over Gussie's mother he'd never seen in her—the genteel languor with which she reclined, the pure satisfaction when she gazed about her, as if a single day could make a life. He'd never, until then, seen her away from the venality and delusion men nursed and petted, had never seen her free from the liver-colored threat of shortage. It could be chased off, shortage, but it never strayed far—the morning's noon, the noon's evening. Midnight, it lurked.

When they'd reached home, spent and salt-eyed, his mother had stacked lime crates three-high beneath the sagging corner of the roof and they had clambered atop and lain flat on their backs in the quiet under the fast-knitted stars. And they had felt yet the enchanting, careless pitch of the sea.

———————

The Aucille. The Ecofina. The Fenalolloway. The wire-grassed Sewanee. The beleaguered cormorants, spreading their wings tentatively to the sun as if before a newly discovered god. The deserted operations at the heads of the unkempt cays for boiling seawater to salt—kettles tall as outhouses, outhouses sun-shrunken and excommunicated.

Julius explored the afternoon and the evening and rode on into the humid night, one hand clenched on the reins and the other loosely propping a bottle to his thigh, feeling a stubborn momentum but also, in larger part, feeling stupefied by fatigue and the sloshing in his brain of the whiskey. His way was lit by a sharp-edged moon, and on occasion the heat lightning out over the Gulf would reveal the entire portrait of the night, from the skunks with their delving black snouts to the taciturn owls in their high hollows. Whenever Julius' chin nodded upon his chest, he revived himself with a slug of his liquor. He hooted into the darkness. Pinched the meat of his arms. Reached high, squeezing his bottle between his legs, to brush with his fingertips the enormous dangling blossoms that stiffened in the breeze like pennants.

The night was neither lengthy nor brief, dawn showing up quietly with no preamble nor invitation, its glow a devoid leitmotiv heralding only itself. Julius rode past vast, unnamed inlets and over tepid freshets so thin the molly mule traversed them with nary a protest and hardly a lengthened step. By the time the land either side the way tapered, the sun had found voice in the treetops, steaming the estuary of its secrets. And it was just past Florimon, the uneven path comprising the entire narrow strip of land, the blanched clay imprinted with a weary cavalcade of prints and tracks, that Julius unsteadily dismounted and pushed his face to the sky and felt a run of hollow cracks speed down his spine. He tipped a long last glug from his bottle and tossed it aside. Unclasped, flipped back the flap, drew forth his blade. Sniffed the handle greedily, which smelled only lightly of sweat and not at all like wood. A crisp smell. Somehow, a blameless smell. Boots below. Knife in hand. Brain steeping. He peered uptrail and down. Spat on the earth beneath him. Peered uptrail again. The unburdened mule looked on confusedly as he flailed his arm in the direction from which they'd come. She ogled him when he stamped his foot. When Julius kicked her flank with all the strength he could muster, she fell dull of eye, collected herself with a strained, soft bray, sidled about, and departed her rider with dignity and without glancing backward, forging off into the given day as if with her own appointments to honor.

Julius sniffed the knife's grip again. He held the weapon at the ready and continued his pursuit afoot, his gait brisk, his mouth a frozen red slash, his weapon grasped rigid, point down, the open sea to the west and the waist-deep sound, flat as glass, to the east.

In full naked day his senses were over-sharp. The harsh yellow cry of the sun. Hornets darting with stupid alarm. Rotting excrement. His nose ran freely and he tasted continually the salty, slick discharge. When travelers began to appear ahead, shapeless bobbing silhouettes and then legged figures in trudge and finally characters in equal detail to Julius himself—one trailing a dog behind, one clutching only a lacquer box, one shirtless and with a patched eye—at any approach, Julius held the blade stiffly against his leg but otherwise did not conceal it, nodding acknowledgment without meeting the other's gaze. He wiped and wiped his palm on his shirtfront, and when his shirt grew too damp, on his pants. The sunlight was a single, slanting tier. It leaned on him with oppressive intent, almost pushing him off course into the shallows. The home he was nearing—it was no earthbound place, but his own contorted soul. His fate, the ancients would say. Authorship and surrender both. If he stopped in the trail, this fate, still and quiet, stopped with him. If he walked on, destruction walked a step ahead.

Abraham was nestled some half-dozen rods from the walkway, behind the found breastwork of a fallen hardwood. He had sat outdoors the night previous and would sit another if needed—another sunset in desperate hues, another twilight calling the night flowers to their posing and the mosquitoes to their onslaught. It was now past noon, the air a dumbing green haze. His spittle was froth. He could not say whether he still sweated—his forehead clammy with chill and pulse sporadic in his skull. The marl he hunkered upon was like spent coffee grounds, his palms impressing countless explicit molds. The sun above had filled the empty barrels of the world to their bottoms like any day, turning over banalities and marvels alike without ceremony, and now the color of the sea matched exactly the hue of the deep shade in which Abraham knelt.

Only lint in Abraham's seedsack and so he overturned it, shook it. Crammed it into his breast pocket, where it didn't fit and would not stay. He watched the same length of trail—travelers one an hour at times, and other times trudging by in dissolute throngs as many as a choir. Each lone southbound soul called him up, eyes hardening, fingers pulling bands of briar from his sightline. Men with the gallant stride of a country swain, men hobbling as if leg-shot, men apparently lost. In the trailside ditches, urn-shaped blooms the pale scarlet of fish blood.

His mind would go white as sky and then he would jerk to, praying not to have missed his office. Boys, to Abraham. Boys the both. One of them the devil he knew. Knew all too well. And none would know Abraham's sin but this very devil who would name it virtue. Abraham's past one epic sharper's play, his future velvety as veal. This one last act. This final service Julius was forcing him to perform, Abraham earning his bread by orders as ever.

When the boy entered the breach, Abraham knew him at once—his bare head slightly bent, the light flashing warmly on his dark hair. When he drew near, Abraham saw the pipe in his mouth, cold, dangling. Hair trimmed sharp and cheeks pink, pack lopsided and seam-split. This was the ice-blooded snipe, full of culprit designs? This was the murderer of bounty hunters and slick eluder of the laws of man and of the American jungle, this poke of bones, seed-eyed, boots a wreck, green as ivy? A babe, Abraham saw. Low fruit, despite his reputation. An easy mark.

Braced on his knees, boot toes dug in, Abraham gripped firmly the contoured wood, felt the grain on the skin of his palm, watched himself with great interest from very nearby—and he knew already that this man he watched did not mean to link his finger into the trigger-guard, knew this as he knew all his own secrets, as he knew his devotion to the old man, as he knew who deserved a father and who deserved an even lesser, even viler world, as he knew that he himself, Abraham Cox, had never strained a wrist to make this earth one iota better. Relief settled over him like clement new weather when he saw the pistol pass to his left hand, when he saw it held there sternly yet absently, a caught serpent that knew better than to foolishly strike and prompt its own clubbing.

And the boy's dust still hung about the way when Abraham sighted the form of his young master—his gait urgent, his posture and bearing full of malice. His shirt, more buttons unfastened than fastened, hung about him like a rent flag. His head was canted toward Abraham, away from the vindictive sun, his nose borne along high as if seeking thinner air. Abraham saw the blade, flashing in the heave and disappearing in the ho. Flashing. Flashing. His smirk grim. His face dark.

Abraham whistled with conviction a decorous old overture he could not have put name to, and this stayed Julius atrail, exposed and liable as a fox on a plowed field. Julius' chin remained high and haughty as Abraham specified him down the dull metal cylinder. As he watched him trapped there in the final stanza of the miscreant poem that was his life. As he watched the antagonist's eyes wheel warily that way, then after a moment, warily this.

IN THE ECHO

HAVING TIDIED UP FROM breakfast and put beans to soak, Abraham installed himself on his peaceful yet cramped portico with a cup of cool water and a neat white cigarette. He struck a match and drew the tobacco to life. Dropped the stick in the dish. Three breakfasts and three suppers now. Abraham's own appetite was returning by bounds—Mr. Searle's not so noticeably, though his demeanor of a visit to table had indeed altered, as he now spent the duration of each meal beaming gladly at the boy's grateful rapacity. Gussie. Abraham had begun calling him by name. This young man he'd spared. Had rescued. He knew better than to deem the youth Mister Gussie, as it would've well leveled him with embarrassment. He made sure, this apprehensive new addition to the household, to grip his fork in the proper way and rest his napkin in his lap, wouldn't so much as sniff the fare until someone else—Abraham, usually—had taken the initial bite. That first evening, he had awaited grace said. Abraham had leaned over and informed him that in this house Galileo, Newton, and Darwin were the only deities. Abraham had needed to act as interlocutor for much of that repast, but by such time as the strawberry pie made appearance, father and son were wading gamely into the seas of confidence, Mr. Searle daring to pose tentative inquiries about the boy's mother, and the boy unguardedly, if a bit timidly, supplying what intelligence he might, both the facts of the woman—her birthplace down Teasdale way, her estrangement from any family but the boy himself, the nature of the illness that had taken her—and also a selection of her outlooks regarding religion, politics, leisure, and general getting on, her sentiments never unctuous nor flagrantly skeptical but managing always to find a self-reliant middle ground. Gussie had noticed the hibiscuses in the gate-beds and instructed Mr. Searle of the revered status that flower had held with his mother, and with earnest countenance the elder assured that each anniversary of her passing the house would be stuffed galley to garret with them. Aside the boy's shy, brave opening line, "I got somethin of yours," and numerous statements of gratitude portioned out over the hours, the burning emotions had mostly visited the father. Indeed, Abraham could tell the new arrival had been rattled at the master's repeated misting up, his abrupt declarations of joy, his quiet looks that were full of awe but tinged with something bleaker. The boy understood better after learning of the prodigal Julius, the severance from Ruth, the recent trials as to his host's health. Over the course of that opening banquet, which had drawn out to three and four hours—Mr. Searle, Abraham noted, tippling his Calvados with a much-reduced zeal—the boy had no doubt grown to comprehend what a kind man sat with him at table. Perhaps Abraham himself was refreshed in this particular knowledge, which he had for a time wished to forget. He saw, watching his master poignantly ogle the visitor, declaring he could find the mother's eyes in the boy's and that mother and son shared the selfsame unassuming grin—Abraham saw that suspicion of the boy was a gainless errand. He found himself occupied, instead of by the accustomed concern for his employer's fortune, by concern for Mr. Searle's eager, vulnerable heart. When the coffee cups were empty of all but the dregs, the windows dark and the world of man quiet, Gussie, with a ceremonial air, insisted on sharing his tobacco with his company and pushed it upon them and upon himself until his holdings were reduced to flecks and grains.

In the days following, as could've been predicted, father and son were inseparable. Mr. Searle had told the boy to keep the gold watch for himself, that a young man ought to have a timepiece, that they would get a new winding key, would sand the current inscription and replace it with G D S. Abraham had witnessed the two splitting

a bottle of ale, had heard from the next room as father offered son
the run of the shelves in his study—never mind that a fraction of
the books were stories, the better part almanacs and treatises—and
had heard Gussie's awed exclamation at the sight of the three long
rows of spines, as if he'd been ushered before the bound holdings of
Jefferson himself. Mr. Searle had walked the boy into town and shown
him about, and the pair had returned with a fine checkers set, pieces
of jade and dark jasper, classified a late birthday gift.

Three breakfasts, three suppers, three nights during which the boy
slept atop his bedsheets and declined to burn a single candle despite
candles being the most abundant resource at the estate. And finally,
just last evening, long after Gussie retired to his room, Mr. Searle
had led Abraham to his own spacious quarters and sat him down
in a box-wing chair and, remaining standing himself, had released
a deep breath and told his servant all. He spoke in a torrent, first of
things of which Abraham was already aware, detailing his crippling
malaise in the workshop, how his brain blanked and imagination
stiffened at the first whiff of the place, spending long hours staring
stupefied at the conversion charts on the walls until he'd memorized
them column and row. He spoke of the caches of liquor, of windows
blacked to conceal delinquency rather than precious scientific gains.
An inventor must be willing to fail, Mr. Searle told Abraham, to fail
much more often than he succeeds, and he had no further taste for
failure. He was no longer young enough, fortune and importance no
longer a fire in his belly. And then he confessed, in a voice thickened but not abashed, what Abraham did not yet know—his legal
ensnarement with the Delawarean cabal, the depth and breadth of
his financial reduction and the fact that he'd worsened the trouble
by his efforts to conceal it, his reprieve during the war and eventual

facing of the music, a music played fortissimo by the low rascals that comprised his former mentor's family. The losses in cattle. The legal fees. He mopped his face thoroughly with his handkerchief—ears, neck—and, sidling yet closer to his aide, disclosed what Abraham was already beginning to make out in the haze: the fact that it would be necessary to put the estate to auction. Mr. Searle looked upward and around, as if from his position in the sitting room of his quarters he could survey the entirety of the manor and grounds. A necessary measure, he said, and perhaps, despite appearances, a not wholly unfavorable one. Abraham had felt dread reflexively galloping upon him, but his master's face had calmed him. His master's self-possessed sigh. He'd understood what bright prospect the older man beheld in his spyglass—the wet and wind of the Ruth Purifoy era finally passing altogether.

Mr. Searle, addressing Abraham as his heart's friend, had bent and put a hand to his steward's shoulder and told him not to fret. The wax and wicks would provide. The three of them, Mr. Searle, Abraham, and Gussie—here he paused, kept his composure—the trio would set themselves up in a dwelling more suitable for bachelors, and henceforth all spirit, toil, and nerve would be directed toward the candle concern. The family candle concern, he amended. The success of the venture had thus far been curbed only by the scarcity of hands to work, of space, by Mr. Searle's own desire to mask from Abraham the true state of affairs. He would always wish to have dear Abe as his manager, he promised. Abraham would learn all parts of the business, keep the books, supervise the workforce, and, if Abraham agreed to it, Mr. Searle was prepared, nay, delighted, to cede him a stake in the earnings, an ownership percentage in the fledgling firm.

Abraham, now, out on the portico, stubbed his cigarette and breathed deep. Somewhere out in the wild pasture was the snippety, sulky quarter horse. They were friends now, Abraham supposed, after their thankfully fruitless venture to see Sir William—friends whether the horse liked it or not. Abraham had had a night to sleep on Mr. Searle's revelations, and to his surprise he felt, along with the lingering disorientation, a distinct relief at the prospect of leaving the estate. It had been Abraham's anchor but also his nemesis—constant upkeep, constant oversight, the air of defeat and sour nostalgia about the place. He had been, early in his life, so destitute that he was obliged, like a stray dog, to defend every scrap he got hold of—then later, he was in charge of such vast wealth that he must worry morning, noon, and night who was scheming to get their own piece of it. He gazed gladly now into a future where he occupied neither of these positions. He welcomed the prospect of being a regular working citizen, of having enough for himself but not so much that he must always look at the world through miserly, anxious eyes.

Abraham would get what he'd wanted, what any would want—a stake, some claim to partnership—and get it honorably. Virtue had been rewarded, and in this life rather than the promised next. Virtue, yes. But nothing was free. Right acts were not free. The universe was not that congenial—its elegance was cruel. Abraham knew that underneath Mr. Searle's bliss at being united with his obscure progeny there lurked a pool of woe at the continued absence of his other son, the one from whom he'd still heard not a word. There'd been no discussion on the topic, but Abraham felt the chill of it in the way Mr. Searle, of late evenings, gaped out the front windows toward all the spread and furtive realms of the North. Felt it in the tense, rigid way Mr. Searle flipped through his post. Julius' bedchamber was still avoided, as if his festering corpse lay within those walls of stone rather than log-pinned, where it in truth resided, under three feet of swamp water. Abraham was the manager, his tasks diverse and often distasteful—would remain the manager, no matter how little there was to manage. He had done his employer well, had confounded the murder of his innocent heir by the murder of his damned other. He had sinned when sin was rightful—part of life for men of many stations and in many centuries, for hordes of men right here in this nation. Abraham would simply bear the ordeal, temper himself against it until it dimmed and assumed its position in the gallery of shadows that was his past. He would slumber and wake, labor and rest, walk slowly under fair skies and hurriedly through rain, and soon enough go unvisited the night through by the image of himself hauling the limp, heavy, ghastly load by one dusty-trousered leg, the fat red brushstroke in the dry dirt of the trail, the victim's arms stretched straight overhead like a child reaching a prize. In time, he would no longer hear the slosh, nor smell the polluted, cankerous odor when he dislodged the sumped log to roll it toward its purpose.

Only a task. And so many more now to check off. This was the trail down which to skelp the mind. There were firstly the routine chores he had left undone these weeks, ample work in themselves, but now the preparations to sell the estate. Sweet, familiar labor. He raised his water cup and drained it, replaced it aside the ash dish. There were lengths of fence that called for painting, lengths that wanted nothing less than replacement. Weed-pulling to fill a day entire—even longer, work boys so scarce. The azaleas and myrtles needed pruning. A clan of moles had taken residence in the side yard. Paint also for the wagon port. The attic to be dealt with—steamy as the Congo. The flashing of the upper-story roof that Abraham had long wished to see. New basins in the kitchen. The boy would throw in his strength—mornings at the candles, afternoons with Abraham. They were unfortunates, some might say, but having one another, they were none of them orphans.

And have each other they did, Abraham knew. Just that morning he had pulled Mr. Searle aside, had stepped with him into the dim study and asked in a firm whisper whether the man had kept him out of the war, whether he'd used his prominence to secretly steer Abraham's fate. Mr. Searle's face had at first clouded over, but his eyes quickly calmed and his posture softened and he reached out to grasp Abraham's arm, looked up into the waiting other's resolved visage, and admitted that indeed he had. The weight of the older man's hand on Abraham's elbow was strange, disarming. He looked down at where Mr. Searle held him. He could hear a moth, oddly loud, thumping against a lamp somewhere.

"I acted selfishly," Mr. Searle told him. "I was afraid to ask your wishes because I wasn't certain what you'd say."

"Afraid?" Abraham had said.

"I couldn't lose you," Mr. Searle stated, obstinacy mellowing his voice. "I couldn't lose my one... my one friend. I wasn't sure how long my influence would last and wasn't sure you'd allow me... I took the choice away from you. It was in my power and I did it."

The word "friend" hanging in the musty air, Mr. Searle said he hoped Abraham would accept his apology, but that he would do the same thing again if the same chance arose, and Abraham said he did accept the apology, cleared his throat, told the other man he knew very well about doing things that were worthy of regret but that one would never, for anything, wish to undo.

And at this, Mr. Searle had released Abraham's arm and stepped aside, his face content, and had motioned to Abraham to lead the way out toward the next new summer day, out to the bright front hall and through to the waiting dining room, whose windows were already full with morning, already full with the retiring, wistful, blue-green sky of the tropics.

ACKNOWLEDGMENTS

The author thanks John McMurtrie, Amanda Uhle, Kate Borowske, Amy Williams, and Heather Brandon. And also Hamline University and the Sustainable Arts Foundation. And also the staff at the Caribou Coffee on Highway 61.

ABOUT THE AUTHOR

John Brandon has published four previous books with McSwee-ney's—the novels *Arkansas*, *Citrus County*, and *A Million Heavens*, and the story collection *Further Joy*. *Arkansas* was made into a movie of the same name starring Liam Hemsworth, Vince Vaughn and John Malkovich. *Citrus County* was a finalist for the New York Public Library Young Lions Award, and was reviewed on the front page of the *New York Times Book Review*.

Brandon has been awarded the Grisham Fellowship at Ole Miss, the Tickner Fellowship at Gilman School in Baltimore, and has received a Sustainable Arts Foundation Fellowship. His short fiction has appeared in *ESPN the Magazine*, *Oxford American*, *McSweeney's Quarterly Concern*, *Mississippi Review*, *Subtropics*, *Chattahoochee Review*, *Hotel Amerika*, and many other publications, and he has written about college football for *GQ* online and *Grantland*. He was born in Florida and now resides in Minnesota, where he teaches at Hamline University in St. Paul.